CW01558540

UK Roof Book

A FOOTPRINT IN THE SAND

THE END OF THE COLD WAR - and an epic political comedy that opens with the death of treasure hunter Graham Dunne on a remote Indian Ocean island. The legendary Fiery Cross of Goa may now never be found. In London, Harry Stone, the Bureau Chief of an obscure Fleet Street agency, says to reporter Robert Walker, "Go to the island, find out what happened to Dunne. Human interest - there's your story, not the treasure. Stay out of politics - and leave the women alone."

Stay out of politics? On far-away Bourbon Island, that's not so easy - where the ruthless, quasi-Marxist dictator-ship of François Bellarmine tolerates no dissent - or journalist.

The Cold War was never quite like this as Robert Walker - an *idiot savant* for Harry Stone's agency - is either helped or hindered by a poly-ethnic cast of characters: meet Mr Swann (the suave, intellectual hotelier), Francis Long (the love-sick bartender), Harry Singh (the subversive plantation merchant), Bishop David Chin (the island's courageous priest), Bugis (the manic Chief of Police), Mr & Mrs Albert Greene (the diffident British Attaché and his wife Liz), Mr Kite (antiquarian map dealer from Berlin), Dr Mobuto (the feathered-man from Zanzibar), Morgan Beaumont (a fall-guy for the Agency), and Barbara West - the perpetrator of a CIA honey-trap to ensnare dictator François Bellarmine, whose regime is about to topple . . .

As for Robert Walker: Brainwashed? "Who, me?"

THE COLD WAR IS OVER! LONG LIVE THE COLD WAR - in an epic political comedy that moves from London and Paris to the far-flung shores of the Indian Ocean . . .

James A. Oliver is an international writer, editor, and journalist. *A Footprint in the Sand* is a political comedy inspired by a "special assignment" at the end of the Cold War. He is also the author of *The Anarchist's Arms* (a play) set in near-future London. . . James Oliver is currently working on a non-fiction title *The Bering Strait Crossing: A 21st Century Frontier* - which is being translated into several languages for release in 2005.

A
Footprint
in the
Sand

For Roy
Exeter (Rare) Books
10 April 2005

James A. Oliver

James A Oliver

THE COMPANY OF WRITERS
2004

First Published in the United Kingdom 2004
by The Company of Writers

www.thecompanyofwriters.com

© James A. Oliver 2004

James A. Oliver has asserted his right under the Copyright,
Designs and Patents Act 1988.

ISBN: 0-9546995-3-X

British Library Cataloguing in Publication Data.
A catalogue record for this book is available from the British Library.

Cover photo: Dan Heller
Snake icon (*ouroboros*): Sarah Cuypers

For my father and mother,
Who took the family three times East
Always East . . .

What is our life? It is a play of passion.
What is our mirth? The music of division.
Our mothers, they the tiring houses be,
Where we are dressed for time's short tragedy.
Earth is the stage, heaven the spectator is
Who doth hold whoe'er doth act amiss.
The graves that hide us from the parching sun
Are but drawn curtains till the play is done.

Sir Walter Raleigh (c. 1552-1618)

This book is about the end of the Cold War. In some way, for both East and West, this was a real conflict engaged in the foreign fields of the imagination.

Bourbon Island is also located in the imagination: exactly on the equator at about 76° longitude in an area of the Indian Ocean along the Carlsberg Ridge (also known as the Socotra-Chagos Ridge). If the island were real, then Seychelles archipelago is scattered to the south-west; and the giant US-UK naval base at Diego Garcia atoll, in the Chagos archipelago, is about 400 miles south-south east.

The characters, their histories and the events portrayed in this narrative are also imaginary, and are not intended to depict real persons or actual events. Any similarities between this fictional narrative and reality should not, therefore, be inferred.

There is an exception. The Fiery Cross of Goa was - or is - a real artefact. A ruby-encrusted cross of solid gold, the artefact was reputed to stand at 4 ft. In c.1720, the relic was transported from the Bom Jesus Cathedral as part of the Archbishop of Goa's manifest bound for Lisbon. The *Virgem do Cabo* was blown off course by a cyclone and becalmed at the island of Réunion (then the real Ile de Bourbon). The pirate Olivier Le Vasseur, whose *nom de guerre* was "La Buse" (The Buzzard), encountered the storm-buffeted ship and its cargo at Port St. Denis. (In today's values, the hoard is said to be worth upwards of US$100 million.) "La Buse" was eventually captured. It has been put to the author that "The Buzzard" is hardly a serious name for a pirate, but that was his name, and that was his name when they hanged him at Port St Denis, Ile de Bourbon, on 17th July 1730.

The Fiery Cross of Goa remains undiscovered.

JAO

CONTENTS

PART ONE
London Terminus   7

PART TWO
Night of the Exiles   26

INTERLUDE
In-Flight Reading   85

PART THREE
The Shoals of Paradise   91

PART FOUR
Missing Cargo   222

PART FIVE
Regime Change   333

EPILOGUE   366

PART ONE

London Terminus

He that seeketh victory over his nature,
let him not set himself too great nor too small tasks.

~ Francis Bacon (1561-1626)

1

HARRY STONE AT THE WIG & PEN CLUB

ON THAT DAY, the yellow disc of the sun was visible through the clouds that shifted high over the River Thames.

Robert Walker made his way along the Strand until he reached Fleet Street. He entered the club, and climbed the staircase to reach the first floor, where he asked:

"Harry Stone? Is that you?" Robert Walker spoke into the shadows: "Are you there, Mr Stone?"

Harry Stone turned: from a cold silhouette, he became smooth, grey flesh but not much in the way of blood.

"I'm here, Mr Walker. So. Anything to report?"

"You recalled me from Paris to ask me that, Mr Stone?"

"I wanted to have a look at you. You're thinner than I expected."

"My expenses?"

Harry Stone either did not hear or did not want to hear. Robert Walker regarded the new Bureau Chief's face, which was broad, flat and grey; and even the smile, which was not real, was a greyish-white. Robert Walker did not know what to say, so he said: "I haven't finished the Wilde piece."

"Forget about Wilde. Wilde's been done a thousand times." Harry Stone turned to the bartender: "Isn't that right, Jenkins?"

"Yes, Mr Stone, if you say so."

"I most certainly do say so." Then: "What are you having, Mr Walker?"

The two men stood by the miniature bar of the International Press Club, which was situated on the first floor of the Wig & Pen Club. A club within a club, it was remote from the office of the Shoe Lane Agency. By the window, a pair of tweed-suited journalists watched the traffic pass each way towards Ludgate Hill or Trafalgar Square. The observers nursed solid tumblers of malt whisky, and talked of the days when Fleet Street had been great.

Robert Walker was sure they were agency directors. On headed paper somewhere, he recalled names - Foxxe and Lambe. Harry Stone seemed unaware of either. "I was asking, Mr Walker, what you would have?"

"My expenses would make a good start, Mr Stone."

"I meant to drink."

"Lager, then, please."

The bartender poured lager beer from a bottle, then gave Harry Stone a measure of Jack Daniels. Foxxe and Lambe ached for privacy, and relocated to the Jubilee Room to watch cricket on television.

"If I may ask, Mr Stone: what's happened to your predecessor?"

"That Wilde thing was his idea, you know, Mr Walker."

"Yes, but I was wondering what happened to him. Vincent Mosley, I mean."

Harry Stone provided Robert Walker with a cold, blank look. "I didn't think you meant Wilde." In the Jubilee Room, the veteran journalists laughed, but not necessarily at the cricket.

"Those days are on their way out," Harry Stone added. "The Cold War is over - or nearly. Mosley's kind are dinosaurs now."

"Are we dinosaurs, Mr Stone?"

"That'll do," Harry Stone warned. "I'm sure he'd be touched by your concern. He's growing vegetables in Brighton." Harry Stone said this with his fake smile which barely concealed relish. "He's finished. It happens to the best of us."

"It happened to him, though."

"That's right, Mr Walker, and if you're not careful, it'll happen to you, too, unless you're prepared to cooperate."

"I'm cooperating."

". . .We don't need you creative thinkers any more. The world has changed. That's why I've decided move you out of investigative and into features."

"That was Mosley's decision, too. That's why I was sent to Paris for the Oscar Wilde piece. Why have I been recalled - and why here?"

"We're cutting costs at Shoe Lane. We're having the office redecorated; that's why I'm meeting you here."

Provoked by the contradiction, Robert Walker asked: "We were talking about my expenses?"

"No, you were talking about them-."

"-?"

"You're costing us enough as it is. That set-up on Long Acre, for example: it's no longer feasible. It was only set up to make you look-."

Harry Stone had glanced outside. On Fleet Street, a taxi passed: the windscreen caught the sunlight, and reflected the beam up into the club. The Bureau Chief, for an instant, was blinded.

"What do you mean?" Robert Walker asked. "To make me look - what?"

"-Respectable. -Normal. Your - ah - I can't see you. Ah, there you are. Your apartment there; we've got to give it the chop. The whole operation . . .is unsustainable and unjustified. If it had been up to me, I would not have sanctioned it in the first place. Your lady friend will have to move, too, and pay her own rent for a change."

"You must be thinking about another reporter. I'm staying at the Fielding Hotel."

"Don't tell me where you're staying. I don't want to know."

There was more laughter from the Jubilee Room.

Harry Stone spoke for a while about rationalisation, downsizing, outplacement, and something he called 'de-layering'. Then, when he had finished, he passed his empty glass across the bar.

"Same again, sir?"

"If you please, Bob."

"My name's not Bob, sir."

"Oh no? What *is* your name?"

"Jenkins, sir."

"All right, if you please, Jenkins."

Jenkins winked at Robert Walker.

"Something in your eye, Jenkins?" Harry Stone wanted to know.

"No, sir. A nervous tick, that's all, sir."

"Stop calling me sir, for God's sake."

The bartender called Bob paused, then said: "Yes, sir."

In the Jubilee Room, someone howled with laughter.

"You find something amusing, Mr Walker?"

"No, Mr Stone, I do not. I know you're new to this - ah, posting, - sir, so you are probably unaware that-."

"-Yes, Mr Walker, what is it?"

Robert Walker hesitated, then said: "I don't know how to tell you this, Mr Stone, but I do not have an apartment on Long Acre, and I do not - as you put it - have a lady friend there."

Jenkins looked, open-mouthed, at his customers. Then Jenkins, though sure he was not needed elsewhere, made an excuse to leave.

The Jubilee Room was silent.

Harry Stone looked into his glass of Jack Daniels: "Of course you have, Mr Walker. I'll think of her name in a minute."

"-?"

"Anyway, by this evening, she'll be packed. Pay the bills, and then we'll close up the apartment. It's all over, you see that, don't you? I've already spoken to the landlord - a Mr Grey. He's been extremely cooperative."

"I don't know him."

"As for the girl - Conny, *that's* her name - be nice to her. If you can't be nice, be convincing."

"Why convincing?"

"Because she thinks her relationship with you - and her situation at the apartment - is genuine. It took a long time to set-up, so don't go blundering in there. We don't want her talking to the press."

"I don't know her. I think you'll find you're mistaken, Mr Stone."

"Oh no, that's not possible. Well, anyway, as I say, try and be as diplomatic as possible. After all, you've been together for three years."

The bartender reappeared from his short tour.

Harry Stone said: "Same again, Jenkins."

"Yes, sir, but my name's not Jenkins."

Harry Stone said: "No? What is your name, then?"

"It's Clive, sir."

"I thought you said your name is Jenkins?"

"No, sir. With respect, my name's always been Clive."

"All right, then, Clive: same again, *if* it's not too much trouble."

A grunt-grunt of laughter came from the two plutocrats in the pit of Jubilee Room.

"Poor, poor Conny, though," Harry Stone said with some insight of his own.

"Yes, poor Conny," Robert Walker seemed to agree. "You have a new assignment for me, Mr Stone?"

"Bourbon Island, the Indian Ocean. A feature article."

"I read something about it in the Tribune by that American journalist. There was a failed coup there only last week. Against the regime of François Bellarmine. A dictator, by all accounts. The infamous French mercenary - Alfonse Trouvères - escaped, but five of his men were captured."

Harry Stone looked into his glass: "You're very well informed."

"There's plenty of talk about it in Paris."

"Well, you can forget about all of that, Mr Walker."

"You want a feature on the island, then? A holiday feature?"

"No one in their right mind would want to go there on holiday," Harry Stone remarked. "The agency wants a feature on Graham Dunne."

"Who's Graham Dunne?"

"That's for you to find out. An Englishman - a professional treasure hunter. He's just died on the island. Find out the why or the how."

"That's investigative. You said you were taking me out of investigative, Mr Stone."

"It's features. Investigative features. Call it what the hell you like. Your subject is Graham Dunne, the man. Human interest. Syndication has already been arranged - worldwide. Women's magazines. You know the kind of thing."

"Well, not really."

Harry Stone removed a manilla envelope from the inside of his jacket. "I've cancelled your credit cards, Mr Walker."

"Yes, I'd noticed."

"No traces. You're to use these."

Robert Walker accepted the wad. "Is it real?"

Harry Stone said: "You think I'm a counterfeiter? Of course it's real. Bourbon Island rupees. Cash all the way. Your flight's covered from Paris."

"-? Why Paris?"

"You're to go back to Paris."

"-."

"Your contact there is a man by the name of Bougainville - an exile from Port Bourbon. He can tell you things."

"Where and when?"

"Tomorrow. Saint Michel, noon. There's a demonstration by the exiles against this fellow Bellarmine."

"How will I know this man Bougainville?"

"He'll know you. Make yourself visible, but not too visible. Wait by the fountain. . .After that, you're to travel to the island. You'll be staying at the Marina Hotel. Stay in the cheapest room. Don't draw attention to yourself. Your contact there is Mr Swann, the proprietor. If you need back-up, there's someone by the name of Mr Kite who might prove useful. Then again, maybe not."

"Kite?" Robert Walker parroted. "Kite?"

"A European of some sort. He's a member of the syndicate that backed the Dunne fiasco. They're not too happy about losing their man."

Robert Walker tried to look unhappy.

"This fellow Kite may be sympathetic to your cause. Or not."

"I don't have a cause."

"Your assignment, then." Harry Stone set the Jack Daniels to one side. "Do you accept?"

"Do I have any choice?"

"No, of course not."

"Then, I accept."

Harry Stone smirked, and said: "You must complete the feature article by or on the fifth of September - and transmit it to the office. No excuses."

"I don't know any."

"There's a bonus."

"A bonus? How much, Mr Stone?"

Harry Stone blinked - slowly - twice, which meant they would both have to wait and see.

"If you miss the deadline, nothing. Stay out of politics, and leave the women alone. And remember - no footprints. Not even one."

2

IN THE KENSINGTON ARCHIVES

ROBERT WALKER MADE his way out onto the street. Across London, puffy white clouds filled the sky at low altitude. After a glance across the road at the Royal Courts of Justice, he turned, and watched: Foxxe and Lambe poured out of the club, and crossed the road to hail a taxi. They took off in the direction of Shoe Lane. After an interval, Harry Stone appeared, and - with his hands in his pockets - crossed the road to catch the next taxi, which rolled away in the same direction. If Harry Stone were cutting costs, it was not on taxi fares.

Robert Walker continued along the Strand: through the Aldwych, he passed King's College, then the Savoy, and onwards. At Charing Cross, he paid a visit to the Intermezzo Sandwich Bar. Behind the tall counter, a jolly woman from Naples seemed to recognise him, though he was sure he did not know her or her husband, who stood sullen behind the counter with a salami knife.

"*Buono giorno!* Long time now, Mr Walker," she said. "Usual?"

The "usual" turned out to be a coffee and a sandwich, after which he left the Intermezzo and made his way to Embankment Underground Station. The brownish grey waters of the River Thames flooded past Waterloo Station - and onwards, beyond Canvey Island, and out to the Channel. Once on the Westbound train, he travelled along the Circle Line. At Kensington High Street, he alighted - and, after passing through the shopping arcade of the terminus - he emerged at street level. There had been a flash shower. A youth with a goatee beard and a pith helmet handed out leaflets to promote a late summer sale. In England, there had been a retail revolution. Robert Walker looked each way along the great street of shops and department stores. Out of sight, somewhere up Old Church Street, roadworks hammered out a steady pneumatic din. An unrelenting stream of the usual traffic passed in both directions. Robert Walker battled to join the pedestrian movement, which turned, flowed over a crossing against the traffic, and seemed to march on Town Hall. A famous actress from the 1960s brought the traffic to halt. He could not recall her name. Diana Ri-? The lights changed, and the traffic and the actress moved on.

Robert Walker found his way into the Kensington and Chelsea Library. On the first floor, he located the reading room. Old folks read magazines. Job hunters hunted for jobs. No experience necessary; but must have a firm grip on reality. Salary according to experience: none. Robert Walker found his way through the dull-eyed unemployed, hard-up teachers, disillusioned lecturers, moth-eaten researchers, and complacent junior civil servants.

The future, from this survey, belonged to the bureaucrats.

Robert Walker crossed the room to reach the archives. These were grey steel cabinets where the microfilm records were stored. Against the *Index* for Bourbon Island, he found *France, Paris: Assassination of Bourbon Island Exile* - 1986 - a year which also yielded *Graham Dunne's Search for the Fiery Cross of Goa.* He found a console, and threaded the microfilm into the machine. He flipped a switch: the device lit-up, and hummed. Robert Walker spooled-forwards the film, until the headlines blurred into a cascade of indecipherable text and images. The microfilm overshot onto the wrong page, and came to a halt, not on Graham Dunne's quest, but on the assassination.

Robert Walker stared into the viewer:

BOURBON RESISTANCE LEADER
SLAIN ON CHAMPS-ÉLYSÉES
From Our Correspondent in Paris

JACQUES SAVVY, an exiled Bourbon Island resistance leader, was slain in Paris yesterday on the Champs-Élysées by an unknown assailant.

Mr Savvy is understood to have been the most committed among the exiled opponents of the Bourbon Island regime.

President François Bellarmine came to power in a 1977 coup after toppling the government of Anthony Montaigne, the first president of the fledgling republic.

At the time of his death, Savvy had become dangerously isolated, and was essentially acting as a one-man resistance movement with little of Montaigne's moral authority - as the first democrat-ically elected president of the island - or, arguably, of Bellarmine himself, the prime minister prior to the coup.

Fellow exiles say that Savvy, as leader of the Bourbon Island Resistance Organisation (BIRO), had paid the 'ultimate price' for his opposition.

The editor of the exiled *Bourbon Island Star*, known only as "Bougainville", had this to say in the wake of the assassination: "We are all deeply shocked. Jacques once said, 'They can kill me, but they can't kill the idea of democracy'. It seems someone has taken poor Jacques at his word."

Inside, the article continued:

A spokeswoman for the Bellar-mine regime today confirmed that the death of Savvy had come as a surprise to the Bourbon Island government, but that any treas-onous activities on the part of overseas Bourbons would not be tolerated. "We Bourbon Islanders are a friendly people," the spokes-woman added.

Ambassador Charles Ram- goolam, who heads the Bourbon Island mission to France, is at present on holiday, and is unavailable for comment.

A waiter, who had been attending M. Savvy outside a café at the time of the assassination, was seriously wounded in the left leg, and is said to be doing well in hospital. Several tourists close to the scene of the assassination are being treated for shock.

(*Continued Middle Pages for features: BOURBON ISLAND ~ BELLARMINE'S LOST PARA-DISE*

and GRAHAM DUNNE'S SEARCH
FOR THE FIERY CROSS OF GOA.)

A photograph of Jacques Savvy stared through the console - from a world beyond - at Robert Walker. Then, he moved the microfilm with a slow-wind onwards, in search of the promised features. A palm-fringed beach in black-and-white appeared inside the viewer. The article recounted François Bellarmine's rise to power. There was, of course, no suggestion of the dictator's complicity in Savvy's early demise. Robert Walker studied the warped features of a cigar-smoking Bellarmine, who looked - from some high-up vantagepoint - over the great Indian Ocean.

Robert Walker recalled Harry Stone's advice - "Stay out of politics" - and moved on to the next microfilm feature. The item scanned:

GRAHAM DUNNE'S SEARCH FOR
THE FIERY CROSS OF GOA
- Our Correspondent reports from
the Indian Ocean -

The article told of how this chartered accountant from Southend-on-Sea, Essex, had realised the equity of the marital home to finance an expedition to the island. Mrs Dunne, a plain Essex housewife - but with ambitions toward property - had sued for divorce. Graham Dunne, on the run from the English courts, had then embarked on a search for a vast treasure hoard: US$100, 000, 000 in silver and gold coin, precious jewels, and the long-lost Fiery Cross of Goa. In excited staccato, the article concluded that Graham Dunne had spent a fortune looking for a fortune, and found . . .nothing.

Back home in Southend, Mrs Dunne remarried: a Ford dealer from Leigh-on-Sea. On the island, Graham Dunne's golden beard turned grey. A final refuge had been provided by the drinking dens around Port Bourbon. That was five years ago, and now Dunne was dead.

It was a start.

Robert Walker turned off the console.

The unemployed had shifted on; the bureaucrats had found new paper pastures; and the library had been left - rightly - to the librarians.

On the Underground once again, he caught the next train on the Eastbound platform. At South Kensington, he changed onto the Piccadilly Line for a Northbound train bound for Covent Garden. He tried not to watch the hard-bitten faces of his fellow commuters. Over the intercom, there came an indecipherable announcement - *WONK! Humfey Dunfey Sat On the Berlin Wall WONK! WONK!*

After a long pause, the voice said: *"Thank you for your attention."* *CRICKLE-CRACKLE.* Robert Walker was sure he had heard something of importance, but it was impossible to say what exactly. He spent the remainder of the journey - six stops to go - looking over the pages he had photocopied. . .He studied the photograph of Graham Dunne. How many tonnes of sand had Dunne shifted to find all but nothing? Among the granite boulders of the island, Dunne had found a single doubloon, which had, shortly after, been stolen from him. An eye in the photograph seemed to wink. Dunne knew, all right, if not where, then how and why.

Over the intercom, another announcement blurted: *WONK! And all Gorbachev's men couldn't put Comrade Mikhael back together again! WONK! The Black Sea coup, it happened today!*

Robert Walker glanced at a fellow traveller's *Evening Standard*: it was the 19th August, 1991. He alighted, and took the elevator to the surface: he emerged from the Covent Garden terminus, and stepped into the streets, where the rush hour had begun. It was time to confront Conny.

3

CONNY TRAPP ON LONG ACRE

ON LONG ACRE, he located the apartment, and climbed past closed, silent doors on the way to the fifth floor. The woman mentioned by Harry Stone was there, sure enough, packing cases. Robert Walker was sure, too, that he had not set eyes on her until today.

"Is that you, Conny?"

"Robert? Robert! Is that you? Where have you been?"

The woman called Conny appeared from behind a packing case. She had long brunette hair, grey-blue eyes, and a pale face. She wore a catsuit of some kind, with a stripy top, and went barefoot. She had long, clear-varnished nails, which did not make the packing any easier.

"I've been recalled. I'm being sent to-."

"-That's a likely story."

"It's a true story."

She looked at him: it was clear that she recognised him, somehow.

"You're looking at me as if I were a complete stranger, Robert."

"Well, that's what I wanted to talk to-."

"-No! Don't come any closer! Can't you see, Robert, that after THREE years, it's all over?"

"I'm not sure," he said, "that it ever really started."

"You-! You-."

She picked up one of her slippers and threw it at him; the missile hurtled past his head, through the still-open door, and onto the landing. From the bottom of the stairwell, someone shouted: "Hey!"

Conny was in tears. "Never really started? You say that after what we've been through? You have a heart of-."

"Harry Stone suggested that I be diplomatic."

"Diplomatic?" She picked up the second slipper, and threw it at him; this time, it bounced off his shoulder, and knocked over a potted palm that he had not seen before. Then, with her eyes flashing all the way, Conny continued with her packing.

Robert Walker took a single step into the apartment.

After a silence, Conny revealed her solution: "I've decided to move out. I'm going to share a flat in Blackfriars with some of the girls at work. I'm fed up with men. . .I want to be on my own for a while."

"Where have I heard that before? You've been on your own since I've been away. Haven't you?"

Conny's eyes flashed: "You're *so* smart, aren't you? I mean, how do I know what *you've* been up to in Paris?"

"I haven't been up to anything in Paris."

"That's what you say. If you ask me, there's something spooky about that agency of yours."

"Spooky?"

She pulled a thin, white hand back through her long, thick hair.

"You look . . .different," she said. "What's happened?"

"I don't know what's happened."

"You've lost weight, Robert. A lot of weight. I barely recognised you when you came in just then."

On her, he could smell cigarettes, wine, and a perfume he could not identify. He had never known the colour of her eyes, which were the blue-grey of her European extraction, and in which he saw the silhouette of . . . Stone. Harry Stone.

She took a step away. "Why are you looking at me like that, Robert? Why?"

"You're being used, Conny, can't you see that? I can see it in your eyes."

"Stop talking like that! You're giving me the creeps! You-?"

"Yes?"

She looked sideways at him: "I'm moving to the new flat. It's in Blackfriars."

"You'll find nothing there, Conny, believe me."

"I'll find the other girls there. It'll be like my college days all over again. You can't stop me."

Robert Walker said to the apartment in general: "Well, I have no reason to stop you."

Conny moved towards the window overlooking Long Acre. She watched the office workers moving along the street. "I'll be one of them again. It's not much to someone like you, but at least *they* know who they are."

She looked across the apartment at him: "You'll have to stay somewhere else tonight."

"I've already made arrangements - elsewhere."

"Where, Robert, where?"

Robert Walker replied: "That need not concern you any more, Conny."

"There's something else," she said. "There's some bills, uhm, to be paid. Over there." She pointed at the floor near the telephone.

"I see them."

"Well, you'll have to-."

"I've been instructed to-. I mean, I'd be happy to cover any outgoings. Ah, how much," he gulped, "in total?"

"I haven't had time to count them up. It's the utilities, mostly." Conny folded her arms, and looked down on to Long Acre. She appeared to be on the look-out for someone.

"I'll leave you to it, then. I hope your next assignment is more rewarding."

"Yes," she said, "so do I. . .But look, we can still be friends, can't we?"

"I'm not sure that's possible, Conny."

She pouted, but her eyes were angry. Big tears dripped out of her angry eyes.

"One last piece of. . .advice."

"Advice?" she said, without looking at him. She had no more slippers to throw. "And what would that be, Mr Robert Walker?"

"You really should stay away from Blackfriars," he advised. "Goodbye, Conny."

Robert Walker had his instructions, but not much else, so he acted on them: he withdrew from the apartment, descended the flights of stairs, and found street level.

Once on Long Acre again, he made his way through the commuters in the direction of Charing Cross Road, where he saw - in fast succession - a courier on a bicycle, a black taxi, and a red double-decker bus. Covent Garden Underground terminus had become choked. Outgoing travellers sought the main-line stations or the suburbs. A flux of incomers represented night seekers of a club or pub, restaurant, cinema or theatre - or a liaison. It was among these that Robert Walker made his way, through Garrick Street, and slipped into the hidden entrance of Rose Street.

4

MR GREY AT THE LAMB & FLAG

INSIDE THE LAMB & Flag, he found Mr Grey, not in the street-facing saloon, but tucked away in the rear-bar area of the tavern. The landlord, reputed to be among the wealthiest men in Covent Garden, was seated at a plain but solid wooden table. Mr Grey wore a grey suit, entertained a grey complexion, and had a *bouffant* of grey-blue hair. By his looks, he might have been Harry Stone's father, which was unlikely.

"You're Mr Grey?"

"Of course. Who else? Have you forgotten what I look like already? Got the keys?"

"Not yet, but soon."

Mr Grey had already set up two pints of beer.

Robert Walker seated himself across the table from Mr Grey.

The two men helped themselves to the beer.

"Cheers."

Mr Grey did not look cheerful.

"I'm not impressed with that Harry Stone. That Vincent Mosley was a regular payer. Mosley kept to his word."

"Mr Stone will keep to his word, too, but in a different way."

Mr Grey, who was not much amused, smirked anyway.

"Where are you staying?"

"An hotel - nearby. "

"The apartment's to be closed down, then?"

"That's the plan."

"Your plan?"

"Not my plan."

Mr Grey took a pause, a sip of beer, and a puff on a cigarette. Then he asked: "What about Vincent Mosley?"

"I understand he's retired to Brighton. To grow vegetables."

"Oh really? That'll be a change for him. Still, the whole world's changing. The bureaucrats are taking over, Mr Walker, make no mistake."

"Vincent Mosley was a bureaucrat."

"Only if you say so; I don't believe it myself."

"Well, then."

"Well, then, indeed."

"Talking of bureaucracy - I've made arrangements to cover the outgoings at the apartment."

"That's very decent of you."

"It seems Conny has run up some bills."

"One of yours, is she?"

"Not really, no."

"I don't understand, then."

"Your not supposed to understand."

"What about you, Mr Walker, do you understand?"

Robert Walker responded only by taking a good look around the place. In the rear-bar area, there were a few other patrons, lost between the limbo after lunchtime and the early evening. Out at the front of the pub, office workers had started to gather in the saloon; others stood with their glasses in the Rose Street courtyard. Robert Walker looked up at the old black timber beam separating the two sides of the tavern, and read the first line of the inscription:

*Meum est propostium in taberna moris**

The ghost of the treasure hunter, Graham Dunne, seemed to speak out from the walls of the inn. Robert Walker guessed that Dunne had died in a tavern, all right - far away.

A thirsty Mr Grey had secured two more pints of beer.

"When you came in just then, you looked as though you'd never seen me before."

Robert Walker regarded the company landlord's face.

"Have you seen me before, Mr Grey?"

The landlord was perplexed. "Why, of course, I-." Mr Grey seemed to look through Robert Walker. "I mean, you're my tenant, aren't you? Or supposed to be."

"You're a company landlord, then?"

"You mean, since we last met?"

"Yes, that's what I meant."

"You're a strange fish, you are, Mr Walker. No offence."

"None taken," Robert Walker replied. "It comes with the territory."

Robert Walker tasted the beer. The time of his passing through London approached its end. The saloon was full of office workers, who told jokes and did impressions - Michael Caine, Sean Connery. Outside, the courtyard was filling up with more of the thirsty office workers. In the saloon, a barmaid and a barman worked in tandem to line up a series of frothy mugs of ale. A young clerical worker was crushed against the bar. The barmaid watched, alarmed. At a nearby table, a couple stared at Robert Walker and Mr Grey, then returned to their conversation, which was about last night's television. In the saloon, a chorus of laughter erupted: a wide-

---

* A rough translation is: *"To die in a tavern is my definite plan."*

boy with a black shirt and white tie had made an office joke: not too funny but very well timed, and the young clerk was released.

Mr Grey asked: "Where're you going this time?"

"Somewhere in the Indian Ocean."

After a while, Mr Grey said:

"It's suddenly become very warm in here."

PART TWO

PART TWO

Night of the Exiles

Men should be bewailed at their birth and not
at their death.
~ *Montesquieu (1689-1755)*

1

AT THE FOUNTAIN OF SAINT MICHEL

ROBERT WALKER travelled under the great city, and emerged from the RER terminus at Saint Michel. A flash shower had refreshed the city, and the noon-sun heated the wet boulevard. Robert Walker entered the Place Saint Michel in search of the man Bougainville, and looked across the river at Ile de la Cité. A grey mass of cloud sailed over the river towards Montmartre. Pigeons flapped, and took to the clearing skies. Pedestrians waited under the rain-dusted plane trees or took refuge in the bookshops and *cafés*. Robert Walker faced the spray of the fountain. A Cold War patriot and his wife wandered by. The patriot looked at the sky, and testified:

"The world's gone all to hell, Mrs W. . .The anarchists will take over when they see their chance. Any day now, you'll see, my dear. "

"As you say, William," the wife replied.

"It's raining," the former G-man realised.

"No, it's stopped now - or nearly."

"Oh Christ," the General said, and looked directly into the sun. "The world has gone mad, and I'm going mad with it."

By the fountain, Mrs W. replied: "Of course you are, dear, dear Bill," and then she led her husband for cover under the rain-splattered plane trees.

"Right, let's get out of here."

Then, from along the Quais, two young Parisienne women skipped and laughed, until their brown eyes settled on the fountain. The girls exchanged whispers, lifted their olive-skinned faces skywards, and then vanished among the pedestrians. Robert Walker watched them pass into the distance. There, the first placards started to appear above the predicted demonstration.

A daubed sign proclaimed: "BELLARMINE DICTATEUR!"

Harry Stone's forecast has been correct so far. Robert Walker turned, and again he faced the fountain. He looked at the weathered-green bronze of the statue. Three drunks were slumped over the low-rimmed edge of the fountain. After the shower, their clothes gave off evil-smelling fumes. They drank wine from a shared bottle. An empty bottle already floated in the fountain.

The nearest of the drunks opened an eye, and in English asked:

"Monsieur, if I may enquire: you are who?"

Under the almost-noon sun, he replied:

"They call me Walker."

"You are lost, Monsieur Walker. Your situation is as hopeless as our own." The *clochard** laughed and showed grey teeth. The nearest of the three, who had spoken, said:

"Do not worry, Monsieur Walker. After the demonstraton, they will find something for you to do."

"They?" Robert Walker asked. "Who are they?"

"They," the *clochard* said with a shrug, "are not sure, either."

The three drunks wheezed with laughter. Robert Walker thought that these men were much younger than they appeared; and, under the rags, athletic-looking. Again, the three of them shared the wine, which passed freely between them and sloshed around inside the bottle.

"You know about the demonstration, then, monsieur?" Robert Walker asked.

"Noon," the *clochard* slurred. "Always noon," and his companions agreed. "Now - look. The spooks are here already."

A group of tourists gathered to watch the encounter.

"Spooks? Where?"

A man with dark glasses and an off-white raincoat appeared from the crowd. Robert Walker, surrounded by tourists, decided he must withdraw. The first *clochard* was drunk all over again, and shouted:

"Monsieur? Monsieur Walker! There is something to say!" but it was too late. Robert Walker crossed the main boulevard in the direction of the rue de la Huchette, and waited outside a *café-tabac*. He turned to look back at the commotion by the fountain. Then the *clochards* were onto the man in the raincoat with a display of coordinated strength.

A proprietor emerged from the *café-tabac,* and said: "Mon Dieu! These Americans with their innovations! The raincoat will do him no good!"and the man returned to the safety of his *café-tabac*.

Robert Walker watched as the American was pushed into fountain. Tourists gathered to observe the spectacle. A photograph was taken, and then another. The man in the raincoat swayed heavily in the fountain, while some of the younger spectators cheered.

An old man, passing through on a bicycle, climbed off the contraption, and announced:

"It is a travesty! So much for the precious raincoat!" he shrugged. "An American, then - CIA, probably."

"Well, what can you expect? Even those three fools who come to watch the demonstration have more sense than to throw themselves into the fountain!"

The tourists laughed and cheered. Then the old local man, who had finished his dissertion, remounted his bicycle and pedalled away through

---

* vagrant or dosser.

the square. The American, his raincoat saturated, waded free of the water to climb out of the fountain. The spectators started to panic and disperse. The first *clochard* shouted that all tourists were cowards, anyway, who lived off the backs of poor bastards like him. As for the man in the raincoat, whether he was CIA or merely an eccentric of the Latin Quarter, well, he decided to join the demonstration at noon.

2

THE STATE IS OUT OF CONTROL, MONSIEUR

ROBERT WALKER REMEMBERED Harry Stone's instructions: he made himself visible, but not too visible, and watched from the side of the boulevard. A patron stepped out from the same *café-tabac*, and said: "The State is out of control, monsieur."

Robert Walker did not respond.

"Café L'Etoile, monsieur - fifteen of your British minutes."

The man who had spoken turned and disappeared along the rue de la Huchette.

There was no traffic: the route had now been cordoned-off along the Quais; and, again, away from the river, at the junction with the boulevard Saint Germain. On the Pont Saint Michel, a mounted division of the National Security force had mustered. Over the hard surface of the road-bridge, the hooves of forty or more horse skidded and scraped with a clatter. The riders were armed with baton and shield, ready for the charge, and now - at the first signal - visors were lowered against the sun. At the far side of the bridge, an infantry contingent had been aligned - transparent shields raised - behind the cavalry.

The target was about one hundred metres away: a crowd of about five hundred Bourbon Islanders, sympathisers, anarchist syndicalists of the Montparnasse Phalange, hangars-on, and stray tourists. Placards were raised over heads to clarify the position: BELLARMINE IS A TYRANT - RELEASE THE FREEDOM FIGHTERS - FREE THE INDIAN OCEAN. Their proposed destination: the Ile de la Cité *via* the Pont St Michel. A tough-looking group of young Bourbon exiles prepared to lead the way.

WHO KILLED JACQUES SAVVY? the leading placard asked.

Robert Walker, distracted, looked across the boulevard at the area of the fountain. The press had gathered with cameras and microphones. A *flash* and again a *flash-flash* emanated - from where? - there, from the balcony apartments which overlooked the boulevard. A television crew, its lights ablaze, was making a live-pan over the distance that so far separated the demonstrators from the police.

By the fountain, the three *clochards* - on duty, it seemed - had been transformed into inebriate television celebrities. An agitator passed by, and shouted: the three *clochards*, he claimed, had organised this whole affair; they should, therefore, of course, and by any natural justice, be garrotted - immediately - in a public place. This place, here and now, will suffice. They are enemies of the people or the State or, probably, both. Then the agitator, in fear of reprisals, disappeared among the line-up of tourists, who watched from behind makeshift barricades along each side of the boulevard.

The ringleaders observed that the press corps was *in situ*. A signal was given from this side, then passed, among the demonstrators. The crowd started moving towards the river, where there was a loud, concerted clatter of horses' hooves.

A second signal came from the area of the bridge.

In response, a demonstrator waved a placard.

The reaction from the bridge was a third signal: the charge commenced. . . A gas mortar popped: a projectile arced, and developed a sickly-yellow trail of smoke as it traced down the boulevard. The capsule bounced once, then twice more: the harmless-seeming smoke coiled after it; then it settled in among the advancing huddle of placard-wielders: those in the centre were blinded and choked; those away from the yellow smoke were safe for now, but confused. The capsule divided the demonstrators against each other; at the outer boundary, all resolve had been lost, except for an isolated protestor, who marched alone with his placard in a droop: HANDS OFF BOURBON ISLAND, Robert Walker thought he could read through the smoke. A young sympathiser shouted and kicked-out at the rolling canister: it skittered across the boulevard, bounced over the barricade, and tumbled into the crowd of spectators. The tourists went wild, and trampled a few of the more peaceable demonstrators: this was not, someone shouted, the reason they had travelled to Paris. What was the reason? someone else shouted back. There was no answer, since the first tourist lay on the ground, unconscious. The demonstration had turned into a riot. A barricade fell, and another, then another in sequence. A woman with a purple face screamed herself into silence. A pale-faced young man laughed hysterically, turned his eyes at the sky, and fainted; he split his head on the ground, and blood gushed over the warm tarmac. The sight of blood caused howls and whistles of derision, but it was too late: there were more pops from unseen tubes, and three capsules bounced, and settled, into the boulevard ahead of the crowd. A visiting anarchist leapt over a barricade, and ran away into an alley, where he was trapped between a baton wielder and a placard waver. After a flurry of smoke, the scene was obsured. The cavalry charge progressed: the enormous beasts passed through the demonstrators with a thunder of hooves. Robert Walker felt a blast of warm, horse-moist air against the nape of his neck. Then he was aware of great, flared nostrils and a heavy, sudden rush of chestnut-brown flank, which charged away along the boulevard and into the thick of the demonstration. The snorting, wild-eyed horses would put an end to that: Robert Walker had a vision of skulls crunching and spines shattering under hard hooves. . .Then a rider was dragged from his mount, away into the centre of the riot, where he was stripped naked to his boots. The horse trotted off at a jaunt, riderless, and seemed to vanish amid the yellow mist.

The demonstrators had become no more than a gaggle of choking, blinded people in a yellow fog.

The charge proceeded on down the boulevard. After an interval, the cavalry reached the junction with the blvd. Saint Germain, and a wave of foot-police moved in to quell the hard cell of activists.

A CANAL PLUS television crew, anxious for unmixed live-feed, scuttled after the foot-police, and recorded the final confrontation.

A victorious battle-cry emanated from the fountain. The *chochards* were so drunk they did not know whose side they were on. Once again, the old local man climbed off his bicycle, and abused them for their stupidity. A freelance journalist had recognised an angle on the day's events: he moved in to interview the *clochards*, and was introduced to the waters of the fountain.

The leader of the charge, as though he had only wanted to exercise the horses, blew a whistle. It was all over. The demonstrators broke up, and the tourists, their eyes streaming with tears of fear and joy, went back to being tourists. The forces of the State had played their part; and the demonstrators, knowing the rules of engagement, threw down their placards. Robert Walker observed a leafleteer limping in the direction of the nearest *café*. The horses, their nostrils flaring for breath, were already returning along the boulevard, and cantered back to the starting point on the bridge. Out of the yellow mist, the foot-policemen reappeared in their blue fatigues, with shields slung low as they re-belted their batons.

The cavalry had now departed from the field of conflict; the policemen, some of whom bled, stalked back along the boulevard, exhausted after the baton charge. Robert Walker turned his back on the boulevard. The yellow smoke from the canisters had thinned to a lemon haze. A light breeze had sprung up from along the Quais.

3

BOUGAINVILLE

OUTSIDE THE DESIGNATED *café*, Robert Walker asked a veteran at a portable newsstand for the *Tribune*. The veteran, who wore the Croix de Guerre on a lapel of his shiny black blazer, searched for and found the last copy, and passed the damp paper to Robert Walker. The front-page headline read:

BOURBON ISLAND MERCENARIES
FACE DEATH DECREE

- *by Morgan Beaumont in Paris*. The report displaced a patchwork of global news, and retold the story of the counter-coup on the remote Indian Ocean island. The infamous Alfonse Trouvères, as leader of the abortive coup, was said (by an unnamed French official) to be an outstanding stain on the national character of France. The newspaper-seller seemed to agree when he exclaimed:

"Trouvères - il y a un fou," and then, guessing Robert Walker was British, half-translated: "Trouvères est crazy. Bonkers, monsieur!"

Robert Walker counted out small change, and paid for the paper: "You may well be right, monsieur. I'll read the report."

The veteran shrugged, and added: "With crazy headlines like this, it is time to retire. The madman Trouvères should also retire."

"It looks, monsieur, as though he has already retired."

The veteran cackled, and started to pack-up the mobile newsstand.

"Well, then," Robert Walker said.

The veteran looked knowingly at Robert Walker. "Ah, merci monsieur. England is a great country. The Britons are a great people! The same, but not the same. Quickly, now, monsieur - inside! - your man is waiting. Do not speak right away; drink a beer, and then wait until spoken to. Just like the old days, ha, ha."

"Thank you for your advice, then."

"Inside, monsieur; no more talk."

As Robert Walker re-folded the paper, he glanced again down the rue de la Huchette: the demonstration had concluded and the normal business of the boulevard was in progress. In the distance, a man in a wet raincoat attracted the stares of pedestrians, who considered the proximity of an unexpected shower.

Inside the *café*, Robert Walker stood at a cool, zinc-topped bar. The *café* was deserted except for a leather-clad Parisian youth, who played *les flippers* or pinball, and a familiar man in a business suit, who was seated at a table, drank from *carafe* of red wine, and read or pretended to read a newspaper.

The proprietor entered from the kitchen.

Robert Walker ordered a half-litre glass of Kronenbourg, then studied the *Tribune*. The proprietor, observing the same headline, became unsettled, and started wiping, unnecessarily, the zinc surface of the bar. Then the man poured out the frothy beer. Robert Walker swallowed-off half of the beer, which tasted good after the riot. Behind the bar, the proprietor had the name *Bernard* embroidered in red on the breast of his tunic. "A disturbance on the boulevard today, Bernard," Robert Walker said in English.

"Qui, qui, monsieur."

The pinball player lost control of the game, and - with a hard *crack* against the glass - the ball was lost to the pit of the machine.

Robert Walker said:

"So much for the Latin Quarter. I'll remember to come here again."

Bernard moved away along the zinc-topped counter.

Robert Walker looked over the *Tribune*: a condensed map of the Indian Ocean region provided an exploded view of the island's location, directly - it seemed - on the equator. Then Robert Walker eyed the famous byline: Morgan Beaumont, who recounted the island's colonial history, leading up to independence, the first republic, then - after much debate concerning the constitution, freedom, human rights and democracy - dictatorship.

The *artiste des flippers* had had enough for now: he slapped the sides of the machine, then made a prompt exit from the *café*, and disappeared along the rue X. Privas.

Robert Walker scanned the columns of newsprint. Behind the bar, Bernard's face shone as though, between them, they would get to the bottom of the Trouvères mystery.

"You know about this Alfonse Trouvères, monsieur?" Robert Walker enquired.

Bernard smiled: "I do not know anything about anyone, monsieur."

"That's very helpful of you."

"You are welcome, monsieur."

A draft came in through the swing-door of the kitchen.

Bernard frowned at the *flap-flap* of the kitchen door, and shouted: "Bebe!"

Robert Walker tried again:

"So, you know nothing about this fellow?"

"Bebe is not a fellow. She is a she."

34

"I meant Alfonse Trouvères."

At the nearby table, the man in the business suit reacted.

Bernard confirmed: "No, nothing, monsieur."

Robert Walker studied Bernard's shiny face, the black strands of hair locked down sideways over a balding pate, and the standard-issue moustache more keenly kept under an expert-sniffer's nose. The man at the table stood, then approached the zinc-topped bar.

"The state is out of control, monsieur."

"So you've already said."

Bernard saw his chance to investigate matters in the kitchen.

"You are interested in our island, monsieur? Harry Stone sent you, then?"

"You are. . .Bougainville?"

"I am."

"And you are a journalist, Mr Walker?"

"I believe I am."

Robert Walker was invited to join the exiled islander at the table. When Bernard returned from the kitchen, Bougainville ordered another *carafe* of *vin rouge*.

"I did not want to say anything in front of that player of flippers," Bougainville explained.

"He looked harmless enough to me," Robert Walker said.

"A good many of Bellarmine's agents look harmless," Bougainville shrugged. "Many took part in the demonstration you have just witnessed; this way, they infiltrate the exiled opposition groups. All very harmless, of course."

"You did not join the demonstration yourself?"

"I have no desire to appear on national television, Mr Walker."

Robert Walker noticed Bernard, whose face was sweaty after the trip to the kitchen to see the invisible Bebe.

"Bernard is reliable," Bougainville assured himself.

Robert Walker remarked: "Bernard is also a man of certain appetites."

Bougainville looked across the table. "It is his inclination. What is your inclination, Mr Walker? You are interested in the regime of François Bellarmine? So was the mecrenary Trouvères, who escaped, but is now a resident of La Santé prison here in Paris. Can you believe it? He hi-jacked a taxi-ing airliner - Air France, no less - to make his get-away; when he landed at Charles de Gaulle, he was arrested. His well-known career is finished after only a single visit to Bourbon Island."

"Yes, I was reading about it in the Tribune."

"Some of his compatriots are not so fortunate."

"I am interested in Graham Dunne."

35

Bougainville looked disappointed, and sipped at his wine. "Another casualty of the island. Dunne was a fool. Let us talk no more about it; there are more serious matters to consider."

Robert Walker rested back in his chair and, watching the exile, also sipped at the wine. It had a brackish taste. Behind the bar, Bernard, with a far-away look in his eyes, polished a glass with a big white cloth.

Bougainville broke the silence: "Let the dead rest, Mr Walker; your subject should be the living."

Bougainville, Robert Walker determined, was ready for a short speech, and the islander did not let him down:

"We live in a time that should present great opportunities. The Cold War is over, Mr Walker, or nearly over. The return of democracy and free speech is our subject - not treasure."

"I'm not interested in the treasure. Graham Dunne is my subject."

"Who is to know the difference? If you are interested in Graham Dunne, then you are also interested in the treasure, eh?"

"I have specific instructions from Mr Stone in this regard."

"Your Mr Stone sounds like one of our own *grand blanc*, Mr Walker."

"*Grand blanc?*"

"These are, of course," Bougainville explained, "the elite of the island, the ruling class, if you like, of French extraction, who engage in a perpetual struggle for power and influence. It is in their blood, I suppose."

Robert Walker speculated: "Plantation owners?"

Bougainville hesitated, then laughed - an islander's laugh. "Yes, you could indeed say *plantation owners*. It all starts there, any way you look at it. Bellarmine's own father was said to be a plantation owner."

Bougainville pushed the newspaper he had been reading across the table. "Read all about it . . . I met your Mr Stone on a visit to London some years ago. I am the editor of this - the free press in exile."

The swing-swang door of the kitchen flew open with a *ba-bong bu-bung*. After investigating the source of the draft, Bernard reappeared, with his face covered in a thin film of sweat. Bougainville and Bernard exchanged winks. A young waitress - Bebe? - appeared at the kitchen door. She rolled her eyes at Bernard, and returned to her work. Bougainville grinned knowingly at the proprietor.

"You see, Mr Walker? Some people never give up."

Robert Walker examined the front page of the newspaper.

"The Bourbon Island Star," Bougainville announced.

"A splendid title," Robert Walker remarked.

"Splendid maybe, but proscribed," Bougainville said: "There is no free press on the island, Mr Walker, so the only free press we have is printed here in Paris." Bougainville added: "One day soon, the Star will be printed in Port Bourbon - where it belongs."

Robert Walker examined the masthead: the sun rising or setting - *rising*, presumably - from behind the cone of the volcano. In this way, Robert Walker surmised, the deep shadows of the Bellarmine dictatorship were soon to be undone by the bright light of democracy. So this was it; this is what free speech in exile looked like, with a virus of typographical errors eating its way through the text.

Bougainville explained: "We do our best in an impossible situation."

Beyond the swing-door of the kitchen, cutlery and crockery clashed. Once more, Bernard ceased polishing the glass, and went to investigate.

"You should come to our conference of exiles tommorow night, and learn more about our island. The famous American journalist, Mr Beaumont, is also attending, with his asssistant - the very beautiful Miss West."

After sipping at the wine again, Bougainville licked his lips.

"Maximum publicity, Mr Walker. The more of you journalists who expose the Bellarmine regime, the sooner we shall all be free. That is what is needed. Instead of telling stories about paradise and lost treasure, you should expose the tyranny of Bellarmine."

Outside, a group of tourists searched for a restaurant, but not, on this occasion, Bernard's *café*.

4

APPOINTMENT IN PIGALLE

AFTER A DETOUR, the destinations became departures, and it appeared that the stops themselves were travelling and not the train. . . Ménilmontant . . .Couronnes . . .Belville . . .Colonel Fabien. . .Jaurès. . . Stalingrad. . . La Chapelle . . .Barbès Rochechouart. . . Anvers - and, the end in sight . . .disreputable Pigalle.

Robert Walker alighted from the train. The ideal of reaching the apartment, without encountering the landlord M. Girouette*, was the immediate consideration. The prospect was about as remote as the landlord declining the rent as a gesture of goodwill. Robert Walker made his way through the subway; then, climbing the steps, he emerged into the twilight street level of the Place Pigalle among blank-faced commuters. Soon, he had found his way along the Bd. de Clichy, turned into the rue des Martyrs, and started up the hill in the direction of Abbesses.

Robert Walker found the entrance to the apartment block. On the ground floor, the *conciergerie* seemed abandoned, and there was no duty-light behind the woman's closed shutters. Robert Walker crept up the stairs, passed the disused elevator (which, he always suspected, was in good working order), and climbed until he reached the first floor.

Once on the landing, he moved, quickly, along the corridor; but as he passed the landlord's room, the door opened.

"So, Mr Walker, you have returned already?"

Robert Walked halted: from the landlord's room, a shaft of yellow light penetrated the dark corridor.

"I was just coming to see you, Monsieur Girouette."

"Qui, I can see that you were! What is that you have there?"

"A newspaper."

"Anything interesting?"

"A coup d'etat. On a remote island republic. . . Alfonse Trouvères."

"Ah, of course! Who else?" The landlord displayed a whiskery, yellow-toothed grin. "Then you must tell me everything. Girouette is very interested in islands and coup d'état and lost treasure and this kind of thing, generally."

"I didn't say anything about lost treasure."

"Oh really? I thought you did. "

"Perhaps you were thinking about the rent? I have it with me here," and Robert Walker reached for his wallet.

---

* Mr Weathercock or Weathervane.

"Oh, never mind about the rent! The light is bad here in this hall. I must fix the bulb one of these days. Step inside; we must talk."

Robert Walker almost remarked on the expense incurred in a change of lightbulb. The landlord stepped to one side. Robert Walker entered the room; behind him, the door closed. Robert Walker turned and stared at M. Girouette. The landlord spoke first:

"How was London?"

"London is fine."

"And your Mr Stone?"

"He is fine also."

"Now the rent, Mr Walker, if you please."

"As you wish." Robert Walker reached, but not too quickly, for his wallet.

M. Girouette's eyes followed every movement. "You have your instructions?"

"I have."

"So have I."

Robert Walker looked up: "You have? From Mr Stone?"

"Indeed. You and I - we must say adieu." The landlord had not yet taken his eyes off Robert Walker's hands. Robert Walker removed the crisp wad from his wallet, and handed over the francs. The landlord counted the notes with his eyes and, like a magician, folded the wad, and made it disappear.

M. Girouette relaxed. "Now, you will have vin rouge?"

"As you decide."

"Well, then, make yourself comfortable - as you English say."

Robert Walker looked the place over. The chamber was crammed with items of unrecognisable furniture and several unpacked crates - some marked FRAGILE. Yellowed newspaper clippings were littered around the floorspace. Crumpled maps and dusty books were spread over the packing cases: M. Girouette, it seemed, was or had been searching for something. On a cluttered mantelpiece, a black-and-white photograph from a studio in Algiers showed the suave diplomat in his prime. On one up-ended crate, an ancient gramophone pointed its silent horn at the low ceiling, and a couple of old acetate discs had slipped outside their brown sleeves: Erik Satie; the speeches of Charles de Gaulle; and - but what was this? - Charles Aznavour. Robert Walker was close to tears. Of seats, there was scant evidence, except for the landlord's special armchair, which was located under a red-and-yellow salon lamp.

"I haven't unpacked yet," M. Girouette explained. "Various artefacts, which I have collected over the years. There are one of two reliquaries I wish to add to the collection, but time is short."

"You mean you keep your collection in these crates? I understood you retired from the diplomatic service twenty years ago, Monsieur Girouette?"

"This is true, although, you understand, I could be recalled at any time for a special assignment. The same as yourself: I am on duty twenty-four hours a day, and I must be prepared to move at short notice. Within, say, one-half of one hour at the most."

"You mean thirty minutes?"

"I do."

Robert Walker looked at the aged diplomatist, and thought this unlikely.

"If I were to unpack, I might then suddenly need to re-pack!"

"I understand your position, Monsieur Girouette. You are very wise."

"You go too far, Mr Walker," the landlord chuckled. "Now, please, take a position of your own. A seat."

Robert Walker searched for a seat. Over the window, which looked down onto the rue de Martyrs, thick musty-smelling velvet curtains had been partially drawn against the early evening. A huge moth, no doubt, lay - undetected - inside the folds of the curtain . . .The carpet, which shifted underfoot, appeared to be made of jute. The wallpaper was just that - wafer-thin paper on a wall. On the whole, the room possessed the atmosphere of a séance parlour, with M. Girouette as *le directeur*. Robert Walker observed a disused banana box (*le produit de Martinique*), which had travelled across an ocean to be up-ended here against this wall in Montmartre. That would do: Robert Walker seated himself on the box, and tried to take as much of his weight as possible on his own legs.

"Do not be alarmed," the landlord said, and lounged back into the special armchair. "The furniture is safe enough. Now, time for some of the *grotte-gorge**?"

This time, it was Robert Walker's turn for diplomacy: "That would be. . . desirable."

Now that the rent had been paid, the landlord reached down beside the special chair, where he found a big, half-empty bottle of *vin ordinaire*.

"You must have some of this; it is good for a broken heart."

"You believe I have a broken heart, Monsieur Girouette?"

"Not you; I am referring to my own heart."

"Ah."

"It is impossible for an Anglaise to have a broken heart. Amour to an *Anglaise* is a foreign country."

"That is harsh with us. What about the Americans?"

The landlord, staring directly ahead, uncorked the bottle with a sharp twist of a yellowed thumb and forefinger, and sniffed at the cork.

---

* Throat-scraper.

"This varies from case to case."

Robert Walker almost groaned at the quanity of rough wine remaining. A zinc tray rested on the table, with a neat white tissue - impressed with HOTEL ANTIBES - set at its base. A couple of plain quaffing-glasses were inverted on the tray. M. Girouette used a thumb and forefinger to upturn the glasses, then poured wine into each, not spilling a drop, up to their brims.

Robert Walker watched with polite interest.

The landlord passed a glass to his guest.

The empty banana box creaked as Robert Walker accepted the glass.

M. Girouette said: "This is a toast to the end of an era. I never thought I would live to see the day."

Robert Walker hesitated before he met the toast. M. Girouette quaffed heavily at his glass, and the wine was gone. Robert Walker took one good quaff, and the rough-tasting wine bit at his lips.

"Now, we speak. I have my instructions. I must leave this place. I am to retire."

"From being a landlord, you must mean."

"I mean, I must retire from this business we are in."

"We? You must have made some error."

"Error? Girouette does not make errors. Of the heart, many. Of business, none."

"Of which you are aware."

"None, I say."

"As you please."

"I have said enough. Harry Stone does not pay me to say these things."

"But *I* pay you."

M. Girouette looked into the distance, which was merely the paper on the wall behind Robert Walker. "The Cold War is over," the landlord reflected. All of us should retire to the south. We should all put fur in our nests, and go."

"Feather our nests, you must mean?"

"What is the difference?"

Robert Walker did not say anything.

"I am saying too much, but what the hell: it is all over. I would advise you, Mr Walker, to do the same thing. Your Mr Stone will have me shot if he knew I were telling you this."

"I don't think Harry Stone shoots people."

"Oh no?"

Robert Walker, who thought of fur and feathers, did not pass any remark. Instead, he took a good slurp of the wine, which scraped - as promised - at the back of his throat.

"It is good, eh?" the landlord laughed.

"It is interesting."

"As for Girouette, there is a woman. Well, that would be telling. She is based now at Antibes. So, I go south, but not as far south as you, Mr Walker!"

"-?"

"Antibes it is, then. That is where I shall go. She runs a hotel in that strange city. There is one small difficulty. She has not spoken to me for thirty years."

"I can see how that might pose a diplomatic barrier."

"Maybe so, Mr Walker, but you forget: Girouette is a diplomatist."

"How could I forget?"

The landlord frowned at his guest. Robert Walker stared at naked floorboards.

"The wine, it does not agree?"

"The wine agrees in its own way."

After an interval, Pierre Girouette made an unusual request: "If you do not mind, Mr Walker, we should continue this conversation later. I have one or two urgent enquiries to make."

5

SHAVING AT MIDNIGHT

THE HEAT WAVE would soon move up from Algeria and engulf the Paris Basin. On the way up the hill, Robert Walker paused to look back over the city, then continued on his route to the *café*.

It was here, at the Place du Abbesses, that he had a late supper of beer and a *baguette* with ham or *jambon*. He was alone, except for the proprietor, and a couple of surly-looking shift workers, who soon finished-up, and departed. A *café*-dog watched him for the entire period it took to consume the *baguette*. After a while, the *café*-dog sniffed at his knees, and then lurched away behind the counter to rejoin its master.

There was time to reflect, but reflect on what, Robert Walker was not so sure, though a rhythm had begun to emerge. Great white puffs of cloud sailed farther on up the hill, over the Sacre Coeur basilica, and away into the night sky. An artificial satellite hurtled through the heavens, and was gone, its mission completed.

Robert Walker, aware of the impossible void, realised it was almost midnight. He settled with the proprietor, a man of few words and a sad face, who regarded him with suspicion. Then he returned to the rue des Martyrs. On the way, he heard the dog at the *café*: "Rough! RoughAAW!"

At the apartment, on this occasion, the *concierge* waited and watched. She was dressed in black and greys, and never smiled. She reminded Robert Walker of Gertrude Stein. This version of Miss Stein, satisfied that he was unaccompanied, shook her head without a word, returned to her station, and closed the door on the world. As he mounted the staircase, Robert Walker felt strangely inadequate.

On the first floor, he encountered M. Girouette, who had apparently walked onto the landing during what is known as a 'dry shave'. The landlord, his chin foaming, held a cutthroat razor in one hand, with a linen towel draped over the other forearm. Robert Walker reached the last step before the landing, and said:

"Shaving at midnight, Monsieur Girouette?"

"Shaving at midnight, of course. I am on the move - south!"

Robert Walker had passed knowing what to say.

"Please, come in: we have not finished our conversation."

Robert Walker did as he was asked. The landlord, in ebullient mood, followed him into the room, but this time the door was left open onto the landing.

"You are feeling restless, Mr Walker?"

"I've been up at the café," Robert Walker explained, "for something to eat."

"That is good. When you arrived, you were thin from your travels."

"Yes, I was-."

"-I know the proprietor. His dog has more personality. It is lamentable. If he had a heart, it would be broken. His wife left him for a man from the Ministry last year - or the year before; it doesn't matter. The man from the Ministry felt entirely justified in his exploit. These bureaucrats are always poking around in other people's business. Believe me, there is no end to it."

"I am acquainted with the dog."

"Well, as I say, the wife has departed. All he has is that chien. I understand he beats the dog, which resents being abused for the bureaucrat's sins. The world, Mr Walker, is a very strange and unfair place."

"I'm beginning to appreciate that more and more, Monsieur Girouette."

The landlord, saying nothing, roamed about the room among the packing cases: he scraped - blindly - at his chin, and lifted the foam to expose a smooth, whiskerless patch of skin. Then he swiped the razor across the linen cloth to remove the whiskered foam.

"You seem in excellent spirits, Monsieur Girouette."

"Please, seat yourself, and pour some of that wine there. I shall finish shaving, and we can proceed. Soon, I must catch the night-train for Antibes!"

"-?"

"Say nothing. I will explain all."

Robert Walker, who had become accustomed to the established procedure, had almost been certain that he was about to be asked for more rent. He poured out two glasses of the rough wine, and, with one of these, he seated himself, as before, on the same banana box from Martinique.

Robert Walker watched as M. Girouette adopted a somewhat exaggerated pose in the middle of the room, and continued shaving, without benefit of either water or mirror. As he observed the performance, he was inclined to wince each time the cutthroat razor scraped over M. Girouette's whiskers beneath the dry-ish foam. After a dozen strokes, M. Girouette had finished, and wiped his face all over with the dry cloth: he presented a reasonably well shaven jaw, with only a few raw wounds. Robert Walker thought Monsieur Girouette looked younger than his years.

"There, now to business," the landlord said, then rolled-up the primitive shaving equipment, which he placed in an old attaché case. M. Girouette dropped into his special armchair with a bounce, showing long legs, De Gaulle-ish to the point of stilts, and helped himself to the glass of the rough wine. Robert Walker imagined the younger Pierre Girouette, poised under the yellow-and-red salon lamp, lounging back in this same chair, years ago, being shaved by a young, dark-haired beauty from Antibes. Girouette in love; Girouette being shaved by the loved one. Now, he could see how M. Girouette had been re-considering the past that day, the glorious, untouchable past, betrayed or missed friends, botched romances, misadventures, lost opportunities, the one-way ferry of life that had now passed the landlord by.

Robert Walker closed his eyes tight shut, then opened them again: M. Girouette was pouring a second glass, which Robert Walker declined, changed his mind, and then accepted.

"You are celebrating?"

"I am always celebrating, Mr Walker! The Cold War is over!"

Outside, a taxi driver *honked* at the bottom-end of the rue des Martyrs.

"You and I," M. Girouette continued, "are on the move, but in different directions."

"-?"

"*Bof!* I have had a lifetime of it; you will never know. I should have joined the merchant marine instead of the diplomatique service. But then - who knows? - for the diplomat is always at sea!"

Robert Walker took a good quaff of the wine, which felt like it lifted the enamel from his teeth.

"Now, you will be pleased to know that I am about to get to the point, as you English fellows say."

Robert Walker watched and waited.

After a very long pause, M. Girouette reported: "I have made several enquiries, Mr Walker. The results are incredible. I am to retire from this business with your agency. I am to relocate to Antibes. The woman Anna had agreed - reluctantly, at first, it is true; but then with enthusiasm. We will end our days together, drinking - not this paintstripper - but champagne, overlooking the blue Mediterranean from her hotel balcony."

"-?" Robert Walker almost gagged on the rough wine.

"-Do not say anything, my friend, for time is short. I linger here only to unload my instructions before embarking. Tonight, you and I, we must say adieu. So I say it now: Adieu."

Robert Walker looked at M. Girouette as though he, the landlord, had lost his mind.

"You are a man who trusts too much. I, Girouette, trust no one." The landlord seemed to look in on himself with great suspicion. "You must leave here."

"Tonight?"

"I leave tonight. You leave tomorrow morning. You are to relocate. I am not to be seen with you; you are not to be seen here in Montmartre. Instead, lose yourself in the crowds for a day or two. "

"Well, then, you will have to explain."

"I have been trying to, Mr Walker. Now, listen, for I have instructions. The world is changing - from political to the economic. As we speak, this realignment is taking place! We must consider our own retirement funds. There. Girouette has spoken. Do not ask me any questions."

"How-?" Robert Walker faltered.

M. Girouette, about to quaff again, realised his glass was empty, and said: "This business of the island, Mr Walker, if I might comment from a personal business perspective. I have heard stories over the years. Treasure? Worth millions. As you know, I am greatly interested in antiquities."

Robert Walker indicated, with a look at the crates and packing cases, that he had not known until today.

"You take my meaning? I mean, if you should hear anything? This matter of the island, it is a very curious affair. . .There are certain geographers who would stop at nothing to-."

"Geographers?"

"Well, perhaps that is not quite the right term, then."

Robert Walker set his almost empty glass to one side.

"You know about my next assigment, then?"

Pierre Girouette looked into his depleted glass, and replied: "You told me today."

"I most certainly did not tell you."

"Then - all of Paris is talking about it. You are being watched everywhere you go. You must be careful, for there is much at stake. You are to relocate: the Levant Hotel on the rue de la Harpe. Your contact there is Monsieur Le Blanc. Find out what you have to and then leave Paris."

"I understand, Monsieur Girouette."

The whites of the landlord's eyes seemed to turn yellow when he said: "If I may ask, Mr Walker . . .have you found out anything. . .yet?"

"About what?"

"Why, about the treasure, of course. The Fiery Cross of Goa: it has been missing for two and a half centuries."

"I am not seeking the Fiery Cross."

"So you claim."

"-?"

"Then you are investigating the Trouvères coup?"

"Monsieur Girouette, I can assure you that-."

"There are those who would pay you well for your information. The syndicate, for example."

Robert Walker replied: "Information? I do not have any information."

"Well, you sound like a man who has a lot of information."

"Really, Monsieur Girouette, I am not interested in the treasure."

"I find that difficult to believe, monsieur."

"What is your own interest, Monsieur Girouette?"

Girouette, Robert Walker considered, was well-named: the land-lord, a twister and turner in any strong breeze, had likely already pre-sold any information in his possesion to the syndicate.

"I have my retirement to consider."

"And I have a feature article to consider, that is all. Graham Dunne is my subject."

"Monsieur Walker, I admire your dedication," the former landlord said, with a dangerous sparkle in his eye. "You almost seem to believe you really are a journalist."

6

YOU ARE NOT WHO YOU PRETEND TO BE, MONSIEUR

GIROUETTE'S DEEP RED wine despatched Robert Walker to the happy-hunting grounds of some far away place. An instant passed, and the neon signs of the Monmartre night were extinguished.

The strong morning light arrived. In bed, he looked up from the hard matress at the cracked yellow ceiling. Outside, it was a fine hot day in the making. The blue skies appeared to suggest that there were possibilities; if not here, then elsewhere. Robert Walker licked his dry lips, and felt raw hunger. Breakfast in bed? Not a chance. His stomach growled for the Café L'Atlantique Bar at the bottom of the hill. Then, he remembered the rough red wine, which had left him groggy but somehow refreshed. As for M. Girouette, he supposed the landlord had by now deserted the apartment block to catch the night train for Antibes.

Robert Walker stood, swayed, and then wandered into the shower cabinet to face a powerful gush of luke-warm water. Then, he shaved, dressed and packed. He fast-packed a single hold-all travelling bag - his all - though he was sure he had not always travelled so lightly: notebooks (3), a wad of mixed currencies, cancelled credit cards, the Shoe Lane News Agency ID Card (which appeared, strangely, to be brand new), a change-and-a-half of clothes, a passport. He did not look much like the images on the ID card or the passport, but at least there was a passing resemblance, if not with him, then between the two photographs.

He reviewed the three notebooks: they were all blank except for a few notes under: OSCAR WILDE (1854-1900). Alien tears, *etc.* Outcasts never mourn, *etc.* In a fresh notebook, with a tremor, he wrote: *The Fiery Cross of Goa, the Search for. . ?*

Then he looked into the fusty mirror: Robert Walker, journalist. Robert Walker, ---------.

For the last time, he looked out onto the rue des Martyrs: it was deserted this Friday morning, but then it was nearly always deserted.

In the dark corridor, he passed M. Girouette's room, where he almost expected the door to swing open with a demand for rent. The door, though, remained closed, and all the rent had been paid. One last time, he ignored the disused elevator and descended the stairs.

"Bon jour, madame," Robert Wallker said to the *concierge.*

"Monsieur," she smiled without teeth, which was much more than he had expected. "Girouette: Gone! Like the wind, Monsieur Walker!"

The woman was clearly elated by Pierre Girouette's Antibesian adventure; or, simply, the landlord's absence from the mezzanine. Robert Walker handed over the keys.

"Spooks," she said in English, and showed purple lips.

"You mean ghosts? There are ghosts here, madame?"

"Girouette is an old fool!" she pronounced.

"-?"

"What ever happened to staff loyalty?" he said.

"Whatever happened to a decent wage?" Then: "Bon voyage, Monsieur Walker!"

Robert Walker stepped out onto the hill. The woman withdrew into her station, where she laughed and then wept the tears of a widow.

Robert Walker left the rue des Martyrs without regret. After a *café-au-lait* at the Atlantique, where the locals put on sad pantomime faces, he made his way to the Pigalle Métro terminus. He travelled down the line in the direction of Mairie d'Issy; he changed at Saint Lazare, then boarded another train bound for Châtillon-Montrouge. On the train, the seats were mostly empty in that carriage, but he chose to stand. He contentedly took in the single interim stop at Miromesnil. A goat-bearded young man boarded, with an armful of leaflets for distribution, and moved, carriage-by-carriage, along the length of the train. The youth spoke of the coming revolution: be prepared, all of you: read our *gazette* and educate yourself - all for only F5!

By noon, Robert Walker had climbed out of the Champs-Élysées Clemenceau Métro terminus. At ground-level, the traffic - a mass of steel, glass, and hot rubber - throttled and vibrated each way along the boulevard, where he made his way to the International Press Club.

At a distance, he recognised a solid-looking figure outside the Press Club. A large man in an off-white suit paused, wrenched his trousers up over a walrus-belly, and looked at his watch. This was Morgan Beaumont, the famous, Pulitzer Prize-winning journalist, and the author of yesterday's *Tribune* headline. Then Beaumont, with a glance at the sky, turned on his heels, and disappeared into the crowds.

Robert Walker made his way through the revolving doors of the Press Club. He approached the reception. The desk clerk, who never spoke, responded with a little lip-whistle of recognition, and checked the pigeonhole marked W.

Then, with another, sad whistle, he indicated that there was nothing for collection *phppfffff!* Robert Walker studied the desk clerk, who reacted with a shrug and a whistle without sound ___.

"I'll wait a while," Robert Walker replied.

The Press Club buzzed with Friday-noon activity. Robert Walker retreated to a corner of the lounge area. Journalists sipped coffee, read the papers in many languages or talked at cross-purposes. One man appeared to argue with himself. A woman studied the elusive pattern in the carpet. Three men, lined-up on a deep leather sofa, discussed French foreign policy in Iraq. An embarrassed silence fell over the group, which - at the sight of Robert Walker - dispersed. Robert Walker sat himself down on the abandoned sofa, and scanned a stray newspaper.

At a nearby table, a silver-haired man and a red-haired woman interrupted their conversation. "Monsieur, with respect," the man said in English: "you look somehow familiar."

"Monsieur?" Robert Walker looked up.

"We are of course both with Le Monde. You are-?"

"Robert Walker. Londres. An independent agency."

"Impossible!" the red-haired woman responded.

Robert Walker thought that the woman, who bit at a fingernail, was waiting for the situation to escalate.

"This cannot be. I *know* Monsieur Robert Walker: you are not he."

"You are the one who said I looked familiar, monsieur."

Robert Walker turned to the newspaper.

"He is an impostor," the woman conferred with her colleague. "What are you going to do?"

"Who, me?"

"Yes, you, of course. Who else?"

"Well, I shall speak with the offcial, of course."

The man stood up, looked at the woman and then again at Robert Walker, and made his way to the reception. Robert Walker heard the clerk, confused by the allegations, whistle like a minor bird. The red-haired woman turned her green eyes on Robert Walker, realised she had been left alone with this *Anglaise* impostor, and grabbed at her handbag. She rose, and walked with steel-heeled steps to the reception, where her male colleague had by now confounded the whistling clerk.

"Still here in Paris, Mr Walker?" A short man with a black moustache had approached. "I was told you were overseas. Your reputation - ah, precedes you. You'd better be careful: a tricky situation over there, you know. Not a game for amateurs, although - in a way, we are all amateurs, are we not?"

Robert Walker looked at the passer-by: "You'll have to speak for yourself."

The stranger took a step back, rubbed at his moustache, and apologised: "I'm very sorry: I thought you were Robert Walker."

Robert Walker did not respond. The short man, whose face had reddened, withdrew from the reception area, passed through the revolving doors, and out of the Press Club all together. He was not alone: the Press

Club regulars - as lunchtime neared - were already emptying onto the Champs-Élysées.

Robert Walker approached the reception desk. The clerk refrained from a whistle. Instead, he shook his head: still no messages.

"I'll call in again before I depart."

The clerk, who stared into the distance, said nothing.

Robert Walker then made his way to the far-reaches of the reading room, where he found a selection of _____ SPECIAL COUNTRY REPORTS. As a republic, Bourbon Island had its own section under B. Robert Walker photocopied the survey for postponed, in-flight reading[*].

Now, it was time to relocate at the Hotel Levant.

---

[*] See INTERLUDE

7

WITH MORGAN BEAUMONT AT HARRY'S BAR

"ALL I'LL SAY," Morgan Beaumont was saying, holding court at Harry's Bar, "is this-."

The famous American struggled to limit his remarks in the presence of his unwanted companions. They were, he suspected, not real journalists, but a pair of stooges assigned to keep an eye on him for the State Department. So much, he thought, for the free press.

Beaumont and his associates stood at the far-end of the bar, away from the entrance on the rue Daunou. It was early, and Harry's was empty, except for the three men, and one bartender - Henri - on duty. The stooges listened: Morgan Beaumont talked a great deal, they thought, but said nothing. In turn, Brad and Dud smiled weakly at their famous countryman, before reaching for a fresh round of frozen daiquiris.

"-You gentlemen are in the wrong line of work," Beaumont said, slurping off a measure of the cocktail. "You'll see - when it's too late."

"How do you mean that, Morgan?" said Dud, a younger man with a crewcut and white shadows around his eyes where he normally wore sunglasses.

Dud did not like being threatened. His expression showed that Morgan Beaumont, in spite of his fame, was still only a journalist

Beaumont added: "Oh, by the way, did I say you could call me Morgan, Dud?"

"Ah, no, may I? "

"Sure, why not? Since we've become so well acquainted lately. Whenever I turn around, there you two are. What is it you're after exactly?"

An older individual with a grey face, Brad, said: "We're on assignment, Morgan, just like you. We're offering you a little friendly advice, that's all. We endeavour to assist our friends whenever - and wherever - we can."

"Endeavour? Now there's a word you don't hear much these days."

"We're only trying to point you in the right direction, Morgan."

"Oh really? And what direction would that be?"

Brad produced a couple of airline tickets, which he set on the edge of the bar. Morgan Beaumont observed, but he did not yet touch. Since when, he thought, had he been so prone to suggestion? He clutched his daiquiri and studied the two men with quiet despair in his eyes. The veteran bartender, Henri, watched from his position behind the bar (ready to serve, never to contradict).

"We have a job to do: the same as you, Morgan," Brad said.

"The same as me? Oh no. You can go back to Washington and tell them it's a no-play. I don't do that kind of work. "

"I don't know what you could mean by that," Dud claimed.

"No, of course not. I don't know what I'm talking about, do I?"

Brad sulked; Dud, he looked agitated.

Then: "You've had a distinguished career - so far," Dud said.

Morgan Beaumont had a vision of a time before he was a journalist: he saw himself standing outside a nightclub. In the here and now of Harry's Bar, he eyed the meniscus of his drink as it approached the bottom of the glass, where the distorted images of Brad or Dud or both appeared.

Beaumont said to the *garçon*: "Henri," and the bartender slid into action: a cold glass in hand, shaved ice, a bottle uncapped, a *slosh* of liquor, the sugared rim, and a frozen daiquiri appeared in front of the big American. Beaumont nodded a discrete *non* and *non* again when the Henri looked sideways at the near-empty glasses belonging to the other men. Beaumont said: "They've had enough," and laughed. The *garçon* returned to his duties. The other two men smirked, wondering at Beaumont.

Then: "I concur, Morgan," Brad said, "but it's all a question of what it is we've had enough *of*."

Beaumont relented: "Encore, Henri!"

"Qui, Monsieur Beaumont. It is done."

Beaumont, his irritation easing, said: "As I was saying, the big question is this: The Iron Curtain has fallen, but will it stay fallen?"

"Ahhh," Brad exhaled as the fresh daiquiris arrived.

"I don't know much about curtains, myself," Dud said, and cleared his throat.

Morgan Beaumont stared at Dud, and said: "Oh no? I thought curtains were your speciality?"

"There's no need to be like, Morgan," Brad said, and shifted his weight from one foot to the other. "I mean to say, we're all on the same side, aren't we?"

Morgan Beaumont glanced outside - at the infrequent passers-by - on the rue Daunou. On the street, a woman appeared: she wore a navy blue blazer, with a pleated skirt to match, and a pearl-white blouse. At the end of a long shoulder-strap, she carried a slim handbag; and, pinned under an arm, a single buff folder. Beaumont thought the woman looked like she had stepped out of the pages of an up-market mail-order catalogue. Then he realised who she was: Barbara West, his very own assistant these last three months. Barbara West was making her way into Harry's Bar. A group of loud New Yorkers followed her in from the street. A tall, Ivy League lawyer-type tried to stand her a drink, but she efficiently declined. Morgan Beaumont eyed his shadowy associates, then said:

"You'll have to excuse me, gentlemen. You can go back to Washington now, and make your report. I'll put those," he said, glancing at the airline tickets, "to good use."

In some way satisfied, Brad and Dud set their respective drinks on the bar, and made to leave. On their way out they passed Barbara West, but pretended not to see her. Outside on the rue Daunou, Beaumont could hear the pair of them laughing.

"Comedians," he said to Henri, the bartender.

Henri, who was a diplomatic sort of bartender, did not say anything.

As Barbara West approached, Beaumont picked up the airline tickets and moved to the nearest table, where he invited her to join him for a drink.

"No, thank you, Morgan. Not just now."

The group of New Yorkers oggled and gabbled at the far-end of the bar. She had excited them almost to a man. After an interval, they turned their attention to their main purpose, and set Henri the bartender to work. There was a lot of talk about what George Bush was calling a New World Order. Morgan Beaumont had heard it all before.

"Who were those two men you were talking with, Morgan?"

"You mean you don't know them?"

She looked across the table at him. "No, I don't know them."

"Oh, I thought you did. They made such an effort not to notice you, I thought it unnatural."

"Who are they?

"Journalists. Myself, I think they're Company men."

"Which company?"

"*The* Company, Barbara."

She showed apparent incomprehension, then asked:

"What did they have to say?"

"They said they admired my work. They said it would be a great shame if I did not continue with the Bourbon Island story."

"I agree: it would be a great shame. Anything else?"

"They wished me well for the journey. They said I deserved every encouragement." He set the two airline tickets on the table. She picked them up, impressed.

"What's wrong with that, Morgan?"

"They don't sound like fellow journalists to me."

"Fellow Americans, Morgan," she smiled. Then: "I've put together some clippings for you." She passed the slim buff folder across the table. It was marked BOURBON ISLAND in her own ornate handwriting. "You can read it during the flight."

For the time being, he ignored the folder. For now, he looked at the shoulder-length brunette hair, the dark blue eyes, the Hollywood-white smile, and wondered who she was, really.

A wave of chatter moved outwards from the group of New Yorkers. Something had happened in Moscow, but Beaumont was unable to hear what, exactly. Out of the hubbub, he could only make out discrete words: Gorbachev, *perstroika*, *glasnost.*

Barbara turned her dark-blue eyes on Beaumont: "I'll have that drink, now," she said.

8

THE MAN WITH THE STRAW HAT
ON THE RUE DE LA HARPE

AT ROBERT WALKER's destination, the many doors of the train rumbled open, and he stepped onto the platform. He passed through the terminus, climbed a flight of steps, and emerged at street-level: it was a fine afternoon, and a strong, warm breeze played along the river.

Robert Walker rested against the cool embankment wall of the Seine. He watched as the other passengers emerged from the depths of the Métro terminus, and then they, too, blended with the pedestrians at street-level. The river at his back, he crossed the Quais, and negotiated the traffic to reach the Place Saint Michel.

Soon, he stood in front of the fountain. Then he noticed the same three *clochards*. One of drunks was less intoxicated than his compatriots. This *clochard* with the brown and dusty head squinted his eyes against the sun, and said:

"That fellow who was following you, monsieur. An American. We took care of him. What do you think of that? He was hot under the collar, all right. We cooled him off in the fountain."

Robert Walker did not yet speak.

"These secret services," the *clochard* slurred, "are everywhere these days."

"I wouldn't know about that," Robert Walker replied. "But thanks for the advice, anyway."

"These - how to do say? - *spooks* are everywhere," the *clochard* related, and commenced the back-slide into delirium. "The Cold War is coming to an end, you'll see. . .They do not know what to be up to any more. They're all lining their pockets. Dollars, Ruples. Both sides. The transfer of funds is as monumental as it is unbelievable," the *clochard* blub-blubbered.

"You and your associates would know?"

"We know, but no one listens. We have been on tv!"

"I can well believe it."

The man squinted at Robert Walker. "You are a spook, monsieur?"

Robert Walker looked away from the fountain, in the direction of the Petit Pont, and then Notre Dame.

"I'm not sure. I don't think so."

"Thaf is god," the man slobbered, and his brown head slumped, unconscious, between his damp knees. The *clochard's* neck, with his head slung so low, had been burnt a deep-ochre by the sun.

Robert Walker picked up his luggage, then made his way to the nearby Levant Hotel on the rue de la Harpe. He found the hotel with its glass *façade*, and entered the lobby. The receptionist, who showed instant recognition, introduced herself as Madellaine, and reached for a key: No 17. She was dressed in red trouser suit, with a white blouse; she wore thick red lipstick, with a white smile to match.

"You recognise me, mademoiselle?"

"Of course, monsieur."

"Passport? "

"Non, Monsieur Walker, there is no need these days; we are, all of us, Europeans. . ."

"We have always been Europeans," Robert Walker said, and accepted the proffered key. "You know my name, then?"

"Of course, monsieur. You are the journalist from England."

"And I made the booking personally?"

The receptionist checked the records. "Ah, non, Monsieur Walker, the booking was made by-. Ah-." Madellaine, aware of company, hesitated:

"Let us just say that the booking was made."

"I understand."

At the other side of the lobby, a well-gutted man in late middle-age - a German or perhaps an American - looked up from a newspaper. He wore a straw hat. After a moment's silence, the fellow juggled with the newspaper and lighted a cigarette from a packet of Camel. Then the straw-hatted smoker moved through the lobby, and found his way out onto the rue de la Harpe. On the street, he looked both ways, and was intercepted by a doorman outside a Greek restaurant. The lobby loiterer was persuaded to take some refreshment.

"This doorman," Madellaine confided, "rarely loses a prospective customer. Unless you are very hungry, keep to this side of the street."

"I'll have lunch in my room, then."

"Very well, monsieur."

"By the way, who is the gentlemen in the straw hat?"

"Which gentleman?"

"The one who was here just now."

"That was no gentleman, monsieur, that was-. I do not know."

"An American?"

"No, Monsieur Walker, European."

"European? What kind of European?"

"I think the new kind," the receptionist replied.

Robert Walker picked up his luggage without comment. Then:

"First floor?"

"Non, monsieur: second floor. It is an anomaly of the hotel."

"I understand perfectly. I'll keep to my room for a while, then. If you would send up a sandwich and two bottles of very cold beer."

"A sandwich? This would be a sandwich *Anglaise*, which we cannot do, monsieur."

"All right, then. A *baguette* of some kind. Ham. Dijon."

"Of course, monsieur, I'll get onto it right away." Madellaine turned, and seemed to vanish behind a vase of flowers to adjust her make-up.

Robert Walker took a serviceable elevator to the second floor. On his way up, he wondered about the man in the lobby, whom he already thought of as Straw Hat. The chamber designated No. 17 was small, but adequate, and the double-bed was an improvement on the wrack he had endured at the rue des Martyrs. At last, he set his luggage down. A desk was mounted against a wall. An ironwork balcony overlooked the rue de la Harpe. This was where, he decided, he would make some preliminary notes on Dunne's quest for the Fiery Cross of Goa. He drew the curtains aside, opened the *porte-fenêtre*, and looked, below the balcony, each way along the street. A warm breeze played up the street and into the bedroom chamber. The doorman at SANTORINI'S ~ MAISON DE GYROS was busy capturing more customers. The ratio was impressive: for every four or five refusals, the doorman had one success.

There was no sight of Straw Hat, which was peculiar, since-. But no - at the farthermost terrace table, the man in the straw hat drank coffee and smoked at another Camel cigarette. He waited, but for what was unclear, unless-. Robert Walker recalled what the *clochard* by the fountain had said: there were a lot of spooks about these days. The brown-headed dosser was right. Straw Hat, he guessed, had to be a new kind of pan-European spook. The Americans watched the islanders, but the French, under deep cover and disguised as *clochards*, watched the Americans, who watched Robert Walker, a Briton, who, really, watched no one, except-.

There was a knock at the door. Robert Walker opened the door, but no one was there: a covered tray, though, had been set on the corridor floor. He retrieved the tray, closed the door, and uncovered the tray: it was the *baguette* and two bottles of fairly cold "33" beer. The considerate Madellaine knew that there was work to be done in this chamber. He unpacked his luggage, which did not take long. Then he de-capped one of the beers. The *baguette* was crusty, and came with plenty of mustard on the ham.

On the rue de la Harpe, the doorman reappeared outside the Greek restaurant, and pulled-in yet another passing couple. This time, he directed the captives to an outside table, and cast his eyes at the warm, blue, empty sky for any sign of raincloud, then - satisfied - passed a pair of menus to the anxious couple. At a nearby table, Straw Hat drank small beer, smoked at another Camel, and read the *Figaro* newspaper, with an occasional glance across the street into the glass lobby of the hotel.

Robert Walker tried to forget about Straw Hat. He turned to one of his almost-blank notebooks, where he had written: THE FIERY CROSS OF GOA. GRAHAM DUNNE (English). ROGER DUPIN (Bourbon Islander) MISSING MSS.* What else did he know? Not much, but this did not matter, for nor did anyone else.

It was now approaching 14:00. Robert Walker made some more notes, and after a while the notebook contained an impressive clutter of stray annotations. In the absence of detailed research, it would have to do for now, and - anyway - he could barely recognise his own handwriting. . . Robert Walker saw fluid versions of the truth mix before his eyes, and stared onto the street below. The balcony ironwork distorted the image of Straw Hat, who seemed to gloat at him from the street, and the doorman, too, seemed to look up, smile, and invite him down for dinner.

It was almost 16:00, which did not seem right - but that was what his watch indicated. There was not much to show for two hours' work, except for dangerous and probably futile speculations without a conclusion.

Again, he looked onto the street, and Straw Hat had disappeared. The rest of the outside tables had been abandoned, and the doorman was not visible. A hungry couple strolled by, passed unmolested, and moved on to dine elsewhere. It was still warm outside. He reached for the second bottle of beer, and found that it was empty.

Almost at once, the telephone extension rang: he lifted the 'phone and listened. It was the hotel reception, but he did not recognise the voice.

"Yes, I was just about to order another bottle of beer. You'll bring one up yourself? That won't be necessary. All right, then, thank you. By the way, there's a man across the street watching this hotel."

Robert Walker waited for the owner of the voice to take a look.

"Not, not the doorman. The man in the straw hat."

Again, Robert Walker waited.

"You don't see anyone? All right, never mind."

Robert Walker set the telephone down on its receiver. Again, he looked at his notes: this fellow Roger Dupin had to be the priority contact on the island.

There was an another, more authoritative knock on the door. This time, Robert Walker was confronted by a well-groomed man in a grey suit, who held a bottle of beer in one hand. This had to be - this was, surely-?

"Le Blanc," the hotel manager confessed.

"You needn't have bothered yourself, Monsieur LeBlanc," Robert Walker said. "I don't know what to say. "

---

* See INTERLUDE - the Bourbon Island bibliography.

"Say nothing, Monsieur Walker," the manager grinned, and handed over the beer. "I have been instructed to afford you every assistance.

"Ah. You have? By, ah, whom?"

That did not, evidently, merit an answer.

Robert Walker tried again: "You are the manager of this hotel, are you not?"

Le Blanc looked surprised: "Of course I am the manager, monsieur. You think I am - what? - one of the chamber maids?"

"No, of course not."

"You are sure you are the Anglaise journalist Robert Walker?" the manager enquired.

"Well, Madellaineat reception checked me in under that name, didn't she?"

The manager looked at him in silence.

"I am. Indeed, I am."

Le Blanc peered out over the balcony in such a way that he would not be observed by the doorman. "We have much larger rooms for special guests, monsieur," the manager confided.

"This room is fine," Robert Walker replied.

"Ah," the manager said, looking at the writing desk, "I can see you have been busy. That is excellent. A man of so many talents is always welcome at the Hotel du Levant.

"There is a back-way out of here?" Robert Walker wanted to know.

The manager shook his head that the idea was unsound. Then: "What does this gentleman - a straw hat, you say? - want from you?"

"I did not say he wants something from me. I said he was watching this hotel."

"Nonetheless, monsieur, it is incredible."

M. Leblanc drew away from the balcony, and brushed micro-dust from a shoulder of his grey suit. The manager happened to eye the notebook, which now held many cryptic and indecipherable anno-tations.

"Some notes," Robert Walker explained. "Who knows where they will lead?"

"Where, indeed? I heard about such a relic when I was a boy, which was a long time ago."

"You know, then, Monsieur Le Blanc?"

"There is a lot of talk about it across the city. The gentlemen you thought you saw watching this hotel may only be a curiousity seeker."

"I saw him, all right. He was in your lobby. Ask Madellaine; she saw him, too."

"A lot of people pass through our lobby, monsieur."

Once again, Robert Walker and Monsieur LeBlanc looked over the balcony onto the rue de la Harpe.

"Well, then the gentleman has gone," Le Blanc concluded. "And I also will leave you to your work. I wish you well with your expedition, monsieur."

"You have something for me, Monsieur Le Blanc?"

"Only this. . ." The manager removed an airline ticket from this jacket, and set it on the desk. Robert Walker examined the specifed route: Paris-Frankfurt-Bourbon Island. Optimistically, the fare showed RETURN.

*

A WHILE LATER, when Robert Walker left the Hotel Levant, it was through the front entrance. He could not see Straw Hat, but the man's presence, if not the man, somehow lingered in the vicinity. Robert Walker took a left-turn into the rue Saint Severin, then another, sharper left-turn, so that he backed up along the Boulevard Saint Michel, away from the river a stretch.

Robert Walker crossed the boulevard, found his way into a bookshop, and waited. After an interval, he headed - in the opposite direction - until he found the nearest Métro terminus. As he descended underground, his knees turned into jelly; he felt like his legs would crumple. The train was already at the platform: from the platform, he hopped onto the deck of the train. After the exertion, his legs started to fold under him, so that he had to press his back up against the carriage. The doors closed with a *whirr*, the carriage shuddered, and the train pulled slowly away from the terminus. Robert Walker watched the posters on the tunnel wall turn to a whitish blur, and the platform was left behind as the train entered the dark tunnel. He looked along the carriage, and there was - who else? - Straw Hat. The German or the American or whoever he was chewed at the remains of a cheeseburger, while engrossed in a newspaper (*France Soir*). Robert Walker remained in a standing position. He closed his eyes, and when he opened them again Straw Hat had finished the cheeseburger. There was no one else in the carriage except two teenage girls, who marvelled at these middle-aged men. Who was following who? they asked each other. And why?

Robert Walker tried to avoid their eyes, which made the girls laugh, but they fell silent when Straw Hat looked up from the newspaper. By the time the train reached the next terminus - the Musée d'Orsay - the girls could not take any more of the intrigue, and so they alighted.

The train lurched, and accelerated along the system of tunnels. There was not much time, and he was heading in the wrong direction for his appointment, which anyway was within walking distance of the hotel. Robert Walker wiped the sweat from his eyes.

The train started away from the platform

At the far end of the empty carriage, Straw Hat regarded his only travelling companion through dry, blood-shot, sky-blue eyes.

Robert Walker straightened his knees, and prepared - when Straw Hat turned back to the newspaper - to alight.

The train decelerated, halted, and the doors slid open: he hesitated, and then stepped out - at Invalides - onto the platform. Straw Hat stood up - too late - and got wrapped-up in his newspaper. The doors closed. Straw Hat, whoever he was, stared out from his glass cage. After a lurch, Straw Hat - his mouth fixed in an O - was whisked away into the tunnel, bound for Pont de l'Alma or even Versailles.

Robert Walker stood on the platform, and considered the situation . . . he changed platforms, and travelled back to the Saint Michel. At street-level, he crossed the road at Grand Augustins. After the riot of the day before, the streets seemed tranquil. At the fountain, the three *clochards* had gone. Robert Walker turned his back on the fountain and started on his way to Saint Germain.

9

RELAIS ODÉON

THE RELAIS ODÉON *café* was the agreed (neutral) rendezvous with Bougainville prior to the meeting of exiles.

Robert Walker approached the *café* from the general direction of the Sorbonne. It was a warm evening, and, from the near east, an indigo-blue horizon raced across the sky towards this part of the city. Soon, it was almost dark. He passed a multiplex cinema. Revivalist posters announced: *Le Patsi avec Jerri Lewis*; *L'Orange Mécanique avec Mal. MacDowell - dir. Stan. Kubrick;* and *Les Vacances De Monsieur Hulot avec Jacques Tati*. Robert Walker looked up at the darkening sky over the Odéon, and breathed the cooller night air.

At the Relais Odéon, it was clear from the tables inside and along the terrace that the islander had not yet arrived. Robert Walker positioned himself at one of the tables, which overlooked the boulevard, and in this way he would not miss the editor of the *Bourbon Island Star*. He attracted the attention of a waiter, and ordered a Leffe *bier*. Then he waited for the beer and the islander to arrive, and watched the lights each way along the boulevard, the flow of the traffic, and the criss-cross of pedestrians as they passed along the *façade* of the *café*.

The Leffe arrived in a glass goblet. Robert Walker took a deep swallow of the beer until his eyes watered.

There was still no sign of Bougainville.

Robert Walker looked at his watch: it was 20:05 hrs, and the islander was late. He studied the faces of the passers-by and the patrons at the terrace tables. A couple of Parisienne girls with olive-skinned faces occupied the nearest table.

And still Bougainville had not arrived.

He looked at his watch: it was 20:15. As he waited, he tried to guess the destination of each pedestrian. This man with the grin on his face is going to see - or has already seen - a mistress. That sad man - the one with a violin case - is a musician on his way to work. Inside the case, there are also narcotics from Algeria, and a violin string would soon break. Those two there are an American couple on honeymoon; they have had an early dinner at the Vagenende 1900 *brasserie*, just along there, and now they are on their way back to their hotel; the girl has the future in her eyes, the boy only the present. That man over there: he has something unspeakable on his conscience. What could it be? It is boring through his mind like hungry woodworm. He is a murderer, but the body has not yet floated to the surface. And that woman there: she should not necessarily be with that man; she should be at home with her children in the distant suburbs. And those two girls, over there, at what are they laughing? Those two, at a terrace table, with olive-skinned faces and white smiles. And who is this fellow here with the *bier,* they say, waiting and waiting. Again, the girls had their dark eyes on him - an eccentric *Anglaise* abroad, then - and laughed. Their laughter made Robert Walker feel warm; he raised the goblet of Leffe at the girls, then drained the glass.

Robert Walker thought of Pierre Girouette on the balcony overlooking the blue Mediterranean Sea, while the former landlord sipped, not the *grotte-gorge,* but chilled *champagne* with his lost love. Well, then, we are old, but not too old, and the *champagne* is cold, but not too cold; look, the breeze comes in off the sea, and our hearts are as warm as the sun that shines down on this balcony. . .

Oh God, oh God. Robert Walker watched the crowds pass before his table. The world was a strange place, full of strange people, and Robert Walker was one of them. He turned to look once more at the two olive-skinned girls, but they had upped and departed. Robert Walker felt an ache of regret. Another time, then, and some other place.

"So," a voice came, "it is our own Mr Walker."

Robert Walker looked up from the table. Bougainville, who sweated from some exertion, had spoken.

"I was just about to leave."

As Bougainville sat down, he caught the attention of the waiter.

"-It is a fine evening, of course," Bougainville remarked. "Good looking girls, too."

"Girls?" Robert Walker said. "What gir-? Oh yes, I agree."

"Now, enough of that: I am speaking tonight along with a few others. You will hear some things about the island that should interest you."

"Not about the Dunne business?"

"No, not about Dunne. But good background material for your article."

"Is it," Robert Walker dared to ask, "in any way relevant?"

"On yes. On the island, everything is inter-connected."

"Inter-connected, you say?"

The waiter arrived with a beer for Bougainville; Robert Walker declined another Leffe. Bougainville's hand was shaking slightly as he reached for his glass. "This is a fine evening. It reminds me of-." Bougainville hesitated.

. "So, you are speaking tonight?" Robert Walker said. "You are nervous?"

"Of course. I am always nervous. Anyone in my position would be nervous."

"I'm being followed."

"Yes, I noticed."

"Not the girls, unfortunately. A man in a straw hat. A European."

"I don't know anyone by that description. Then again, if you are researching the treasure, a lot of people are sure to follow."

"I'm not researching the treasure. I'm looking into the Graham Dunne case."

"You surprise me, Mr Walker. Tell me, who is to know the difference?"

After a while, Bougainville said: "All right, let us go. The conference venue is not far from here."

Robert Walker turned away, and looked across the boulevard. Bougainville was right; it was a fine evening. Robert Walker decided, then, that whatever happened to him, and wherever he went in the world, he would never forget this time and this place, here on the terrace of this *café*.

10

NIGHT OF THE EXILES

ROBERT WALKER guessed that about two hundred exiles were present in the ballroom. An aisle ran between two blocks of seats, up towards a stage, where the various speakers were positioned at a long table. Over the stage, a blow-up photograph of Jacques Savvy, the assassinated resistance leader, looked down on the exiles. An almost invisible smile played over the lips of the dead man.

On the stage, the Editor of the samizdat *Bourbon Island Star* positioned himself with his fellow speakers at a long table. One seat remained vacant: ANTHONY MONTAIGNE. Behind and above the speakers' table, a broad white banner was emblazoned with the words:

CONFERENCE FOR THE RESTORATION OF DEMOCRACY ON BOURBON ISLAND

Below the banner, the symbols of the young republic made up a crest: a silhouette of Mont Pomme d'Or; twin coconut trees; a turtle on a deserted beach, and a pair of giant marlin fish, rampant with crossed swords.

Robert Walker tried to locate a seat. The eyes of many strangers scanned his features. On the perimeter of the audience, a man in loud, check-jacket stood up, and invited Robert Walker to take a place. The only available seat, he discovered, was situated beneath a formidable chandelier. Robert Walker, once seated, took out a notebook. He looked up at the many facets of the chandelier, which, he supposed, was well anchored against the ceiling.

"No one else will sit there," his neighbour advised.

"That's reassuring. Thanks, all the same."

"You are a journalist?" the man whispered.

Robert Walker nodded that, yes, he was a journalist. The man in the loud jacket indicated that he had nothing against journalists in particular. For Robert Walker's information, the man pointed: a two-man video crew had established itself at the head of the aisle. The camera was focused, not on the speakers, but on the famous American journalist and his glamorous assistant. Both Americans slanted their faces away from the camera.

"Morgan Beaumont," the man in the loud jacket informed Robert Walker.

"Yes, I've heard of him. Who's the woman?"

"I don't know. His secretary - or something. Nice to look at, eh?"

"Yes, very nice."

"Dangerous to look, eh?"

Robert Walker looked at his neighbour. The man's face sparkled with perspiration under the diffuse light of the chandelier.

Up on the stage, a large woman inside a substantial dress approached the microphone stand.

"It begins," Robert Walker was advised. "This is Mrs Smith, it is true."

The chatter of the audience increased in both volume and scope. Anthony Montaigne, the chatter seemed to agree, had decided not to attend. How dare he snub the exiles. No wonder Bellarmine is on top - and we are here. If Montaigne is not here, then why are *we* here? If Montaigne is not interested, then why should we be interested? Bellarmine will have a good laugh when he finds out. So, it is another small victory for Bellarmine! It is a disgrace in the face of poor Jacques' memory! Look at him, up there on the wall! What would he think?

The image of the dead man, Robert Walker thought, did not appear moved one way or the other. What do I care? he seemed to say. Mrs Smith reached for a glass of water. She drained it, with a rattle of beached ice-cubes, in a single gulp.

"Don't worry, sir," Robert Walker's neighbour said. "Montaigne will be here soon enough. You'll see. He never lets the ladies down. Never."

Mrs Smith *rap-tapped* the stage microphone with a long, purple fingernail. "All right, enough discussion!" she announced.

The film crew took its cue . . .

Mrs Smith, encouraged, reached for the microphone: it howled with feedback, but she seemed to choke it off with a big hand.

"There, silence, at last. . . "

The audience cackled. Mrs Smith implored:

"Now, please, ladies and gentlemen! I must call for calm! I am sure," she continued, "that some of you may find all of this very amusing, but - I can assure you - that there will be little to laugh about during the rest of the evening."

The audience, fickle-hearted, agreed to silence.

"Thank you, everyone. Now, I would like to welcome each and every one of you here on this extraordinary evening. I see many familiar faces here, as well as some guests, who are interested in the plight of our island."

Yes, yes, yes, some people at the front mumbled.

A round of light applause came from the middle and rear of the ballroom: the proceedings, at last, were under way.

"All right, I see we have one or two jokers with us tonight," Mrs Smith said. "There will be plenty of time for that later on - when you all, no doubt, will be going on to the nearest nightlcub."

Mrs Smith cleared her throat, and said:

"Ladies and gentlemen, I give you the late Jacques Savvy, who paid the ultimate price in the struggle . . ."

"You see," Robert Walker's neighbour whispered, "how she would introduce a dead man?"

Mrs Smith's face twitched with emotion; she raised her eyes to the photograph of Jacques Savvy, while the audience tested its five-year-old grief.

Robert Walker studied the face of the dead man. There was a spark in Savvy's eye, for sure, the same spark the agents of Bellarmine had snuffed out that day on the Champs-Élysées. In those grim moments, Robert Walker heard the sound of the film as it moved through the camera, an occasional cough, and the rustling of feet at the rear of the ballroom. Jacques Savvy, the founder of the Bourbon Island Resistance Organisation (BIRO), had been no match for François Bellarmine, the leader of the Bourbon Island People's Party (BIPP). . .

"So, first of all, our thoughts are with poor Jacques. . . "

In a flash, she made the Sign of the Cross.

"We can now proceed. I do not think we should wait any longer for our guest of honour," she said, and glanced at Montaigne's unoccupied seat.

Then Mrs Smith made a formal opening:

"My dear friends, one and all, the time has come when we must confront the very serious and sad situation on our island. Our first speaker this evening requires no introduction, but I will introduce him anyway. . ."

"Well, now, the first speaker is our old friend, the editor of the famous Bourbon Island Star, who was imprisoned by the regime not long after the coup, and then subsequently deported. Since that time, there has been no free press on the island, and Bougainville has continued his work here in Paris under difficult circumstances and at great personal sacrifice. . .at the very forefront of the resistance against a cruel and unjust regime."

The speakers, Bougainville included, had adopted expressions of solemn concentration. The stage microphone emitted one more little wail of acoustic protest, and settled down for the evening.

"I give you - Bougainville. . ." Mrs Smith withdrew for more water.

Bougainville moved to centre-stage. He was greeted with polite applause and a few cheers. The video crew fixed its lens on the first speaker's face.

"My fellow Bourbons," Bougainville commenced, "I must first of all say I consider it a tragedy that, after all these years of exile, I cannot at this time be addressing you back on our beautiful island . . .However, we could say that if we *were* back on our island, there would be no need to address you at all!"

Thunderous applause bounced around the ballroom.

At the speaker's table, a man in a grey suit and slicked-back hair sweated under the stage lights. This was, a place-name revealed, CHARLES RAMGOOLAM.

"Let me assure you all," Bougainville continued, "that the Bourbon Island Star will continue - and, what is more, it will one day soon be printed in Port Bourbon - where it belongs!"

Charles Ramgoolam, who wore a haughty smile, looked some-where off-stage, and folded his arms.

"Who knows," Bougainville added in a low voice, "it might be easier: for, here in Paris, the whereabouts of our print-room has been betrayed to the regime many times."

The audience gasped. Bougainville glanced at Charles Ramgoolam, whose haughty smile had turned into a snarl.

The audience reflected on that revelation. Who was the traitor? Who?

"We at the Star believe that Bellarmine's 'Revolution', as he calls it, has come full circle, and ended up nowhere - where it started!"

Excited, nervous laughter was heard at the rear of the ballroom.

"The great collectivist experiment . . .has been an equally great disaster!"

"Bellarmine has spoken many times of justice for all, and he has given us tyranny in its place. But what can you expect when you import your ideas from places like Cuba and North Korea? Some experiment this has been! Some revolution that was!"

There was strong applause at this benchmark in Bougainville's address.

"The brain-washing that the one-party state passes-off as education in our country must come to an end . . . The torture and corruption must stop, and on that day soon, let me tell you, BELLARMINE CAN GO BACK TO THE FISHING VILLAGE WHERE HE WAS BORN!"

This brought rapturous applause. Charles Ramgoolam shook his head in strong disagreement. The din echoed around the ballroom until the big chandelier shook. Robert Walker looked up at the ceiling. The man in the loud jacket shifted one-seat sideways away from Robert Walker.

Bougainville concluded: "There, I have said everything I want to say!"

"Succinct and to the point," the man in the loud jacket advised Robert Walker, and then joined-in with the substantial applause, which turned into wolf-whistles, and a concerted stomp-stomp of feet.

Bougainville took one step back from the microphone, and returned to his seat. Charles Ramgoolam glowered at him.

The response was ecstatic. Everyone in the ballroom clapped, except Charles Ramgoolam, who kept his arms folded in defiance.

Mrs Smith, anxious to maintain protocol, lumbered to her feet. The video crew panned - then zoomed-in on Charles Ramgoolam, whose well-oiled hair had started to unfurl in the heat of the ballroom.

The audience, without instructions from Mrs Smith, calmed itself. Charles Ramgoolam checked his wristwatch.

Someone shouted: "Please, Charlie, tell us the time!"

Mrs Smith approached the microphone once again, and said:

"If you please, whoever that was, His Excellency is not ready to speak just yet, but he will be heard!"

An outraged Charles Ramgoolam got to his feet, approached centre-stage, and took the microphone stand from Mrs Smith. He barked at the audience:

"You talk of free speech! But I suppose I, too, will be denied a voice by your illegal forum in the face of these unfounded charges! Where is your evidence?"

"Please, ambassador!" Mrs Smith pleaded, but she surrendered the microphone, and returned to her seat.

Charles Ramgoolam spoke direct to camera: "I have only been invited here to be ridiculed by this treasonous talk! I must be allowed to put the government's case at this illegal gathering."

Bougainville shouted:

"So, Mr Ramgoolam, why would you stand on an *illegal* forum? You are with us, then?"

"GENTLEMEN!" Mrs Smith cried. "I must . . .call this meeting to order!

Ramgoolam responded to camera:

"I would stand on this forum to answer these absurd charges! I ask you again, where is your evidence?"

Bougainville stood up from the table; he pointed at the big photograph of Jacques Savvy: "There is your evidence!" and sat down again.

Ramgoolam glanced at Savvy's image, and explained: "This man's - ah, demise - came to as a great surprise to us all! In the past five years, I have made many enquiries in my official capacity, and no one knows who is respon-."

"YOU MUST BE JOKING!" someone shouted. There were more heckles, but then the audience turned sullen, and decided to listen.

The ambassador, his face running with sweat, cleared his throat, and addressed the audience:

"My fellow Bourbons. . ."

There was a single, strangulated laugh from the middle of the ballroom.

"Please, if you will hear me for a moment! It is my duty to repeat to you the offer made by our leader only recently. That all of you who call yourselves exiles from our homeland. . .are welcome to return to our island at any time!"

The audience greeted this announcement with silence.

"Some of you, I know, have already resolved to make the trip."

The audience was not so sure. Was this true? Who among us?

Robert Walker heard the *rinkle-tinkle* of the chandelier above his head.

Charles Ramgoolam, encouraged, seemed to think he had won over the audience.

"We must all work together in helping our leader work . . .for the benefit of our country. . ."

Feet rustled somewhere near the front of the ballroom. Robert Walker thought he could hear footsteps - from above - a guest, perhaps, lost in a corridor on the first floor. Again, the chandelier *rinkle-tinkled.*

"We Bourbons must learn to forgive. We must stop hating each other. On your return, you will be treated as any other citizens of the republic. The law-abiding individual has nothing to fear. There will be no reprisals. The criminal element will be treated like any other criminal element. Those involved in the recent coup attempt will be tracked down like dogs. No one else has anything to fear. . ."

Fear? Ramgoolam, once he had said this, did not look so sure, and his eyes shifted over the crowd of heads. The audience scented the diplomat's treachery. Hoots and whistles moved from the rear of the ballroom towards the stage. Ramgoolam coughed, and ran a hand through his mess of hair. "Now, we must realise the truth of the matter. Our President François Bellarmine-."

The truth? This time, the audience exploded.

"Please, my friends! Listen to me! He is a fine man who has dedicated his life to the making of our country. He is misunderstood. He is a kind man who has always had the welfare of his people close to his heart. He is a hero among heroes."

That was enough; Ramgoolam had gone too far. The group of women in the front row all stood up from their seats. The first egg hit Ramgoolam in the face, and splattered, bright-yellow, against his grey suit. The camera crew zoomed-in on the action, and panned from the throwers of the eggs to the target.

"AHG! Ugh! You DISGUSTING people! I say again, the offer-."

A salvo of eggs - close-targeted - plastered the lonely figure of the diplomat: his face was a yellow mass of scrambled eggs and white shards of shell.

"Let me finish-! This is a disgrace-! "

The audience looked on, fascinated by the procedure, and only a few at the rear of the ballroom cheered as the eggs broke over the diplomat.

"SOMEONE CALL SECURITY!" Ramgoolam howled.

The egg-throwing women operated as a firing squad:

SPLAT! Splag! Splaf!

Mrs Smith, about ready to faint, made no attempt to control the women. The eggs were nearly all extraordinarily well aimed. A shell-fragment bounced off Ramgoolam's shoulder and hit Bougainville on the side of the face. Bougainville reached under the table, found a telephone extension, and called for assistance. After an interval, two doormen appeared from the lobby: they dived into the ballroom, and manoeuvred towards the stage.

"Get - . . .OUT of here!" Bougainville ordered.

The two doormen clambered up on to the stage, and made a grab for Bougainville, who shouted again:

"Not me, fools! Ramgoolam!"

The security men turned, wild-eyed, and pounced on the diplomat. The bombardment continued. The doormen dragged Ramgoolam off the stage, and hustled the egg-splattered diplomat out of the ballroom.

Bougainville wiped the egg-splash from his face to see the egg-shelled stage.

The audience watched, fascinated, replete. "This is more like it," someone said.

"Is it over?" Mrs Smith enquired. She fixed her hair, and reached for her fifth glass of water

"It's over for now, Mrs Smith" Bougainville confirmed.

The women in the front row had depleted their bags: they returned to their seats, and waited for the proceedings to recommence.

"Ladies and gentlemen," Mrs Smith panted, "it is my special pleasure to introduce our next speaker. Anthony Montaigne, the first president of our island republic."

In the audience, the man in the loud jacket whispered at Robert Walker:

"You see? Montaigne never lets the ladies down. Never. Not even a big one like Mrs Smith."

11

MONTAIGNE SPEAKS

AFTER A PERFECTLY timed late-arrival, Anthony Montaigne stood under the stagelights, and smiled statesman-like at the audience of exiles. Montaigne was dark-bearded (tinged with grey) and barrel-chested inside a very expensive-looking lightweight suit designed for extensive travel. The applause rose to a feverish pitch, wore itself out, then settled down to a respectable thunder. In the front row, the group of women egg-throwers shed tears, and chanted:

"VIVE MONTAIGNE! VIVE MONTAIGNE!"

Anthony Montaigne ignored the video crew, which, he seemed to sense, was the glassy eye of Bellarmine. Montaigne kissed each of Mrs Smith's substantial cheeks. Then he turned to shake hands with each member of the speakers' table. He paused at Ramgoolam's empty place, and smiled again at the audience. Approaching the microphone stand, he remarked:

"I see His Excellency has an urgent appointment with the dry cleaners!"

"VIVE MONTAIGNE! VIVE MONTAIGNE!"

The deposed president blew a single kiss, and no more, at the women in the front row. The audience calmed down. Those who had been standing returned to their seats; the young men at the rear of the ballroom tried to appear unimpressed with the former leader.

Montaigne wasted no time on preamble:

"My fellow country women and men - and, distinguished guests - it is indeed a long time now since I have spoken to you, and I must say it does the heart good to see your faces again. . ."

The audience, happy to be recognised, applauded and cheered.

"Here, in this great city, many of us have found a home from home. We are here, and they are there: the majority of our fellow nationals remain on the island of tyranny, in a state of repression. This is the regime of François Bellarmine."

The audience remained silent. Robert Walker made a note, but he still did not recognise his own writing. Next to him, but one, the man in the loud jacket noticed, and became unsettled.

". . .This is the same Bellarmine," Montaigne was saying, "who I felt obliged - for the sake of peace, but against my better judgement - to make my prime minister when I was elected the president of our young republic. At that time, there were issues of national security that had not yet been resolved, and so I must accept that great burden of conscience.

"All of you here, of course, know how Bellarmine rewarded my misplaced trust in him . . .

The audience recalled, and grumbled.

"While I sought to launch our administration in a spirit of high endeavour, it was Bellarmine who looked to a different kind of politics. In doing so, he brought the dark forces of the mainland to bear on our island. Then came the intrigue and conspiracy that has brought our small country such great shame."

That Bellarmine, he is a devil, an older woman whispered.

"There is no need to list again in detail the catalogue of crimes he has perpetrated against our people and the law of our island. Most of you know these things well enough by now. Some of you know, but are not here to tell."

-?

"But are we able to find an explanation or a root cause for all this infamy? What kind of bizarre psychology is it that motivates such men to do what they do? It is, my friends, a deeply disturbing subject."

Oh yes, oh yes, the audience agreed (hush).

"I am not sure I am able to explain these things, but at least I can share my thoughts with you. After all, we have all had long enough to reflect on the nature of the whole sad situation."

Yes, yes indeed, the audience muttered. Too long. Far too-. Long-.

"-To the one we know as Bellarmine, the prospect of high office has always been a bright and shining thing. In power, Bellarmine's dictatorship is a uniquely personal business. In power, it is no coincidence that he now lives on top of our highest peak - Mont Pomme d'Or. Not for him, the low coastal plain of our island. Oh no! His vaulting ambition takes him to the skies. "

"What is this?" a heckler asked. "A geography lesson!"

"More like history!" someone else remarked.

"Politics is our subject here, my friends. Politics. Believe me, when I hear people say - usually politicians - that the business of politics is not about personalities, it is about the issues, I do not believe them!"

The audience seemed to blink as one: What? How? When? Wher-?

"For it is the individual man or woman who holds any given belief, and not the other way around."

The audience blinked again, undecided.

"Except," Montaigne added, "that in the one-party state, it IS the other way around! The belief holds the person! And it is this false ideology that was made up somewhere else - and imposed on our island."

The audience listened, detached, remote - safe here in Paris.

"But there is a deeper truth."

What? the audience wanted to know. What is that truth? Robert Walker thought that Jacques Savvy, from his position up on the wall, looked as though even he waited for the answer.

"That Bellarmine would impose *any* idea from outside that would give him power. This is what happens when you are incapable of having ideas for yourself!"

There was nervous laughter in some quarters of the audience.

"It is of course reasonable to expect that those who are aiming for high office are men and women of genuine ability and integrity, who must be prepared to subject themselves to the greater will of the electorate. It will not do to say - as Bellarmine says in private - that the foolish electorate must be guided by the superior intellect! His intellect! We have seen this before many times in this cruel century. Thank God we are near the end of it!"

This baffled the audience. The end of tyranny? Or the end of the century? Or the end of both? Montaigne pressed on:

"Once we have chosen our leaders, then these, hopefully, will be men and women whose vision for their country can help mould and shape the destiny of the people as a nation; otherwise, we shall always be the pawns for some other nation. It does not matter that we are one of the smallest nations on this globe. We are still a nation!"

This brought loud, formal applause. The man in the loud jacket kept checkered-arms folded. When the applause had faded, Montaigne continued:

"These are worldly matters, but in some ways they are reasonably straightforward, so that even I can understand them."

The women in the front row laughed merrily at this assumed modesty. Montaigne smiled at them, raised his dark eyebrows, and continued.

"I have never been of the view that our island is any place for ideology, and - unlike my opponent - I have never tried to force our people to accept any ideology. The fish of the sea have no ideology, as far as I know, and the people of the island live on these same fish from the sea."

Montaigne looked straight into the audience:

"After all, what do I know?"

This brought good-natured laughter and uncoordinated applause. The islanders looked at each other - bewildered or laughing - and some of them slapped each other's backs. Beaumont heaved in his seat until Robert Walker was sure its legs would break. Then Robert Walker looked at the ceiling: the chandelier had started - ever so slightly - to swing. Sabotage?

"And I say to you, my fellow islanders, the time for candour and strong language is long overdue. The time for tea-party chit-chat is over. I do not approve of violence and I do not support adventures of any kind; but I am fond of the truth, and I am against injustice in any form.

"Many of you have criticised my position in the past for not taking stronger action against the Bellarmine regime."

The audience grumbled, doubtful and embarrassed. Who? Us? Surely not?

"Oh, yes, oh yes, my friends . . .

There was some light applause from the middle rows.

"Many of you may not approve of my ways; but I can assure you, whether you like the course I am taking or not, I shall always keep to that course, and I will always keep my rudder straight!"

This brought loud, formal applause.

"In the meantime, I say what I cannot say: change is on the way, but not by violence or the ways of the mercenary!"

The audience signalled disappointment.

"It is Bellarmine who will undo himself!"

"Oh yeah? How?" someone asked.

An uncertain applause rippled through the audience.

Anthony Montaigne conncluded: "I will be charitable by being brief. Over the years, those who do not know what they are talking about usually make the longest speeches. So, my friends, I end there."

The former president turned, and vanished through dark stage-curtains. The audience laughed, cheered, and applauded empty space. It seemed then that they were alone again in exile, and some were disgruntled by the sudden departure.

"The people want revenge," the man in the loud jacket whispered. "Not talk. Put that in your notebook."

Robert Walker interpreted this as: Talk, Not Vengeance - and the man, sullen, looked away.

The audience seemed to take an interlude of deep sleep. The group of women at the front sighed, woke up, and the older among them stared into the downstage distance. The audience groaned: Mrs Smith was introducing a man in a tight-fitting, light-blue suit.

"Oh no," the man in the loud jacket advised. "John D'Ory. A nice man, but a fool. Don't bother to write anything down."

Robert Walker complied, and put away his pen and notebook.

The former fisheries minister took a step upstage. His dark hair was set into a wavy quiff, with a crest flecked with grey.

"There is plenty more I could say," John D'Ory said, "but I think everything has been said by the previous speakers."

The audience, relieved, erupted with laughter.

The man in the loud jacket said: "This fellow would turn humility into a vice."

Robert Walker smiled and said nothing.

The video crew zoomed-in on D'Ory's nervous features. The next words were slow to come:

"The years of exile have been difficult . . . I-. I-."

The audience waited, sullen.

"Let's all go onto the night-club," someone suggested.

Mrs Smith thumped the table: "Please! The former fisheries minister shall have his say!"

The years of exile, it was true, had been hard on the former minister of fisheries. He reached for the microphone - and it howled at him.

"Agh!" John D'Ory recoiled, but forced himself to continue:

"You must excuse me if I seem a little nervous. It has been a very strange evening, for sure."

The audience, bored, remained silent.

John D'Ory looked, open-mouthed, at the audience. In the front row, the women talked among themselves. At the rear of the ballroom, a few notes of dry laughter erupted, then failed. Bougainville had his face in his hands. Mrs Smith frowned at the back of D'Ory's head.

The former minister of fisheries removed a thick sheaf of papers from his light-blue suit; the audience, at sight of the wad, gasped.

"Now, my fellow islanders. . ."

An angry delegate bleated: "You said you had nothing to say!"

"Please!" Mrs Smith bellowed. "I must have order!"

Bougainville lifted his face out of his hands, stared up at the photograph of Jacques Savvy, and shook his head.

John D'Ory's subject matter had been well prepared: the state of the Bourbon Island fishing fleet, which lay in dry dock, while far-flung fishing rights were auctioned to the highest overseas bidder.

Robert Walker looked up at the steady pendular motion of the chandelier. On the stage, Mrs Smith adjusted her messed-up hair-do. Above the stage, the photograph of Jacques Savvy seemed to reveal a quirky smile at the corner of the deceased resistance leader's mouth. The evening held the promise of a long night ahead.

12

AMBASSADOR RAMGOOLAM & MADEMOISELLE RECHERCHEFORT

THE WELL-HEELED men and women of the worldly diplomatic elite moved into the foyer of the embassy. In a foyer corner, Brad and Dud waited, and observed and listened to the multitude of pre-dinner exchanges as the guests hovered over the thick blue carpet of the residence. What would Gorbachev do next? The Soviet Union does not look like it can last in its present form. Yeltsin waits in the wings. Operation Desert Storm has been a qualified or even great success, though the clinical battle would never have been fought but for *perestroika* in the USSR. The battle, surely, was uneven. A competent enemy with a moral purpose would have made for a different prospect. This, we know, from the Asian theatre of operations. There is nowhere to hide under the parching sun of Iraq. The world has changed; the New World Order is here to stay, perhaps. Do not say that too loudly in front of our host. The Ambassador likes straight talk, but not that straight. Those bunglers at the State Department got their signals mixed up as usual. (It was the same when the Berlin Wall fell). Why would Saddam have supposed the West cares about the Al Sabah family? A family, it might be said - but not by this observer - who is not renowned for its commitment to democracy or the free press. It is fundamentalism that is the enemy - the enemy of thought. This is the real enemy of the West. Why so? Fundamentalism of any kind is the enemy of reason everywhere. It creates distortions in the free market. Governments, too, create distortions in the free market: they're called taxes, excise, tariffs, duties and rates. Then again-?

In Moscow, retranchavism could yet undermine *perestroika*. Where is the Soviet ambassador, anyway? Indisposed. Is the Cold War really over or was it an illusion all along? It was no illusion, Your Excellency, but it is not over yet. Whether it is truly over remains to be seen. In the meantime, many civilian populations are placed on the front-line by their góvernments. It is true, though, that many one-party states continue to crumble. A long winter in Moscow lies head, whatever happens. History is unfolding before our very eyes. We no longer have to ask what the future holds. This *is* the future. Since November 1989, when the Wall came down, we have been living in the future. Wait and see. What about the North-South divide? What about China? She's waking up after a long sleep. What about East and West? Where does one end and the other begin? At the Bering Strait, of course. . .at the Diomede Islands. The International Date Line is, of course, invisible. There was polite laughter.

These were the younger diplomats.

Then it was the turn of the older diplomats: grey-templed, they spoke in measured tones of comparative trifles. The future is unknown; it is the present we have to live in, my dear. Paris is very warm for this time of year, don't you think? Not as warm as some places I've been recently.

"There he is Brad."

"Where, Dud?"

"There? With the Italian suit and slicked-back hair."

" I see him."

In a break-away group of dilplomats, the word 'coup' was heard, to which the diplomat with the slicked-back hair responded:

"This Alfonse Trouvères, who is now detained at the pleasure of the French authorities, is a madman, a fool, and a pawn of reactionary forces."

"How do mean that, Ambassador Ramgoolam?" a cocktail-sipping woman diplomat enquired with a smile.

"The French are inclined to make heroes out of the strangest of individuals. Our own President François Bellarmine, on the other hand, is a hero of the republic, and a great man. As with many great men, he is sometimes misunderstood."

"Sometimes?" the women diplomat enquired.

"There are forces that would overthrow the government, most sponsored by the exile Anthony Montaigne, who is unable to relinquish the past - and a renegade."

The woman diplomat drew closer to Ramgoolam. "It is true, Your Excellency, that it was Montaigne who first appointed you to-."

"-In time, our people will learn to forget him."

"You make him sound like a tyrant, Excellency," a short-legged diplomat, who was almost out of sight, said.

"If that is so, Signor Gambini, then-."

The short-legged diplomat persisted: "I have always understood Montaigne is a true democrat and a peaceable man. He has denied any connection with Trouvères, whom I believe he has denounced as an irresponsible adventurer of the worst kind."

"Well, of course Montaigne would deny any connection," Ramgoolam explained, loftily, "and such denunciations are easy to make."

"You will forgive me, Ambassador Ramgoolam, if I were to suggest that Trouvères' actions were possibly encouraged by a third force."

"A third force?" Ramgoolam asked. "I have no knowledge of any such third force, Signor Gambini."

The short diplomat was not for giving up: "The name of, ah, Jacques Savvy has been posited in some circles. . . "

"Savvy? Jacques Savvy? So now we enter the realms of fantasy? The third force of which you speak acts, then, from beyond the grave. The poor fellow was killed in a shooting accident some years ago."

"Surely," the woman diplomat interjected, "you have read the Beaumont report?" She sipped, gamely, at her *champagne* cocktail. At her proximity, Ramgoolam's brow tightened.

"Indeed, I have, Madam-?"

"-*Mademoiselle* Recherchefort."

"Ah, well then. Indeed I have, and I am sorry I wasted my time doing so. There are too many such journalists filing bogus reports. Now that I think of it, first thing in the morning, is it my intention to post new instructions: no visa will be issued to any journalist wishing to travel to Bourbon Island. "

On the other side of the foyer, Brad said:

"You hear that, Dud?"

"I heard, Brad."

"You'd better give the signal, Dud."

"She's already onto him, Brad."

"She is? Which one?

"The tall lady."

"Lady? Ah, I see her. At that altitude, good-looking, too."

"In the morning, he won't be able to remember his name. For twenty-four hours, anyway. Long enough to delay those new visa instructions. She's very good at what she does."

"This Mademoiselle Recherchefort, Dud, you would have direct personal experience?"

"Regrettably, no."

"It is self-evident," Ramgoolam was saying, "that Mr Beaumont's best days as a newspaperman are well behind him. There is nothing in his report of any consequence. Beaumont has a past, but no future."

The short-legged diplomat took a step forward: "You discount the possibility of Trouvères' sponsor being anyone other than Mont-?"

"-I do. Categorically, as the Americans say. Now, where was I?"

"And the aftermath of the coup?" someone from the Foreign Office enquired.

"You must mean the failed coup?" Ramgoolam considered, and said: "From the British perspective, a most unfortunate development of a personal nature, if I may say so."

The individual from the Foreign Office withdrew, and settled in another part of the foyer.

". . .There is the sad case of a Mr Saunders - or Sanders - who was until recently attaché with the British High Commission in Port Bourbon. It has been reported that there were no casualties during Trouvères' absurd invasion. That is not entirely the case. Mr Saunders has been replaced as attaché. (Mr Greene, of the FO, I understand - first time out.) High Commissioner Browne, I understand, is not faring much better. An attack of the nerves. The jitters, the British say. He confines himself to his garden these days. The British, I suspect - our former colonial masters - know more than they are saying. It is what they do not say that is important. Perhaps you, sir, and you - mademoiselle? - should direct your questions there."

The representative of the Foreign Office, though, was no longer visible or audible anywhere in the foyer.

The woman diplomat, who towered a head-and-a-half over Ramgoolam, drew closer again. "How your people must have suffered, Ambassador Ramgoolam."

"We have all suffered, Mademoiselle Recherchefort."

The short-legged diplomat had become jealous, and now said:

"Well, whoever was the prime-mover, Montaigne is unequivocal in his denunciation of the entire episode. Such adventures, he seems to maintain, only serve to reinforce the plight of the Bourbon Islanders."

"The p-p-plight?" Ramgoolam stuttered. "You dare to speak to me of a plight? Why, I myself received a most friendly welcome at a meeting of my fellow nationals - only last night."

"If you insist." Signor Gambini retreated, in search of the Yugoslavian Ambassador, whom he could not locate.

"Montaigne? Quite the ladies' man, I understand." Mademoiselle R. had spoken; now, she bit her tongue, and stared at the blue carpet.

Charles Ramgoolam provided Mlle. Recherchefort with a short lecture:

"As for President Bellarmine, he does not have the time for such things, Mademoiselle Recherchefort. *He* is dedicated only to his people. He is concerned with regional security. In this way, the United States is grateful to him."

"- On an annual cash basis," someone whispered far too loudly.

"!? . . .He is very much of the view that the small nations have an important role to play in the global scheme of things - besides, if I may say so, providing fish for the dinner tables of the West."

Charles Ramgoolam turned to face the deserted foyer doors. The ambassador, for an instant, was certain someone - but who? - had been listening to his discourse. Brad and Dud, though, were already on their way back to Washington, D.C.

An electronic-gong sounded for dinner.

"This way, Charles?" Mademoiselle Recherchefort offered, with her generous smile.

13

ON THE CHAMPS~ÉLYSÉES

AFTER A SUBSTANTIAL feast of salami, bread rolls, and coffee, he made his way from the Levant Hotel to the nearest Métro. On board, he travelled to Concord, where he changed trains, and continued along the track of the Champs-Élysées. The rue des Martyrs seemed a distant place, where he had found a kind of anonymity, and no one followed anyone else, necessarily. Those days, though, were over. There was no indication of the Camel-smoking, journal-reading Straw Hat, whom he had not seen since the earlier encounter on the Métro. So far, the motives of Straw Hat, the industrial snooper - or whatever the man's occupation - remained unknown. Tourist resort development? Land, where land was scarce? Fishing rights? Offshore banking? Arms? A consortium to locate buried treasure? (If the Fiery Cross had not been found, then where *was* the precious cargo that had destroyed Graham Dunne?) As the train moved through the system of dark tunnels, he guessed that Straw Hat - or the consortium he gave a face to - was most likely after fishing rights. In the event Bellarmine were toppled, the fishing rights would be up for grabs. The Republic of Bourbon Island, though a small island, was surrounded by its own Exclusive Economic Zone (EEZ): this extended 200-miles off-shore, which equated to an area of over 125,000 square miles of the Indian Ocean.

As he emerged from the Métro, his head swum with a million unhooked tuna. In the way of such things, he felt strangely alone. There was nothing remaining for him in this city, but to leave.

One last time, he chanced his way through the hubbub of traffic - across the boulevard - and into the International Press Club. The establishment had been evacuated for the hot month of August, and he caught the clerk by surprise.

A whistle echoed around the reception area.

It was the desk clerk, who was dressed in black, and sported a new hairstyle. In this way, Robert Walker thought the clerk resembled Bela Lugosi. The fellow looked as though he were in mourning, probably for the absentees, who wrote - if at all - their columns on remote location. The clerk turned - with a whistle - and studied the array of pigeonholes, which were crammed with uncollected messages, except - that is - for W, which was empty.

The desk clerk whistled a sliding scale of disappointment.

Robert Walker would be glad to get out of that place.

The revolving doors, caught by a light breeze from the boulevard, continued to revolve. Behind the reception desk, the clerk watched, mesmerised.

There were no messages, no mail, and no faxes; there was nothing, then, no more business, to detain Robert Walker any longer. He provided the clerk with a forwarding address in Covent Garden, and attached a modest gratuity: a F50 note. The clerk whistled a note of his own, smiled, and could not stop smiling.

Robert Walker, with some judgement, passed through the revolving doors and out onto the boulevard. The traffic raced by, halted, waited, and - after a short interval - started racing again. Robert Walker could feel the breeze on his face. Soon, it would be time to check out of the Levant Hotel, collect his luggage, and catch the RER at Saint Michel for Charles de Gaulle Airport.

In a short time, he would be underground again.

At the nearest *café*, he sat down at an outside table. He looked up at the azure sky above the boulevard, and, with the sun on his face, he waited, and watched the breeze play through the plane trees. The stop-go-stop-go of the traffic rolled down this side of the boulevard, while, on the other side, it climbed. A waiter limped into view, and stood by his table. The waiter took the order for a *demi* of Stella, and limped away. After a while, the waiter reappeared with the beer. "Monsieur."

Robert Walker tasted the cold beer.

"Monsieur?"

"Qui?"

"Monsieur, you are all right, monsieur?"

"I'm fine. The beer is also fine."

"Monsieur, you are looking for a-?"

"-Not at this time."

" . . .Then, you were wondering about my limp, non?"

"I would not think to mention your limp. It is a visible affliction. There are other afflications - invisible to the eye."

"Ah, mais qui, monsieur."

"Well, then?"

"I can still hear it now, monsieur."

"Hear . . .what?"

"The screams. . .the tourists; they scream louder than anyone else. I don't know why. The man who died made no sound."

Robert Walker remembered the news report about Jacques Savvy's assassination: "This is the very same location?"

"It is indeed, monsieur. That day, it was much like today. It was five years ago, but I still have the limp. And to think that my wife asked me to stay at home that day."

Robert Walker realised what the waiter was talking about. This was the waiter, then, who had taken a bullet, while the tourists, unharmed, screamed for their lives.

The traffic rumbled on and on. . .

"You are wise to be married."

"You have not seen my wife, monsieur."

"No, I haven't."

"I have not been much good to her in that way since-. Still, in other ways-. The are said to be other things in life, monsieur, though at the moment - I cannot think what, exactly."

The waiter brought the empty tray up against his chest, then limped away, back to the *café*. Robert Walker looked across the boulevard. From the south, an unsteady breeze played through the plane trees.

INTERLUDE

In-Flight Reading[*]

---

[*] These are some excerpts from materials photocopied by Robert Walker at the IPC in Paris. A Bourbon Island bibliography of sorts is included, which provides the only clue to the missing MSS. by Roger Dupin.

BOURBON ISLAND SPECIAL REPORT

/ last

The Republic of Bourbon Island in the Indian Ocean is among the most isolated islands in the region, and lies on the equator at about 67° of Greenwich. At least one amateur geologist has speculated that, while today the anomaly comprises a single extinct volcanic outcrop, it may at one time have been part of an archipelago, extending north by north-west towards Socotra Island (Yemen).

The islands of this region were noted on the charts of early Portuguese explorers, notably Vasco da Gama, whose epic voyage of 1497-98 opened up the oceanic route to India.

The island remained unexplored until a ship of the East Indian Company, which surveyed the area in the mid-1600s, was blown off course towards its remote shores. On making land, the crew found fresh water and victuals in abundance. A famous story is told that the captain of the vessel, as he looked down at the beach of virgin white sand, was amazed to find a single human footprint - only to discover that it was his own. There were no signs that the island had at any time been inhabited, except by the indigenous birds and turtles.

. . .In the late 18th and early 19th centuries, the superpowers of the day - Britain and France - fought for supremacy over the Indian Ocean region, culminating with the Treaty of Paris (1814).

. . . In the 1930s, the island finally became a British Crown Colony, with Sir Godfrey Smythe-Smith as first governor. In the following decades, little was heard of the island, except for news of the occasional expatriate scandal. In the modern era, the island has become known as an ornithologists' paradise, and is a much-prized source of copra, cinnamon and vanilla.

In the Cold War years, the island's true value, as seen through the eyes of the superpowers, is strategic.

... In 1977, barely a year after independence, François Bellarmine, then prime minister, mounted a *coup d'etat* with assistance from a revolutionary group based on the African mainland. The president, Anthony Montaigne, who had been outside the country at time of the coup, claimed a Moscow-backed conspiracy, and has remained in exile ever since.

At home, Bellarmine acted swiftly to abrogate the country's constitution, created a one-party state with himself as president, outlawed all other political parties, and banned any expression or manifestation of the free press as "the pawns of imperialists". Bellarmine announced to the world's press: "The situation here has changed."

The changed situation allows for elections, but Bellarmine, as the only candidate, has understandably won every election held since the coup. In addition to Head of State, Bellarmine is also Commander-in-Chief of the Armed Forces, and Minister of Finance, among various other portfolios. François Bellarmine has consistently defended "La Revolution" as promulgated by his Bourbon Island People's Party (BIPP). At a recent party rally at the National Stadium, he made clear his policy to pursue "ever purer forms of collectivism".

In the face of such rhetoric, diplomatic acquaintances have related that, deep down, François Bellarmine is that living contradiction - a revolutionary conservative. An intensely private man, who remains a bachelor at the age 50, he is said to appreciate fine wines and "antiquities". . . but, above all else, he is considered by friend and foe alike as a supremely practical politician exercising the levers of power. The resident Catholic prelate of the island, Bishop David Chin, has remarked in a recent sermon that "a woman's touch would not go amiss up at the dacha".

In stark contrast, there are reports of a dark side to Bellarmine's nature, which opponents claim informs the essence of his regime. There have been numerous counter-coups aimed at unseating Bellarmine and restoring multi-party democracy: all have failed. The exiled Anthony Montaigne has protested allegations (as a man of non-violence) that he is the moving force behind any of these coup attempts.

In November 1985, Jacques Savvy, the youthful leader of the exiled Bourbon Island Resistance Organisation (BIRO) in Paris, was assassinated on the Champs-Élysées.

The exiled BIRO was dealt a severe body blow, and active opposition to Bellarmine effectively ceased. A spokesman for the regime denied all knowledge of the assassination, and Bellarmine himself is said to have expressed surprise.

Since the fall of the Berlin Wall, the exiled islanders have found new hope that political change may be on its way to their remote homeland.

The island's strategic geo-political location, with tension growing in the Gulf region, continues to act as a boon to the ruling elite. A Russian naval base, according to an unconfirmed report, is under construction at Sans Souci Bay, on the eastern coast of the island. This, despite the protests of the Americans, who maintain a satellite tracking station in the shadows of Mont Pomme d'Or, the island's extinct volcanic peak.

This unlikely accommodation illustrates the Cold War tightrope that Bellarmine has succeeded in negotiating with the superpowers. The regime continues to collect substantial rentals - albeit with no direct aid - for the US installation.

The latest consensus (c.1990) reveals a predominantly Catholic population of some 70,501 persons. (An estimated 10-12,000 islanders are living in exile). Among the home population, about 80 per cent are of African extraction, with other ethnic groups, including Chinese and Indian, making up the remainder. A small proportion of the population (about 2-3 per cent) is of European extraction, mostly descended from the original French settlers and plantation owners. The ruling elite, including Bellarmine himself, is almost exclusively of French origin - and is known as *grand blanc*.

The ordinary people of the island, who are known to have a low regard for ideology, tend to meet their predicament with a detached irony. Visitors to the island, however, report that the miniature capital, Port Bourbon, is deserted of its people, even before the 18:00 curfew (which is still imposed). A vital centre of island life, Saturday market, with its once-bustling mêlée of buyers and sellers, is now restricted to a showcase of stale produce. The prices of foodstuffs are said to be even higher under the Bourbon Island Marketing Board (BIMB) parastatal than under the despised merchant classes. It was this group that Bellarmine identified as the traditional enemy of the people. Even so, a small number of privileged private operators are allowed to exist under special licence. Party favourites are reputed to enjoy large incomes from tariffs imposed on the import of staples, such as rice and potatoes. The BIPP can be relied on to vehemently deny these allegations.

Trade missions have observed that the old entrepreneurial spirit of those driven into exile has created a vacuum on the island. The vacuum, Bellarmine's overseas critics maintain, has been filled by systemic corruption. Millions of rupees, they say, have been siphoned-off into Swiss bank accounts by the governing elite, which, again, can be relied on to deny any such charges.

The Bourbon Island Philatelic Bureau (BIPB) has, on a number of occasions, attracted the special attention of INTERPOL.

The collectivist philosophy of the umbrella BIMB parastatal has generally not been regarded as an outstanding success.

The main exports are copra and other coconut products, cinnamon bark, canned tuna fish, and vanilla pods. Imports include rice, textiles, fuel oil, and manufactured goods. Tourism has proved difficult to develop, largely because of Bourbon Island's remote location and micro-climate - which many visitors find intolerable, especially during the doldrums. As a travel destination, the island is considered strictly for the occasional treasure hunter or the outwardly adventurous.

BIBILOGRAPHICAL NOTE: *Orchid Life of Bourbon Island* (1965) by The Very Rev. David Chin; *A Bird Watcher's Guide to Bourbon Island* (1970) by George Peck; *Seashells of Bourbon Island* (1972) by C.A.G. Flute; *The Shoals of Paradise: A Geological Survey of a Submerged Archipelago* (1973) by Edmund Hughes-Peke; and, in the political arena, *Confessions of an Exile* (1978) by Anthony Montaigne. The latter's arch-opponent, Bellarmine, is said not to be the memoir-writing type. Note: A local man, Roger Dupin, is reputed to be working on a MSS. about the elusive Fiery Cross of Goa.

PART THREE

The Shoals of Paradise

This is . . .the year of living dangerously.
~ *Achmed Sukarno (1901-1970)*

1

THE SHOALS AND MR WILSON

AT THAT ALTITUDE, what did it all matter anyway?

Then the cloud-shrouded cone of the extinct volcano heaved into view. The aircraft circled high over the island, the engines whined, and the long descent continued. The aircraft banked, and the clouds parted to reveal strange white flashes far below. . . strips of coralline beach, studded with what, at this altitude, were miniature palm trees.

Robert Walker rested his head against the *antimacassar*. Again, the aircraft banked, and moved into a tighter arc.

Robert Walker caught sight of a long, white stretch of a beach, fringed with an irregular line of palms, which followed the edge of a great, sweeping bay, and disappeared into the dark blue horizon of the ocean. His stomach sank. The aircraft shot over the roof the island, and entered the dense white cloud. Then, the massive cone of the dead volcano appeared: a big grey, wrinkled eye, which stared up at the sky, with the iris of an unfathomable black lake at its centre.

The crater seemed to pull down on the aircraft fuselage.

A passenger wailed, and was comforted by a stewardess.

The NO-SMOKING and SEAT-BELTS signs were illuminated with a *bong*.

The aircraft was buffeted by turbulence as it slipped over the crater, and reached the far side of the wind-shedding cone. At this apogee, Robert Walker observed an ancient pine forest, dark-green and dense in the foothills, but brown and thin near the wind-swept rim of the crater. Then the view was obscured. The aircraft dipped, Robert Walker's ears popped, and they re-entered the island's shroud of moisture.

Robert Walker turned away from the opaque porthole. This part of the cabin was occupied only by himself and - across the central aisle - a man by the name of John Wilson. An international stamp dealer, Wilson had boarded at Frankfurt, consumed two bottles of champagne, and fallen asleep - strapped into his seat - for the remainder of the journey. Robert Walker, then, had been left with his in-flight reading as they flew far to the south, over the Red Sea, the Arabian Sea, and across the maritime wilderness of the Indian Ocean. It was only now that Wilson awoke: he stared through the nearest porthole, and was alarmed to see nothing but a white glare of nothingness. He was, was he, de-? John Wilson turned a groggy head to leer across the aisle, and was grateful for sight of a fellow passenger. The philatelist raised an eyebrow, which fell, and tried a smile, which faded.

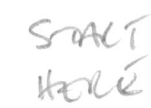

"Mr Walker, isn't it?"

"Yes, Mr Wilson."

"I thought I recognised you from somewhere."

"I was on the aircraft from Paris. You boarded at Frankfurt."

"Yes, Mr Walker, I know where I boarded. Are we there yet?"

"We're here, Mr Wilson."

John Wilson awoke from a time-warp of his own making, and was anxious to continue the conversation: at the exact-point where they had left off some hours ago:

"A specimen."

"I'm sorry?" Robert Walker responded across the aisle.

"You asked about my mission to the island. I didn't answer. Now I'm telling you: a specimen stamp, Mr Walker. VERY HUSH, HUSH, you know!" Wilson shouted over the noise of the turbines.

"I understand," Robert Walker replied, but his mid-air thoughts were far-away from specimen stamps.

"What are you thinking about, old boy?"

"Nothing."

"Really? I knew a girl like that, once. Not a thought in her pretty little head. Talked from sunrise to sunset. Lived in a perpetual present, you see. No past, no future. I'd say to her, what are you thinking about, my dear? And she would reply: Nothing. And I'd say, I'll give you something to-! Well, never mind what I said. That was in another country, and - besides - the wench is dead."

Robert Walker, with a measure of patience, smiled at Wilson.

"You're a treasure hunter, then?"

"A journalist."

"Those notes you have there," Wilson observed with one eye closed: "you're following the clues, aren't you?"

Robert Walker did not reply. John Wilson was not sure how to react; above his head, he studied the fresh-air nozzle, decided it was not as fresh at it might be, then looked across the aisle.

"A journalist, you say?"

"The Shoe Lane News Agency."

"Never heard of it." John Wilson leered along the aisle at a stewardess with green eyes and auburn hair. "Well, what have we here?" he said. "A lass from the Valleys, is it?"

Robert Walker asked. "Staying on the island long, Mr Wilson?"

"As long as it takes."

John Wilson studied the stewardess. "I haven't been here for some months now, but a few days ought to do it - after which, I'll be flying on to Mauritius. Got a girl there, you know."

"Oh really? Mrs Wilson?"

"Of course not. Need all the sleep I can get before landing on *that* island, I can tell you."

"You must have a fine collection by now," Robert Walker said.

"I *do* beg yours?" Wilson responded. ". . .Oh, I see what you mean. I should apologise, but I won't," Wilson went on, and - reluctantly - turned away from the sight of the stewardess' long, lithe legs. "Of, ah, what?"

"Of stamps, of course."

"Not really. I'm not a collector; I'm a dealer. Quite a different thing, old boy. Do you collect yourself?"

"No. Not my line. I don't collect anything. And I'm not *looking* for anything, either."

"Ah," Wilson said. The stamp dealer's eyes were the non-colour of coals.

Robert Walker chanced: "There are some interesting specimens on Bourbon, then?"

"I'll say."

"Stamps, I meant."

John Wilson raised both eyebrows. "You're sure you're not a collector?"

"No - as I say, I'm a journalist."

"Well, all right, then, since you ask. . .There's not many, but there's one or two - *one*, really - of, shall we say, special interest?"

"We're still talking about stamps?"

"We are, Mr Walker." John Wilson looked, with searching, philatelic eyes, across the aisle at his fellow traveller. Robert Walker felt uneasy under the blood-shot gaze of the stamp dealer. "You see," Wilson whispered, "there's a new issue coming out. I've got to get my hands on-," he stopped - then calmed - himself. "I mean, I aim to acquire a first proof of the stamp; it is, you know, distinguished by the fact that it bears a design for . . .the Fiery Cross of Goa. I aim to secure the specimen, I'm telling you."

Wilson watched Robert Walker for a reaction.

"I can see that you do, Mr Wilson."

"This particular piece of gummed paper might, Mr Walker, even be of interest to your good-self."

The whine of the aircraft's turbines seemed to fade. The cabin lights flickered. The cabin crew watched these two passengers, and listened without hearing.

"Why do you say that, Mr Wilson?"

"Well, it's obvious, isn't it?"

"I'm not sure that it *is* obvious."

"Well, don't you see? " Wilson sat upright, and leant - part of the way - across the aisle. "No one in modern times has ever seen the Fiery Cross.

There are no drawings extant, as far as I know, only vague descriptions. So, how come - I ask - is it, that there is an exceptionally ornate design for the Cross on the stamp?"

"I have no idea. You have seen the stamp?"

Wilson withdrew to his own side of the aisle: "Not yet, not yet."

"Then how to do you know . . .the design is ornate?"

"It's my business to know, you could say. I've been told by someone who knows."

"The Bourbon Island Philatelic Bureau, no doubt?"

John Wilson pretended he had not heard.

"I would say, then, the most likely explanation. . ."

"Yes, yes?" Wilson stiffened.

" . . .is that the engraver has used some imagination. Artistic lic-"

John Wilson baulked: "Imagination? Well, I wonder, Mr Walker. You journalists always have an easy explanation for everything. You'll see soon enough; there are stranger things in this old world than lend themselves to explanation. I can explain that much to you, old boy."

Robert Walker asked: "What makes you think I would be interested in the design of the stamp, anyway?"

John Wilson smiled: "Now, really, Mr Walker, you don't need me to tell you that."

The blast of the gas turbines resumed.

The belly of the aircraft tilted against three o'clock, took an anti-clockwise turn, and leaned into the course set for it by the pilot at a radius from the crater. A break appeared in the mist, and Robert Walker observed a canopy of mighty conifers.

The pilot spoke over the intercom:

"*This is your Captain, Roger Chance speaking . . . The local time is approaching four o'clock on a balmy afternoon, and the temperature has just slipped below eighty-five degrees . . .Now, rest back, and we'll try for the smoothest landing possible. . .*"

"Don't like the sound of that," Wilson remarked.

"*On behalf of the crew and myself, we hope you have had a pleasant flight.*"

"I don't remember a damn thing about it," Wilson offered.

"*. . . and thank you for travelling with our airline.*"

Captain Roger Chance's intercom crackled, for the last time, into silence.

Robert Walker held back a painful grin. John Wilson did not look so assured: he called the stewardess, a young, green-eyed Welsh girl with her hair cropped short, who had previously supplied the stamp dealer with *champagne*. This time, Wilson - who looked into those enquiring green eyes from the Valleys - ordered water. "Water, water, everywhere - and not a drop to drink!" Then: "Dying of thirst," Wilson explained. He ran a hand across the top of his impressive domed head, and repositioned - Roman Emperor-style - a hyacinthine bang of grey hair. "Used to know one just like her," Wilson confided, "a long time ago. Born with grass on their backs, don't you know?"

Robert Walker replied - the blast of the jet turbines drowned-out his voice - that he did not know, but that he-. The Welsh stewardess, who was all smiles, arrived with a tray, which bore a single paper cup of cold water.

"Yaki Dah, what?" John Wilson watched the stewardess retreat to the cabin crew's station, where she conferred with an effete-looking male steward. John Wilson shook his head with disapproval, and mumbled: "What a damned waste." Then, more clearly, he remarked:

"Bloody hot down there on the island, Mr Walker," and then Wilson, a victim of a powerful thirst, slurped away the water. The stamp dealer's throat, it seemed, was on fire.

Robert Walker looked through the porthole at the shifting horizon . . . The aircraft banked, and circled along the western aspect of the island. John Wilson was able to look across the aisle - past Robert Walker's taut chest - and out through the same porthole. Below, he saw the foaming ocean floor of the Carlsberg Ridge.

The water seemed to invigorate John Wilson. "Look, Mr Walker - The Shoals of Bourbon."

"Yes," Robert Walker said, "I see them now."

John Wilson had sobered up, although - for some reason - he was becoming drunk again. Excited, he said: "Death by a thousand cuts, old boy!"

"How do you mean, Mr Wilson?"

The gas turbines howled, so that Wilson raised to his voice to explain:

"Think of - the whole Indian Ocean pouring across those coral shallows! A swimmer or a boat caught in the shoals doesn't stand a chance! You would. . . be dragged across the reef! You wouldn't need to worry about the sharks!"

"Why?"

"BECAUSE THERE'D BE NOTHING LEFT OF YOU BUT SAW DUST AND FISH BAIT!"

"-!"

The Welsh stewardess reappeared by stealth. She looked at Wilson from a strange angle: "Please, Mr Wilson, there's no need for alarm," and she reached to tighten the stamp dealer's seatbelt.

"I'M SORRY!" Wilson shouted. "Didn't mean to - shout. Don't know what came over me. Please, I'll be all right. I was just explaining the general situation to Mr Walker here."

The stewardess spoke with a lilt: "There, there, now, Mr Wilson, everything's going to be just fine."

"Just fine, you say? There's no 'j' in Welsh, I'll tell you that much."

She looked at passengers Wilson and Walker. "You gentlemen really must behave yourselves," she advised. "We're coming into land very soon, and we mustn't disappoint the Captain, must we?"

"Some chance," Wilson smirked.

"Well, that's his name, isn't it, Mr Wilson?" the stewardess cooed. Then she returned to her seat by the Emergency Door, and belted herself in under Wilson's watchful eyes.

The aircraft found a level horizon. Captain Roger Chance had manoeuvred onto the unusual alignment for Bourbon Island International Airport. John Wilson rested his damp head against the *antimacassar*, which soaked up sweat from the back of his neck. Then the stamp dealer looked sideways across the aisle: "Sorry about that, old boy."

"I understand," Robert Walker said.

"Well, I'm not sure that you do, you see?"

Robert Walker re-arranged his notes, and said: "Please, explain, then."

"They also call them the Shoals of Paradise . . .but bad things have happened down there, believe me."

The Welsh stewardess, from her station, kept an eye on Wilson. The stamp dealer hesitated to smile reassuringly at her.

"I've seen the photographs."

"What photographs?"

"Opponents of the regime in so-called fishing accidents. Foolish treasure hunters caught up in the chase. Stay away from that sort of business, Mr Walker - that's some free advice from John Wilson, Esquire."

Robert Walker reacted to a change in cabin pressure. It was, he supposed, nothing more than Wilson's high-strung presence - whom he now saw with two heads. So it was a two-headed Wilson who reminisced:

"I miss Blighty, sometimes, but it's good to get away from all that misery, and try someone else's misery for a change, don't you think?"

Robert Walker accepted this without comment.

"I used to get homesick for Blighty, but not any more. I keep moving, that's my secret. If you keep moving, you've got no right to be homesick for anywhere. That's what I say, anyway." John Wilson smiled twice, greatly satisfied with this reasoning, based as it was on years of international travel.

The aircraft started on the ramp to a lower altitude, ready for the final haul before landing.

"You know," Wilson said, "there's only one island here. Solid granite, that's why it's still here. Some geologists believe that, thousands of years' ago, there was a whole necklace of coralline islands here, too, but that these have been eroded away to leave only this grand edifice. . .Look-"

The aircraft flew out from a wall of cloud into clear skies.

The massive peak of the extinct volcano - Mont Pomme d'Or - appeared outside Wilson's porthole. Below, plantation terraces appeared, then disappeared. A great estate or farm was gobbled up by the high-velocity fly-over, and left far behind. A white telecoms radome bubbled into view, and then collapsed in the distance. A mountain reached for the sky, and was turned into sandy rubble. A jungle flourished, then decayed. Only the ocean remained steady.

On the coast, the grey structures of a naval base came into existence, and perished. Robert Walker watched the exposed landscape, and said: "I'm not sure; I might have read something like that, somewhere."

"That's what the shoals are; that's what's left of them. . .You know, I'll tell you something funny. Do you want to hear something funny, Mr Walker?"

"Of course, go ahead."

"Well, a well-placed acquaintance of mine told me-."

"-Yes?"

"- that Bellarmine loses sleep at night: he has nightmares about the fact that he might have been the master of a whole archipelago, instead of just the one island in the middle of nowhere."

"Bellarmine?" Robert Walker, the ingenue, asked.

"Why, yes," Wilson said, with an insider's knowledge. "President François Bellarmine - he who rules this granite roost. It just goes to show; you can't have everything, even when you do."

John Wilson paused to sip-up the last of the moisture from the cup; then he crushed the empty container in his fist. . .Robert Walker thought Wilson, whose seatbelt could not be much tighter, was again half-drunk. An irascible man, Robert Walker thought.

"I miss everywhere, except the place where I am," John Wilson continued on his prior theme. "You can't win, you see that, don't you?"

Robert Walker agreed without saying anything.

"Best to keep moving. I deal in stamps, but you don't have to travel to do that, you know; not really."

Robert Walker thought: landing nerves? The reluctant philatelist, perhaps, saw himself on the tarmac - or spread over a thousand square miles of the Indian Ocean. The aircraft's nose dipped, then rose again. A line of palm trees rushed past the cabin portholes as Capt. Roger Chance brought the aircraft into land.

"Well, old boy," Wilson said, "I wish you the best of luck."

"Luck?" Robert Walker asked.

John Wilson tried to sit-up straight, and stared directly across the aisle - at Robert Walker's papers. "With the treasure.'

The aircraft hit the runway, bounced, and skidded. The gas turbines roared with reverse thrust.

"I mean, you're not really a journalist, are you? You're one of these treasure-hunter types, aren't you?"

"Not me, no, Mr Wilson," Robert Walker replied. "I'm not interested in treasure. My story is about Graham Dunne, the man."

John Wilson persisted: "Same bloody thing, isn't it? You're after the Fiery Cross, aren't you? I've seen you trying to work out the clues. The only place you'll find the Fiery Cross is printed on the new stamp - believe me, I know," Wilson explained in a panic.

"It's not like that."

"Studying the clues," Wilson surmised; "trying to decode them. I've seen your type before on this same flight. They come here, trying to pick up where that chap Dunne left off. They all think they're cleverer than the last fellow, and that what happened to Dunne won't happen to them. Dunne was no fool, though. A City man; a trained accountant - but no ordinary bean-counter. Oh no. Met him once. Stood him a beer or two. Skint, he was. Those who follow - if you'll forgive me - are the fools, but not Dunne. He had brains."

"I'm not looking for any treasure, Mr Wilson."

"That's what they all say," Wilson said.

John Wilson cocked his head to one side. His face was covered with sweat. He implored: "Well, what *are* you looking for, Mr Walker?"

Robert Walker studied Wilson's ageing face. "I'm not looking for anything."

"Everyone's looking for something. Even if it's only a stamp."

"I'm here to write a feature, that is all."

John Wilson raised his head: "Well, that's as good a cover as any, I suppose. It's usually bird watcher - ornithologist, I mean - marine biologist, something like that. But what they're really after-."

"It's not a cover; it's my prof-."

The aircraft performed a final SKID-SKID, and made its heavy rumbling way along the hot, wheel-melting runway.

Outside, the palm trees seemed to pass by in a blur. John Wilson could not see the trees, because his eyes were shut-tight. . . while both his hands were white-knuckled from his grip on the armrests. As the aircraft air-braked along the runway, John Wilson had achieved a kind of stasis, whereby he could not be harmed.

Then it was all over: the aircraft taxied for a while, and then halted. John Wilson opened his eyes. He released the armrests; his knuckles remained white. The stamp dealer, only slightly put-out by the knowledge of being seen in deep trauma, explained:

"It's ridiculous, I know. A fellow like me, having flown hundreds of thousands of miles around the world, and still I can't stand it."

"Flying?"

"No, Mr Walker, *landing*."

The stewardess got up, and started along the aisle, but Wilson waved her away. Robert Walker realised that the stamp dealer was over-the-moon happy - or delirious, anyway - from an outpouring of nervous energy. Now, Wilson was ready to talk:

"Journalist, eh? Well, whatever next?"

Through the porthole on Wilson's side, Robert Walker observed a low-lying terminal building across the runway. An airport vehicle had set out from the terminal, in no particular hurry, with a set of disembarkation steps in-tow. On both sides of the articulated steps, large white letters announced: WELCOME TO BOURBON ISLAND.

"Like hell," John Wilson complained.

2

BUS-RIDE TO PORT BOURBON

THE AIRLOCKS OPENED, and a barrier of heat engulfed the passengers from Europe. A smell of lush vegetation hung in the air over the island, and was blown away at intervals by the trade wind. The edifice of Mont Pomme d'Or climbed from the depths of the ocean and stood against the sky over green-brown and grey foothills. Behind the island's blanket of mist and cloud, the rim of the crater appeared and disappeared.

Robert Walker's clothes stuck to his stiff, flight-bound limbs: among the last passengers to leave the cabin, he was confronted by the green-eyed stewardess from the Valleys. Those passengers that had already alighted commenced the slow march across the runway towards the terminal building. The yellow-white sun, even at this late-afternoon hour, grilled the passengers' heads. A bird - a sooty tern, he heard a bird-spotting tourist claim - flew high overhead, and angled against the steady breeze, where it looked down at this other flight from London *via* Paris and Frankfurt.

The journey was over, then, at least for now, before Captain Roger Chance and his crew flew onwards for the sugar-island of Mauritius.

The aircraft's fuselage was covered with a thick film of moisture, which dripped onto the hot, dry runway. Near the under-carriage, a group of technicians in red overalls carried a long hose. A smell of kerosene mixed strangely with the sweet, lush, salt smell of the island and the hot concrete of the runway. The runway, which was of military dimensions, pointed straight out to where the shoals foamed white, and - beyond - the dark blue of the ocean.

John Wilson appeared, blinking, from the cabin: "Impressive sight, old boy. It takes everyone that WAYYYY-!"

The stamp dealer staggered, and nearly went over the side of the articulated steps; the stewardess from Wales reached out, and saved Wilson from the runway. "OOOPS! Touch of the Hong Kong Gallop, old girl! Had to GO!"

The stewardess tried to smile as she assisted Wilson: down the flight of steps, and onto the runway.

"Are you all right, Mr Wilson?" Robert Walker asked.

Robert Walker watched as the barrier of heat enveloped Wilson. The stamp dealer, who had put on a panama hat to secure his wayward bang of hair, ignored Robert Walker, and doffed his headgear at the stewardess:

"Thank you, Miss, for being - well, such charming company."

"Well, we'll see you again soon, Mr Wilson," the stewardess cooed. "Have a pleasant stay on Bourbon Island."

"Is that where we are? Fly me, I'm Wilson. . .And Yakky Dah to you, my dear."

The stewardess turned sullen, and climbed the steps to rejoin her crewmates. Passengers Wilson and Walker started on their way across the runway. A bronzed, white-toothed Captain Roger Chance emerged from the cabin, and stood at the top of the disembarkation steps. Something that the stewardess said made Captain Chance laugh, and take off his cap.

The stamp dealer hot-footed it across the sun-parched runway; he looked back that way, and said:

"I don't know what he's laughing at. Not such a *smooth* landing at all! Not as smooth as he is, anyway. Nearly swallowed my bloody teef, I did. I know what he's got his mind *on!*"

The two Britons turned their backs on the aircraft, and crossed the runway against a balmy breeze, which persisted, as did the Captain's laughter.

"I'll give him something to laugh about," Wilson slurred.

Robert Walker studied the slopes of Mont Pomme d'Or, which, as he watched, turned from grey to a reddish-brown. In that instant, the wind rose high over the island, blew away the cloudbelt, and revealed the stark grey cone of the volcano. He fancied he could make out François Bellarmine's *dacha*: there, at the uppermost edge of the green-belt, where the ancient forests gave way to weathered, mineral-streaked rock. Robert Walker closed, then opened, an eye on the mountain. Wilson watched, not the mountain, but his travelling companion, but - for once - said nothing.

As for the other passengers, they had almost reached the terminal. This was crowned with the parched white letters: BOURBON ISLAND INTERNAT AL AIRPORT. (The missing letters, the Bamboo - or rumour - Mill said, had been a covert sign - *Charge!* - for Trouvères and his mercenaries.) At the rear of the column of passengers, a wealthy looking honeymoon couple, from the London suburbs or thereabouts, were blissfully ignorant of any coup-attempt. The bride, disgusted by the surprise destination, had wanted instead to go to Seychelles, and an argument unfolded there on the runway.

"Young love," Wilson chuckled, and winked. "There's nothing quite like it."

"No, I suppose not, Mr Wilson."

"-Knew one like her, once. Never stopped bloody talking from sunrise to sunset. Would have talked the head off a rhinoceros . . .What I've been through in the name of love, Mr Walker, you would not believe."

The bridegroom, broad-shouldered, but numb from the rebuke, looked at the sky and said nothing.

"If he doesn't assert himself now, he's fu-."

Up ahead, John Wilson had spotted a nun - a Sister of Mercy - who was as cool as a cuttlefish with a flowing rosary. In tropical whites, she strode across the runway at the heels of an elderly French couple, who were undertaking the last leg of a grande tour of *l'Ocean Indien*. Ahead of them, a team of drunken government officials had returned from an overseas promotional trip at taxpayers' expense. At the very head of the column, an over-weight European businessman led the way. He had a rolled-up newspaper under an arm, an attaché case, and . . .wore a distinctive straw hat.

Robert Walker halted on the hot runway, and watched as the fellow disappeared inside the terminal.

"-What in the name of-?" Wilson started. "You're not giving up already, Mr Walker? You've only just arriv----." The breeze almost took Wilson's words, along with his panama hat, away across the runway.

"No, of course not."

"You know that chap?"

"What chap?"

"Him, there -? Oh, he's gone inside."

"No, it's all right - I thought he was someone else."

"Well, maybe he *is* someone else, eh? -You're pulling my wire, old boy. Really, Mr Walker, you can't stand out here on the runway all day," Wilson advised, and wiped his face. "You'll never find the treasure with that sort of attitude."

"Attitude? I told you, Mr Wilson; I'm not looking for any treasure. Really, I'm not."

John Wilson smiled knowingly at his fellow passenger.

Robert Walker started again towards the terminal building, but it was John Wilson who took the lead. "In the footsteps of the great Trouvères, eh?" The stamp dealer grinned at the sky.

Robert Walker thought that, so far, there was scant evidence of Bellarmine's unsmiling dictatorship.

John Wilson had recovered from the lapse into drunkenness, and walked tall. He looked at Mont Pomme d'Or when he remarked: "You seem strangely subdued, Mr Walker. Something I said?"

Robert Walker, disarmed, said: "No, of course not, Mr Wilson. The heat, maybe."

"Ah, the heat: soaking up the atmosphere, that kind of thing?"

"If you like." Robert Walker regretted he had told Wilson anything of his mission to the island; already, he knew, he would pay heavily for divulging that confidence.

The two men walked in silence until they reached the terminal.

It was at this point that Robert Walker's first impressions started to change. Inside the terminal, three substantial, dark-faced islanders in starched khaki uniforms represented the Bourbon Island Police Force. On Bourbon Island, this was - Robert Walker supposed - maximum security in the aftermath of the Trouvères' invasion. A young officer, with a Sam Browne belt in a state of high polish, smiled, and said:

"Ah, Mr Wilson, welcome once again to the Republic of Bourbon Island. It has been a while since we last saw you."

The other passengers had already collected their luggage; up ahead, they moved, in obedient silence, through an umbilical marked ARRIVALS into a hallway.

"Well, I've been elsewhere, haven't I?"

"Passport please."

"Ah, yes, of course," Wilson obliged, and fumbled for his travel documents. "And how is our Chief of Police these days?"

"He is in excellent health, as always," the officer said. Then the smile disappeared. "Chief Bugis has started a small stamp collection of his own since you were here last. I am sure he would appreciate your *expert* advice. That last one you sold him: he said it tasted like liquorice. "

John Wilson looked straight through the officer. The two constables had nothing else to do but watch Robert Walker, who remained motionless.

John Wilson reported: "How extraordinary that is."

"Yes, isn't it? Maybe you would like to speak with the Chief about it."

"Yes, yes, I'll do that. First opportunity," Wilson consented. The constables smiled, but did not yet show teeth. "Always happy to be. . . of service-. You know, always a pleasure-." John Wilson, international stamp dealer, shut himself up, and stood aside.

Robert Walker reached for his passport, which he handed to the officer: the officer declined, so he passed the document to the constables, whose eyes shifted beneath cap visors. One of the cons-tables stroked at a side-arm.

"I see you have company on this trip, Mr Wilson," the officer remarked.

"Oh, you mean-?" John Wilson was quick to disown his travelling companion: "We happened to be on the same flight, that's all."

John Wilson's passport was returned to him.

The young officer snatched Robert Walker's passport from the constables. The officer looked at the passport photograph and then at the real-life Robert Walker. Then he checked the visa slip. "Welcome to Bourbon Island, Mr Walker."

"Thank you. It's a pleasure to be here."

"And is it business or pleasure, Mr Walker?" the officer asked. "Your purpose in visiting our island?"

Robert Walker thought this was going to be difficult to explain. The whole story? No, of course not. Already, the equatorial heat seemed to be affecting his state of mind; he sweated, and the sweat made him look guilty of every conceivable crime against the island republic. He looked into the three sets of curious, unforgiving eyes.

"Pleasure, certainly," Robert Walker remarked.

The young officer looked - high-up - at the hangar roof.

"Primarily, I am on assignment."

"The visa here says - September Sixth. Any reason?"

"I am at the mercy of my news agency."

The officer stared into Robert Walker's eyes. The officer's eyes read: YOU, SIR, ARE AT THE MERCY OF THE BOURBON ISLAND POLICE FORCE.

"I see. And what is the precise nature of your assignment, Mr Walker?"

"He's a journalist," Wilson volunteered.

The officer rebuked the stamp dealer: "With respect, Mr Wilson, I did not ask you. We know very well why *you* are here, so now we want to know why Mr Walker has come all this way to visit our small island." Then: "So, you are a journalist, Mr Walker? Is that correct?"

"Yes, it is."

"You look nervous, Mr Walker. Do you have something to feel nervous about?"

"Too much bloody champagne on the flight," Wilson volunteered. "He's got the shakes from dehydration."

"Mr Wilson, please be bloody quiet!" the officer grimaced "This is not England, you know. Now, there's a good British gentleman."

"Sorry," Wilson gulped.

Robert Walker felt like the sole, unwelcome representative of the former colonial power.

John Wilson tried, but could not keep quiet: "Where have. . .all the other passengers gone? Where are the civilian immigration officials?"

"So, you are asking the questions, Mr Wilson?"

"No, not me, of course not. Please, continue."

The young officer gestured at two pieces of luggage.

"These are yours?"

"That one's mine," Wilson confessed. "Where did you-?"

Before Robert Walker could comply, the officer had seized on his travel-grip, while the two constables pounced on Wilson's suitcase. "So," the officer said, commencing his search, "you travel light, Mr Walker?"

"Always."

"And you are going to write some journalism about our island, Mr Walker?"

"That's why I have the special visa."

"Mr Robert Walker," the officer pointed out, "the mercenaries who attacked this island only recently *all* had special visas."

. "I'm not a mercenary," Robert Walker stated. "I'm a journalist."

"And who's to say which is worse, Mr Walker?"

"Easy," Wilson warned. "We are both British subjects, you know."

The officer closed, then opened, his eyes. "Mr Wilson, *please* shut the hell up! For the last time!"

"You can't speak to me like that. I won't have it, you see."

"It's all right," Robert Walker reasoned. "Mr Wilson is still suffering from landing nerves."

"We know all about Mr Wilson's landing nerves," the officer said.

On a nearby desk, the two constables were making a hash out of the contents of Wilson's case, which seemed to contain a selection of useless travel paraphernalia.

"Be careful there," Wilson whispered. One of the constables had found a deck of playing cards showing 52 different women in various states of undress. The bladder-wielding joker was a depiction of -. "If you don't mind-. I'd rather you didn't touch that, gentlemen."

"You see, Mr Walker," the young officer was saying, "how Mr Wilson calls my constables gentlemen?"

One of the constables had found something in Wilson's case: an artefact, the purpose of which was unclear. A mermaid's purse? A-? The policeman, gripped by susperstition, tossed the unknown item back into the suitcase, half-closed the lid, and shoved the luggage across the desk. An agitated John Wilson reclaimed his luggage.

In Robert Walker's luggage, the officer had located some papers of interest. Photocopies, from Kensington library; more from the IPC in Paris.

⸰ "Ah," Wilson said.

"So," the officer beamed, "you are following the clues - just like our friend Graham Dunne from England? Everything becomes clear."

At this latest development, the constables joined their superior, and displayed healthy white teeth.

"So, Mr Walker, you are a treasure hunter? That is more like it! This business about being a journalist - really - do we look like fools?"

Robert Walker did not respond.

"I wouldn't answer that, if I were you," Wilson advised.

"It's background research, for the article. I'm a journalist, not a treasure hunter. There is no treasure, anyway."

The officer spoke to his subordinates, which, in Creole, was something about the British stiff upper-lip. The policemen had a good, solid laugh at that, until an announcement came over the PA system: an Air India Flight was on its way in to land. The officer, now determined to conclude this business, said:

"This is all very well, Mr Walker. You may proceed. But you will need a permit, of course."

"A permit? A permit for what?"

"Why, for hunting treasure. Five thousand rupees is all."

"And if I decline?"

"Then you shall of course not be permitted to enter the country."

"You would deport me in such a circumstance?"

"That is . . . up to you, Mr Robert Walker."

"I would, of course, be speaking with the British High Commissioner on the subject . . ?"

"You would," the officer grinned, dangerously, "find His Excellency, High Commissioner Browne, much preoccupied."

"Oh Christ, I'm getting out of here." John Wilson picked up his ransacked suitcase. Then: "Browne's had a bloody nervous breakdown, even I can tell you that. Listen, old boy, I'll meet you in the arrivals' lounge. Over the other side there."

"Yes, yes. Please go ahead, Mr Wilson."

"And you, Mr Robert Walker, will come with me," the officer directed.

Robert Walker was escorted into a small room marked IMMIGRATION. By the time he was allowed to leave the room, he had been issued with a government permit (with rules of trove and conditions attached) to search for treasure on dry land only, properly stamped and sealed, with a receipt for BIR5,000, which the officer claimed was excellent value. The permit was valid for a period not to exceed the limit of his current visa. In the event of serindipidy, the government was to have its share.

"Excellent, excellent," the young officer had said. "That's what I like, Mr Walker: cooperation."

In the ARRIVALS lounge, John Wilson said: "Thought we'd lost you there, old boy . . .What's that you've got there?"

Robert Walker revealed the scroll: "A permit."

"You're joking? I thought you said you weren't a treasure hunter?"

"Mr Wilson, I repeat for the sake of clarity: I am not a treasure hunter."

"Then why the permit?"

"You heard: I would have been deported."

"And you paid good money for a piece of paper?"

"You, Mr Wilson, pay good money for smaller pieces of paper."

"Ah, point taken. But there has to be more to it. What baffles me is - well, why would you want to-?"

"-Cooperate?"

A tall black man, with startling green-grey eyes, and a coffee-coloured business suit, approached the Britons.

"Secret service," Wilson whispered. "Don't say anything unless asked directly."

"Welcome to Bourbon Island, gentlemen." The man, who towered over even the fairly lanky John Wilson, flashed an ID card. "Ahhhh, Mr Wilson, it is *you*?"

"Yes, yes," Wilson said, flustered, "I know it's me."

"You are here on stamp business again?"

"Why, yes, I'm always on stamp business. A new issue, you see, which I must have for, ah, a special client-."

"A new issue? Really? I haven't heard about that. My eldest boy collects all of our national stamps."

"Not like this one," Wilson said. "It hasn't been issued yet."

"Ah, you are unusually candid, Mr Wilson," the agent said, and fixed his green-grey eyes on the stamp dealer. "Commendable. A new issue that hasn't been issued yet? This is all very interesting and very clever, of course. You excel yourself, Mr Wilson."

"Any, ah, news about the, er, coup?" Wilson ventured. "Any idea who was behind this Trouvères fellow?"

"I don't know anything about any coup, Mr Wilson." The secret serviceman's face tightened, and seemed to turn blue. "You know anything about the coup, Mr Wilson? Strange how you should turn up so soon after event. "

"No, of course not," Wilson blubbered.

"Then you should not talk about it any more, Mr Wilson. Put it out of your head, entirely. Stick to the stamp business, and you'll be all right." The secret serviceman grinned at his own lame joke; then, with a look across the top of Robert Walker's head, he said: "Passport?"

"-?"

"Show him your passport," Wilson fussed.

Robert Walker handed over the document for examination by those green-grey eyes.

"And you are staying *where*, Mr Walker?" the secret serviceman enquired, and searched Robert Walker's eyes.

"The Marina Hotel," he answered.

"You have a reservation?"

"No, but it came recommended."

"Who recommended it to you?"

"I did," an eager-to-get going Wilson said.

"You are staying there also, Mr Wilson?" the agent enquired.

"I always stay at the Marina," John Wilson said, "as I am sure your people are very well aware."

After a pause, the secret serviceman noted: "I see you also have a special permit, Mr Walker."

Robert Walker handed over the scroll.

"This is also very much in order." The agent's wry smile meant that this particular visitor was not to be taken too seriously. "I wish you luck, Mr Walker. You'll need it."

Robert Walker saw now how the permit might, after all, have its advantages. Its job done, he slipped the scroll into an inside pocket.

Wilson took command: "All right, let's get going."

As they strode across the lounge, Robert Walker said: "Thanks, Mr Wilson."

"Don't mention it, old boy. It just came out. One of these days, you may be able to do *me* a favour. In fact, there is something. . .About what I said on the aircraft. About the Fiery Cross stamp. I was a little tipsy, you see. I didn't mean to-."

"You want me to keep quiet about that?"

"If you would, old boy."

"Yes, of course."

John Wilson, his secret regained, *hum-hahed* with satisfaction. The two men reached the main terminal hall. A few outbound passengers stared up at an analogue timetable that flap-*flap-flapped* for no apparent reason. The Air India flight from New Delhi and the outgoing BA London-Frankfurt flight bound for Mauritius were the only events on the board. At strategic points around the teminal, Kalashnikov-armed members of the khaki-clad Bourbon Island People's Defence Force (BIPDF) watched the two Britons pass through the hallway. Above the main exit, a giant portrait of President François Bellarmine levelled his eyes at the transient inhabitants of the terminal. Robert Walker could feel the eyes of the dictator follow their every step towards the exit.

"You'll get used to it," John Wilson advised. "His portrait is just about everywhere."

"Ever . . .met him, Mr Wilson?"

"Oh no. He's not much of a mixer. In *his* position, he has to be careful."

They stepped out into the harsh sunlight, and John Wilson was blinded.

Robert Walker looked across the coastal plain, then upward, and then again up, onto the slopes of Mont Pomme d'Or's exposed, ragged, wind-torn crater.

"If you don't mind my saying so, Mr Walker," Wilson was saying, "you seem rather anxious. Any, ah, particular reason? Secret service bothering you?"

"It's nothing, Mr Wilson, really."

"You needn't worry about that, old boy. Bellarmine's still very much in control around here. I believe it was more of a skirmish than a coup.

You know how these journalists build things up out of all proportion, don't you?"

"Yes, you're quite right."

Across the road, a bus driver honked at the pair of Britons.

"They'd have to pay *me* to travel in that jalopy," Wilson remarked.

Outside the terminal, the old British Leyland bus - painted red-and-white, the colours of the Bourbon Island People's Party (BIPP) - was ready to leave. In front of the bus, a white Mercedes taxi (diesel, air-conditioned) had been spared the red brush of the BIPP. The taxi driver, keen-eyed to divert this prestigious double-fare away from the state-owned bus, blasted his own klaxon. The advance party of passengers had already departed for Port Bourbon, while the remainder - the nun, the elderly French couple - waited inside the bus. Robert Walker checked for any sign of Straw Hat - the European - who was, evidently, not a rider of buses. Neither was Wilson, who said: "Taxi for me, old boy. Care to hitch a lift?"

Again, the bus driver honk-*honked* for attention.

"I'll take the bus, Mr Wilson, if you don't mind."

"Take in the local colour, that kind of thing?"

"Yes, that's the idea."

"All right, catch up with you later. I'm off to the Philatelic Bureau. Urgent business. Buy you a drink. The Marina Hotel - this evening. Quench that damnable thirst once and for all, eh? There's someone I'd like you to meet. Someone who knows things about things. An Italian - but nobody's perfect, are they, old boy?"

"I suppose not, Mr Wilson."

The bus driver *honk-honked*, which made the nun scowl, and revved his engine so that blue smoke spluttered from the exhaust. John Wilson clambered into the rear of the taxi, which took off along the coastal road for Port Bourbon. Robert Walker, who had not liked the look of the hair-primping taxi diver, headed for the bus.

"You get on board, man! Pay later!" the bus driver shouted above the roar of the engine. Robert Walker lumbered along the aisle. The bus accelerated along the coastal road in pursuit of the white Mercedes. Robert Walker was thrown into the nearest seat.

Again, the nun scowled.

A while into the journey, the roadside coconut groves yielded, and a long stretch of white coral beach opened up to the east. The automatic door, which was not working, remained open, and a powerful draught flowed through the length of the bus. Robert Walker tried to take in the topography of the island. The passengers bounced - over hard, wooden seats - as the scenery flashed by. In an unequal competition with the taxi, the manic-obsessed bus driver pressed on towards his destination. The smooth-rolling Mercedes swerved to block the passage of the bus. John

Wilson appeared to instruct the taxi driver to slow down, and then the bus, too, was forced to deccelerate, and the powerful draught dropped to a steady breeze. Along the coast, a bay opened up, and seemed to show the way.

The old bus, unable to out-manoeuvre the Mercedes, slowed to a steady crawl. The nun commenced a decade of her rosary. The elderly French couple peered at the island's hinterland. Robert Walker opened-up his travel-grip, and removed a map of the island - which he folded across his knees. This bay was Anse Venus. The capital, Port Bourbon, lay at the southern escarpment of Mont Pomme d'Or, which had created the deep-water harbour. At the interior of the island, the USAF's radome was indicated at an elevated position, sheltered - high up in the foothills - to the west, away from the shadow of the crater. On an eastern aspect of the island, a cove named Sans Souci Bay was marked as a harbour facility - reputed, again by the Bamboo Mill - to be a Russian naval installation.

On this open stretch of road, the bus driver shouted, changed gears in fierce, quick-fire succession, and at last succeeded in overtaking the coasting white Mercedes. Robert Walker looked back along the road, where the taxi had been left behind, and where John Wilson was fast asleep in the back seat. The hair-primping taxi driver, for fear of waking his passenger, shook his fist - in silence. The bus-driver, with his euphoric, sweaty features visible in the rear-view mirror, *honk-honked* abuse, and then accelerated to open up the distance between the two vehicles.

Once again, Robert Walker was thrown back into his seat.

A boy appeared from the rear of the bus, and took up a position in front of Robert Walker. Robert Walker re-folded, then put away, the map. Over the seat's handrail, the boy said:

"You looking for a guide, mistah?"

There was something about the boy that Robert Walker thought unnatural. The nun, who had finished her prayers, watched the boy for signs of misbehaviour.

"No, thank you. I'm not going anywhere."

The boy rolled the whites of his eyes at Robert Walker.

The bus pounded and rattled onwards, way ahead of the white Mercedes, so that the beach rushed by in a ripple of featureless sand.

"What's your name, sonny?"

"Charlie!"

"Charlie who?"

"Charlie the Fish!"

"That's a strange name."

"What's yours, mistah?"

"Robert."

"Which Robert?"

"Just Robert."

The nun was leering across the aisle at Robert Walker. The potential for wickedness, her face made clear, was never far away.

"My father will put you in his jail, Mistah Robert."

Once again, the boy rolled an eye at Robert Walker, and then crossed the aisle to sit with the nun.

The bus driver howled as he encountered a double-buckle of a turn in the road, which marked the outskirts of Port Bourbon. Up ahead, a promontory rose from the ocean, where the long beach had reached its end. The tyres of the bus squealed. A canopy of trees obscured the sunlight. The old Leyland passed though a dense corridor of palms either side of the road. After a darkened interval . . .the bus reappeared on the other side of the promontory, and hurtled through a rich grove of coconut. Then the palms gave way to the expansive gardens of a church, with banana trees, flowers of many kinds - gold, white, yellow, pink - and a rolling lawn, which was kept verdant against the harsh sun of the equator. A gold-painted sign showed THE CHURCH OF MARY MAGDALENE. A spire above a bell-tower pointed at the tropical heavens. The bus swerved, trundled onwards, and entered Port Bourbon.

The manic driver became calm. The bus was made to cruise responsibly along the main street. This was Revolution Boulevard. The square buildings were of the early French and later British colonial periods. Eslewhere, everywhere, a patchwork of red-, blue-, and green-painted wood frames supported rust-stained, sun-baked roofs of corrugated iron. The more severe architecture of Bellarmine's "La Revolution" was represented by utilitarian breezeblocks combined with indifferent overseas aid. A legacy of colonial decadence had been allowed to coexist with the harsh reality of the collectivist state. The bus rolled on. A dilapidated wall showed the eroded remains of advert-isements for various foodstuffs - BRO KE BO D and BOV IL. A more recent, Party poster boasted: BIPP Rally - National Stadium, Revolution Day, 5th June. The boulevard, with its many side streets, was mostly emptied of its people. An occasional tradesmen, an unarmed soldier, a pair of ambling policemen, and then. . .goose-stepping along the main street, as though to meet the bus, a troop of Bourbon Island youth in the uniform of the Party. These adolescent troops took a lazy, pigeon-toed about-turn, and disappeared up a side alley - bound for their state camp in the foothills.

"Okay, Port Bourbon, everyone!" the bus driver announced. "One stop only this side of town!"

The nun, the elderly couple, and a few disconsolate locals stood up from their seats, and all climbed off the bus. The bus driver, who still grinned from his triumph, turned to see the white Mercedes finally crawl into town. He clapped his hands - once - sharply, and bounced on his seat.

Robert Walker caught sight of John Wilson in repose. The panama hat lay askew over the stamp dealer's head. The taxi driver shook a fist, and honked at the bus driver. This time, the bus driver banged his fist on the centre of the steering wheel, which produced a single bark of the klaxon. The nun, whose turn it was to alight, stared at the bus driver with careful rebuke in her eyes. Then the nun urged the boy to climb off the bus - at this stop, not the next one.

"Where you going, man?"

"The Marina Hotel," Robert Walker divulged, but that could not be helped. The boy, he guessed, was a bus-riding spy in the pay of the regime. The child performed as he was told, but then made a devil-face at the nun, and scampered away.

"Other side of town, man. I'll bring you there, man, you'll see. Get your ten rupees ready now, man!"

"Okay, thanks."

The driver adjusted his rear-view mirror, and - with a steady lurch - the bus moved slowly, slowly - speeding on the coast? not me, sir, no, sir - along the length of Revolution Boulevard.

The bus reached an unmarked stop at the crossroads. Robert Walker handed over a BIR10 note to the driver, and alighted. By the crossroads, he could hear, and then smell, the old port area. An unseen tugboat *chug-chugged* out of the unseen harbour. The boat hooted a plaintive welcome to a much larger vessel out at sea. In search of a berth, the ship blasted a deep-bass reply. The bus driver continued on his way along Victoria Street, past a Police Station, and then - after a lurch - out of sight. Robert Walker looked across the street at the veranda of the Marina Hotel, where a sign announced: "SOON TO BE FULLY AIR-CONDITIONED".

3

MR SWANN AT THE MARINA HOTEL

A HIGH WIND tore over the cone of the extinct volcano. The sun continued on its downward slope over the Indian Ocean and, beyond the horizon, the mainland of Africa. At sea level, a salty breeze had sprung up from beyond the harbour, and crept through the town. The Marina Hotel's abandoned veranda seemed to whisper something at Robert Walker. The tourist brochures that had not yet been written would one day refer to the hotel's 'faded elegance' and 'former grandeur'. The enormous wood-frame had, though, been restored, and presented its magnolia *fascia* to Revolution Boulevard. In the 1930s, the building had been - the same unwritten brochures would say - the residence of the Governor, Sir Godfrey Smythe-Smith. The structure revealed four storeys with balconies, and an observation deck - which could be taken for a fifth - with cupola. Robert Walker guessed that the original construction dated from the middle British colonial period, that is to say about 80 years' ago.

Times changed, even here; but somehow the Marina Hotel, an insulting anachronism - to the BIPP's eyes anyway - had been allowed to survive.

A well-established hornet's nest hung from an edge of the cupola. In the breeze, the paper pod wobbled; its fierce occupants buzzed. A single hornet went into orbit around the nest. The creature was the size of a small, hairy bird. Then Robert Walker, from the aspect of the unmarked busstop, noticed an unusual outcrop from the roof of the hotel. A craftsman had positioned a life-size gargoyle - a gesticulating monkey or chimpanzee - on the western side of the observation deck. The gargoyle had, he supposed, passed unnoticed, for the figure's dissent was surely aimed at the one-party state and - somewhere on the slopes of Mont Pomme d'Or - the dacha of François Bellarmine.

Robert Walker had seen enough: he picked up his travel grip from the roadside. He heard a sound of sandals over grit. It was the boy, Charlie, who had changed into a stripe-top tee-shirt and pair of shoddy shorts, and play-picked at his nose. Robert Walker wondered if this boy, too, had seen the treasonous simian on the roof. But no; the boy was too short, by about one-half.

"Why are you following me, Charlie?"

"I'm not following you, Mistah Robert, I'm waiting for the bus."

"The bus has gone."

"The bus will be back. The bus always comes back. Round and around it goes. . ."

"Round and around, you say?"

The boy made hand-circles above his head and rolled his eyes.

"You looking for somewhere to stay, Mistah Robert?"

"Sure."

"My Papa's prison is over there."

Beyond the crossroads, the dirty-whitewash of a single-storey block dominated that side of Victoria Road (another permitted anachronism). The Police Station, then, added its ballast to the unintentional cubism of the post-Revolutionary era.

"No thanks."

"You're welcome any time, Mistah Roberts!" The boy, anticipating sudden violence, turned and ran away over the crossroads.

"Please, sir? You should stay away from that boy. Bad luck."

Across the road, a man in a fine white suit had appeared on the hotel's verandah. The man's dark hair was combed-back from his face and set in brilliantine. A smile played over one side of his face, while the other was set in a rictus of despair.

"Bad luck, I say."

Robert Walker looked each way along the boulevard - there was no traffic of any kind - and crossed the road.

"I am Mr Swann. Mr Robert-?"

"No, Walker. Robert Walker."

"Ah, I heard the boy-? Then, welcome, Mr *Walker.* You are in search of accommodation?"

"I am. On your roof - I was just looking at that-?"

"Watch out for-?"

Robert Walker had climbed the short flight of steps onto the veranda - and tripped over a loose plank.

"Please. If you please, Mr Walker!"

Robert Walker regained his balance.

"Our carpenter . . .he is away," Mr Swann apologised, and showed the grim side of his face.

The sinking equatorial sun seemed to bite at the back of Robert Walker's neck.

"Why is it so quiet around here, Mr Swann?"

"You think it is quiet?" Mr Swann checked his watch, took a step back, and watched over the boulevard. "Now, you see: almost five o'clock."

The seconds ticked by in a kind of silence. A bus backfired somewhere in the distance. A whistle sounded in the harbour. An invisible light aircraft buzzed somewhere high above the island. Its engine performed a doodlebug cut-out. The hornets' nest seemed to respond. Beyond the crossroads, a shriek of laughter erupted from inside the general Police block. In the sky above the hotel, a bird squawked - and flew away. There was a rustle at the far end of the veranda: Robert Walker looked to one side: a pith-helmeted gardener hoed away at a sun-blanched grass verge. Mr Swann hissed at the gardener:

"Not here, George! The hornets' nest. Go now!"

The gardener showed liquorice-blackened teeth; and, with his hoe, disappeared around that side of the hotel - but not to destroy the hornets' nest.

Mr Swann explained: "George is lonely. He wants to listen to a British fellow speak English."

"All gardeners are lonely," Robert Walker supposed. "Aren't they?"

Mr Swann examined Robert Walker's white, sweaty face with interest. The proprietor added: "His only friend was the carpenter," and looked down at the loose plank.

"What happened to the carp-?"

"-Now," Mr Swann reiterated: "observe!"

At 17:00 exactly, the offices and stores along Revolution Boulevard disgorged their human contents. A swarm of pedestrians and bicycles invaded the streets. At the end of an official day's work, men and women of all ages - but mostly in their 20s and 30s - made their way homewards. The old British Leyland bus, with a cloud of dust in its wake, rumbled along the boulevard - and braked across the road from the hotel. It was the same driver, who had already completed a circuit, but this time he had a full busload - standing and seated - of passengers. There was no laughter or gossip among the passengers; only a cough or a sniff broke the silence. The bus driver - ready to be on his way again - honked the klaxon. "There she is," Mr Swann observed. "Dead on time - as usual."

"-?"

A girl in green fatigues alighted from the bus and approached the hotel. In one hand, she carried a basket of assorted vegetables; in the other, a sheaf of printed matter for night-study.

"The kitchen, if you please, Danielle," Mr Swann directed. She skipped over the loose plank, glanced with light-grey eyes at Robert Walker, and made her way into the hotel. "The growing of private vegetables is no longer permitted," Mr Swann remarked. "Our housegirl. She is a typist by day at State House. At week-ends, she is a soldier. For most people, office hours end at five, as you can see. Curfew starts at six. There is not much time in between to have any fun - so, no fun."

Along the road, the bus had disappeared behind a cloud of dust, and embarked on another circuit with its silent cargo. The blank-faced office workers headed for the harbour area, the fishing villages along the coast, and the foothills outside of town. A few commuters were hauled into the Police Station, and others wandered into alleyways.

"Now, Mr Walker, without further delay, it is time we checked you in."

Mr Swann led the way into the lobby, where he took up a position behind a reception desk. An abacus and a ledger rested on the desk. Mr Swann ignored these, and opened a leather-bound register.

Mr Swann coughed into a closed fist, then said:

"Your passport, please, Mr Walker."

Robert Walker reached into his jacket: he removed the passport and - by chance - the special permit for treasure hunters.

"The rules," the proprietor said. "You can have it back when you leave. Sign here, if you please."

"Of course. I understand. Please, would you keep this permit for me also?"

Mr Swann examined the permit. The proprietor's thin eyebrows rose, and froze, but otherwise he made no comment. The pen slipped through Robert Walker's fingers as he signed, such that his signature was a mess: ROBOT WALK.

"How long will you be staying with us, Mr Walker?"

"September the Fifth or Sixth."

"Well," Mr Swann explained, "we may be able to be offer a discount. I will need to perform some calculations." Mr Swann reached for the abacus, but glanced outside: a big, shambling islander in a light khaki uniform with massive, starch-stiff baggy shorts had emerged from the Police Station. The policeman twisted his cap firmly over a large head; then he lodged a rattan cane under an armpit; and, casting a substantial shadow, started out in the direction of the crossroads.

"Oh no," Mr Swann whispered. Then: "Mr Walker, I have urgent business. Also, please forgive me; you must be very thirsty after your long journey. If you please, refreshment - on the house - the Marlin Room is there behind you. My nephew - Francis Long - is the bartender. Here, allow me to take your luggage."

Robert Walker passed the grip over the reception desk. Mr Swann stowed the luggage out of sight. Robert Walker moved through an archway, and entered the lounge area of the Marlin Room. Inside, a fan buzzed from the ceiling, and Robert Walker's face was cooled by the downdraft.

Mr Swann observed the progress of the policeman. The fellow waited in the middle of the crossroads. A steady stream of cyclists parted to avoid the khaki obstacle. One among the cyclists appeared drunk. This cyclist was stopped, and ordered to dismount. The offender was lashed once, and then again, across each of his arms. The cyclist howled; the bicycle fell awkwardly against its owner's thighs, and caused more pain. The policeman pointed his rattan cane in the direction of the Police Station. "There is your destination. The bike is to be impounded. Walk, don't ride, WALK! WALK!"

The policeman walked, too, in the direction of the Marina Hotel.

Inside the Marlin Room, Robert Walker waited for service, and listened.

In the lobby, Mr Swann's abacus commenced the calculation, and the beads flew back and forth along the many rods of the device. Soon, the sound of heavy boots on the veranda signalled the arrival of the Chief of Police. The Chief entered the lobby, and set about the rapid questioning of the proprietor on the matter of the hornets' nest. There have been many complaints. One day, someone will be badly stinged. Stinged? Stung? I say, stinged, which is many times stung over. A public nuisance, then, for which there are severe penalties. Mr Swann explained that the gardener was too frightened to tackle the problem, since the hornets had become very, very angry in recent weeks. So have I, the Chief announced. Mr Swann, the Chief suggested, should hire a more courageous gardener. There was another possibility: the hotelier could always go up onto the roof and deal with the situation himself. No chance. Mr Swann continued with the abacus calculation. The Chief remarked that the infernal device was like another bloody damned hornets' nest. Mr Swann, he said, should stop playing around when serious business was under discussion. Mr Swann was only an hotel proprietor, nothing more. He, Bugis, was, well, Chief of Police, as anyone could see with their own eyes. Mr Swann looked at the Chief with his own eyes, and saw . . .nothing. Insulted, the Chief rapped his rattan cane across Mr Swann's nicely polished reception desk.

Then: had the stamp dealer by the name of Mr John Wilson arrived yet?

No, Chief Bugis.

Then: had a gentleman by the name of Mr Robert arrived?

No, no one by that name.

Then: the register, if you please.

A struggle over the register ensued; a series of spats and counterspats unfolded between hotelkeeper and policeman.

Robert Walker had heard enough. He looked around the place. The big room was named for the stuffed marlin that hung from the main lounge wall. Above the glass-eyed monster, a fishing net with floats had been positioned to suggest the fish had - just then - escaped from the sweep of the net. In reality, this could not have been the case. A pole and a hook had finally caught this creature. Elsewhere, the walls of the lounge were covered with photographs, charts, clocks, and compasses. Assorted paraphernalia made up a jig-saw of the island's maritime heritage. On the wall, by the archway entrance, the same photograph of President François Bellarmine had been positioned with care. In this way, the leader of the BIPP confronted the guests when they arrived, and again when they departed. Robert Walker stared into the cold blue eyes of the master of this island, then moved on - to the lounge area. Near a bay window, a parrot's perch lay abandoned. The bay window overlooked the marina. Outside, several yachts were moored, and which belonged, no doubt, to the influential polity of the island, and the occasional wealthy visitor from abroad. At the centre of the bay window, a brass telescope on a tripod looked out over the expanse of ocean. Robert Walker stooped to look through the device, which, he discovered, was focused on a craggy, pillar-like rock, which lay about a league off-shore from Anse Venus. The coral sand glowed blue-white and ochre as the sun continued on its path beyond the Indian Ocean. Then, a double-flash of red, crystalline light emanated from the tip of the craggy rock - and then ceased.

Robert Walker turned away from the brass tube. He faced a horse-shoe shaped bar, which dominated this end of the Marlin Room. The bar was made of a solid bamboo structure. An array of cabinets and shelves were generously stocked with sprits, beers, cordials, and liqueurs, but not much in the way of wines. The local beer was called Bourbon Island Brew or "BourBrew". He looked over the counter, and - set into the floor area - a trapdoor started to open. The trapdoor lid was pushed back, and flapped onto the floor with a clatter. A head appeared - it was, presumably, the nephew, Francis Long.

"Excuse me, sir. Busy in the cellar. How may I help you?" The bartender faced his only customer.

"Beer?" Robert Walker asked. "I'll try the local."

Francis Long heard Chief Bugis in the lobby. He did not move and he did not speak. Then: "You staying with us long, Mr-?"

"The name's Walker. I'll be staying for a while."

"At your service, sir."

Robert Walker sat on a stool by the horse-shoe shaped counter.

"You'd better close that trapdoor, Francis, before someone falls into the cellar."

"Someone like me," Francis Long smiled, and closed the trapdoor lid without sound. Then he poured out a glass of the Bourbon Island Brew.

"Your boss said this one's on the house."

In the lobby, there had been a pause in the fiery exchange. In measured tones, the two men had, for now, reached some form of rapprochement.

Francis Long poured, and said nothing. His hands shook. Robert Walker sweated, and waited.

"There you are, sir. Welcome to the Marina Hotel. I hope you enjoy your stay with us."

"Thank you; I'm sure I shall." Robert Walker tasted the beer. It was good. He took a good long swallow, until the glass was almost empty.

Chief Bugis stepped into the Marlin Room. The policeman waved his rattan cane at nothing and everything. In the lobby, Mr Swann resumed his abacus-crunching calculation. Robert Walker had never seen anyone who looked quite like the policeman. The Chief was a horse-faced man of about fifty. He had big, heavy-lidded eyes, with dark bags of pure kohl; the eyelashes, long. The head was jug-eared, sketched-in with thin (plucked?) eyebrows. The Chief's cap had a big, super-shiny rim. The frame of the body was rectangular; the paunch, a reliable witness to the demolition of many powerful curries and gallons of this same local beer. The Chief wore big, baggy shorts, heavily starched to provide a rigid buttock-box with sharp creases, which reached to just above knee-level, the half-way points of somewhat bandy, hair-free, stockinged legs. Back on the face, the smile - which was not a happy smile - was made up of tombstone-teeth. The eyes were beyond any reasonable assessment. The orbs looked in - at what? - as much as they looked out. And, even then, it was still not over: the Chief opened his mouth to reveal an ox-tongue, bright orange from the prolonged chewing of betel nut, which he sucked-on even now. The Chief was about to spit on Mr Swann's french-polished pine floors, changed his mind, and swallowed the red liquor.

The Chief pounded across the floorboards to confront Robert Walker.

"Hey, you there, are you Mr Robert? "

Robert Walker set his beerglass on the counter: "I am Mr Walker."

"Then who is this Mr Robert I hear about?"

The Chief brought his long face close to Robert Walker's.

"I have no idea."

"Maybe you see something you don't like around here, Mr Walker? You a journalist or what? There are too many bloody journalists around here, if you ask me! Far too many!"

Robert Walker reached inside his jacket.

"Hold it!" Chief Bugis swashed the rattan cane over the edge of the bar. Robert Walker thought a fly caught at the end of that cane would not stand a chance. Francis Long retreated, and found a corner of the bamboo bar.

The Chief produced the passport, but not the treasure permit.

Mr Swann *clack-clacked* away in the lobby.

"I am indeed a journalist," Robert Walker ventured. "And that passport is-?"

The Chief raised his plucked-thin eyebrows, and deployed a massive smile.

"Oh yes, oh yes?"

Robert Walker's beerglass was beaded with moisture. The Chief took a step backwards. "Your glass is empty, Mr Walker, perhaps you'd better have another. "

"I'm all right, thank you."

The policeman looked across the counter at Francis Long. "What have you got to say then, man?"

"I've got nothing to say, Chief Bugis."

"Well, *I* have! One Blue Marlin, if you bloody well please!" The Chief, along with his order, rapped his rattan cane over the counter. Francis Long did as he was told, while the Chief studied the passport.

"So, so, a visitor from England, who has come all this way with Mr Wilson."

"I was not with Mr Wilson. I mean, I was on the same flight. He joined the flight at. . .We arrived together, but are we not travelling together. I only met him on the flight." Robert Walker relented; anything he said would sound suspicious to the Chief's jug-like antennae. As for Francis Long, he stood well away from this exchange.

"Yes, yes, you may well look baffled, Francis," the Chief assured the bartender. "Everything is a big bloody mystery these days, isn't it? When I was a young policeman - oh yes, I was young once - we were satisfied with one or two mysteries, and now everything is a mystery. Like who sent Trouvères is a mystery. . ."

The Chief waited for a reaction from either of the men.

The *clackety clack-clack* of the abacus in the lobby paused, and then continued, as did the Chief:

"But let me assure *you*, Francis, that mystery is *my* business."

The Chief, after all that, swallowed at something, so that his large adam's apple moved up and down behind his starched shirt collar.

"Now, what have we here?" the Chief, from a flap-down breast pocket, removed a second document. "Ah yes, I almost forgot." He unfolded the permit. "So, another *treasure* hunter . . .This explains your suspicious conduct, Mr Walker, if I may speak so bold."

In the lobby, the abacus clack-*clack-clacked* in a frenzy. From the ceiling, the fan buzzed away merrily - too small for the job.

"I've only just arrived. I - came in on the bus."

"I know when and how you arrived, Mr Walker. However, I am not sure . . .this permit . . .is in order."

"It was sold to me at the airport."

"*Sold* to you, Mr Walker? You mean *issued* to you?" The Chief's eyebrows were raised so high they had disappeared under the brim of his cap.

"Yes, that's what I meant: it was issued to me."

"You don't look like a treasure hunter, Mr Walker."

Robert Walker decided not to volunteer any information.

Francis Long had opened a bottle of the Chief's favourite beer from Mauritius, and set the bottle and the glass on the counter. The Chief ignored the glass, and snatched the bottle by its neck; he up-ended it, sucked the moisture out of it, then slammed the empty bottle onto the counter. Francis Long looked uncomfortable.

"What the hell is wrong with you, Francis? Still looking for a girl?" The Chief tipped his great head back, and howled with laughter, so that tears came into his black eyes. "If you were the Chief of Police, they would be crawling all over you! Maybe you should be helping Mr Walker here find the treasure. Girls like treasure, Francis!" The Chief cackled some more, so that the cheeks of his face were wet with tears.

"They will come like bloody moths to a light!"

The Chief, entertained and diverted, calmed down: he had spotted a dish of green Manzanilla olives on the counter, and helped himself to a fistful. He stuffed the olives - one by one - into his face.

"About the permit?" Robert Walker asked.

The Chief wiped at his mouth, rubbed his hands on the permit, and glared at this foreigner's insolence.

"About the passport, then?"

"Oh no. Oh no. I have to keep these two for close inspection. You have a cash receipt for the permit?"

"I have."

"Then you must give it me," the Chief smouldered.

"I can't help you there."

Francis jumped in with: "Mr Walker-!"

"-Francis," the Chief barked, "you mind your own bloody business!"

"Yes, Chief." Francis Long sulked, and started to clean some glasses which did not need cleaned.

"You should complain," Chief Bugis advised Robert Walker, "to Deputy High Commissioner Greene, if you like - if you can separate him from his bloody missus. I really don't care, you know," and the Chief rolled his eyes in the vague direction of the stuffed marlin on the lounge wall.

"It's not mine, you see."

"Not yours? Not yours?" The Chief looked at the passport, and then at the real-life Robert Walker. "What are you? Some kind of impostor?"

Robert Walker chanced on an idea:

"It belongs to Her Majesty's Government. I have no say in the matter whatsoever."

The words started to work on the Chief of Police. Francis Long stopped what he was doing, and stared across the bar at Bugis. The Chief's face flushed purple, his adam's apple bobbed, and his eyes became misty, while his eyebrows seemed to swim away in either direction. In the days of the Colonial Police Force, Robert Walker guessed, Bugis had sworn an oath of allegiance, when both he - and Her Majesty - had still been young.

From the lobby, Mr Swann appeared at the Chief's side, and reached for the well-thumbed passport. The policeman snarled, then pouted, but offered no more resistance. "And in the meantime," Mr Swann stated in a high-handed way, "it is I who am responsible. I, who am anxious to avoid any trouble with the British High Commissioner or his deputy, who, as you know, is a regular customer in this very establishment. . .We all have to be accommodating in these situations."

"Enough of this talk, Mr Swann," the Chief demanded. The policeman had recovered from a bout of nostalgia, and eyed the proprietor with suspicion. The Chief breathed in, and then out. He fondled the rattan cane under his armpit, changed his mind, and instead took off his cap; he inspected its rim, and dusted away some particles. Robert Walker stared at the Chief's haircut - a short-back-and-sides in the George Formby fashion, well-oiled, and then quaintly parted down the middle.

"What are you looking at?" the Chief enquired.

"Nothing."

The Chief turned to the proprietor. "You have some very strange guests around here these days, Mr Swann."

"I have heard the same said about your own police station, Chief Bugis."

"In that case, Mr Swann, I shall leave this matter in your, ah, capable, ah, hands. But all visitors must report to the Police Station when requested to do so," he added, without looking at Robert Walker. Mr Swann did not say a word; he stood there, straight and formal in his white suit, and waited for the Chief to be on his way.

Then the Chief grinned, put on his cap, gently rap-tapped his cane on top of the bar, and was gone. Mr Swann, with the passport secured, followed the policeman into the lobby. The Chief, though, Robert Walker realised - too late - had retained the permit.

"Well, how about another beer, Mr Walker?" Francis suggested. "You look like you need it."

The housegirl, Danielle, entered the lounge: she had changed from her green fatigues into something more traditional - a white blouse and light-grey skirt. She ran a feather duster over François Bellarmine's photograph.

"You see this, sir? Such a beautiful girl, who never smiles. Always dusting the President's face, even when there is no dust. *Grand blanc*, for sure."

Danielle ignored Francis Long, and found work to do elsewhere. Francis Long, with the eyes of a fisherman or a hunter, watched her go. Then Francis Long said:

"So, Mr Walker, you are a journalist?"

Robert Walker replied: "I am to write a feature article on the subject of Graham Dunne."

"Graham Dunne is dead. As dead as can be."
"Yes. Yes, I know."
"The Chief will go crazy when he finds out, Mr Walker."

4

A QUESTION OF ACCOMMODATION

"THE AMERICANS ARE here?" Robert Walker asked in a low voice.

Francis Long looked in the direction of the lobby, where the *clack-clack-clack* of Mr Swann's abacus calculation progressed.

"You mean who, Mr Walker?"

"Mr Beaumont? He is here?"

Francis Long tossed the Chief's discarded beer bottle into a skip under the counter. He glanced at Bellarmine's portrait on the wall, and said: "I don't know anything. I have been abroad. I only returned to the island recently."

"You were an exile?"'

"Not any more."

"About the American?"

"Yes, an American journalist. A woman, too. Good looking, all right. An assistant of some kind."

"Yes . . .?"

Francis Long wilted under the eyes of François Bellarmine's portrait.

"You were saying?"

Francis Long grabbed at a stray glass. "I wasn't saying anything. I am not an informer, Mr Walker, I am only a bartender."

"I didn't suggest that you were, Francis."

"Now that I am back home, all I want is a boat and a wife."

"Ambitious. You should start with the boat."

Francis Long, his face covered with sweat, had become excited by mention of a boat. "How do you mean, Mr Walker? Explain, if you please."

"We could come to some arrangement over that."

"All right, then. Mr Beaumont takes long walks. The woman disappears, too, but not in the same direction. Her name is. . .Miss Barbara West. Very beautiful. Only for looking at, this kind."

Francis Long's hands were shaking.

"Yes, I know what you mean. Go on."

"Something is going on, but it is none of my business, and I don't want to know."

"About Miss West?" Robert Walker enquired. "Disappearing where?"

The rattle of the abacus ceased. Mr Swann entered the Marlin Room. The proprietor said:

"Francis, please try not to provoke the Chief. Look, you are still sweating with fear."

"Uncle Jeff, I-."

"You will only end up staying at his place again."

"That I would not like."

"We at the Marina Hotel must avoid any confrontation." Then: "Wouldn't you agree, Mr Walker?"

Mr Swann faced the new arrival: "Mr Walker?"

"I understand."

Mr Swann waited in silence.

"I agree," Robert Walker added.

"Excellent," Mr Swann smiled. "I am able to tell you, then, that I have a solution to the question of accommodation."

"Well, that's good, Mr Swann."

"First, please be assured that your passport is once more safe in our safe."

"Safe in your safe? And the permit?"

"I was unable to retrieve the permit."

"The permit was in your safe keeping, Mr Swann."

"It was, Mr Walker, and I apologise. But the permit - strictly speaking - belongs to the authorities. Also, the Chief has a special grudge against treasure hunters-."

"But I'm not a-?"

"-or, indeed, anyone who might be interested in treasure or treasure hunters. The Dunne case brought him all kinds of problems. In truth, he is not at all keen on foreigners. You must be careful, Mr Walker. Now that he has your treasure permit, there is the possibility that he will arrest you for searching for treasure without a permit."

"I'm not looking for any treasure, Mr Swann," Robert Walker explained. "Please be assured of that fact before we proceed any further. The permit was sold to me at the airport - almost, you could say, as a pre-condition of my entry into your country."

"My country, Mr Walker, but not my pre-condition." The two sides of Swann's divided face struggled to form a complete smile, then failed. Robert Walker was beguiled Mr Swann's Confucian banter, which, however, was not getting them anywhere. Mr Swann's dark eyes shone at the prospect of treasure. It was, though, nightly room rental that was on the innkeeper's mind.

Francis Long observed the negotiations from behind the counter.

"I am interested in Graham Dunne, not the treasure itself. Chief Bugis probably finds himself in the same predicament."

"In what way, Mr Walker?" Francis Long asked.

"Yes, in what way, Mr Walker?" Mr Swann wanted to know.

Robert Walker replied: "Policemen are interested in clues, too. Just like Dunne."

"Not this one," Mr Swann advised. "He learnt a lot from the Englishman: not to chase after so many shadows. The Chief prefers to eliminate all clues and go straight to the target, which is usually to be found . . . inside his own prison cell."

"Ah," Francis Long motioned. "Should we be talking like this, Uncle Jeff?"

"Probably not, Francis," Mr Swann agreed. "The Chief is beyond our help. Now, if you please, to business."

"Please, Mr Swann, proceed." Robert Walker turned to look at the veranda: already, it was almost dark outside.

"Here, Mr Walker, is my solution. If you are staying until the fifth or sixth day of September, your stay could prove expensive. That is - fifteen nights."

"I am open to any suggestions, Mr Swann."

"Very well. There is a room, a rather unusual one, which no one else - not even among my staff - seems to care for. It is yours, for the period, at only a modest tariff."

"How modest is the tariff?"

Mr Swann rubbed his well-manicured hands together. "The calculation shows that this would be only five hundred rupees per night."

"That's what I call modest. What's the-?"

Mr Swann looked affronted. "Mr Walker, really, there are no catches at the Marina Hotel. If you want a catch, you can always go fishing with my nephew."

Francis Long smiled at this talk of fishing.

Robert Walker asked: "All right: let me put it another way: why is no one, not even a member of your own staff, interested in this particular room?"

"Superstition, I suppose you could say."

"Why is that?"

"Well, the room has an unfortunate location: it is under the stairs."

"Under the *stairs*?"

"Tell him the truth, Uncle Jeff," Francis Long urged.

"All right," Mr Swann relented. "The superstition is *not* about being under the stairs, Mr Walker."

"Well, what is it about, then?"

Mr Swann looked at his wristwatch; he had, it seemed, lingered for too long already. "The room, you see, used to belong to the hotel carpenter."

"Ah. The only friend of the gardener?"

"This is true. Some believe he was a genius in the business of wood."

"And now the carpenter," Robert Walker interpolated, "has left your employment - and so his room . . .is free?"

Mr Swann's unusually cool forehead had become moist.

Robert Walker paused to consider: there had been a word there: the carpenter *was* - not *is* - a genius. "Mr Swann, you are suggesting the man lost his ability?"

"Oh dear, dear," Mr Swann sighed. The proprietor took out a silk handkerchief, which he dabbed at his forehead. "The poor man has lost everything. He *was* a genius: he restored this entire hotel, single-handed."

"It's true, Mr Walker," Francis Long said: "this carpenter fellow restored this whole place over many months."

The image of the chimpanzee gargoyle came gesticulating into Robert Walker's mind. "Is this carpenter the same man who carved the chimpanzee on the roof?"

"Chimpanzee?" Mr Swann asked. "There is no chimpanzee on the roof, Mr Walker."

"All right - monkey, then."

"No monkeys, either. Hornets, yes."

"I noticed it when I got off the bus."

"Then you're the only one who has seen it," Francis Long said.

Mr Swann said: "I shall ask George one more time to go up on the roof and take a look."

Francis Long reminded his uncle. "George won't go anywhere near that hornets' nest."

"Yes, of course, Francis," Mr Swann admitted, "you're quite right."

Robert Walker asked: "How long ago did the carpenter leave?"

"Mr Walker, if you please," Mr Swann explained: "The carpenter did not leave in the way you must suppose."

"-?"

"-He's gone - for good."

"-? You're offering me a dead man's room? That's the reason why no one wants to stay there?"

Mr Swann said: "I did not take you for the superstitious sort, Mr Walker, and it is the best deal in the house. That is to say, the other rooms are three or four or five times more expensive - even at a term discount. I'd be very happy to book you into one of *those*."

Robert Walker considered the unexpected expense incurred by the treasure permit. Then he thought about Harry Stone in London. "I'll take the room," he agreed.

5

THE ROOM UNDER THE STAIRS

THE ROOM THAT Robert Walker had accepted sight-unseen was located beneath the great British colonial staircase. The room, Mr Swann disclosed, had been the wood-cutting bachelor's permanent accommodation. It is all very mysterious. The body was never recovered, so the carpenter cannot, reasonably, be pronounced dead. Robert Walker recalled the words of John Wilson: a thousand cuts; fishbait and sawdust!

A hefty deposit was agreed - BIR5,000 - which Robert Walker passed to the white-suited proprietor in a single, uncontested wad. Harry Stone would, no doubt, be charmed by the deal - in so far as that were possible. A receipt would be prepared, of course, in due course. Fifteen days it is, then, half-board included (along with three bottles of beer *per diem*). The remainder of Robert Walker's rupees would take him that far, and no farther. . .As for this evening, dinner is about to be served. Our chef, Sami from Mauritius, he is *this* island's best.

The fingers of the proprietor's right hand still twitched with nervous energy from the number-crunching abacus. Mr Swann escorted his guest to the rear-base of the staircase, and opened a portal. Robert Walker had expected no more than an extended broom closet. Mr Swann thrust a hand into the dark interior, and flicked a switch: a lightbulb came to life, and revealed the complex hidden inside the staircase's overall, cheese-slice volume.

This was no ordinary utility cupboard.

The proprietor indicated the room's contrived facilities. An upright capsule of varnished mahogany turned out to be a shower unit; this was no botch-job, for it was crafted in high-style with brass fittings, and perhaps it had been filched from a rich man's gin palace or cabin cruiser, and then plumbed into the Marina Hotel's water supply.

"I allowed him that," Mr Swann explained. "It hardly uses any water. On this island, that's important. Please, Mr Walker - try."

Robert Walker, in a stoop, stepped inside the cabin. The door of the capsule swung open on silent bearings. He reached for a shiny brass chain, and pulled: a fine aerosol mist sprayed down from a recessed showerhead. He released the chain, and felt at his barely damp forearm. This would have to be tested in full, and soon. Robert Walker marvelled at the deceased carpenter's obvious ingenuity; a master plumber, too.

"There is space also to work, Mr Walker." A neglected desk occupied a dark corner. "Your research?"

"Yes, Mr Swann, I'd like to get started as soon as possible. There's a lot to catch up on."

"Catch up? Yes, all of us should catch up." Mr Swann's face shone with a powerful work ethic. "But first, you will want to try out the shower. After that, dinner. The chef's special: chicken madras, with basmati rice and lime pickle, chapatti, yoghurt with sliced cucumber; cold beer or iced-water. For dessert: baked banana with coconut milk. There - now enjoy your stay, Mr Walker."

An aroma of curry floated along the corridor. Mr Swann turned, and followed the aroma's trail in the direction of the kitchen. Robert Walker's empty stomach heaved. He was still thin - very thin - from those last days in Paris. He turned sideways, and disappeared into the cabin. He closed the door against the aroma, which, anyway, crept beneath the floorboards.

Robert Walker was alone. He sat down - on a chest of some sort - and studied the carpenter's domain. The yellow tungsten filament of the lightbulb burned its way into the recesses of the cabin. A writing desk was secured against the hotel's exterior wall. On the desk, a small compass showed the way across the surface of a tattered map. A thick red sash dangled from the underbelly of the sloping staircase, which formed the 'ceiling' of the cabin: this, he pulled, and a full-length bed flexed outward from strong hinges. In one smooth, well-beeswaxed motion, the entire structure swung downwards - two legs on brass hinges clicked into place - and the bed settled onto the deck. A canvas mattress was made of sailcloth stuffed with coconut coir. A pillow was podgy with kapok or - more likely - marine sponges. THE MARINA HOTEL was embroidered crudely over its surface. A headboard had been carved with a relief: a shipwreck going aground on the island's shoals. The year of the wreck was indicated: 1730. The headboard was embellished with strange symbols. Robert Walker counted twelve of the icons, two of which remained blank tablets - or had been later blanked-out with a chisel. A sow. Then again: a flying horse. . .mighty oxen. . . Stars in the sky. . .A plough. . . A dog with three heads.

Robert Walker looked at the dead man's well-sprung bed. So much for Mr Swann's low-rent strategy, but it was too late now to withdraw. Jet-lagged sleep tugged him towards the bed, but he resisted, and checked the exterior wall of the cabin. There was, he discovered, a double set of shutters built into the wall, although not even a crack of light was permitted to enter.

The carpenter had thought of almost everything.

There was evidence of the man's belongings spread around the cabin. Relatives? A sweetheart? Had no one dared enter the cabin? He opened the chest, and found more formidable possessions: tools of the trade, from apprentice to master, sought-after, expensive. Robert Walker closed the lid.

If ever he needed a hatchet or a rasp, he would know where to look. A washbasin nested against the shower capsule. A circular shaving mirror had been affixed above the unit, but there was no razor or brush. A lump of coal-tar soap rested on the basin; and, on a nearby shelf, a packet of BAND-AID, unused and now no longer needed; and a jar of palm oil, which, in the trapped heat of the cabin, had turned into rancid palm-gunge. A compact refrigerator hummed beneath the basin unit. He looked inside the ice-box: it was empty.

There were no papers or photographs evident, but there were books, lined-up on a fine bookshelf, which ran the length of the interior wall beside the articulated bed. Robert Walker fought-off sleep as he stretched out onto the bed, and lay flat on his back: the coir mattress was comfortable, albeit a little wiry, and gave under his weight. The whole structure bobbed on mighty timber-spring hinges until it found equilibrium.

Robert Walker studied the eclectic collection. A selection, probably, from the ocean-going libraries of a hundred passing ships. *Woodcraft Wisdom* by J.G. Cone, Fully Illustrated by the Author, a 1960 reprint of the original 1952 version. The yellowed pages of its innocent advice must have been child's play to the advanced notions of the deceased carpenter. *The Land, Sea & Air Survival Handbook* (1944), published by the US Bureau of Aeronautics, was undeniably the most useful volume among the entire collection - and it was waterproofed. On page 43, there was the revelation:

> " . . .Crabs and lobsters can most easily
> be caught at night, as that is the time
> when they generally move about."

The same, Robert Walker thought, might be said of political dissenters. There was nothing, though, that betrayed the carpenter as having been anything of the sort, except - perhaps - for the simian gargoyle on the roof.

The row of books slumped onward - *Le Grande Meaulnes* by Alain-Fournier, and a dog-eared Jules Verne paperback, *Twenty Thousand Leagues Under the Sea,* an American edition - until they reached, intended as a book-end and nothing more, a second edition of *Seven Pillars of Wisdom* (1935). Behind the bookshelf, a single sheet emerged, which did not seem to belong. Robert Walker, with care, pulled at the onionskin, until it yielded. It was a title page, knocked-out on some old typewriter, which read:

THE TERMINAL ODYSSEY OF GRAHAM DUNNE

by Roger Dupin

The discarded folio appeared to be from an unpublished, missing or abandoned manuscript. The carpenter's name had, he supposed, been Dupin. Roger Dupin had been a friend, then, not only of the gardener, but also of the wayward Englishman. Robert Walker set the onionskin on the writing desk. He got up from the bed, and flipped the structure - with a bounce - into position inside the staircase. He had his title. It was a start, but that was all.

Robert Walker unpacked his own belongings. After the long journey from London, he took off his suit - and entered the shower capsule. Once again, he pulled the chain, and was blasted by high-pressure mist. A film of moisture enveloped his body. He stepped out of the capsule, the film evaporated, and he was - dry.

After a change of clothes, he was ready.

In the dining room, he found a table, which overlooked the marina. Outside, the lanterns on some of the yachts shone over a long, T-shaped pontoon. A radar reflector clattered against a masthead until it was secured by unseen hands. Beyond the marina, the Indian Ocean was a moonless expanse. In these equatorial heavens, the stars of the Southern sky emerged to prick-out the dark-blue canopy. A yellow-white arc of light gripped at the distant horizon, and at last gave way to total night. A tugboat hooted from the harbour. Robert Walker was distracted by movement on the pontoon. A pot-bellied yachtsman clambered out onto the stern-deck of a long sloop. On unsteady sea-legs, with a cocktail glass poised in one hand, the yachtsman ignited an extra lantern. The keen-eyed mariner looked up from the pontoon, and waved. Robert Walker saluted the fellow, who turned, sipped at the cocktail, and stared at the stars. After a while, the yachtsman slumped back over the rudder, unconscious.

Robert Walker's bamboo seat creaked against the silence of the dining room's crisp white linen, sparkling glasses, and shiny cutlery. At the centre of the room, a fan wobbled, and below the fan there was a man with a sunburnt forehead and streaky, yellow hair: it was the European businessman, whose straw hat rested on the table. The man he thought of as Straw Hat had twinkling, pale-blue eyes fixed on a spot somewhere far beyond the marina, his thoughts - Robert Walker guessed - on the cash value of a million unhooked tuna, while he, the German, spooned away a large plate of soup. Bouillabaisse? Robert Walker wondered at the greed of men: a million fish, where a plate of soup might do. Robert Walker, who had lost his appetite, looked elsewhere. . . On a grand tour of the Indian Ocean, the elderly French couple had located a table nearest the kitchen. In this way, they had less time to wait, and the waiter a shorter distance to walk. The man provided his more animated spouse with a short lecture on French foreign policy in the region. The elites of France have an historic duty in this area. The Indian Ocean is like a lake - at the centre, the Ile de France - he was saying. In this big lake, there are many Francophone nations, which float in this lake like ducks, which need to be cultivated like-. Like what? the spouse asked. Like ducks? The woman advised her husband that if he was to make a fool of himself, then he should do so in a lower voice. The man flashed angry dark eyes at his wife, then remembered his wedding vows from long ago. He took his anger out instead on the edge of a bread roll, and cast his dark eyes in the direction of the soup-spooning Straw Hat, whose eyebrows were raised in silent dissent: What you know about foreign policy, monsieur, would not fill this soup-plate. You, a German, tell me this?

There was no sign of the Americans.

Robert Walker became restless. Bon appetite, Monsieur Walker. There was something not quite right in all of this: a pan-European alliance to suck the fish out of the ocean? Sustainable development? You must be joking, monsieur. Why the plankton pyramid will one day collapse, so short-term profits are just that - short-term, then lost, forever. The elderly French couple, who studied Robert Walker across the dining room, were no ordinary tourists. Straw Hat, who turned to look - over a soup spoon - at Robert Walker, was no ordinary soup eater. On an ornate bamboo menu-bracket, he studied a typed white card, which described what Mr Swann had already promised.

It was no good: Robert Walker's appetite was shot.

When a waitress - it was Danielle - arrived at the table, the honey-moon couple from Greater London had replaced Robert Walker. Straw Hat, aware of the transformation, spluttered into his soup plate. By the kitchen, the elderly French woman spoke to her husband - the world belongs to the young; life is the concern only of the living - and squeezed his hand. We have, she said, our memories, which are rather splendid. The French man replied: Oh, yes, yes, my love - if only I could remember them!

Robert Walker had made his way to the reception. Mr Swann handed over a receipt for BIR5,000, with compliments of the Marina Hotel. Inside the Marlin Room, guests - in huddles around the lounge - drank thirstily and talked excitedly.

The ceiling-fan blew down on the hubbub.

Robert Walker paused to ask: "The gentleman in the dining room, Mr Swann? The fellow with the straw hat?"

"You must mean Herr Papier-Drache? Our German visitor?" The proprietor covered the hotel register from any probing eye.

Something about that name prickled at Robert Walker's thoughts. A German-English dictionary from the bookshelf of Roger Dupin might yield a clue.

Mr Swann spoke up: "Another gentleman was here asking for you - a Mr Wilson. British. He has stayed with us on a number of occasions over the years."

Robert Walker had forgotten all about the stamp dealer.

"You'll find Mr Wilson in the Marlin Room."

"We met on the flight. I'll speak with him now."

"You wish to leave a message for Herr Papier-Drache?"

"No, Mr Swann, I do not. Thank you all the same."

Robert Walker entered the Marlin Room. François Bellarmine's image presided over a *mélange* of guests, local visitors, expatriates, diplomats, and assorted hangers-on. Through a blanket of smoke, drink and talk, Robert Walker saw the American, Morgan Beaumont, who stood under the stuffed marlin fish, and spoke at length to a group of diplomats. The woman known as Barbara West fended off the wives. Robert Walker moved towards the bamboo bar. Beaumont spoke of Cold War's end. A grey haired diplomat in a coal-black suit considered the question. In the end, he was unable - or unprepared - to draw any conclusion from the American's hypothesis - that the Cold War was already over. Who told you that? someone asked. A man with a beard in Harry's Bar, the American replied. You're joking? No, I'm not; I don't think the man with the beard was, either. The American went on to discuss the balance of power in the Indian Ocean. The diplomats listened with cocked heads, while the wives spoke to Barbara West about the possibility - sometime soon - of a coffee morning. Barbara West listened, her eyes glassy, until her attention settled on the portrait of François Bellarmine.

Robert Walker moved unobserved through the lounge. By the bar, John Wilson, who wore a white tuxedo, passed a peanut to a parrot, which stood on the perch that had, earlier, been unoccupied. The parrot took the nut in its beak, broke open the shell, found two nuts, swallowed one, then the other, and set the shattered shell in a little copper fount at its feet. John Wilson guffawed. "Ah, there you are, Mr Walker! Here, you have a try."

Robert Walker declined the offer. John Wilson shrugged, took out another peanut from his tuxedo pocket, and passed it to the bird. The bird performed the same routine, and - again - John Wilson guffawed.

"Mr Walker?" Francis Long asked.

"Beer, please."

"I'll get that," the stamp dealer ordered, "and same again for yours truly."

Francis Long looked at the stamp dealer.

"Yours truly - that's me, see?"

"Yes, Mr Wilson." Francis Long set up the drinks.

John Wilson cackled at nothing.

"A fine specimen," Robert Walker chanced.

"Sorry, old boy?"

"The parrot, I mean."

"Oh, I see: I thought you were alluding to-. No, of course not. Yes, I concur."

"It wasn't here when I arrived earlier."

"Oh no?" Wilson asked. "I thought it had been here for years."

"This one was donated to the hotel by Mr Beaumont," Francis Long reported. "That makes it Number Fifteen."

"And what happened to the other fourteen?" John Wilson wanted to know.

Francis Long looked at the deck beneath his feet.

"Extraordinary," the stamp dealer concluded. "But why would our American friend make such a bequest? We have a mystery on our hands, gentlemen. What about the girl? What's her part in all of this?"

Barbara West was engaged in conversation with a stick-thin, blond-haired woman who wore a lemon dress. This wife looked as though, over the years, she had been gently abused by the expatriate life, since the tropics - her face told - were only something to hanker after from higher latitudes. She pined for England. Fish & chips (though probably not). The smell of fresh-cut, proper, green grass. Black taxis with reliable fare-meters. The BBC World Service. Fair play (or not). A log fire in winter, the snow thick on the ground outside, a group of friends about to arrive for sherry and a chat, and then a visit to a remote country pub - The Diggers Rest at Woodbury, say. A deep, January frost. Parish democracy. On this island, there was no frost, and no democracy, except for the brittle constitution of the BIPP. Robert Walker read her lips: This is a dreadful place, full of dreadful people - you'll see, Barbara, soon enough. Your husband, does he like the island? He is the British Attaché; it's his job to like the island. We've just been drafted in from London; his predecessor - Saunders, Sanders? - had a nervous breakdown brought on by the coup attempt. Can you believe it? I could have a breakdown here *without* a coup. As for High Commissioner Browne - Old Badger Browne, they call him (tee-hee) - I'm not able to say. . .Haven't met him yet, oddly. Imagine that, a diplomat who won't speak with anyone. So, you see, my Albert has got plenty to do, and when he's got nothing much to do, he comes here. I'm not complaining; it's all part of the job, really. What about *your* husband? Barbara reponded: I have no husband; I have only my work, Mrs-. Please, call me Elizabeth, Barbara. Elizabeth Greene. As I say, my husband is Albert Greene - the British Attaché. There he is, talking with your colleague, Mr Beaumont. Mrs Greene fiddled with her cocktail glass. The fan, which fluttered above the women's heads, seemed to blow away the rest of the conversation.

John Wilson was saying something. ". . . Jet-lagged, old boy?"

"Yes, that must be it. What about you, Mr Wilson?"

"Who, me? I've been jet-lagged most of my adult life. And, I'll tell you what, Mr Walker, I wouldn't have it any other way. Now, I promised you a drink, and I'm a man who keeps his, ah, promises. Old fashioned, call it. A beer for Mr Walker, Francis."

"You've already-."

"-Never mind about that, old boy. Who's counting, eh?"

"Right away, Mr Wilson." Francis Long poured out another BourBrew.

"By the way, Francis, where d'you suppose our American friend acquired the parrot?"

Francis Long set the frothy beer on the bar in front of Robert Walker.

"Harry Singh's place."

"Oh really? Well, that is interesting. Met him a few times. That man could sell sand to the Saudi Royal Family."

"Any luck with your own business, Mr Wilson?"

"Luck's got nothing to so with it, Mr Walker. If it had, I would have fallen destitute years ago. . .Anyway, since you ask . . ."

John Wilson removed a slim black wallet from his tuxedo, and revealed a rectangular piece of paper. "Don't touch, just look." Then John Wilson put the stamp away, and slipped the wallet inside his tuxedo. "What do you think of that, then?"

Robert Walker, in that instant, had seen an image of what he supposed was the Fiery Cross of Goa. No head of state - no Bellarmine - no one at all. A signal to the oustide world? John Wilson looked greatly impressed with his achievement. "Got to think about my retirement, haven't I? Not going to stay young forever, am I?"

"I'm not sure I understand, Mr Wilson."

"Well, that's too bad, old boy, because I'm not going to say anything more." John Wilson was happy to contradict himself: "Anyway, good thing those goons at the airport didn't go through my luggage more thoroughly. . .For that very reason, I usually include a few items of paraphernalia in my suitcase for no good reason, you see. A piece of black coral in a glass bulb, that kind of thing. An Arctic trout with a coat of white fur. Better yet, a deck of lewd cards. Gives them something to look at, you see. Same as a conjuring trick. If you repeat any of this, I'll deny it. Say I'm drunk and jet-lagged, both of which of course I am."

Robert Walker looked around the room. The guests had started to form cliques and sub-cliques. John Wilson might as well have been talking about the weather. The younger diplomats fêted Morgan Beaumont. Barbara West and Mrs Greene exchanged further, eye-widening intimacies of no obvious importance. The older diplomats soaked expatriate traders for information. BIPParty-snoopers and other locals remained aloof, and listened. A dangerous-looking man in a weather-bleached shirt stood by the bay window, and peered into the night through the telescope.

"Anyway, I was going to say: in my humble opinion, that's the only place you'll find the treasure - on a piece of gummed paper!"

The various conversations in the Marlin Room faltered, and then ceased... John Wilson became the focus of attention.

"I say something out of order?"

Robert Walker replied for all to hear: "As I've said, Mr Wilson, I'm not looking for any treasure."

The guests resumed their conversations.

John Wilson said: "I'm sorry about that, old boy. It just - slipped out."

Robert Walker ignored the stamp dealer, and - over the bar - said: "You were saying, Francis?"

"I wasn't saying anything, Mr Walker. I don't know anything about any treasure. I'm only a bartender."

John Wilson retorted: "I believe you, Francis, though millions wouldn't." The stamp dealer winked at the bartender.

"About the parrot," Robert Walker clarified.

"This an angle on the story?" Wilson asked. "The bird got some information that could, er, lead somewhere? Or not? Pity it doesn't talk then, eh?"

Robert Walker did not respond.

John Wilson, quick to rebound, said: "I mean to say, gentlemen, are you aware of how much these birds are worth on the open market?" Then: "Doesn't say much, does it?"

The bird seemed to squawk a rebuttal.

"Well," Wilson continued, "what would you say, Francis, if I told you that parrot is probably worth as much as, say, a fishing boat, with an outboard thrown into the bargain?"

Francis Long stared at Wilson. "What fishing boat is that, Mr Wilson?"

"Why, the one you were telling me about earlier. The one you're going to buy when you've enough saved up. That one."

"Oh, that boat," Francis Long smiled.

John Wilson turned to Robert Walker: "Don't think for a moment I'm putting any ideas into Francis' empty gourd."

"No, of course not, Mr Wilson. I'm sure you wouldn't do anything like that."

Beyond the bar, Francis Long's thoughts raced way ahead of him. The bartender was partly relieved when the stamp dealer added:

"Well, that's the price of them in England, anyway. Saw one once at Woburn Park. How much the American paid for it on this island - well, I have no idea. Depends where he bought it, really."

"At Harry Singh's place," Francis Long reiterated. "You can buy just about anything there - as you know, Mr Wilson."

"I don't know what you mean by that." John Wilson studied Fran-cis Long's face. "I mean, how *do* you mean that, Francis?"

Francis Long replied: "Well, you've been there before, Mr Wilson. You know what I mean."

"No, I do not know what you mean. No, I've never been there. Never."

"Whatever you say, Mr Wilson."

John Wilson relaxed, and stared into his glass, which he saw as half-empty. The stamp dealer looked up without comment. After a moment, he asked: "Is that old crook Harry Singh still business?"

"Oh indeed he is, Mr Wilson."

The stamp dealer relished the counter-thrust: "Ah, so you would agree that Harry Singh, one of the most respected merchants on the island, is a crook?"

Francis Long's face fell: "I did not say that, Mr Wilson; you said that."

"I made no such assertion; I merely asked you a question."

"Ah, you had me fooled there, Mr Wilson. I know this one: I only meant to agree with you that he is still in business."

"Well done, Francis," John Wilson said. "There's hope for you yet. I'll have another, thanks."

Robert Walker asked: "Who is this Harry Singh?"

"Someone," Wilson slurred, "who could probably be of a great deal of assistance to yourself, Mr Walker. Maps, and so on."

Francis Long, who had refreshed Wilson's drink, added: "He is among the very few independent store keepers on the island. Up on the plantation. You can buy just about anything there so long as you have enough rupees."

"An extraordinary fellow, by all accounts," Wilson said. "But why, you might ask, does this gentleman of commerce maintain a general store up there on the plantation, rather than here in Port Bourbon?"

"Why?"

"Well, don't ask me," Wilson slurred. "I haven't the faintest idea. But I'll guess this much: that it's a condition of his independence. All other traders are obliged to do business through the-."

John Wilson, aware of the BIPP-aligned locals, decided to say nothing about the monolithic parastatal known as the Bourbon Island Marketing Board (BIMB). Instead, he offered:

"Well, you know what I mean."

"I might just take your advice, Mr Wilson, and go up there tomorrow."

"I'd come with you," John Wilson said, "but I've got to get moving before that Chief Bugis catches up with me. They say I sold him stamps that taste of liquorice. Well, he shouldn't be licking them, should he? The

Chief's tied up in some investigation on the other side of the island for a couple of days, so I'm clear. But not for long. Next stop - Mauritius."

Robert Walker said: "So soon, Mr Wilson?"

"Mission accomplished, old boy," Wilson said. "And there's a lady waiting on another island. Well, a woman anyway . . .Good luck to you, Mr Walker, that's about all I can say. Speak with you before I depart. One for the road?"

"No, thanks; I think I'll call it a day."

John Wilson said: "Anyway, don't worry, your secret's safe with me."

"I don't know what you mean, Mr Wilson. Really, I don't."

By the bay window, the man in the weathered shirt swivelled the telescope over the dark horizon. The movement caught John Wilson's eye.

"Ah, before you retire, there's someone I'd like you to meet, old boy."

"Mr Wilson, I really must-."

"-Back in a tick." The stamp dealer made his way over to the bay window. The man at the telescope turned a longish grey beard and kohl-black eyes on the stamp dealer.

"Go now, Mr Walker," Francis Long whispered. "This is not a good man. Don't wait."

Robert Walker said: "I'll see you tomorrow, then."

Francis Long said: "I'll show you the way to the plantation. I've got the half-day off. Now, good-night, Mr Walker."

John Wilson returned from the bay window. "Where the bloody hell is that fellow?"

"He's gone, Mr Wilson," Francis Long reported.

"Gone? Gone where?"

The man with the longish beard and weathered shirt waited by the telescope.

"I don't know, Mr Wilson. I turned around from my duties, and he had vanished."

"Vanished? Into thin air? You mean that literally? I was going to introduce Mr Walker to Signor Colon."

"Why would you want to do a thing like that, Mr Wilson?"

"*Why*, did you say?"

The man with the kohl-eyes, Signor Mario Colon, abandoned the telescope and approached the bamboo bar.

"Oh Mario, there you are," Wilson said. "Been looking all over for you. Thought you might have gone back to Italy."

"Well, where is this Mr Walker of yours? You're playing jokes on me, Mr Wilson? I know some good jokes. You know the joke about the stamp dealer whose stamps taste of liquorice? Bloody funny, eh?" Mario Colon said with a stony face.

Francis Long polished a glass until it sparkled.

6

A MONKEY ON THE ROOF

THE NIGHT-HEAT of the island embraced Robert Walker. John Wilson's stamp inspired a dream of an untouchable Fiery Cross of Goa, and then the image vanished. The structures of the hotel creaked and groaned; the bed bounced on its timber springs, and then settled down for the long night. The miniature refrigerator hummed on until dawn, when the unit fell silent.

The sun rose over the Indian Ocean, and the temperature soared. The unit under the sink re-activated itself. Outside, the commercial noises of the harbour brought the neighbourhood to life. A conveyor belt, somewhere in the vicinity, shifted thousands of bottles of BourBrew into the lives of the thirsty islanders.

Robert Walker awoke: this was not, he realised, London - or Paris. This was. . . where? Inside the cabin, the enclosed volume of air was musty with the smell of dry wood-shavings, beeswax and the carpenter's oiled tools. The carpenter? So, he had spent the night in the bed of a dead man. The timber springs shook: he rolled off the bed, and stood on the naked planks of the deck. He pulled on a short-sleeved shirt and a pair of shorts. Inside the desk, he discovered a blank wad of onionskins; these would do for the task ahead. He placed them, ready for the day's work, on the desk. He could smell fresh-brewed coffee. He opened the portal. In the corridor, no one was in sight. On the floor, though, a covered tray held a pot of coffee and a round of cucumber sandwiches. He was almost sure he had never had a cucumber sandwich. He brought the tray inside the cabin. A white card read: *With Compliments of the Marina Hotel.* The night before, he recalled, he had not eaten: he devoured the sandwiches, and drank half of the coffee, which was excellent. Then he reached for the first onionskin, which he had - the day before - hidden under the mattress. Then he up-ended the bed, flipped the structure into the under-belly of the staircase, and sat down at the desk. He adjusted the cover sheet so that it read:

THE TERMINAL ODYSSEY OF GRAHAM DUNNE

by Robert Walker
with Roger Dupin

Credit, then, where credit was due, even to a dead man. Robert Walker needed more light and air: he unlatched the shutters, which opened inwards: strong daylight poured into the cabin; the air smelled of salt-spray; and the parched grass was greener on this side of the hotel. Outside, the pith-helmeted gardener - George, an early riser - whitewashed the hotel's boundary wall. In the near distance, the dock facilities rose beyond a cramped, tin-roofed residential area. Across the road, the bottling plant's slack conveyor belt shifted its precious cargo from the factory to a distribution bay. A sign over the plant reflected the morning sunlight: BOURBREW - THE REAL TASTE OF THE ISLAND; and another - BOURBON ISLAND BREWERIES (PTY) LTD. Est. 1971

Robert Walker, from this ideal hide position, could observe without himself being observed.

"Good morning . . ?"

The gardener heard, but did not respond.

Robert Walker spoke from the side of the hotel: "George, isn't it?"

George stiffened, and waited: he dropped the bucket, and a great gush of whitewash splashed his legs. The brush hung limply from his hand, until it, too, hit the grass. Then he turned, and ran. This was a man, Robert Walker realised, who lived in fear - of the hornets' nest, of his dead friend's ghost, *ju-ju*, anything. Robert Walker closed one of the shutters, left the other partially ajar, and withdrew. He considered the pile of onionskins. So much for the whitewash. On the next, blank skin, he made a start on the feature article, and wrote

The-

when a voice outside the portal asked:

"Mr Walker, you have arisen?"

Robert Walker set down his pen, stood up from the desk, and re-opened the portal.

It was Mr Swann in an immaculate sandy-yellow morning suit. He asked:

"You slept well, Mr Walker?"

"Yes, Mr Swann, and thank you for the cucumber sandwiches. A surprise."

"You are most welcome. The British, I understand, are very keen on the cucumber sandwiches."

"Well, I. . .How can I help you, Mr Swann?"

Mr Swann saw the onionskins on the desk. "You are busy? I am interrupting?"

Robert Walker looked at the proprietor, whose face had already adopted its customary double-sided expression. Joy, at his guest's work ethic; despair, that he, Swann, had disturbed his guest's labours.

"I've made a start, Mr Swann. That's something. Now, how might I help you?"

"Very good, Mr Walker. Yesterday, when you arrived, you mentioned a monkey on the roof."

"I was tired from the flight. A trick of the setting sun. I did not mean to cause any concern."

"You do not strike me, Mr Walker, as a man who sees things."

"Kind of you to say so, Mr Swann."

"If you wouldn't mind . . ?"

"The roof?"

"It is still early. We won't be seen. We must not be seen."

"I understand. Well, let's go, Mr Swann."

Proprietor and guest climbed the great colonial staircase. On the way, Robert Walker confessed: "I think I may have frightened your gardener."

"George? He is always frightened, Mr Walker. If not this, then that."

"In the cabin. I opened the shutters. He was there. He must have thought I was a-? His friend, the carpenter-?"

They had reached the second floor, and it was clear that Mr Swann did not want to hear any more.

On the third floor, the proprietor found a better mood: "A ghost, Mr Walker? You were going to say my gardener took you for a ghost?"

Robert Walker, so soon from Europe, was aware of his very white limbs. On the fourth floor, Mr Swann said:

"Now, Mr Walker, if you please. . .we go to the roof."

At this level, and at this hour, they were alone. They passed the Presidential Suite, where Morgan Beaumont no doubt slumbered, unless the American had already taken to the hills. The climb had loosened the proprietor's tongue: "Castro, oh yes. Sukarno. Both stayed in this room. In the old days, Montaigne. In the very old days, when I was a boy, Sir Godfrey Smythe-Smith."

Robert Walker was unable to see Mr Swann as a boy, ever. He asked:

"This was the governor's private room?"

"It was. . . Sir Godfrey Smythe-Smith and Lady G-. Ah, Gertrude or Gwendolyn, something like that. A sad story. There was love affair, as they called such things in those days, with a plantation owner. The woman Gertrude, I mean, of course. The lady went astray. The officials blamed the heat, and Sir Godfrey blamed himself. Sir Godfrey shot himself in that same room. I do not usually tell this story, Mr Walker. Not good for business."

Robert Walker chose not remark on the subject. So much, he thought, for the Governor's apple-blossom spouse. But then (as an aide to Sir God might have said), what else could you expect of a French planter? The past seemed to whisper at him from along the balcony terrace. But it was Mr Swann who whispered:

"I have said enough."

Robert Walker looked each way along the empty corridor, then - over the balustrade - onto the deserted stretch of Revolution Boulevard. At the far end of Victoria Street, a detachment of the island's National Youth Corps marched into the distance, and disappeared along a dirt track. Robert Walker looked in the direction of Mont Pomme d'Or, which was invisible behind a shroud of moisture. Then, he turned to look into Mr Swann's dark eyes, which seemed to say: These are the party *apparatchik* of the future. The individual must be suppressed - and then absorbed. Ants, bees. Any form of individual expression must be eliminated - or anyway projected onto the Leader. The cult of personality, no less. . . The Leader is the embodiment of the BIPP or Bourbon Island People's Party. If you are not with us, you are against us: the Party will not tolerate opposition of any kind. If you wish to oppose us, we shall dissolve your brain in a bath of sulphuric acid at party headquarters. It was just the way Harry Stone had said: Stay out of politics, and leave the women alone - and to hell with liberty. Mr Swann - or the Party - had spoken, without saying a word. Robert Walker - or his Agency - responded: That is all very well for your *apparatchik* goonsquad, but the human creature is neither an ant nor a bee. In time, the collective suffocates without dissent or random mutation. He had started to perspire - with heat or fear or both - and it was still only short of 07:39.

On the balcony, the air seemed to buzz at the prospect of noon; but no, that was the awakening hornets' nest, out of sight on the fifth deck.

"The roof, Mr Walker, if you please."

The proprietor led the way towards a door marked LINEN. Mr Swann produced - from deep a trouser pocket - a bunch of keys on a long chain. He selected a key, opened the door, and entered. The linen room was piled high on both sides with fresh sheets on wooden racks. At the far end of the room, a dumb waiter or laundry chute was set into the wall beside another door. A second key opened the portal. Mr Swann mounted a spiral staircase, which he climbed to reach an observation deck beneath the hotel's cupola. After an interval, Robert Walker appeared from the staircase: he stepped onto the observation platform, and stopped. He looked up at Mont Pomme d'Or; the mist had cleared from the foothills, but the cone of the extinct volcano remained obscured.

"Do you see the monkey, Mr Walker?"

"I see the. . . hornets' nest."

Mr Swann turned: "Yes, unfortunately, they seemed to know we are here."

Robert Walker looked down onto Revolution Boulevard. Beyond the crossroads, the Victoria Road Police Station had not yet opened for business. Robert Walker tried to gauge angle and distance from road-to-roof, but he was distracted by the buzz of the nest.

"Do not be alarmed, Mr Walker. I have a solution."

"A solution?"

A single hornet emerged from the nest. It had a body the size of a bullfinch.

"Whatever you're going to do, Mr Swann, please do it now."

The hornet performed an acrobatic loop, and dived back inside the crumply, *papier-mâché* nest.

The proprietor searched himself: he found a packet of 555 State Express, and a lighter. Mr Swann lit-up, and blew the smoke in the direction of the hornets' nest. The proprietor puffed, and the hornets grew sleepy.

While Mr Swann smoked, Robert Walker looked over the roofs of Port Bourbon. A metal patchwork of blue, green, red and yellow corrugated-iron sheets (in the rain, the sound of a thousand drums) paved the way from the State House bureaucracy, across town, to reach the port area. In the harbour, a single container ship of the Blue Star Line had berthed overnight. In the marina, a flotilla of yachts nudged against the pontoon, where smaller craft were also moored. Beyond, the blue horizon of the Indian Ocean opened the way to Antarctica. Robert Walker's eyes followed the rugged shoreline from the promontory by the Magdalene Church, into the consecrated gardens, through the coconut groves, then along Revolution Boulevard, and arrived once again at the unmarked bus stop.

Mr Swann said: "There - the hornets are asleep. But not for long. You see anything yet, Mr Walker?"

The buzz of the nest had subsided into a dozy hu*mmmm*.

Robert Walker looked down at the bus stop: the boy, Charlie, had appeared, and waited for transport. Then: the boy raised his eyes at the cupola. Mr Swann rubbed-out the cigarette between a thumb and forefinger, and placed the stub - for now - inside the packet of 555 State Express.

"We are betrayed. Quick now. You are mistaken, after all this?"

One again, Mr Swann's expression was divided: this time, between treachery and discovery.

Charlie had already started in the direction of the Police Station. Papa! Papa! Old Swann and that English fellah are on the roof! Why are they on the roof, Papa?

Robert Walker took in the scope of the roofspace: he looked and looked, and then - out of the corner of an eye - a shape became manifest among the rafters below the eaves. Mr Swann followed his guest's gaze: "I see it, Mr Walker, but I do not believe it."

Robert Walker, even with second sight, did not believe it, either: high treason, on the roof of the Marina Hotel.

The hotelier's licence was in jeopardy; he said:

"The boy. He has seen us. He has seen . . ?"

"He's seen us, all right, Mr Swann; but I don't think he's seen that thing. The boy's too short."

"When the Chief comes, he'll see!"

"The hornets' nest, Mr Swann," Robert Walker reminded the proprietor. "No one will come up here."

"Except us, Mr Walker. So, then: this nest stays where it is," Mr Swann decided.

From the observation deck, the two men studied the sculpture. It was a chimpanzee; its hollow features, though, were those of François Bellarmine.

Mr Swann's oil-stiffened quiff resisted the coastal breeze. He said. "This can only be the work of one man."

A cluster of wood shavings, trapped for months by an eddy, circulated at the base of the gargoyle. "Roger Dupin did this?"

"You know his name, then," Mr Swann realised. "Of course. Who else? Look, it is a work of considerable accomplishment. Only *he* had such ability. I have seen some things in my time, Mr Walker, but this goes too far. Let us get down from here at once. Look, the hornets are waking, and I only permit myself one cigarette each day."

Office hours approached: from the side-streets, workers started to file onto Revolution Boulevard. The morning procession towards State House had commenced.

7

DUNNE ON THE PROMONTORY

BY THE TIME of the second call of that day, Robert Walker had written

The map

- when a voice outside the cabin announced: "Beer supply, Mr Walker!"
The voice belonged to Francis Long.
Robert Walker got up from the desk, and opened the door. Francis Long grinned, and clasped three bottles of beer between the digits of one fist. This was the first daily instalment of Mr Swann's promised package.
"You've been up and about already, Mr Walker?"
"Yes, Francis. Up and about. You can put those in there."
"Nothing strange going on here?"
"No, everything is all right. You knew the fellow who stayed here?"
"No. I cannot remember. I've been away a long time. Everything has changed, except for my Uncle Jeff - he still pays low wages."
Robert Walker returned to the desk. Francis Long located the refrigerator, opened the cabinet, and set the three bottles inside the unit.
"His name was Roger Dupin."
"I've heard the name, but I did not know him. He has a nice-looking sister somewhere - I don't know where. "
"How do you know she's good-looking?"
"Someone told me - I don't know who." Francis Long closed the cold-cabinet, then stooped against the slope of the overhead staircase. "It's none of my business, Mr Walker, but why doesn't your agency pay for a nice room?"
"The same. Low wages. Low or no expenses."
"Then why do you do it?"
"I don't know why I do it. I really don't. A bonus, maybe. I've got fifteen days, then I'm out of here - away. Anyway, this is a nice enough room. By the time I get used it, it'll be time to go."
Francis Long relaxed: "If you say so. This Dupin has something to do with the treasure?"
"Something, but I'm not sure what."
"Harry Singh has maps."
"What kind of maps?"
"Treasure maps."
"Are they real?"

146

"I don't know if they're real, but he has them. He has everything. He sold that parrot to Mr Beaumont, but Mr Beaumont is not happy."

"Why is Mr Beaumont not happy, Francis?"

"Because the bird won't talk."

"Won't? Or can't?"

"I don't know."

"What do you recommend, then?"

"About the bird?"

"No, about the maps."

"I recommend we go see Harry." Francis Long re-opened the portal. "We'll go up to the plantation store. I want to speak with Harry Singh, too. About a boat."

"All right, then."

"I've got to get back to the cellar. There's a shipment of beer coming in from Mauritius today. After that, I have the rest of the day off work."

"I'll meet you in the Marlin Room at noon." Francis Long closed the portal, and departed.

Robert Walker tried to continue with the feature article, but it was no good, and the cabin had become oppressive. It was time, anyway, to explore the immediate locale before noon. A normal person, he guessed, would go out and buy a newspaper - or something. There was, he recalled from yesterday's bus journey, a newsagent half-way along Revolution Boulevard.

The cabin did not have a lock, so he merely closed the portal.

Behind the reception desk, Mr Swann was preoccupied with the nightsafe. Robert Walker passed - unseen - through the lobby, and stepped onto the veranda. This time, he avoided the loose plank on the steps, and found his way onto the main street. Then he made his way - away from the crossroads - into town. The streets of Port Bourbon were empty of pedestrians or any kind of traffic.

After a while, the old British Leyland bus lumbered into view, *honk-honked* at the crossroads, and - with a splutter of blue smoke - crawled up Victoria Street, and along past the Police Station. The driver was the only passenger on board.

The sun burned Robert Walker's face. The sweat basted his flesh. He made his way along the empty street. In the distance, the bus driver *honk-honked* as the vehicle commenced or completed another lap of the specified route.

Once again, the streets were silent and empty. Robert Walker was sure he was being watched, but from where and by whom and why, he could not say. Office workers, without much work; shopkeepers, with hardly any customers. . .A bus without passengers. Then, up ahead, he saw the newsagent. He looked back the way he had walked: the boy Charlie had appeared on the crossroads. Robert Walker stepped out of view - and into the newsagents. A fan cooled the shop; he stood under the fan, and waited. The fan precessed, gyroscopically, on its gimbals. In front of an old-fashioned counter, two matriarchs and a younger Bourbon woman gossiped. A stern looking woman with horn-rim glasses kept shop. The group of four exchanged various, serious whispers. On a wall behind a Post Office cage, a portrait of François Bellarmine seemed to watch over the premises. The shopkeeper's magnified eyes examined Robert Walker's white, British legs. The women customers made adjustments to their hairstyles. The youngest of the women glowed under the disapproving eyes of her companions.

Robert Walker studied the contents of a newspaper rack.

On the other side of the rack, an overweight European man with a straw hat read a magazine. The phlegmatic Herr Papier-Drache, for it was he, looked up from a copy of *National Geographic* with a tuna fish on its out-of-date front cover. He glanced at Robert Walker; then he returned the journal to the rack, raised his hat at the women by the counter, and departed. The European's face, he observed, had become reddened, damp and very shiny.

"These foreigners should know," the shopkeeper informed her regulars, "that this is not a public library!"

The women continued with their whispers.

Robert Walker surveyed the island's press.

The proscribed *Bourbon Island Star** was not, of course, in evidence. A fortnight-old copy of *The Times* of London had become acquainted with the censor's scissors. A more recent copy of *Le Monde* (who knew more, he suspected, than they were prepared to admit about all of this) remained more or less intact. An enchantingly titled *Echoes of the Island*, he discovered, was the monthly Catholic newspaper of the Diocese of Bourbon, Edited by Bishop David Chin: a publication, Robert Walker suspected, barely tolerated by the regime. A single, long sentence in Chin's Editorial had been felt-tipped beyond legibility. Robert Walker glanced over at the counter: the shopkeeper's eyes bulged behind her horn-rim glasses. In abundance, the newspaper rack held numerous copies of *Le Peuple*. This was the weekly organ of the Bourbon Island People's Party (BIPP), uncensored and free of charge (since, he heard one of the women laugh, no one would pay for the paper). A lower section of the rack provided a few comics - *The Beano, The Dandy* - but these, too, had been

---

* The organ of the exiled opposition to the Bellarmine regime. The longer-established Bamboo Mill reports that the *Star* is printed in a Paris basement by the pseudononymous editor "Bougainville".

well-scissored by the censor. A whole episode of Desperate Dan had been excised from the opening section of *The Dandy*. *Batman* and *Superman* were both absent (confiscated, probably, for the Chief of Police's own collection,). There were a few harmless puzzle books, a copy of *Lady*, and a set of Tide Tables for Port Bourbon. There was no vestige of an independent local press of any description whatsoever.

Robert Walker purchased the set of Tide Tables. The women watched him go as he turned left outside the shop, and continued on his way.

Outside, the day was already much hotter.

Behind him, the boy-spy was not visible. Ahead of him, Herr Papier-Drache slipped into a barbershop. As he passed, Robert Walker glanced into the parlour. A few old local men watched as the European, seated in a grand leather chair, read a newspaper, while his yellow-blond hair was clipped by a bald-headed barber.

Robert Walker had reached the immediate outskirts of Port Bourbon. At almost 11:00, the sun toasted his limbs, the back of his neck, and the crown of his head - which stung. This side of the main street gave way to a much older alleyway, along which there were several small stores, forgotten, extra-legal left-overs from the pre-Revolutionary days. A bicycle-repair shop (always good business). A dry goods store - stuffed to the ceiling with unwanted produce; a cloth shop run by a burly local, who waited inside, rubbed at a piece of calico, and smiled from the shop's shadows; and named, so the sign indicated, Jimmy Ramgoolam Co (Pty) Ltd. A spice emporium (Robert Walker sniffed, and detected vanilla, cinnamon, chillies, garlic, ginger) called Lee Kuan Yew Spices (Pty) Ltd. A stall selling small fish (not for eating) off the reef. A brightly coloured fruit shop, with bananas, plantains, coconuts, bizarre tubers, small fruits, big green melons, and small fruits, which Robert Walker did not recognise. The proprietor of this shop bore the unlikely name of J. Smith, Esq. - Fruit & Veg - Port Bourbon.

These shops had provisions, but no customers; in time, but not yet, the tourists would arrive. In the meantime, these men belonged to the despised merchant classes - enemies of the State - bourgeois criminals!

Robert Walker had reached the coastal road's junction with Revolution Boulevard, where a lanky man with a tricycle had set up a mobile stall. Refreshments, salty nuts, iced-coffee or iced-tea. The vendor fiddled with a paper - *The Black Turtle!*, the masthead read - which he shoved into an upright Huntley & Palmers biscuit-tin of refuse. Robert Walker asked for cold lime juice, which he swallowed-off, and then passed the empty cup to the vendor. The man accepted enough change for the drink. Then the vendor packed up the mobile stall, and pedalled the tricycle into an alleyway, where - out of sight - he crashed into a fence. Inside the small stores, the merchants applauded and cheered their mobile colleague. The man from the bicycle repair shop spotted an opportunity, but did nothing. Robert Walker crossed over the hot concrete of the coastal road, and made his way into the environs of the Magdalene Church. A breeze came in off the shore, and cooled the lush yellow-green of the gardens. The sun and salt spray fought against the bishop's efforts. The wind ripped at the steeple of the church, where the belfy groaned but the bell remained silent. Built prior to 1814, the church still stood up against the elements and the termites - a miracle.

A traveller's palm waved the way through a grove of magnolia.

Robert Walker made his way through the grounds towards the shore. Beyond the promontory, the ocean opened up, and the shore churned and foamed against the rocks. Far away over the shoals, a dark belt of cloud, heavy with moisture, unloaded its burden onto the flat surface of the ocean. On the far side of the promontory, a group of palms spread over a cove at strange angles, and sheltered a miniature beach. The cove marked the beginnings of the greater Anse Venus, which swept away out of sight along the coast. Off-shore by about a league, the same jagged rock rose from the ocean floor and broke to the surface.

Robert Walker angled his way along the promontory. A cluster of stone slabs had been upended to form an informal graveyard. These stones, he gauged, faced anywhere but East. The promontory, he supposed, was unconsecrated ground.

Robert Walker edged, against the ocean spray, towards the nearest stone. The surf pounded at the rocks. There was no living creature here - not even a crab or a bird. In the swell, a dead jellyfish of an unknown genus floated nearby. Robert Walker examined the epitaph, which read:

LIGHTHOUSE KEEPER

- but the name and dates had been blasted away by the ocean-spray. Robert Walker moved away from the lighthouse keeper's grave. He wondered where Sir Godfrey was buried. Then he realised the former Governor was probably interred, not here on Roman turf, but elsewhere, in an indifferent Anglican graveyard.

The next stone, freshly carved, read:

GRAHAM DUNNE
Treasure Hunter,
who searched for the Fiery Cross
b. Southend-on-Sea, England, 1946
d. Bourbon Island, 1991

So, Robert Walker deduced: this promontory, this unwanted patch of ground, was Bishop Chin's burial ground for what might be termed 'special cases'.

"You are looking for someone, my friend?"

Robert Walker jerked away from the stone. A man in a white cassock had appeared from the other side of the promontory.

"I thought I was, er, alone."

"Almost alone," Bishop David Chin smiled. The priest took up a position beside Robert Walker, looked first at the gravestones, and then across the Indian Ocean. "None of us is ever as alone as we might suppose."

"You caught me by surprise."

"Sometimes, I catch myself by surprise," ~~The~~ *Chin* Bishop laughed into the wind.

"I can see that you do," Robert Walker remarked.

Bishop David Chin was a solid-looking priest from good eating and drinking. He was unshaven and appeared tired.

"You are Mr Robert Walker from London."

"And you are Bishop Chin of this diocese."

The two men shook hands. The bishop, polite but not shy, was possessed of ruddy good health, had strong blue eyes, and solid white teeth of pure ivory.

"Excuse my appearance. I have been up all night. I have just now returned from an all-night parish visit."

The priest looked up in the direction of Mont Pomme d'Or's summit. Its bleak cone had been exposed by the wind. "I was making my way back through the gardens, when I saw someone - yourself - out here on the rocks. You're a relative of the deceased, perhaps? A descendant?"

Robert Walker replied: "No, neither a relative nor a descendant, Bishop Chin, I'm a -."

"Yes?"

"A visitor to your island."

A jet of ocean spray came over the promontory and caught Robert Walker on the side of his face.

Bishop Chin stared up at the burning sky.

"You're standing too close to the rocks, Mr Walker."

"I was curious about Mr Dunne's endeavour."

"Curiosity, you say? Mr Dunne's curiosity was his undoing, Mr Walker. Now, we should let the poor fellow rest in peace. He's earned that much."

"Yes, you're quite right, Bishop Chin, except that-."

"Except that, you cannot?"

"I'm a journalist."

Bishop Chin's dark-blue eyes cut through Robert Walker. "You don't look like a journalist, Mr Walker. Mr Beaumont, the American, he looks like a journalist."

"Yes, I suppose he does."

"One day, you know, all of this will be gone. There is no question about it. We arrogant men will be long gone by the time this piece of land is washed away, taken back by the Indian Ocean, which by then will have no name. These things are inevitable. Many things are inevitable, but people do not always see them coming. Good-day to you, Mr Walker."

"And to you, Bishop Chin."

The priest's cassock billowed in the wind. Soon, Robert Walker was alone on the edge of promontory. The wind was up, and the surf dashed against the rocks. A great plume of spray shot up into the sky. Robert Walker turned slightly to face the ocean. There was another stone, set close by the water's edge:

GODFREY SMYTHE-SMITH, Kt
(1898-1938)
Governor of the Crown Colony
of Bourbon Island.

Robert Walker had imagined someone older. There was no mention of Lady Gwendolyn or Gertrude. A high wind blew in off the shoals. A wayfaring stranger might have taken the salt spray on his face for tears.

8

THE LISTENING BIRD

"IF YOU ASK me," John Wilson was saying in the Marlin Room, "I think the fellow's got ideas about himself. Met the type before."

Robert Walker entered the lobby from Revolution Boulevard, and stepped into the lounge. The stamp dealer, who was positioned at the bamboo bar, swivelled over his stool. "Oh, there you are, old boy."

"Mr Wilson." Robert Walker passed the Tide Tables over the bar to Francis Long. "It's a start, Francis."

"And cheaper than a boat," John Wilson slurred. The stamp dealer had already embarked on a forenoon course of frozen cocktails

"I'll have a BourBrew, please, Francis."

"Thirsty work, eh?"

"What's thirsty work, Mr Wilson?"

"I saw you-? Ah, you don't catch me out this time. Not a dickey bird, that's what I say." Wilson glanced at the parrot: "No offence."

The book of Tide Tables had silenced Francis Long. He set these to one side, and - still silent - poured out a glass of beer. Robert Walker looked around the lounge area: the ceiling fan churned steadily at the moist air. Morgan Beaumont, who was feeding the parrot at its perch, merely provided a nod as between strangers. On the other side of the lounge, Barbara West relaxed on the sofa, where she studied various documents and made notes. The frond-patterns of the sofa's upholstery seemed to embrace her. She glanced up from her papers, smiled at the Marlin Room in general, and returned to her studies. Over by the bay window, the telescope pointed in the direction of the promontory. John Wilson's right eye-socket was still reddened from its eyepiece.

"Met our American cousins, have you, Mr Walker? Mr Morgan Beaumont and his assistant, Miss West."

"A pleasure, I'm sure," Robert Walker said. Francis Long's smile agreed: a pleasure, indeed.

Both Americans smiled at the Britons without remark.

"Something going on here," John Wilson observed. "I can tell."

Robert Walker paid for, and then tasted, the beer. "There's nothing going on, Mr Wilson."

"Oh really?" John Wilson stared with cocktail eyes at Francis Long, who moved to re-examine the Tide Tables.

"I thought you were travelling today?"

"Mr Wilson's flight is delayed by one hour," Francis Long reported.

"Yes, that's right, I'm having one for the, ah . . .You know," and the stamp dealer looked at the Americans in turn, then Francis Long, and again at Robert Walker. "Something not quite right here. Something very fishy."

"One for Mr Wilson, Francis," Robert Walker offered.

"Damned decent of you and all of that, old boy."

"You're welcome."

Barbara West re-positioned herself on the sofa; the bamboo creaked.

"Anything, Missy?" Francis Long asked.

Barbara West shook her head: no, and returned to her papers. The portrait of François Bellarime stared down at her from the wall.

"Couldn't sit there under that gaze myself," John Wilson remarked. "Still, I'm not a woman, am I?" The stamp dealer winked at his companions.

"No, you're not, Mr Wilson."

Barbara West's concentration broke: she gathered up her papers, stood up, and departed with: "I'll see you later, gentlemen. You too, Morgan."

"Sure," Morgan Beaumont replied, but she had already disappeared through the archway.

"I didn't scare your secretary away, did I, Mr Beaumont? Not talking to that bird, are you?"

The American shrugged at both questions.

Francis Long said: "Thanks for the Tide Tables, Mr Walker."

"You never know: you might need them one day soon."

"You two are up to something, aren't you? I know for a fact that our bartender-friend is saving up for a boat. So, why, Mr Walker, might he need the Tide Tables so soon?"

Robert Walker did not say anything. Instead, he looked over the memorabilia behind the bar: a maritime chronometer showed a time of 11:55; a cigar presented to Mr Swann by Fidel Castro was mounted in a smoky glass case; a newspaper cutting of Kim Il Sung referred to the Great Leader's recent fiftieth-birthday gift to François Bellarmine - six personal bodyguards, North Korea's finest.

"Well, I'm right, aren't I? Planning an expedition - something like that?"

Robert Walker glanced at John Wilson: the stamp dealer's bang of grey hair was damp and heavy with perspiration.

"Time for your flight, Mr Wilson?" Francis Long prompted.

"Not at this moment, Francis. All in good time. It's my intention to stay away from that runway until the last possible moment."

Morgan Beaumont had had enough: "I can't get a word out of that bird. I'll see you later. Have a good a flight, Mr Wilson. Speak with you another time, Mr Walker. Francis, anyone want to know where I am, tell them I'm at Silent Pete's."

"Yes, Mr Beaumont."

The American marched through the lobby and out of the hotel.

John Wilson remarked: "Strange fellow. That's Americans for you: high expectations. Bad losers. He won't get anything out of Silent Pete, either. That Australian hasn't uttered a word since Nineteen Seventy-Seven. As for the bird, it doesn't matter how many nuts he gives it - that thing'll never speak."

"Why not?" his companions choroused.

"Well, how can it talk," John Wilson guffawed, "if it's eating nuts all the time?"

Francis Long and Robert Walker looked at each other. Then all three of the men stared at the parrot known as No.15.

"You're right, Mr Wilson," Francis Long agreed. "This is not a talking bird.

"Oh no? What," Wilson wanted to know, "kind of bird is it, then?"

Francis Long replied: "This one is a Listening Bird."

"A listening bird? You're kidding?"

"No kidding, Mr Wilson."

"Well, I never: a fellow wants a bit of a laugh, and you go and take it all the wrong way. That's bartenders for you: no sense of humour, eh. Or decorum."

"This bird only *listens*," Francis Long explained.

"You can't mean that? Really, did you hear what he said, Mr Walker: it's outrageous."

"Yes, I heard, Mr Wilson."

Francis Long explained: "This bird does not talk. This bird only listens. It listens to everything. Look, it's listening now - to everything you say, Mr Wilson - or to anything anyone says."

"I don't quite like the sound of this," John Wilson remarked. "It's some kind of plant - or bug - that's what you're implying, aren't you? When Harry Singh recovers the bird, it tells ALL! . . .I've heard this story before, you know - about the listening bird, I mean - some years ago. It seems most unlikely to me, but you never know with these things. Harry Singh, despite what I might have intimated about his character, is a man who knows many secrets. . .It becomes clear to me - at last - how he came about these secrets. It is quite possible Mr Singh trained this bird only to listen. If it does speak," John Wilson concluded, "then it's only to *him*. So, you see, Francis, there's listening - and there's *listening*. Knew a fellow like that once. Wouldn't pay a damned bit of attention to you unless he heard something he could use against you at a later date. Well, that's friends for you."

The three men studied the creature on the perch. No one said anything; the only sound in the lounge was the slow churn of the ceiling fan, which seemed almost at a standstill. . .Francis Long returned to his duties; he found a glass, which he polished in a leisurely way.

"Anyway, anyway, I wasn't talking about that. You're trying to distract me, that's what."

"Distract you from what, Mr Wilson?"

"Well, I can't remember now, can I?"

The stamp dealer was anxious about his imminent flight.

Francis Long glanced at the chronometer; his shift was almost over.

"All right, all right," Wilson agreed. "I should be on my merry way, I suppose."

The housegirl, Danielle, entered the Marlin Room, ready to relieve her colleague. She feather-dusted the President's portrait.

Francis Long said: "That's enough of that, girl." She ignored him, then approached the parrot's perch, as though ready to dust the creature, too.

Robert Walker said: "Well, it's been a pleasure making your acquaintance, Mr Wilson, and thanks for the . . .advice."

The two Britons shook hands. Then John Wilson reached across the bar to shake hands with Francis Long.

"A pleasure seeing the back of me, you mean."

"-."

"I know too much, don't I? About your mission. If I were to speak with the press, they'd be all over this island."

"Speak to the press about what?"

"About the you-know-what. The, ah, A-R-T-E-F-A-C-T. I'm not a fool, you know. Can spell, too."

"Well," Robert Walker concluded, "have a good journey, Mr Wilson."

John Wilson, international stamp dealer, readied himself for departure: he climbed off the barstool, and lifted his suitcase.

"Anyway, don't worry about me, gentlemen, I won't say a word. Never let it be said that John Wilson, Esquire, cannot keep a secret!"

John Wilson grinned with enormous satisfaction.

9

HARRY SINGH'S GENERAL STORE

SO, HARRY SINGH's general store was located on the edge of plantation country. The extinct volcano's escarpments provided some of the richest soil on the island, perhaps even in the whole Indian Ocean region, and this was where the merchant held a captive, highly lucrative base of custom, tied as it was to the virtuous circle of the plantation economy.

This was a real achievement, since visiting professors from overseas agreed that the plantations had undergone structural decline for a generation. The professors would not admit, however, since they were recipients of a bourse from the regime, that the advent of the Bourbon Island Marketing Board (BIMB) had hastened this decline through management techniques unknown even to the craziest of European bureaucracies. Instead, the professors blamed 'volatility in the world markets, combined with widespread product substitution in the West'.

The same double-pronged thesis, naturally, omitted any reference to the instruments of the one-party state for the enrichment of well-placed officials at the heart of the Bourbon Island People's Party (BIPP).

The BIPP was sometimes depicted as the snake that swallows its own tail[*] - an icon, in this instance, of corruption - which had started to appear as *graffiti* on the walls of Port Bourbon:

Some *graffiti* artists preferred (since snakes were not indigenous to the island) an octopus, not with eight arms, but with ten or twelve or maybe even more tentacles. It was generally accepted that the snake was the work of a disaffected plantation worker, while the octopus was the projection of a stevedore agitator.

---

[*] *ouroborus.*

One or the other, these images outraged the chairman of BIMB - F. Bellarmine, LLB. - who had hired the distinguished professors to attach the plumes of academic respectability to the greatest of all 'parastatals'.

The exiled *Star* countered that the BIPP-BIMB's tentacles - favouring the octopus motif - sucked the lifeblood from the people, while pretending to give them succour. So much, the exiled *Star* taunted, for the integrity and independence of academics, while the Party place-men and -women grew rich off the backs of the workers.

The professors had received a handsome grant for their massive, passive field-study *Economics of a Micro-State*, which, at over 1,000 pages, had become bloated on subsidy.

In this sea of state-run enterprises riddled with corruption, Harry Singh, a free-marketeer, prospered.

So the *Bourbon Island Star* said, from its basement printing press in far-away Paris.

In this way, the *Star* singled-out Singh without condemning the merchant, since, as the editor knew, Harry Singh, whether or not the merchant sat on his plantation fence, might prove useful when the Bellarmine regime was overthrown, and democracy returned to those distant shores.

The professors had referred to this well-known local trader as 'a niche player'. Harry Singh, who had not published a paper on this or any other subject, related in private that these 'old men with nothing to do' were 'frauds and impostors, who do not know what they are talking about'. That risked the wrath of Bellarmine; but, soon after, the professors fell out of favour, and had fled the island to leave behind them one of the island's few advocates of the mixed economy.

Harry Singh, it was said, had the ear of the president - but only when it was to Bellarmine's advantage.

As for the plantation workers and stevedores, these were the only groups who performed any real work on the island, and were represented by the mostly silent voice of the Bourbon Island National Workers' Union (BINWU). The BINWU was mostly silent because its secretary-general was . . . F. Bellarmine, Esq.

The plantation workers spent long days out on the estates, where they cut sugar cane and gathered coconuts. The estates were largely government owned, ever since they were seized by the Bellarmine regime on the night of the 1977 *coup d'état*.

On that night, too, the regime outlawed the Planters' Association - an elite club of *grand blanc* - made up of fat British growers and wealthy French plutocrats.

On the fringes of the giant estates, vanilla and cinnamon were also cultivated. These were traditional crops revitalised under an initiative of the Lôme Convention, which also benefited the Party place-men and - women of the Bourbon Island Marketing Board, who laughed at the European bureaucrats, while ready to accept subventions from long-suffering European taxpayers.

After the harvest, the workers were compelled by statute to deliver the valuable produce to the BIMB's main depot in Port Bourbon. The produce was then transhipped to Europe, sold, refined, sold again, processed, packaged, and resold and retailed, before ending up in a multitude of confectionery and beauty products. These products were then consumed by the same European taxpayers, who in effect subsidised corruption in places like Port Bourbon - and Brussels.

That cycle, Harry Singh whispered, was what happened when governments intervened to distort free markets, with monolithic structures like the BIMB, which cast a long shadow over those who preferred, like himself, not to cooperate.

In this way, the exiled *Star* claimed, the eccentricities of the bureaucrats in Brussels supported the self-willed madness of the BIPP-BIMB's *apparatchiks*, who lived a life lavish beyond the imaginings of most European taxpayers and plantation workers - that is, the consumers and the producers.

These excesses irritated Harry Singh, an enemy of bureaucrats everywhere, who was therefore considered dangerous by the civic authorities: a man, then, to be kept out on the plantations, and away from the town.

Some of the islanders wondered why Harry Singh was not in jail. Others guessed that the merchant knew something about François Bellarmine that ensured his, the merchant's, survival - not in the commercial sense, but in the biological sense.

In Silent Pete's - a disreputable drinking den that had done for Graham Dunne - they said that one day Harry Singh would go too far. These days, a lot of talking and drinking - more so than usual - was going on at Silent Pete's. The stevedores and plantation workers were on short-time because of 'turbulence in the world markets and product substitution'. Family men, patriots, or those islanders who did not care for Silent Pete's, spent their time with the Bourbon Island People's Defence Force (BIPDF), which organised pointless manoeuvres among the deserted plantations in return for a daily bounty from the regime.

The country, the exiled *Star* said, had become morally and financially bankrupted under the regime of Bellarmine and his murderous goons.

Le Peuple retorted that 'La Revolution' was not a luxury cruise for lazy capitalists; and, that by definition, the revolution must go on and on. . .

Harry Singh maintained that Revolutions, by definition, do not go on and on, but round and round, until they ended up where they started - nowhere!

Harry Singh always had the final word on this subject. An unconfirmed source had quoted the merchant as saying: 'If the government leaves me alone, then I shall leave the government alone'. If true, this suggested that, should the government not leave Harry Singh alone, then something of an unspecified nature - perhaps malignant - might happen to the government or its agents. For this reason, many people in the BIPP, the BINWU, BIMB, and BIPDF feared Harry Singh.

At Silent Pete's, an unnamed bar-room philosopher remarked that this was an irrational fear, which was all the more effective for that, and this was the real reason the merchant was left alone to enjoy his virtual monopoly on the plantation.

The plantation, on the edge of dissent and subordination, was a grey-green world, set on the margin of island politics.

The older and sometimes wiser islanders, who had not had their minds adjusted by the Party, believed that ghosts roamed the plantations at night. Only the drinking of the toddy, these older folks claimed, could protect you against the ghosts, who were the spirits of dead workers from the days when slaves were used on the estates.

The subject of ghosts, and the inter-related matter of excessive toddy drinking, had been the theme of many of Bishop David Chin's sermons. A recent sermon had implied that Harry Singh himself was an agent of dark forces, who encouraged stories of plantation-ghosts as a way of shifting excess stocks of the powerful palm-toddy - which was another of the merchant's monopolies (*see below*). The bishop had then gone on to suggest that Harry Singh was the owner of so many toddy tree licences only as a consequence of his liaison with the devil, who might or might not be François Bellarmine, who was, anyway, only a man.

This was dangerous talk, some people said, for a man who was only a bishop.

The toddy of Harry Singh, the bishop warned, would not only swell your tongue and stomach, it would also empty your wallet, and it might drive you mad by rotting your brain. On the other end of the argument, some among the congregation whispered, at least Harry Singh practised what he preached - to the extent that he had consumed so much of his own product that he had probably driven himself mad.

Harry Singh had asserted, for the benefit of the moralists, that he could not expect the workers to drink the brew if he were not prepared to drink it himself, and that anyway it was good for the health. Palm toddy, he appreciated, was not 'everyone's cup of tea', as he put it, and added - with a counter-thrust - that the drinking of *champagne* and fine claret was not as commonplace on the plantation as it was in church or governmental circles.

This barbed remark had stifled the debate for a good while, although, from high-up on the mountain, the dispute had provided François Bellarmine with an opportunity to proscribe the drinking of toddy. An instrument of policy intended to force the workers onto the relatively expensive BourBrew - or the even more expensive imported Blue Marlin - the decree had instead encouraged such a rash of petty thievery throughout the island that this particular Presidential Decree had been promptly dropped - or lifted.

It was prior to the lifting or dropping of the decree that Harry Singh had made his bid for, and then acquired, the bulk of the government's licences for each of the official toddy trees.

The moralists and bureaucrats, then, had inadvertently provided Harry Singh with one of his greatest commercial victories.

The Bamboo Mill had more to say: an expatriate Italian businessman, as a way of cashing-in on the proscription of toddy, had ordered a large shipment of Blue Marlin beer all the way from Mauritius. The Italian, it was said, had been ruined by the transaction - because of the unanticipated lifting of the decree. The cargo of beer was expected at Port Bourbon any day now on a boat called the *Maputo*. . .That was all that was known - so far. The Italian - a Signor Mario Colon - had played a key role in the coup that had first brought Bellarmine to power, but the expatriate businessman was no longer friends with the president. In this way, the Italian was the laughing stock of the whole island. There was talk, too, that the mothers of the many under-age daughters the Italian had seduced during the immediate post-coup days were looking for Signor Colon. The idea was that these mothers, when they caught up with the seducer (now himself naked without the protection of the president) would hang him upside-down by the feet - or some other part - just like Benito Mussolini.

On the plantation, the Bamboo Mill reported that Harry Singh was planning a disposal of toddy tree licences by way of a Palm-Toddy Lottery. The rumour, which was not true, had become true by giving the merchant the idea. In a double-swoop, then, Harry Singh had privatised the entire stock of the government's holdings in this sector, which was seen by the regime - too late - as a dangerous precedent on the road back to the *laissez-faire* system.

The Harry Singh General Store provided, as the proprietor often remarked, 'everything in this creation a body and soul could want'. If by chance a specific item was not in stock, then the merchant had an impressive library of mail order catalogues from Europe, the United States, Bombay, Colombo, Singapore (C.K. Tang's) and Hong Kong.

Harry Singh never criticised his customers for buying things they did not need, since the impulse-purchase was essential to his livelihood, and that of his extended family. Harry Singh had imported and read all the books from the United States on the subject. The books attempted to explain the psychology of the consumer, which Harry Singh thought was bogus-*grandiose* - as he put it - and, anyway, all very elementary in his league of thought. Harry Singh's equation was that of human love or hate, which demanded various forms of expression, and manifested itself between merchant and customer in the form of - a purchase. The simple mechanism of simian greed was only a part of the equation, since this was subsumed by greater forces, such as desire, rather than need, and *fear,* which could be allayed by something termed 'conspicuous consumerism', which was an even greater mystery for most islanders than plantation-ghosts. It was much more complicated than that, but none of Harry Singh's secrets had found their way into the books from the United States. The secrets of Harry Singh, then, the greatest salesman in the whole of the Indian Ocean, were safe inside his own head.

Harry Singh's status had grown with the islanders' fast developing thirst for what were known in the world outside as consumer goods or sometimes as consumer durables. Harry Singh detested both these terms; he preferred the traditional, simplified form 'goods' - or, better yet, 'merchandise'. According to the Bamboo Mill, the plantation people would often go into the store for one item and come away another, entirely different item. If you went into the store for one thing, it was said, you could come out with just about anything. The Bamboo Mill reported that, only recently, an American gentleman had visited the store in search of a certain kind of hair-tonic, and had instead emerged with a parrot, which had not to date, despite Harry Singh's claims, spoken a single word. When the American had returned to the store to lodge a complaint, Harry Singh reasoned that the American was feeding the bird the wrong kind of nuts. The American had re-emerged from the store with the right kind of nuts, which Harry Singh claimed were "special nuts " - and therefore not cheap - but still the bird would not speak. On a third visit to the store, the American was told that the parrot was 'not a chatterbox', and would only speak when it had something important to say.

"Well, then, why didn't you say so in the first place?" Morgan Beaumont had demanded.

"You didn't ask me," Harry Singh had spoken up. "Or the bird."

By this time, the American had developed a taste for long walks, and set out in a different direction every day, but not in the direction of Harry Singh's General Store on the plantation.

The stories of Harry Singh's legendary salesmanship were legion on an island hungry for information of any kind, true or untrue, but the story about the American was true "- as you know, Mr Walker."

Francis Long and Robert Walker had trekked through the foothills above the town. After a while, a terrain of moss-covered boulders gave way to a jungle path. Francis Long took the lead. A pig - a regular commuter along the pathway - saw the men, retreated - and then trotted with a squeal in the other direction. Francis Long chased the pig, but the animal took a sharp turn into the dense jungle, and disappeared.

"What would you have done if you had caught it?" Robert Walker asked.

"Sold it," Francis Long panted. "A deposit on the boat, maybe. . . Okay, Mr Walker - nearly there now."

Francis Long did not say anything more until they had reached the eastern aspect of plantation. "This is it, Mr Walker."

Robert Walker looked back over the way they had hiked: the jungle trail, invisible from sea-level, snaked back towards the foothills, through the green-belt of vegetation, until it merged with the wider track outside of town. In the shimmer of distance, at the end of Revolution Boulevard, the observation deck of the Marina Hotel was just discernible by the crossroads. On Victoria Street, someone seemed to scream from inside the Police Station - but, no - overhead, it was only a hungry gull. The great white stretch of Anse Venus pointed the way - along the coast - to the airport. The Church of the Magdalene's spire pointed at the sky. The promontory, where Sir Godfrey and Graham Dunne were buried, jutted into the sea. Off shore, the jagged pinnacle of rock stuck up from the ocean floor: something - for an instant - sparkled from its pinnacle. The sun burned down on Port Bourbon's patchwork of metal roofs, which generated a mass of thermals. A few puffs of cloud hung over the distant horizon. In between, nothing, except the vast, uninterrupted expanse of grey-blue ocean.

"Mr Walker, you okay? Mr Walker . . .?"

Robert Walker turned: for a moment, he did not recognise Francis Long, who waved for him to follow. Over a ridge, the plantation estates opened up onto a plateau, which rolled out of sight into acres of dense cultivation. Out of the direct sunlight, it was cooler, and a steady air-flow breathed through the trees.

"How far?"

"Five miles, maybe. On the way back - downhill all the way."

They approached the eastern gateway of the plantation. The high canopy filtered out most of the sunlight to form streaks of white light on the forest floor. Underfoot, the grass was soft and springy.

Ahead, a palm-thatched, single storey building on stilts bore the sign: H. SINGH GENERAL STORE ~ Independent Trader. Est. 1970 & 1977

Robert Walker listened: the plantation's movements of air, water, earth and wood might easily be taken for restless spirits.

"What is it, Mr Walker?"

"Nothing, Francis, really."

A warm, steady breeze persisted, and found its way up the great slope from Port Bourbon and onto the plateau, over the canopy of the plantation and, higher yet, into the conifer belt. From the shade of the plantation, Robert Walker looked out over the almost featureless trough of ocean. A ship moved into view, exposed its diesel-driven screw in a churn of white sea-foam - and then somehow disappeared. The *Maputo*?

"Thirsty work. Let's go inside and have a beer," Francis Long suggested.

Robert Walker listened: nearby, a chicken or something scratched at the dry earth.

"Please, Mr Walker, this is spooky."

"All right," Robert Walker conceded.

The two men climbed a short flight of steps to mount the platform. The storefont was protected from rare flash-floods by great, thick stilts, which raised the building from the forest floor. The store's walls were fashioned from the products of the plantation, and supported a high, sloped roof.

The men entered Harry Singh's domain.

Yellowed palm-fronds hung from the eaves of the roof, and tickled their sweaty faces. Ahead of Robert Walker, Francis Long disappeared. Out of the darkness, a shiny face with a gold tooth appeared. As Robert Walker edged into the store, something tugged at his arm.

"Let's get out of here," Francis Long panicked.

"You're the one who wanted to come in here."

Robert Walker felt ahead of him, but Francis Long was out of reach. Sweat ran down Robert Walker's backbone; he stopped, and held his position.

"Francis?"

There was no answer.

Then: a skylight swung open, and admitted a dusty, yellow-brown shade of light from the forest canopy over the store's roof.

Francis Long stood - rigid - at the centre of the store. A second skylight opened, and a narrow shaft of plantation light imparted a kind of sense to the store's interior. Around the store-perimeter, racks occupied the space from deck to roof, and supported complex arrays of dry goods, packets and bottles of various sorts, and merchandise of all descriptions. The skylight revealed the store's atmosphere as a suspension of spices, dried herbs, grains, oils, and plantation grit.

"No air conditioning here, gentlemen." It was Harry Singh, who appeared from the shadows. "Ah, it's you, Francis! And you have a guest with you from far away. How marvellous. Welcome, welcome."

The storeowner pulled and pushed a few levers, and more skylights opened at locations around the store's structure. "I was, you see," he said, "having my afternoon kip. I thought maybe you were representatives of the People's Militia."

"Hello, Mr Singh," Francis Long managed to say. "We're not the militia."

Harry Singh had a good look at Robert Walker. "Yes, I can see that, Francis."

"This is Mr Walker - from London."

Harry Singh stood out from a substantial-looking counter, shook Robert Walker's hand, and turned to face Francis Long: "You seen any militia, Francis?"

"Not today, Mr Singh."

The storeowner, satisfied, returned to his position behind the counter. "Manoeuvres, you know. They like to scare away my customers," Harry Singh explained. "They find it very amusing. I do not."

Harry Singh pressed a well-formed toddy-belly against the counter. He wore simple cotton shirt open at the collar. Around his trouser-waistband, an elasticated belt showed a sideways-S-shaped buckle. The man's teeth, except for a single gold incisor, were strangers to the dentist's drill, and showed good and white. The whole set was directed at Robert Walker.

"You two gentlemen are perspiring very, very heavily, if you do not mind the observation. Something cool to drink, I think." Harry Singh reached into a cold-chest, and removed three bottles of BourBrew. A bottle opener was produced, and the BourBrews were - *one, two, three* - de-capped in series. Robert Walker had never seen three bottles opened so quickly. Francis Long merely stared with his mouth open. "You're catching flies, Francis," Harry Singh laughed.

The bartender of Marina Hotel closed his mouth. The two men approached the counter. Harry Singh allowed his guests to satisfy their thirst; then, protocol observed, he took a fast swig from the third bottle. Robert Walker, with tears in his eyes from the cold beer, studied the store. Behind the counter, the same portrait of François Bellarmine looked over the store. It was mounted in such a way that indicated rotation was possible: another portrait, perhaps, of Anthony Montaigne?

"So?" Harry Singh started.

"The boat, Mr Singh?" Francis Long proposed: "I want to buy the boat as soon as possible."

"Now, hold on, Francis, not so fast!" the merchant insisted. "You walk all the way from Port Bourbon, and it is straight to business. Don't you ever think of anything else besides? Patience, my friend, patience!"

Francis Long's silent, sweaty face looked from Harry Singh to Robert Walker.

"All right, then, Mr Singh; we'll have two more beers, if you please, and then-."

"THREE BEERS COMING RIGHT UP!" Harry Singh confirmed.

Harry Singh reached for the cold-chest, and set up three more of the bottles. Again, he de-capped the bottles in fast succession. This time, he blasted himself with the foamy gas from the unsettled third.

"There," he said, "just the ticket!"

Then the merchant reached under the counter, and produced a notebook and pencil: he scribbled a sub-total for six bottles.

"That's the price of four beers maximum, Mr Singh," Francis Long said with the sharp eyes of a bartender.

"My mistake." Harry Singh corrected the subtotal. "Sorry about that; I'm still dreaming from my afternoon kip."

"Oh really?" Francis Long laughed. "I heard Harry Singh never sleeps, that he cannot afford to."

"This is a good joke, Francis Long, to tell anyone except me."

Robert Walker detected a void behind Harry Singh's eyes that spoke of treachery, but then the merchant broke into a big, white smile. "You see?" he said: "this is my idea of a joke. Ha, ha."

"Ha, ha," Francis Long echoed. Then Francis Long, careful in Harry Singh's presence, raised his bottle at the portrait. The merchant turned, and he, too, raised his bottle: "To our President. A hero among heroes."

Another framed photograph, smaller and much older, was set deferentially below Bellarmine's image. "And to my grandfather," Harry Singh related with a smile, "another great man. Gentlemen, I give you the Doctor from Bombay."

Francis Long and Robert Walker raised their bottles.

Harry Singh allowed his ancestor a respectful pause, while Dr Sanjay Singh of Bombay looked back at them from the past, and seemed only slightly less impressed with his descendant. The grandson continued:

"A great man, deeply flawed as we all are, but still great, although not as great as our own François Bellarmine. Where would we be without our great men?"

"Where?" Francis Long asked.

Harry Singh watched Francis Long's features for traces of dissent.

"Sweating so much, you look," the merchant observed, "as though you've been swimming in deep water, Francis. You should be more careful. How about another beer?"

"Not yet."

Harry Singh did not like to miss out on a sale. He studied Robert Walker's silent, sun-reddened, British features. Robert Walker shifted his weight from one foot to the other, and rested an elbow on the counter. Instead of meeting Harry Singh's eyes, he glanced outside onto the serene plantation.

"You have many great men - British fellows - in your country, Mr Walker? Sir Walter Raleigh, for example, who invented America?"

Robert Walker smiled, but did not say anything; Harry Singh's face told of a long inquisition in store involving many 'special offers'.

"A long way from home, then?" Harry Singh probed. "I have for many years been meaning to travel to London to see Oxford Street and Regent Street. Also Covent Garden market for the fruit and veg."

Robert Walker spoke up:

"The market is no longer there, Mr Singh."

"It still exists?"

"It is still called Covent Garden market, but it is not in Covent Garden any longer."

"This is amazing," the merchant said. "The English are a very strange people."

"This is true, Mr Singh," Robert Walker agreed.

Francis Long became unsettled; the subject had drifted a very long way from the business of the boat.

"The tourists have taken over."

"Tourists have taken over the whole world, Mr Walker. Not here yet, but soon. I shall sell them sun-lotion and sunglasses - and maps."

Robert Walker continued: "It's been taken over by boutiques and street performers."

"Well, then, I shall visit Oxford Street and Regent Street. These places are still there?"

"They are still there," Robert Walker confirmed.

"Good, then I shall go next year," Harry Singh decided. "How about another beer, gentlemen?"

"Why not?" Robert Walker said.

"Why not, indeed? Or maybe something stronger?"

"The beer's very good," Robert Walker replied.

Harry Singh prepared another round of BourBrews.

Robert Walker cast his eyes around the store. The split-level racks of produce contained an unbelievable diversity goods. Tins and jars and packets and bags of various kinds: oils for cooking, including vegetable ghee, biscuits from England, noodles from the Far East, basmati rice from India - "The Prince of the Rices" - lime and mango pickles from Malaysia, and chilli sauce and soy sauce from Singapore. Robert Walker's eyes were lost for a place to focus.

Harry Singh closed the flap of the cold-chest with bang. Then the merchant adjusted the steadily growing sub-total on the notebook, passed two of the bottles over the counter, and raised the third in a toast:

"All political careers end in failure."

At the counter, no one moved.

The merchant added with care: "I quote this English chap, but this - you understand - will never happen to our President. Some say Anthony Montaigne is coming back, at any time now, but I am not one of those people who say this. You understand me, perfectly, of course. I am not one of these people who say the opposite of what I mean to make a point - do I or don't I?"

"You do," Francis Long guessed. "You don't," he tried again. Then again: "Whether you do or don't, what about the bo-?"

"-You're going to start on that again, Francis?"

"That's what I came here for, Mr Singh."

"Oh really? I thought you came here to drink all of my beer?" Harry Singh did something to the tab that made the sub-total reach the bottom of the page; then he flipped the notebook over onto a fresh page. Francis Long looked nervous.

Harry Singh cleared his throat, and asked: "So, you have your eyes on this boat, my friend?"

Francis Long said: "I'll paint eyes on it."

"Not yet, you won't."

"You have the photograph, Mr Singh?"

"I do." Harry Singh about-turned, searched along a shelf, and located a colour photograph the size of a postcard. He shielded the photograph from Francis Long's eyes.

"What? You won't let me see?"

"You understand: I am merely acting as broker; this is not my own property."

"Who owns the boat, then?"

"That is confidential. My client's anonymity must be respected, as I am sure you understand, of course."

"How much?" Francis Long asked.

"Fifty rupees."

"Fifty rupees? How can that be?"

"-For this photograph," Harry Singh revealed.

Francis Long's face clouded over. "Well, -?"

Robert Walker interjected: "I don't understand, Mr Singh."

"That's okay, Mr Walker; nor does he."

"You mean, you're going to sell Francis the photograph of the boat - and not the boat itself?"

"Mr Walker, I am selling Francis the boat when he can afford it; the photograph is an essential first part of the transaction. Also," the merchant added, "I had to arrange to photograph the boat at my own expense. The ultimate vendor was out of the country at the time. Even this, I should not tell you."

"-?"

Francis Long was in torment: he stared at Harry Singh's clasping hand, and - irrationally - tried to see through the back of the concealed photograph.

"Well," Robert Walker suggested, "perhaps you could just let him have a glance at it - after all, he is only a potential purchaser."

Harry Singh almost took offence. A foreigner - ready to tell he, Harry Singh, his own business. Robert Walker relented; Harry Singh held his breath; he waited, while his pencil-hand hovered over the notebook.

"ALL RIGHT!" Francis Long agreed.

"It's a deal!" Harry Singh marked BIR50 on the notebook, and - simultaneously - handed over the photograph to Francis Long.

Harry Singh created a new subtotal, and showed his gold incisor to his customers.

"I've seen this boat in the marina!" Francis Long realised.

"That," Harry Singh said, "does not surprise me in the least. You think - what? - I would keep it up here on the plantation?"

Francis Long scanned every detail in the photograph. "She's a beauty," he said. "Bigger than I expected, but not too big. Manoeuvrable. Needs a coat of paint. Who's the owner, My Singh?"

Harry Singh folded his arms over his toddy belly. "I'm not telling."

Francis Long groaned into his beer.

Robert Walker was sure the merchant was about to request at least another fifty rupees for this information.

"Inspect the craft by all means. Look, but do not touch."

Francis Long handed over the photograph to Robert Walker: a five-metre skiff, with two sets of oars, but with no outboard engine. It was a handsome-looking craft for in-shore or coastal purposes. As for the search for a potential wife, Robert Walker thought Francis Long would need a much larger vessel made for, as it were, rougher seas.

"It's a fine boat," Robert Walker agreed, and returned the photograph to Francis Long. To the merchant, he said: "If I might ask, Mr Singh: if the image of the boat is fifty rupees, then how much is the actual boat?"

"The deposit you mean, Mr Walker?"

"No, I mean the full asking-price, for everything we see in that photograph, including the oars. I don't mean the purchase of this photograph or a copy of it; I mean the actual wooden boat, in reality, of which this photograph is merely an image."

"Ah, yes, you mean the boat itself, which can be used to float on the sea and from which to catch fish?"

"Yes, that's the idea."

"No, not the idea, Mr Walker: you mean, the *boat*."

"Yes, that's what I meant, Mr Singh."

Harry Singh placed both palms of his hands on the counter. "This is a matter of much delicate negotiation, wouldn't you agree?"

"No, not really. There must be a straight-price the mystery owner wants, on which you, presumably, as broker, earn a commission."

"This is not the case, Mr Walker; rather, the owner has granted me exclusive rights of negotiation on his or her behalf."

"You mean, the owner is a woman?" Francis Long enquired.

"I know what you're thinking, Francis: two birds with one shot. But, no, I did not say that. Whichever, I shall then negotiate with the former owner when the sale has been completed, and the individual is satisfied. This is my own method."

Robert Walker shrugged: "Well, what's the notional guide-price, then?"

"Ah, that is more like it," the merchant grinned. "So, you are now also bidding for this boat, Mr Walker?"

"No, I am not," Robert Walker replied. "What would I need with a boat? I'm only visiting this island."

"How long are you with us, Mr Walker?"

"A couple of weeks.'

"Well," Harry Singh suggested, "you could purchase the boat, use it for a week or two, and then re-sell the boat at a profit - or not."

Francis Long looked up from his beer.

"I don't think so."

"Well, then," Harry Singh said: "that's that then - as you say in England."

"Yes, that's that."

Harry Singh turned to his real buyer: "Well, then, Francis. Do you wish to know the notional guide-price as we shall call it?"

"You say what, Mr Singh?"

Harry Singh would not repeat himself.

Francis Long looked again at the photograph.

"I don't know, Mr Singh." Francis Long avoided the merchant's eyes. "Maybe not."

"You say what, Francis?"

"In a small way, you have already sold me this boat."

"You mean what, man?"

"I have it here for fifty rupees."

The merchant stared at his customer. Then Harry Singh frowned: "Well, you have not paid yet, Francis."

Francis Long reached into his pockets and found a BIR200 note. "There you go, Mr Singh. Enough for the beers also."

The merchant accepted the note: "This banknote is damp, Francis. Sweat in your pockets, no doubt. This is no way to treat money."

"You don't want it? I'll take it back."

"No, no - I'll dry it out. No problem." Harry Singh looked with dismay at the damp banknote, then made it disappear beneath the counter.

"Take this wet money for the beer and the photograph. Then use the dry change for more beer."

"Well," Harry Singh said in a sulk, "there won't be much left, that's for sure." The merchant drummed the fingers of his free hand on the counter, then he placed the same fingers at his left temple: "I have a number in mind."

Francis Long looked up from the photograph. "What number?"

Harry Singh closed his eyes: "The number is called the guide price."

"You can't fool me, Mr Singh."

"Guess anyway."

"I don't know."

The merchant opened his eyes: "I see ten-thousand rupees before my eyes."

Francis Long stared at Harry Singh: "Is the engine included?"

"No, the outboard engine is a further three-thousand rupees, optional. If not the engine, then a couple of oars to paddle with."

"Oh, no, no."

Harry Singh returned to normality: "Yes, oh yes, Francis, this is a good price. The best price. Everyone will be happy. You, me, the owner. Even Mr Walker here will be happy."

"The *guide* price," Robert Walker responded.

"As you wish," Harry Singh admitted.

Francis Long tried to work out how many months - or years - it would take to raise that sum of money working at the Marlin Room Bar. "Does any one else want to buy this boat, Mr Singh?"

"I have had several excellent offers," Harry Singh exaggerated.

"If I could make a suggestion, gentlemen?"

Both islanders looked at Robert Walker.

"As a gesture of good will, perhaps Mr Singh would accept a small deposit?"

"There is no good will on this island, Mr Walker," Harry Singh replied. "Even so, it is an idea. What do you think, Francis?"

Francis Long did not want to commit himself - at least not today.

The merchant said: "You see, Mr Walker? It is all talk."

"After I've looked over the boat," Francis Long decided.

Harry Singh smouldered: "You have the photograph. Look at it there."

Agent and potential buyer had reached an impasse.

Robert Walker had begun to stew in the dark heat of the store; he ran a hand over the back of his neck.

"All right," Harry Singh agreed. "Have a look at the boat, then we'll agree a deposit."

"A deposit of how much against how much?"

Harry Singh closed, then opened, his eyes: "X against Y for now. Go look at the boat, but don't touch, then we'll talk again."

Harry Singh tried to work out how many beers he had sold, and at what profit, then realised he had consumed the profit - and more - himself. The storekeeper's eyes bulged; was he, the great Harry Singh, losing his touch?

Robert Walker wondered if the merchant had any business selling the boat.

"I agree. I won't take her out."

"You'll just look at the boat - don't touch - and then decide?"

"I'll look at the boat, and then decide!" Francis Long agreed.

"Now, we celebrate," Harry Singh decided. "I think," he said, "enough of this beer. Something more interesting is in order, I believe."

Francis Long laughed, and studied the photograph of the boat. Robert Walker (taking the bait) asked: "What do you have in mind, Mr Singh?"

Harry Singh did not reply; instead, he moved to the far end of the counter, lifted a latch, and swung open a palm-thatched door onto the store's exterior. Harry Singh descended a short, steep ladder from the platform-level of the store, and - with a final jump - disappeared onto the plantation floor.

Left alone, Francis Long and Robert Walker watched, waited and. . . listened - to nothing. Then they heard the sound of spirited digging, then something was removed from the ground. After a pause, the something was a given triple-slice or chop.

Harry Singh reappeared at the top of the ladder with a coconut husk in his hands. "You see, Mr Walker? The champagne of the plantation!" The merchant closed and secured the doorway, then approached his side of the counter with the giant husk.

"You'd better stick to the BourBrew, Mr Walker," Francis Long joked.

The coconut had been cleaved open with a *machete* to form a lid.

"Now this," Harry Singh said, and lifted the lid of the nut.

"Coconut milk?" Robert Walker asked.

"Oh sure, if you say so. I would say, a Harry Singh Special. I take this nut, cut it a bit, then I bury it in the ground. Three days. On the third day, I dig it up, like this one here. It is only by coincidence that you two

172

gentlemen happened to come by on the third day - at *exactly* the right time. Now, Francis, you first; we must not force our guest to taste if he does not want to taste."

Francis Long took the husk from the merchant, raised it to his mouth, and slurped at some of the liquid.

"Well, Francis: you a democrat now?" Harry Singh teased.

Francis Long wiped his mouth, but did not say anything, for the effect was almost immediate. Harry Singh took the nut away from Francis Long, then passed it to Robert Walker. Robert Walker took the smooth husk into his hands, and sniffed at the aperture, which had been cut into the roof of the nut - the aroma was coconut milk-plus - then raised the husk to his lips. The liquid, which seemed to flow of its own volition, moved into his mouth: it was cold and hot, and the whole plantation went into a spin around his head. He took another sip, to make sure - it tasted better than the first - and the spin turned into a wobble, and his head went into an Indian Ocean free-fall. He could see Harry Singh say something - the merchant's lips moved - but there was no sound. Robert Walker's hands stuck to the side of the husk, so that Harry Singh had to prize his guest's fingers loose. Robert Walker watched the storekeeper take a single, delicate sip, and then set the husk to one side - just out of Francis Long's reach.

"This . . . is the . . .co-co-nut . . .toddy?" Robert Walker asked. He looked at Harry Singh, but the merchant had gone wandering around the store.

In that instant, Robert Walker was able to form a mental inventory of every item held in the general store, including the curry power from Madras, the lime pickles from Sri Lanka, the soy sauce from China, and bombay duck, which were not ducks, but little dried fish, and not from Bombay, but from Goa. Goa? Like-? This made Robert Walker start to laugh, but he stopped himself, since storekeeping was a serious business.

"Now, who are you?" someone asked. "And why have you come to this island? You have, haven't you, come as - not a treasure hunter - but as a cunning assassin? Revenge for Savvy? Trouvères has sent you? Montaigne? What are Montaigne's plans? He will land on the beaches at night? Which beach, and when? Stay out of politics, you bloody Englishman with white legs, if you want to live. Drink tea, not this stuff, and do not cross the BIPP.

"Now, tell us the name of the high-level American operative based on this island?"

Robert Walker's lips were hot and numb. "Stay out of politics," he parroted.

A burst of laughter came from the rear of the store.

"That's good advice around here," he thought he heard Francis Long say.

"And leave the women alone," he added. Harry Stone had said something like that - a long time ago.

"That's even better advice!" he thought he heard Harry Singh laugh.

Robert Walker saw an empty perch in a corner of the store, and understood: he had been programmed - Harry Stone's stooge - and there was nothing, not now, that he could do to erase the protocol. Unless-?

"More toddy?"

"Not on your Nelly," Harry Singh said. "No bloody chance, that is."

He was nothing more than a prawn - *pawn* - of the Yanks. The other Harry - Harry Stone - had sold him down the river, out to sea, and - over an ocean! Fishbait and sawdust! Homesick? John Wilson seemed to ask. You've got to keep moving, you know that, don't you? If you keep moving, you've got no right to be homesick for anywhere. It's a Honey Trap, Harry Stone's voice seemed to say, that's all I can tell you. A honey trap - the sweetest!

"I can see everything now," he said. "You shouldn't have done it, Harry."

"Where have I heard that before," the merchant taunted.

Robert Walker looked over the counter - his eyes damp - at the portrait. Bellarmine's hard blue eyes watched, over Harry Singh's shoulder, every customer who passed this way. Foreign usurpers, too. We're all bloody foreigners here, he thought he heard John Wilson say. Originally uninhabited, don't you know? Then Robert Walker caught sight of the elusive merchant, who had grown three Harry Singh heads. Six eyes blinked, and three gold teeth smiled along with the other teeth. Three sets of lips moved. Questions, questions. Who are you? I am nobody. I am a dead man - since before I was born. You are indeed a dead man - just like Jacques Savvy. Since you will soon be joining him, how about a short vacation - before infinite one.

Robert Walker was sure, though, that no one in the store had said anything. He sucked at numb gums until it hurt, and he began to see sense: the inventory had been itemised with each point of origin lodged. The Doctor from Bombay smiled over the counter - jolly good show, Mr Walker, and welcome to the entrepôt economy. You have been initiated; there is no turning back. Not now, not ever!

"Now, now, now," Harry Singh was saying.

10

THE PEOPLE'S MILITIA VS. THE JU-JU STICK

ROBERT WALKER'S HEAD seemed to rebound from the store's rafters.

"Now . . . to . . .business, Mr . . .Walker."

Robert Walker turned: Harry Singh was back on duty, with his feet anchored on the deck, and his belly set against the counter. A bleary-eyed Francis Long smiled at nobody. Harry Singh *tsk-tsk-tsked*. "You stick to your boy's beer, eh?" Then the merchant unfolded an oblong document.

"How can you say these things, Mr Walker?"

"What . . .things? I haven't said a word."

"It is a good thing I did not let you finish the free sample. Visions, old boy."

Robert Waker thought John Wilson had spoken.

"You would see the green grass of England again - just like that," and the merchant clicked a thumb-and-finger together, but there was only the dry sound of leather.

"Be assured, gentlemen," Harry Singh repeated: "I am the discretion of soul."

"I'm pleased to hear that, Mr Singh, but-?"

"-Now, to business. Look, I had almost forgotten where I put this map. Only fifty rupees."

"For what?" Robert Walker wanted to know.

"This treasure map, here," Harry Singh said, and spread the document over the counter.

"Ah." Robert Walker glanced at Francis Long, who stared, not at the map, but at the photograph.

"Keep on looking, Francis," the merchant laughed: "soon, you will see the boat slip loose from its mooring, and go out to sea. . . Now, the map. Fifty rupees only."

Robert Walker had removed a BIR100 note from his pocket. Harry Singh accepted the note, tested it for moisture content, and counted out change of five - easy-to-spend - BIR10 coins. Robert Walker thought the coin-count took a long time. Then Harry Singh started a fresh column of figures in the notebook. Robert Walker checked the map for authenticity. In the Legend, a number was printed: No 508, beside which were the words *From the Original*.

"This number here, Mr Singh? You have sold this many maps to date? Five Hundred and Eight?"

"You think I would start the series at five-hundred, Mr Walker?"

"Five-O-Seven, maybe," Francis Long joked.

"What happened to the people who used the map?" Robert Walker wanted to know.

"Nothing!" Francis Long laughed. "None of those fools found any treasure because they cannot read the map!"

"Then it is not the map that is at fault, Francis," Harry Singh said. "This map was drafted by the pirate La Buse's own hand."

"La Buse?" Robert Walker asked. "Then you have the original?"

"Since you ask, the original is in a museum in Mauritius. It is much better to buy this copy here than to travel all the way to Mauritius to see the original. That is a much more expensive exercise, and even then you would not be permitted to make a copy. Then you would have to come all the way back here to buy this map."

"There is much in what you say, Mr Singh," Robert Walker remarked.

"Oh I know, Mr Walker."

"You believe this map to be accurate?"

Behind the counter, Harry Singh shifted. "I am a merchant, not a cartographer."

"Why," Robert Walker reasoned, "don't you seek the treasure yourself?"

"How about another nice drop of toddy, Mr Walker?"

"No. No, thank you."

"Then . . .This is a good question, Mr Walker."

"You have a good answer?"

Harry Singh smiled: "I have to admit . . .that I am in the same position as everyone else: I do not understand the map, either."

Francis Long let out a bark of laughter then fell silent.

"You see this fellow, Mr Walker? You see what the juice of the coconut does to him? Boat crazy. Girl crazy. You see? And now toddy crazy!"

Francis Long recovered, and said: "The only one to make money out of this bloody treasure is Harry Singh. Fifty rupees times five-hundred and eight. Not bad for a lot of rubbish!"

Harry Singh looked at the deck beneath his feet, then at the ceiling, and then at Robert Walker. "This is a public service. I could easily charge many times this price."

Francis Long did not seem to think this deserved an answer; he looked again at the photograph of the boat, which, in his eyes, had become much larger.

Robert Walker's head spun, but he made an effort to look the map over: the chart was a rough schematic of Bourbon Island from the purported era of 'La Buse', the *nom de guerre* of the pirate Olivier Le Vasseur. The map was dated 1725. The extinct volcano was at the epicentre of the island. A smaller version of Port Bourbon was shown to the south. The map, real or not, was at least consistent in that there was no indication of the Russian naval base at Sans Souci Bay - or of the International Airport on the south-west coast. In every detail, the chart appeared to represent the island as it might have existed in the early 1700s. . . .Robert Walker checked again for any obvious anach-ronisms, such as the USAF's satellite-tracking station. . . Even so, the map might be entirely bogus. He had, anyway, already paid his BIR50.

". . .You will not see any such map in any of the shops in town, Mr Walker. This is a direct copy of the real thing."

Robert Walker studied the borders of the chart: there were symbols, related to several points of reference around the island, presumably - clues. He had seen depictions of some of these before: on Roger Dupin's bedstead, under the stairs at the Marina Hotel. The symbols bore annotations in the original French, with translations in English, added - it would seem - much more recently. Robert Walker's head throbbed; he reached for cold beer, and swallowed.

"Mr Graham Dunne," Harry Singh explained, "your fellow countryman, wrote those words there in English."

The north-east corner of the map - spread over an empty space in the Indian Ocean - bore a splendid illustration of the Fiery Cross of Goa. If it were real, then it differed in some respects from the motif on John Wilson's specimen stamp. A product of the imagination, he suspected, since it was heavier on the encrusted rubies, and thicker at the staff of gold.

Robert Walker looked up from the map and into Harry's Singh's eyes.

"So, now, I answer your question: I am a merchant, not a treasure hunter. But if I were a treasure hunter, then I would be very, very happy with a map like this, which is nearly three-hundred years old." Harry Singh showed a broad, white, very, very happy smile.

"Well . . ?"

"All very interesting," Robert Walker replied. His head was almost clear of the effects of the fermented coconut juice, which had swollen the inside of his mouth and left him thirstier than before: "More beer, if you please, Mr Singh," he asked. Harry Singh reached for the cold chest, set up the beers, and then adjusted the loose change on the counter - that left only BIR30 in coin - and the tab in the notebook. Again, the sub-total had been zeroed.

"So," Robert Walker asked, "you say the Englishman Dunne made use of this map?"

"Mr Dunne? Of course. I sold him map Number One myself. After he made his comments on it, I, - ah - reacquired his only copy. . and re-issued the map in this improved form. His estranged wife, from a place called Southend-on-Sea, tried to sue me for copyright infringe-ment. Imagine that, if you will, Mr Walker - but I was able to demonstrate that this is a map from antiquity, not from her belated husband's imagination. It is all very complicated. The lawyers made fools out of themselves on that case, let me tell you. Mrs Dunne made fools out of them, too."

"So, then, Graham Dunne actually used this map?"

Francis Long spoke up: "He used it all right, and look where it got him!"

"Please, Francis," Harry Singh said, "let us stick to the facts, if you don't mind. The facts can stick up for themselves, all right."

Harry Singh pointed: "These symbols here, for instance: they could be interpreted in many ways; they do not necessarily align themselves with the ambitions of mortal men, wouldn't you agree, Mr Walker?"

"I don't know. Men created the symbols. Others follow. It depends if the symbols are intended to lead or mislead."

"That is very true," Harry Singh admitted.

"Poor Dunne," Francis Long remarked, then took a long swallow of beer.

Harry Singh sighed, and continued:

"Mr Dunne used to come in here occasionally and drink like we are drinking today, but only because one of the clues was supposed to be up in this direction."

"Which clue, Mr Singh?"

"Ah, I say no more. You have paid your fifty rupees, but only for the map. . . not for information."

"Poor Graham Dunne," Francis Long repeated.

Harry Singh said: "If you ask me, he was only trying to get away from his bloody missus. . .What about you, Mr Walker?"

"I'm not married."

"You're not looking for the treasure?"

"No. I'm a journalist."

The merchant stood away slightly from the counter.

"I'm doing a feature story. Anyone who follows in Dunne's footsteps is - in my opinion - asking for trouble."

"Mine, too," Francis Long said.

"You are really a journalist?"

"Yes."

"You do not look like a journalist."

"Oh no? What *do* I look like."

"You look like a man who needs a haircut."

"You may be right."

"All right, then. What about you, Francis? I have more maps, but there are not many copies remaining. When you save up enough money, you can go looking for the treasure in your boat."

"-? -?"

"-But, for that, you will also need a map. For you, fifty rupees. Special price."

Francis Long replied: "No, thank you, Mr Singh. If Uncle Jeff found a map like this on me, he would throw me out of the hotel and into the sea."

"Mr Swann does not think there is any treasure? I would very much like to know what your uncle thinks on this subject."

"I cannot tell you what Uncle Jeff thinks," Francis Long said. "I can only tell you what *I* think."

"All right, that will have to do. What do you think?"

"Well, I don't think anything at all. It might be at the bottom of the ocean, for all I know. All I care about is the boat."

"Which is not yet yours," Harry Singh said.

"Soon enough; you'll see."

Harry Singh said: "Well, you have the map anyway, Mr Walker. That is something to be going on with."

Robert Walker folded the map into its reduced format, and placed it inside a breast-pocket. Francis Long, too, tucked the photograph of the boat away.

Robert Walker explained: "I'll keep it as a souvenir, and that's all."

"So you will not then be needing any extra equipment, Mr Walker?"

"What kind of equipment?"

"The usual things: pick and shovel, ropes, compass - maybe a donkey? Explosives?" Harry Singh added, and showed strong, white teeth.

"No, I won't be needing any of those things, Mr Singh."

"Oh," Harry Singh said, "then you won't be-?"

"-No, I won't be."

Harry Singh said: "All right, then. How about that haircut?"

After refusing so much, Robert Walker relented: "How much?"

The merchant glanced at the loose change on the counter: "Thirty rupees."

"All right, then."

The merchant took a step away from the counter, reached for a lever, and jerked. A traditional barbershop chair rotated - outwards, away from the store's wall - and snapped into place with a triple-click. The whole unit contained a great shaving mirror, various tonsorial apparatus, and racks of vials and jars with red, blue and green balm and lotions. Around the great mirror, there were paper cut-outs of vaguely erotic forms, set in a pastoral scene, with a goddess and several maidens in attendance. The kohl-eyed maidens of this heaven, if that is what it was, invited Robert Walker - through a gauze of diaphanous veils - to have his hair trimmed. In the circumstances, Robert Walker was pleased to accept.

Harry Singh pulled a rope, and a controlled shaft of sunlight entered a skylight in the palm-thatched roof - and illuminated the barbershop chair.

Harry Singh took a deep breath through his nostrils. "If you please, Mr Walker, step this way."

Robert Walker climbed into the seat. Francis Long merely watched as Harry Singh flipped-open a linen cloth. The merchant said: "Roger Dupin, the handyman. He built this barbershop for me a few Christmas's ago. Poor fellow."

Robert Walker looked through the sunlight and into the mirror: he did not know himself.

"Now, Mr Walker, make yourself comfortable."

Robert Walker felt the luxurious leather of the cool barber's chair.

"What's so funny, Francis?" Harry Singh snapped.

"Nothing, Mr Singh."

"Well, have another beer there, and keep quiet. I must have complete silence." Harry Singh prepared his instruments. "So, so, Mr Walker. We have established that you are not interested in treasure. What, then, shall we talk about?"

"I don't know."

"Ask me a question. Any question you like."

"Well . . ." Robert Walker considered.

"Yes? You have you question ready, Mr Walker?"

"They say you are an enemy of-."

"-Yes . . .?"

"- bureaucrats everywhere. Is this true?"

"An excellent question, Mr Walker. Yes, it is true, I am pleased to say. In fact, I am an enemy of both bureaucrats and bureaucracy in general."

"Why?"

"That's two questions."

"All right, then: please continue with the first question."

"Bureaucrats, by their very nature, are not to be trusted. These are what we might call the administrative classes, who live inside other people's pockets. . .When a politician says something like, 'We must fight bureaucracy', then what - I ask you, Mr Walker - is the first thing that happens?"

"A new department is set up - staffed by friends - to deal with the initiative - if ever it is implemented."

"Excellent, Mr Walker! You are a bloody genius, if you will excuse me for saying so! So, I say to you: show me a bureaucrat who wishes to cut back on bureaucracy, and I will show you either a fool or a liar."

"Thank you, Mr Singh."

"You are most welcome, Mr Walker."

"You may proceed with the haircut now, Mr Singh."

Harry Singh raised a set of battery-powered clippers, and set to work. Robert Walker could feel the metal teeth buzz over the nape of his neck.

"A light trim, Mr Singh, that's all for now."

"As you wish."

Robert Walker studied the barbershop unit. A miniature red-and-white striped barber's pole protruded, above the great mirror, over the heads of the goddess and her kohl-eyed maidens. The clippers buzz-buzzed. Robert Walker, in the deep comfort of the barber's seat, started to feel drowsy. . .The kohl-eyed maidens with blue-black hair and shell-white skin seemed to welcome him into their idyll. If not the inaccessible goddess, then one of her lovely maidens-! That one, there, with the smile-! Then he awoke:

"Any extras, sir?" Harry Singh was saying.

"No thank you, Mr Singh. Thanks anyway," and Robert Walker was asleep again.

"Our guest is prone to suggestion, Francis. It is very strange. I am quite sure he is not a journalist."

"What do you mean, Mr Singh?"

"Never mind what I mean, Francis. Now, what about you? I understand you are looking for a girl as well as a boat."

"Not just any girl."

"I have something that may be of help," Harry Singh explained.

"And what is that, Mr Singh?"

"Tiger pills," the merchant replied. "That fellow Mr Wilson was here in preparation for his trip to Mauritius, and-." Harry Singh held his tongue. He passed the sample to Francis Long.

"MADE IN HONG," Francis Long read. "These are for old men."

"You think so? Harry Singh whispered. "Have you ever met an English woman, Francis?"

Robert Walker started to wake up. Francis Long set the Tiger Pills well out of sight.

"Almost there, Mr Walker," Harry Singh continued "There is just one little lock of hair I've missed there on the side. Hold still now."

Robert Walker looked at his reflection: there were tears in his eyes, real tears, which rolled down his cheeks. Harry Singh saw his customer's tears for what they were, and smiled. This time, Robert Walker saw, not the kohl-eyed goddess pastoral, but Lady Gwendolyne or Gertrude.

In the reality of the general store, someone entered from the plantation. Robert Walker turned, and Harry Singh's clippers moved up and over his customer's scalp to create a deep groove. Two soldiers of the BIPDF or People's Militia had entered the store.

"Oh no! What have I done?" Harry Singh turned off the clippers, and tossed the device aside - out of sight.

The khaki-clad soldiers moved quickly through the store. They laughed as they approached the counter. Francis Long started to move away. "Stay where you are, boy!" one of the soldiers shouted.

The soldiers sweated, grunted, and positioned their weapons at the base of the counter.

"Don't move, I said!"

"I'm not moving," Francis Long complained.

"I saw you blink! Don't move and don't speak."

The other soldier said: "I know you, don't I?"

"No."

"I said don't speak," the first soldier said.

"He's one of these exiles," the one said to the other.

"Gentlemen?" Harry Singh asked.

"The People's Militia," the older of the two said, "are not known as gentlemen, Mr Singh."

"If you say so, sergeant," the merchant was pleased to agree.

Robert Walker wiped the moisture from his face. As he stood up from barbershop chair, he felt one side of his head. A deep furrow extended along the length of his left temple.

"No charge, Mr Walker," Harry Singh whispered.

"What's going on here?"

"This gentleman's just had a haircut, sergeant," the merchant explained.

"We can see that!" the corporal laughed. "Even in the militia, we don't have to go through that!" The corporal, who stared at Francis Long, laughed and then suddenly stopped.

The sergeant demanded: "Cold beer. Very cold, Mr Singh."

Harry Singh pulled a lever, and the barbershop unit triple-jerked and disappeared into the wall cavity.

"This is a madhouse," the sergeant remarked.

Robert Walker reached along the counter for his bottle of beer. The sergeant observed, hesitated, but said nothing. Harry Singh retrieved two more BourBrews from the cold-chest, and set the bottles up on the counter.

"That's twenty rupees," he said.

"The People's Militia, Mr Singh," the sergeant explained. "Plantation manoeuvres. Thirsty work. We don't carry cash."

The merchant did not say anything.

"This fellow here can pay," the corporal suggested.

"-?"

"Who are you, sir?"

"I'm a visitor to your island."

"I asked who are you - not what are you."

"Walker."

"Well, Mr Walker, what do you think of my corporal's suggestion?"

"I'd be happy to buy you a beer, sergeant, but I don't have any cash, either."

"Well, then."

Francis Long had not moved from his spot. Harry Singh still did not say anything.

"What's your recommendation, then, Mr Walker?"

"I do not have any recommendation, sergeant."

"You hear that, corporal? Mr Walker does not have any cash. He does not have any recommendation, either."

The corporal stared instead at Francis Long.

The sergeant asked: "What's that you've got in your pocket, Mr Walker?"

"Which pocket?"

"You know which pocket."

Harry Singh moved towards the portal.

"What are you doing, Mr Singh?"

The merchant kicked-open the portal.

"Hey! Hey!" the sergeant yelled.

Harry Singh explained to the troops: "These gentlemen were just leaving. Some urgent business in Port Bourbon, you understand."

The corporal grabbed his weapon: an advanced Kalashnikov model - or a play version of the same. There was something on the Bamboo Mill - that everything Soviet on the island was made of wood or rubber, including the naval base at Sans Souci Bay.

"What are you gong to do?" Robert Walker asked. "Shoot us? With that thing?"

"You don't think I'll use this?" corporal challenged. "I could poke out your ribs, mister!"

Francis Long and Robert Walker made for the portal. They jumped from the platform of the store, and landed on the floor of the plantation. Inside the store, there were some erratic movements - then silence.

The militia moved through the trees. In seconds, thirty or forty soldiers had surrounded the escapees from Harry Singh's General Store. Francis Long swayed from the place where he had landed, and was kicked back into place. The troops stared, sweated, and grunted. Robert Walker tried to look down the barrels of several more ersatz Kalishnikovs.

The troops crowded around until the two men were boxed-in.

"Got to be going now," Francis Long joked.

The rifles were replicas, but the butts were real. Francis Long took one across across the face, and collapsed onto the plantation floor - where he was kicked senseless. Soon, he was beyond pain. Robert Walker was next in line. Out of the trees, a young officer appeared in a tight, shrink-to-fit uniform:

"Okay, okay. At ease, men," and he swished the air with a rattan cane. *Swish, swish - swash.* "Okay, okay."

The militia relaxed, though by not much, and some of them drank from canteens; the soldiers closest Robert Walker smelt of toddy.

"What the hell's going on here?" The young officer removed sunglasses. "Who's that there lying down on the job?"

"Francis Long, sir."

"Oh, I hardly recognised him. Fall down and have an accident, did he?"

"Yes, sir - he ran straight into that tree there, sir, and then fell down and smashed his face, sir."

"I see, I see. Well, the girls won't be looking at him now, will they?"

The soldiers cackled and made anatomical remarks.

"Bloody civilians, see. Weak-minded. Weak-willed. A puff of wind, and they all fall down. No fibre."

The group of soldiers listened to what the young officer had to say.

"This is an excellent job you men have done up here on the plantation. I told you, see? This place in not haunted - unless by spies."

The troops were less sure now; with nervous giggles, they cast dark glances into the trees in the vicinity.

"And - what - do - we - have - here?"

The soldiers around Robert Walker parted.

"Nice haircut," the officer observed. "The girls won't be looking at you, either."

Robert Walker realised he had taken a blow on each of his kidneys. His legs weakened, buckled, and he fell to his knees.

"You see?" the officer gestured. "The slightest puff of wind, and these civilians are over."

The soldiers cackled, snorted, and some spat.

The young officer pressed the rattan cane against Robert Walker's forehead, and continued the lecture: "But this is no ordinary civilian, men. This is a spy. A real spy. A plantation spy."

The officer moved closer, and - with arrogant, over-promoted eyes - looked into Robert Walker's face. Robert Walker saw a double-flash of light behind his face, and he was over. Dry palm fronds tickled and stuck to his face. A sweet, metallic taste filled his mouth. The floor of the plantation was springy under his weight. He rolled over - a pig among truffles - and stared up at the forest canopy. A flash of wet fire splashed across his face and into his eyes. Stale toddy washed from a soldier's canteen.

The young officer stooped to whisper: "Welcome to paradise."

Documents were passed among the soldiers. A photograph of a boat. Not much of a boat, but a boat all the same - probably stolen or about to be stolen. A map. A spy's map. Out of date by a long way, though.

"A beach boy," a voice observed, "who is now nothing more than a junior officer in the People's Militia."

It was Harry Singh who spoke from the open portal. The merchant looked down on the soldiers from the raised platform of the store.

"Ah, Mr Singh, no less."

"What are you doing here?"

The soldiers aimed their mock rifles at the merchant. The young officer waved his rattan cane, and the rifles drooped.

"I am an officer, as you say, in the People's Militia. I am usually addressed as sir."

"Not by me. I know who are you, Tommy Jones. A delinquent in a tight-fitting uniform who likes to beat up civilians for no reason. As I've always suspected, there is no substitute for hard work or a good upbringing. Your father would be ashamed of you. What are you doing here?"

"You talk too much, store keeper."

"Again, I ask: why are you here?"

"Two of my men are missing."

"Funny you should say that: two of my customers are missing."

"Where are my men?"

"Behind you."

"Where are the two soldiers who came this way, and then disappeared?"

Harry Singh, who had a stick or rod of his own, waved it over his shoulder:

"They're inside. Too much to drink. They're sleeping it off now, Tommy-boy."

"You would call men that in front of my men?"

"I would."

The young officer moved a free hand over the holster-flap of his side-arm. Instead, he swished the rattan cane through the air - *swash*.

Harry Singh laughed at the posturing.

The young officer signalled that Robert Walker, who groaned just then, should be made unconscious.

Harry Singh jumped from the platform, landed on the plantation floor, and waved his stick. The bamboo totem was wrapped with different coloured yarns, with black and white feathers attached at intervals along the shaft. Instead of the brass-cap of the officer's cane, the stick was fitted with lapis lazuli.

"What the hell is that thing, Mr Singh?" Captain Tommy Jones wanted to know.

Harry Singh raised the totem so that it was visible to the troops. The militia became unsettled.

"You must be joking, Mr Singh," Captain Tommy Jones snorted. "A ju-ju stick?"

"Call it whatever you like," Harry Singh advised. "Now, hand over that map, which does not belong to you. Then you can help me take both these injured men to the Infirmary at Port Bourbon."

"You made this yourself!"

"You have your cane," the merchant explained, "and I have this stick. It was a personal gift to me from Dr Mobuto."

"Dr Mobuto?" Tommy Jones asked. "I thought he was gone - back to Zanzibar?"

"Oh yes, but he has returned."

"You can't fool anyone with that thing. Don't you know that those days have gone, Mr Singh?"

"And so have your men, Tommy."

Harry Singh's laugh was heard, though not by by the People's Militia, throughout that part of the plantation.

11

A VISITOR AT PORT BOURBON INFIRMARY

"SO, IT HAS come to this, has it?"

Mr Swann, his face stiff with anger, had arrived unannounced at Port Bourbon Infirmary.

"Beaten up," the hotelier summarised, "by the forces of the state - and now fixed-up by the state." He bit at his lip, but felt no pain.

A petite nurse in a starched white uniform attended Mr Swann, who surveyed the two beds occupied by Francis Long and Robert Walker.

On the wall, a portrait of François Bellarmine watched over the patients: robust stevedores; sturdy plantation workers; lithe, well-muscled fishermen.

The ward was more popular even than Mr Swann's Marina Hotel or Silent Pete' Bar at the habour. A big nurse appeared - the ward sister:

"Mr Swann, is it? This is not an hotel. This is an infirmary. This is not visiting hours. These two patients are, anyway, not permitted visitors."

Mr Swann ignored the woman. The ward sister whispered - loudly - into the petite nurse's ear, and went in search of a strong-armed porter. The hotelier folded his arms, and looked down at the sheen of his patent-leather shoes all the way from Hong Kong.

"So. So much for free health care," Mr Swann observed. "The only difference is that you two are actually in need of treatment."

The petite nurse covered her mouth.

"Yes, it is all very amusing, Nurse Dupin. Look at the state of them. My own nephew, who does not surprise me; I am aware of his pre-disposition for misadventure. But you, Mr Walker: you have been on this island for twenty-four hours only, and look what happens. . ."

Robert Walker tried not to move; Francis Long could not move.

"As for you, Francis, I would not even have recognised you. Sometimes I wonder if you are my nephew at all."

Francis Long's eyes showed through the mask of bandages. Again the petite nurse - Nurse Dupin - covered her mouth.

Mr Swann continued his assessment: "The girl Danielle has taken over your shift. Perhaps I should let her take over your wages as well."

Francis Long reacted; a bone lightning-rod conducted white sheets of pain through his jaw.

"Ah, so you are still alive, after all."

Francis Long's tortured eyes stared out from behind bandages.

The big ward sister reappeared; she had failed to find assistance. She pressed in between Mr Swann and the petite Nurse Dupin.

"Their injuries are cosmetic," the big nurse insisted.

Nurse Dupin moved to Robert Walker's bedside.

"My God, woman," Mr Swann retorted: "I wonder at your definition of a *serious* injury. "

The big nurse bridled, saying, "I am not to be referred to as 'woman', Mr Swann. I am to be called-."

Mr Swann said: "Cosmetic, you say?"

The petite nurse made dab-dabbing movements all over Robert Walker's face.

"Those," the big nurse replied, "are the words of Dr Marigold."

Mr Swann's faced reddened: "Dr Marigold? Really? Does he still have a licence to practise medicine on this island?"

The big nurse, outraged by the remark, stood away from the hotelier, who added: "I will not have that man near my employees or my guests."

"Dr Marigold has dedicated many years of his life to the sick and infirm of this island, Mr Swann. You, who are never sick, perhaps do not appreciate that."

"I do not have time to be sick." Mr Swann said. "Unlike most of the patients on your ward."

At the far end of the ward, the stevedores grumbled, while the plantation workers - a more placid group - stared at the man in the white suit, the two nurses, and the two men who had been beaten-up by the People's Militia. A rumour had spread over the island that these two fellows here had frightened away the entire BIPDF by themselves alone. It was, a dock worker behind a screen volunteered, better than television. A man with a mop and a bucket remarked that anything was better than BIRTV. The plantation workers and stevedores all laughed. That was the first time, the man with the mop said, he had heard anyone laugh on that ward for years, and went back to his work.

"You are having an unsettling effect on the ward, Mr Swann. I must ask you to leave."

"Ask away."

"You surprise me, Mr Swann. You used to be such a polite gentleman."

The hotelier regarded the woman, and shook his head. "We do not," he said, "live in polite times, sister."

"I am matron, not sister."

"As you wish. Now, if you succeed in finding Dr Marigold, please inform him that I shall be observing these patients on a regular basis. You understand? I would not want them to meet with an unfortunate accident while in the care of the good doctor."

"You have no authority here, Mr Swann," the matron retaliated. "Your comments will be reported to-."

"-The Party? Oh yes - I know."

The little nurse, Nurse Dupin, pretended not to listen - Robert Walker saw - to every word of this exchange. In the next bed, Francis Long's eyes bulged at his uncle's unusually provocative manner.

The big nurse stared at Mr Swann, and then withdrew to an administration area to make an urgent telephone call. Where - oh where - was Dr Marigold?

"So, Francis," Mr Swann whispered, "perhaps it would have been better if you had stayed in exile, after all."

Nurse Dupin's eyes widened; she hastily applied ointment to the groove somewhere - there - along the side Robert Walker's head.

"Cosmetic, indeed," Mr Swann fumed. "I know very well what she would mean by non-cosmetic: injuries resulting in death. Injuries, shall we say, from which the patient stands no chance of recovery. You two will recover, therefore your injuries are cosmetic." One side of the hotelier's face had returned to its usual stiff smile.

Francis Long's bandage-mask had become irritable. He shifted against an unscratchable itch, and felt more pain. "Ahhhhhg," he groaned, which exerted unwanted pressure on his shattered ribcage. "Ahh."

Nurse Dupin stood up from the bedside, smiled at Mr Swann, and disappeared into a darkened corridor. The ward sister looked up from her futile telephone call, and realised she was alone.

Mr Swann continued: "Oh yes, now you suffer. You take one of our guests up to the plantation, and look what happens." The hotelier seemed to wince with anxiety. "All I can say is, thank God things are not worse than they are. You know what those militia are like. The two of you could have been killed. Now they are saying the pair of you are heroes; that you stood up to the Bourbon Island People's Defence Force all by yourselves. Well, we all know what happens to heroes on this island, don't we? I say no more about it."

Francis Long could not speak and Robert Walker did not try to speak.

The big nurse approached, and advised: "If you please, Mr Swann, there will be no talk of killing on this ward."

"-?"

"You'll upset the other patients."

"The only thing that would upset these fellows, matron, is a hard day's work."

The big nurse, who seemed to agree, dipped her eyelashes at Mr Swann's patent leather shoes.

"Now, where was I?"

Francis Long grunted; he was trying to say something, but every time he tried to speak, the pain intensified.

Mr Swann said: "Be still, Francis, if you want to get better. Recover quickly; there is plenty of work to do. Now, if you cannot speak, listen: I must go back to the hotel. Before I go, there is one question."

Francis Long and Robert Walker looked at Mr Swann through their swollen eyes.

"Mr Walker, who shaved your hair like this? It was part of the torture? The soldiers did this to you?"

, Robert Walker found his voice: "No, Mr Swann, it was Harry Singh. He gave me a haircut for thirty rupees."

The hotelier and the big nurse looked at each other.

Francis Long's chest heaved; his eyes welled-up, and he howled with the pain.

12

WELCOME TO RADIO BOURBON

"WELCOME TO RADIO Bourbon Island, listeners. This is your old friend Johnny Savvy here again, who these days is no longer making government announcements or playing songs nobody likes . . . Johnny Savvy is his own man. So, this next song is called '_____'. I am sure many of our older listeners will remember that this was the favourite song of . . . Anthony Montaigne . . . the first president of our island republic.

"This is also the first time the song has been broadcast on the BIRTV network for many years, so we are especially pleased . . .to be able to play it once more . . .on this beautiful early Saturday evening . . . as we listen to the voice of _____ . . ."

Inside the small studio, the turntable spun, the acetate crackled . . .and Johnny Savvy sat away from the control panel. The sweat streamed from the DJ's bright, shiny face. The voice of the station controller came over the headphones: *"I know you're taking a qualified risk, but it's your risk. I'm outta here."* Qualified? They might kill him for his trouble. The Party newspaper had probably already prepared the copy: DJ IN FISHING ACCIDENT. . . Outside the acoustic insulation of the studio, a basement door slammed, and the (former) studio controller fled.

In that interval, the people of Port Bourbon listened to static . . .On that hot August evening, the radio waves emanated from the government-controlled transmitter, up on Mont Pomme d'Or, to reach an audience that included: high up in his dacha, a cigar-smoking François Bellarmine, resplendent in a fan-backed bamboo chair, with a woman at his side; the assorted guests at the Marlin Room of the Marina Hotel; the regulars at Silent Pete's Bar; the hardened *apparatchiks* at BIPP headquarters; Chief Bugis and his constables at the Victoria Road Police Station; Harry Singh's crowded store on the plantation; and - far out at sea - the crew of a passing ship, who heard only the tropical crackle and hiss of the station's carrier wave.

This was free expression, not of the printed variety as espoused by the exiled *Bourbon Island Star*, but an audible, tentative start to a new era of broadcasting for the island republic. Johnny Savvy was a made man or a dead man. That very night, there was a promise - or not - of a tidal wave of political change, but only if Bellarmine permitted the broadcast, for the mostly good-natured islanders - as the BIPP well knew - would never rise up against the regime.

In the dacha, a woman's hand pressed against Bellarmine's shoulder, and so the broadcast was allowed to continue.

At the radio station, Robert Walker realised he was next on air. As the show's special guest, the radio station's hostess had escorted him into Johnny Savvy's overheated studio. A girl called Sylvia in a blue silk dress, she looked somehow familiar. Robert Walker, though, could not recall where he might have seen her before today.

"There you are, friends," the DJ announced: "we're still here, after all. The Johnny Savvy Show stays ON-AIR!"

Robert Walker touched, self-consciously, the side of his head, where he felt the overgrown groove left by Harry Singh's clippers. John Savvy observed, and said:

"A close shave, listeners, but let us press on into the evening. I am staying on duty - twenty-four hours. Until-."

That - the DJ decided - was going to too far. "Yes, until."

Johnny Savvy's hands shook. The old acetate skidded-off the turntable, and hit the deck.

"Okay, sorry about that, folks. A slippery record, all right. Now-."

The announcer had forgotten his script.

"Oh yes, and now -."

Outside the studio, someone thumped on the main door. The People's Militia? The Police Force? Agents of the BIPP? Robert Walker looked through the soundproof glass screen: the hostess answered, and turned away a man with a mop and a bucket. A cleaner, that was all, ready to start his shift. The DJ looked as though his heart had stopped.

The hostess, Sylvia, returned to her desk, and signalled her colleague.

The 18:05 interview commenced:

"Now . . .listeners, we come to our special guest this evening. . ."

Robert Walker sipped at a cupful of sugar-cane juice provided by the hostess.

". . .all the way from London. Welcome, Mr Walker, to Radio Bourbon, the Voice of the Island."

"Thank you, and Good Evening, Mr Savvy."

Johnny Savvy's expression was that of man who had been allowed to live. "Yes, it is a good evening, that's for sure. . ."

Again, the DJ had forgotten his script. The hostess signalled through the screen that he should look at his cue sheet; he did so:

"Ah, yes, now, as our regular listeners will know, we have many unusual visitors to our island from all over the world. Explorers, big game fishermen, stamp dealers, and so on. And this evening we are speaking with - a treasure hunter, -."

Robert Walker interjected: "That's a journalist, not a treasure hunter. I'd like to get that straight from the outset."

"Well, you've put me straight, all right, Mr Walker." Johnny Savvy checked with his cue sheet, then frowned through the screen. The hostess was applying clear lacer to her fingernails.

"You are then-?"

Robert Walker helped out: "I'm here to write a feature story about Graham Dunne. I'm not looking for the treasure itself. That would be quite a different thing."

"Yes, yes, I can see that it would, Mr Walker." John Savvy chuckled; his shiny face beamed under the dim lights of the studio.

"I mean to say, the treasure may not even exist. Whether it exists or not, I still have my feature."

Johnny Savvy brooded; a few silent moments passed. Around the island, and out at sea, listeners everywhere looked at each other.

"That may be so," the DJ continued, "but there are rumours - we call it the Bamboo Mill here - that you are following in the footsteps of the Englishman."

"What happened to Graham Dunne is very sad. That is one good reason not to follow in his footsteps."

The hostess by the name of Sylvia looked up from her nail lacer.

"Well, I can see what you mean, Mr Walker, but you have not really answered my question."

"I've said it before, and I'll say it again. I am not here looking for the treasure of the pirate 'La Buse' - or anyone else's treasure. . . It is an interesting story, about the Fiery Cross of Goa, and it is part of your island's history. As I say, I am employed by my press agency to cover the story - not to look for treasure. I am not interested in looking for the treasure. I do not have the resources to undertake such an expedition. Graham Dunne spent ten years on his quest. I am here for fifteen days only."

Johnny Savvy found his wits: "Some people say the entire story has been fabricated to promote tourism."

"Then the story is not working. I have not met any tourists here at all."

"I meant, the future tourism industry. The traditional industries are in decline. Tourism is the way of the future."

"My research to date indicates that the story of the Fiery Cross of Goa is not a fabrication. Whether the artefact is here on not is another matter."

"Where, then?"

"I don't know. Madagascar. Seychelles."

Quickly, Savvy observed: "Even if you are not looking for the Fiery Cross, you might find it by accident."

"In my opinion, that is the only way anyone would find it."

Johnny Savvy laughed into the microphone. The girl in the blue silk dress smiled through the studio screen. She was, Robert Walker realised, a *doppelgönger* for Nurse Dupin at the Port Bourbon Infirmary.

"You see, Mr Walker, how people would misinterpret your motives?"

"Perhaps it's time you played another record."

"-?! In due course, Mr Walker. Now-?" The microphone hid Johnny Savvy's nervous grin. The hostess - Sylvia Dupin, it had to be her - was preparing to leave the station. An urgent appointment elsewhere?

"-There is another rumour that you have a treasure hunting permit in your possession. How do you respond to that?"

"I have no such permit in my possession."

"Oh really? I understood that-?"

"-You have been misinformed," Robert Walker said.

Sylvia Dupin was about ready to abandon the studio. She waved through the glass screen at Johnny Savvy and Robert Walker.

Johnny Savvy considered his whereabouts - a glass cage - prison.

"If I might explain?" Robert Walker posed.

"Please do, Mr Walker."

"In my opinion, such an endeavour is futile. Naturally, I say this with all deference to Graham Dunne's family. But his story, I think, should be taken as a warning."

John Savvy cued the next record.

"What about the clues?" the DJ asked.

"Why leave any clues at all?" Robert Walker replied. "Why, unless to mislead? Why follow twelve clues when you could go straight to Clue Number Twelve?"

"Yes, perhaps you are right, Mr Walker. Thank you for coming all this way to talk with me. So, listeners, this next record is a very special request for my auntie in Sans Souci. Strangers on the Shore, by Mr Aker Bilk."

"-?"

13

SILENT PETE GREETS THE PRESS

IT WAS A fine, balmy evening, cooled by the trade wind from the south west, and the curfew had been imposed.

Almost fifteen years' ago, the curfew had been François Bellarmine's first decree. It remained unpopular with nearly everyone, except for Chief Bugis, who derived considerable authority from its enforcement, with the erratic support of the militia, and that part of the population - about 10 per cent - who were members of the Bourbon Island People's Party.

The exiled *Bourbon Island Star* said that fifteen years of the decree was long enough. Dissidents who remained underground, such as the faceless local editor of *The Black Turtle!*, pointed out that the exiles were not affected by the decree any more than Bellarmine and his stooges. This exemplified the conflict of opinion, between the many anti-Bellarmine factions at home and abroad, which guaranteed the regime's grip on power. Each of the underground factions was almost as jealous of each other as they were of the BIPP, though they were not jealous any more of Jacques Savvy who - the wits at Silent Pete's observed - resided permanently underground. Outside of Silent Pete's, no one spoke of Jacques Savvy any more.

In recent days, through some creeping process, the enforcement of the decree had been noticeably relaxed - or ignored. Chief Bugis and his special constables had made some arrests, to set an example, but it was clear that transgressors would soon fill the jails of Port Bourbon if this policy continued - and so all of the curfew-breakers had been released. A pamphleteer, however - who had misjudged the moment - had not been seen since his arrest. The BIPP elite, *The Black Turtle!* warned, were not about to surrender their hard-grabbed privileges so easily.

So, Robert Walker left the studio *after* curfew-hour, and went unmolested. Charlie the Fish, the boy-spy who would betray a man for a gob-stopper, waited outside the BIRTV station. The boy had a toy radio at his ear, and pretended to listen-in on the broadcast.

"You found any treasure yet, Mistah Robert?"

The toy radio, he suspected, had been a bribe. "I'm not looking for any treasure, Charlie. Now, why don't you go home?"

"My Papa wants to talk to you about the treasure, Mistah Robert."

"He sent you over here?"

"I was just walkin' by, Mistah Robert."

"Why don't you go home, Charlie?"

"Yankee Go Home!" The boy laughed, then pretended to tune-into another radio station.

Robert Walker ignored the boy. The final descent of the sun cast dark shadows along Pedro Mascarenhas Street. He turned, but the boy and his radio had gone. He started along Victoria Street. There was no way to avoid the Police Station, except by trespass over a hurdle of private garden walls, so he passed the general police block - unchallenged. Inside the station, the electric strip-lights of 24-hour administration buzzed, while papers shuffled and chairs scraped over concrete floors. A powerful smell of curry wafted onto the street. It was almost time for dinner, though for Chief Bugis it was almost always time for dinner.

Robert Walker reached the intersection with Revolution Boulevard. Beyond the crossroads, the Marina Hotel looked busier than usual. The British Leyland bus pulled-up opposite the hotel. A group of reporters and photographers bounced-off the bus, and crossed the road. On the steps, a photographer tripped over the loose plank, and head-butted a colleague between the shoulder-blades. The rabble poured into the lobby. So far unobserved by the press, Robert Walker instead headed in the direction of the harbour. The radio interview with Johnny Savvy had left him thirsty. The BourBrew bottling plant was silent except for a few crates being shifted. A man emerged from the loading bay, and wiped the sweat from his face. He gave Robert Walker the thumbs-up, and then returned to the crates with a smile. The treasure, the Bamboo Mill reported, was to close to being found.

The establishment known as Silent Pete's Bar overlooked the grey, oil-filmed waters of the harbour. Every berth in the harbour was empty. The oily grey water took on a silver sheen. The orange disc of the sun dipped into the ocean. From Silent Pete's, yellow lights shone over the black surface of the deserted harbour. Maritime commerce might be slack, but trade at Silent Pete's was booming.

Robert Walker stepped inside. By the bar, Morgan Beaumont cast the longest shadow. One the other side of the bar, the landlord - Silent Pete - did not say anything. Robert Walker could feel real sawdust beneath his feet. An advance party of foreign correspondents had already established a private drinking club in a corner of the room. The correspondents were too busy chattering and joking to notice anything. There were other cliques gathered around tables or perched at the bar. Stevedores, warehousemen, plantation workers, and idlers laughed at old jokes, or whispered widely-known secrets at each other. The older men stared into the middle distance or at the floor. On a wall over the doorway, a flaxen-haired Englishman stared out from a cheaply-framed photograph. Robert Walker recognised the man as Graham Dunne of Southend-on-Sea. Of François Bellarmine's official portrait, there was no evidence.

"Robert - here - join me for a beer."

The group of foreign correspondents had become aware of the encounter.

An Australian expatriate in his late fifties, Silent Pete revealed _himself as pustule-faced, beer-gutted, and strong-armed. The landlord reached for the controls of a big radio, and turned-off the set.

"We've all been listening," the American related, "to your broadcast."

The Australian landlord grinned, but did not - of course - say anything. Morgan Beaumont signalled that he wanted two more beers, and the landlord set them up. A good evening was in store, for sure; sales of beer had already exceeded projections. An emergency consignment was being arranged. Silent Pete's face showed all this without a word being spoken.

Morgan Beaumont paid for the beer. The Australian turned away to tend a thirsty cutting crew at the other side of the bar.

"Hasn't spoken for years, not since-."

"So I understand."

"Pete's intimated that he won't speak again until-. Well, I'll follow his example, and say no more."

One among the foreign correspondents had taken a step closer. A bald-headed young man with thick glasses, Robert Walker recognised the fellow as a hack from *The Telegraph* of London.

"What are you doing here, Morgan?" Robert Walker asked.

"Having a beer or two."

"I meant, on the island?"

"I'm on assignment. I was on assignment, anyway, until . . .I haven't been feeling myself lately."

"You've lost weight."

"I walk plenty."

The bald-headed fellow had recognised Morgan Beaumont.

"Excuse me, Mr Beaumont?"

"Not now," Beaumont said without looking at the man from *The Telegraph*. A cheer erupted from the group of stevedores. A bet had been placed - and won or lost.

"Excuse me, Mr B-."

"I said not now."

A pustule-faced Silent Pete stared until *The Telegraph*-man had backed-off to rejoin the group of correspondents. The landlord looked as though he might speak, but then said nothing.

Robert Walker glanced over at the group, and was recognised by the bald-headed reporter.

"Pete intimates that there's going to be trouble."

"Why's that, Morgan?"

"They don't like journalists around here."

"What about you?"

"I'm with you."

"What about me?"

"They won't touch you."

"Why not?

"They think you're looking for the treasure."

"-."

"Don't tell anyone you're not looking for the treasure, okay?"

"But on the radio, I said that-."

"-They think you're bluffing."

"What about those fellows over there?"

"Well, they're all in trouble, aren't they?"

Silent Pete had given the signal to a group of stevedores around the table where the bet had been won or lost.

The man from *The Telegraph* had his magnified eyes fixed on Robert Walker.

"What's up?"

"I think I've been recognised."

"So, what about it? A Fleet Street colleague, that's all."

"I don't want to be recognised."

"Why ever not?" Morgan Beaumont had a good look at Robert Walker. "You're one of these special correspondents, aren't you?"

"I can't say."

The bald-headed man from *The Telegraph* crossed the room. On the way, he took out a notebook, and licked at his limp moustache.

"You're British, aren't you? Have we met before-?"

"No, I don't think so."

"We've been listening to your broadcast. Haven't we, Mr Beaumont?"

The American did not respond.

"Listen," Robert Walker explained, "I don't have anything to say to you."

"Yes, yes, of course." The man from *The Telegraph* fixed his glassy, bug-eyes on Robert Walker. The journalist removed the glasses, which revealed the same-size bug-eyes. Robert Walker studied his glass of beer: Blue Marlin, all the way from Mauritius.

"I think we've met before, you know."

"I have no recollection."

"I just can't place you. It'll come to me in a moment. Until then, I'd like to ask you a few questions about the Fiery Cross of Goa and all that."

"What is this?" Beaumont complained. "The press interviewing the press?"

Silent Pete grinned at the smoke-yellowed ceiling.

The bald man said: "Well, I don't see how-? You mean you're a-."

"If you don't mind," Robert Walker said. "I've said what I wanted to say on the Johnny Savvy Show."

"The story goes. . .that you represent a Franco-German syndicate with some sort of London tie-in . . .that has been formed to look for the treasure, not just the Fiery Cross, but the rest of the hoard, too. One hundred million dollars - *at least* - in gold and silver." The journalist's glassy eyes sparkled. "Really, Mr Walker, while you've been confined to this island, you have no idea how big this story has become in the world outside. I had assumed you were a geographer of some sort. But come to think of it-."

Robert Walker said nothing.

"Yes, I remember now. You were with-." The man from *The Telegraph* hesitated. "Oh, oh. Vincent Mosley. It's Harry Stone's show now, isn't it? The Shoe Lane Agency. You're not a journalist, you're-? There's something not quite right about all of this."

"I'll have to ask you not to say anything more."

"If you're not here about the treasure, then you must be here to-."

Robert Walker asked: "Who told you about the treasure?"

"You can't expect me to divulge my sources, old boy. That's not on."

The man's exposed head was covered with sweat.

"'Old boy?' You been talking to Wilson, haven't you?"

"I don't know who you mean."

"John Wilson, the international stamp dealer."

The bald-headed man leered at Robert Walker, then withdrew to rejoin his colleagues. Silent Pete signalled at the stevedores' table where the bet had been made. The group of men set down their drinks, and stood up from the table. In the corner, the foreign correspondents were unaware of the development. Then: Silent Pete signalled with his eyes - not yet, not yet - and the stevedores returned to their table. A pair of local men entered with a giant PYE television set.

"Pete intimates," Beaumont explained, "that a presidential broad-cast is imminent. Can't miss that now, can we?"

The landlord set-up the television on the centre of the bar. One of the locals plugged the unit into a wall socket; another man configured the aerial; and the Australian twisted the controls.

"That's what I like to see," Beaumont observed. "Teamwork."

Then: "It's got to be Wilson," Robert Walker concluded. "He talks too much."

"That stamp dealer who was here?"

"That's him: John Wilson, Esquire. He must have returned to London from Mauritius. Once in London, he contacted the press. The media will drive up the value of his Fiery Cross stamp."

"How so?"

"By telling the gentlemen in the corner there that the treasure is close to being found."

"That's one thing you can always rely on: rabid self-interest."

Silent Pete had waved for complete silence. Every head in the tavern crowded around the television. Above the main doorway, even the photograph of Graham Dunne seemed to stare in that direction. The foreign correspondents would end up in the harbour, all right, but not until the transmission was over. The landlord had almost located the island's only channel. The television showed static, which cleared to show a light grey screen. The landlord thumped the clapped-out PYE, and the image revealed:

BIRTV

CHANNEL ONE

Silent Pete, whose bright green eyes were lit-up by the flickering screen, folded his arms, and stood to one side. A female voice-over from cold storage announced:

"*Comrades, we are this evening privileged to listen to our own President François Bellarmine as he addresses his people from the National Stadium . . .on his return from the archipelago of Indonesia, where he personally negotiated a successful treaty in respect of cooperation and trade. . . "*

Out of nowhere, a black & white image of François Bellarmine appeared. The clientele of Silent Pete's did not pass any remark. The stevedores watched the foreign correspondents, who in turn watched Ballarmine.

"*The announcement this evening, however, concerns the mercenaries who invaded these peaceful shores only weeks ago. Comrades, our leader speaks to you directly by live broadcast. . ."*

There followed what sounded like a pre-recorded roar of approval. The television image cut sharply away from Bellarmine's head and shoulders. Stock film, cleverly done but not seamless, had been spliced into the programme to show the National Stadium packed with an ecstatic, cheering, arm-waving crowd of men, women and children - the same stadium, but at an earlier time of day or on some other day on another occasion. A sporting event? The Indian Ocean Games?

The film-splice jumped, and the real-time camera went into a sudden, cack-handed close-up of François Bellarmine.

The face of the president dominated every television screen on Bourbon Island: the portable colour screen out at Harry Singh's General Store; the Russian-made screens at Sans Souci Naval Base; the Japanese-made screens at the USAF satellite tracking station; and on the Dynatron -

by HM Appointment - screen at the British High Commission; and - set up by Francis Long - a portable screen at the Marina Hotel.

On this PYE screen at Silent Pete's, François Bellarmine accepted the contrived adulation as his due. Among the plantation workers, there were dangerous whispers of dissent.

"My fellow Bourbons. . ."

The crowd, on the television at least, went crazy. François Bellarmine urged his countrymen to hold onto their seats. The camera did not pan too far across the real-life audience behind their president.

The President of the Republic stared - unflinching - into the hot, glassy eye of the camera, and said:

"My fellow Bourbons. . .I have only today returned to you from a journey I made to the islands of the great Indonesian archipelago, where I attended the Non-Aligned Movement conference in Jakarta.

"I could not help but notice that, while our Indonesian friends have thirteen-thousand, six-hundred and seventy-seven islands, fate or geology has decreed that we Bourbons have only one island. . ."

"He's gone loco!" a stevedore volunteered. No one agreed or disagreed. Silent Pete remained steady - there was the question of his licence - and, true to form, said nothing.

On the screen, the stadium crowd seemed to have gone home *en masse.* A sleepy cadre in the group behind Bellarmine yawned - then sat upright.

". . . But their President Suharto was good enough to tell me that we have this in common: we are both great island nations!"

The response of the stadium audience: silence. The select BIPP entourage behind Bellarmine performed a polite, rehearsed applause. An off-screen rent-a-crowd joined in, but the applause degenerated into an erratic hand-clap. Off-screen, the BIRTV-BIPP media coordinator had missed his cue. Bellarmine smirked where he had meant to smile, and his eyes lost focus. The stadium crowd roared - at nothing. A sound engineer silenced the mob with a single twirl of a dial.

Bellarmine looked into the BIRTV camera, and continued:

"Now, my fellow islanders, with that thought in mind, let me turn to the main point I wish to convey to you this evening . . .

"I have had good cause to think deeply on the subject of the attempted coup against our country. At first, I was of the view that I should take my own counsel and hand the invaders over to the judiciary. . .for proper trial and sentencing. . .while others advised me that the people should decide."

The audience listened, confused. Decide? Who are we to decide? Decide what? In Silent Pete's, some of the warehousemen had started to fidget. The television camera cut away from Bellarmine: another splice of stock-film revealed the central field of the National Stadium bathed in powerful spotlights. A group of men - with their hands bound behind their backs - were shown on their knees. A frantic crowd seemed to bay for the disposal of the prisoners - mercenaries to a man. An executioner waited nearby. In his hands, a garrotte. The executioner looked up at the crowd for a decision.

The BIRTV camera cut to a close-up of the five condemned men, the remnants of Alfonse Trouvères' invasion force. The captive mercenaries were shown as nothing more than half-starved scarecrows in rags, sweating, bruised and bloodied. Deprived of sleep, their heads hung low, ready - by chance - for the garrotte. Then the splice broke, and flickered. The picture cut back to an angry François Bellarmine, who barked into a clutch of microphones:

"*These are the criminals who would despoil our shores! These are the adventurers who would take your freedom from you, the people! So, it is the people who shall decide the sentence! What is your sentence?*"

"*Death! Death! DEATH!*" the crowd roared.

The camera zoomed over Bellarmine's shoulder. The rent-a-crowd fanatics of the Bourbon Island People's Party seemed to agree:

"*DEATH! Oh yes - DEATH! DEATH, is it . . ?*"

In Silent Pete's Bar, the stevedores became agitated. They swallowed more BourBrew, and showed signs of instability. Another bet had been placed - and won or lost - and it was time to act. The winner of the wager looked at the landlord for a signal. Not yet, those bright-green eyes indicated, but soon: the broadcast is almost done. Then it was done: the transmission had failed, and the screen of the big PYE television showed:

POGROM WILL
BE RESUMED SOON

Next: *Sea Hunt* with Lloyd Bridges

The female voice-over from cold storage said:

"The outside broadcast has . . .run into some technical difficulties caused by sun spots. The president has decided to continue his address to the nation from the State House studio later this evening. Thank you for watching-."

The sound had failed, too. After an interval, the screen reverted to its natural static. Silent Pete laughed - though he did not say anything - then flicked-off the PYE set all together.

The clientele cheered: "Sunspots! Sea Hunt! Beer, more beer!"

"I'll drink to that," Morgan Beaumont remarked. "What about you, Robert?"

In the corner, the man from *The Telegraph* was ready to consolidate his exclusive angle on Robert Walker, but by then Silent Pete had already signalled the stevedores. These men had worked hard, and were thirsty for entertainment. A large, muscle-bound stevedore asked the man from *The Telegraph:*

"You know the way to the harbour, man?"

"Oh God, no." The bald-headed journalist removed his spectacles. The first of the foreign correspondents was escorted to the dark waters of the harbour.

"I'll see you back at the hotel, Morgan," Robert Walker said.

*

IN THE NATIONAL Stadium, no one except a handful of die-hard BIPP supporters and technicians heard what Bellarmine had to say next:

"My friends, we have known fear, and now these invaders know fear. Now let me say this to you: these men here are but pawns of powerful forces. I proclaim the death penalty, not on these men, only on Alfonse Trouvères. . .their leader who has abandoned them. Trouvères is now in jail where he belongs. Let the French authorities deal with Trouvères as they see fit, but let him not set a foot on these shores again!"

"Death to Trouvères!" a BIPP cheer-leader shouted. Out in the darkness of the wider stadium, there was no sound from the great terraces of empty seats.

François Bellarmine smirked, shrugged his shoulders, and continued:

"As for these so-called mercenaries, I say death is too good for them! If they had been lucky, they would have died like men - these Chiens de Guerre! I say, Chiens only!"

"Now, in the days when I was a young lawyer, -. "

A wave of laughter passed through the group of BIPP faithful.

"We'll have to stop you there, sir. Technical difficulties."

"Very well, then. How did it go?"

"It went very, very well, sir," a voice from the darkness replied.

"I can't see anything. Cut those lights, will you?"

The technician knocked-out the spotlights.

Behind the podium, the rent-a-crowd remained silent in the narrow set of stall seats within view of camera. The BIPP cheer-leader handed out wrapped gifts to everyone who had participated.

Bellarmine spoke to his close allies:

"We are the BIPP. This island and its Exclusive Economic Zone belong to the Party - the only party. The mercenaries have been ransomed. We are the honest Bourbon Island people, who are able to show mercy and generosity even to the enemies of our country. Those of you who have shown mercy will be rewarded. You may choose to distribute these gifts to your constituents. My fellow Bourbons, thank you for coming along, and I bid you a peaceful good night."

The exodus from the National Stadium commenced. A convoy of air-conditioned limousines made its way into Port Bourbon. A group of vehicles separated from the main convoy, and travelled at speed, beyond the town, along the coastal road, in the direction of the international airport.

François Bellarmine walked through the stadium tunnel. Outside, the presidential limousine was ready with a chauffeur and four or five armed bodyguards. The foreign woman occupied the rear passenger seat. A BIPP security agent opened the door. Bellarmine sat next to the woman. "I must prepare for a press conference at State House, my dear. . . I'll drop you off on the way."

The chauffeur accelerated the vehicle headlong into the night.

"If you don't mind, François," Barbara West said, "not too close to the hotel. I'll walk the rest of the way."

14

MR & MRS ALBERT GREENE

ROBERT WALKER MADE his way through the congested dining room. He found his usual table, which was still free, and took a seat over-looking the marina. The menu for the evening was typed-out on an immaculate white card:

~ SATURDAY, 25th August 1991 ~
Sop of the Day
*

Hungarian Ghoulish
Crammed Potatoes + Gorden Herbs
Mange Trout
*

Red Snapper
Sea Salad
*

Creme Camel
Vanilla Icy-Cream
*

Goulash? This far south, what did it matter? As for the typist - well, Danielle - as she passed, flushed the colour of paprika, and avoided Robert Walker's eyes. A mixture of aromas floated in from the kitchen. Robert Walker stared over the dark waters of the marina. Along the pontoon, the yachts had put out to sea, and a single skiff remained - tied up at one end of the T. The skiff, Robert Walker knew, was still up for sale. In the dining room, most of the tables were occupied by the sudden influx of off-island visitors: South Africa, Mauritius, Australia - exiles and expatriates from farther afield. The visitors were hungry and thirsty, and exchanged controlled whispers. At one point, Sami - the chef - emerged from the kitchen to see if anyone was still there, and was alarmed to find a full house. A sea of hands waved for attention. The chef nodded at Robert Walker - who nodded back - and withdrew behind the swing-door of the kitchen. By the door, the elderly French couple engaged in a long discourse about the importance of diplomacy, which ended in a bad-tempered silence. As for the English couple, they had cut-short their honeymoon and returned to London. In a corner of the dining room, Straw Hat - Herr Paper-Drache - concealed a sizeable paunch under the veil of the tablecloth. In the way of a Rhine riverboat, he spooned at soup until the plate was dry. The soup - minestrone? - looked complicated. On the table, outside the splash-zone, the German's straw headgear had become battered and wilted by the tropics. At a nearby table, a second group of reporters discussed the fate of their advance-party colleagues, who had ended up in the harbour, and were now - this exchange revealed - being escorted to the airport by police van for deportation. In this way, Robert Walker knew that the man from *The Telegraph* would be temporarily silenced. So much for John Wilson's big mouth. A blonde waitress approached the table. Imported from Paris by Mr Swann, her name-badge showed 'Bebe'. Robert Walker recognised her, of course, from the *café* in Saint Michel. At last, then, Bebe had escaped Bernard's hot breath on her neck. She took the order, and disappeared through the swing-swang door of the kitchen. Sami, a dedicated family man, provided no such distractions, although-. Dishes rattled - followed by a mighty crash of cutlery. The diners' whispers rose to loud murmurs: what, everyone wanted to know, was going on in there? A red-faced Mr Swann appeared out of nowhere, went to investigate, and re-emerged - satisfied that the situation was under control.

Robert Walker was served with goulash. He made a start on the dish - which was magnificent. At a nearby table, a fresh phalanx of journalists watched everyone else. The dining room had reached its capacity. Danielle and the French girl, Bebe, criss-crossed the dining room floor in a blur of activity. Steam belched out from Sami's kitchen. The door swung open to reveal George, the gardener, who had been drafted-in as stand-in dishwasher. A group of diners finished-up, and departed.

Fresh-in from the airport, new arrivals: from Cape Town, a nervous ornithologist - a woman of uncertain years - wandered among the tables; a devious-looking geologist from Frankfurt; a well-tanned priest on a pastoral visit; a trader from Mombassa, another from Antananarivo; a dyspeptic USAF captain outbound, a well-fed French captain (civil), inbound; a copper-headed South African businessman. The South African, so he said - to the alarm of dining room in general - was here to buy the granite base of the island for use as aggregate in the construction industry. "The hardest stoone known to min," he claimed. (At that, the geologist snarled that this was untrue. There are some that make granite look like butter, fool.) The new South Africa would be built on solid foundations. Why though, a local at an adjacent table challenged, must that foundation be our island? There are plenty of rocks in Africa. You could grind up Table Mountain, and use that instead!

The copper-headed businessman did not take that too well, but managed to say, "I was only kidding, min. Don't take it too personal. You kint blame me for the free markit, min."

"To hell with the free market," a State-employed bureaucrat responded.

"And to hell with you too, min!" the South African fired back.

"Peace?" the priest suggested.

"Sorry, father."

At a separate table, a group of Belgian bird fanciers were planning an expedition into the foothills.

"Do not go up to the plantations," someone warned this group. "A British fellow was badly beaten-up there only recently."

"Who would want to beat us up?" one Belgian enquired.

"You would be surprised, min," the South African countered.

"They would assume," someone exlpained, "you were looking for the treasure."

"Oh?" another Belgian wanted to know. "What treasure is that?

"I thought you said you were looking for birds?"

"Well, we are, we *are*. . ."

"Who isn't?" someone quipped. Then: "Sorry, father."

"Some say," a detached voice reported, "that Bellarmine himself has already found a rare bird - the rarest of them all. White-faced, with red markings. Blue eyes. Good plumage, full-breasted. Brains, too - and impossible to catch."

The priest dabbed at his lips, stood up from his table, and departed.

"Sorry, father."

"*What* treasure?" the Belgian enquired again.

"Will someone, for Chrissakes, tell this bird-watcher where the treasure is?"

"No one knows. Maybe that guy over there knows. He's with the consortium, isn't he? Perhaps we could all buy shares in the Fiery Cross!"

Robert Walker sipped at a glass of ice-cold water. On the far side of the room, another soup-eater caught his attention: a man in the grey silk tunic suit of a BIPP commissar. A disguise, Robert Walker was sure. The fellow wore what appeared to be a receding toupee. The man looked nervous, joyful, and thirsty. He became aware of Robert Walker, stood up from the table, and deserted his soup - and the dining room.

"Him there - ask him. He ought to know. Maybe he's the same guy who was bashed-up on the plantation."

Robert Walker decided it was time to leave.

"Monsieur? You are-?"

One of the Belgian birdwatchers had approached.

"No, thank you," Robert Walker said. "I won't be having dessert."

"But, monsieur, you are mistaken: I am not a waiter."

By then, Robert Walker had already departed.

The Belgian rejoined his colleagues.

"What did he say?" one wanted to know.

"He said he would *not* on this occasion be having dessert."

"Oh really? It must be some sort of code."

Out in the lobby, Mr Swann was saying, "Ah, Mr Walker - there you are. Mr Greene was enquiring after you. He and his wife are in the lounge."

"Yes, of course . . .By the way, Mr Swann - if I might ask - you know of a girl by the name of Sylvia Dupin?"

"How could I forget, Mr Walker? She tended your injuries at the Port Bourbon Infirmary."

"I didn't have an opportunity to thank her," Robert Walker chanced.

"No need," the hotelier advised. "She was only doing her duty."

"She has always been a nurse?"

Mr Swann paused, then said: "She has had many occupations. At one time, an airline hostess maybe."

"She is, maybe, the sister of-."

"-I say no more, Mr Walker."

Robert Walker, certain Mr Swann would say no more, entered the Marlin Room. The lounge was packed with regulars and visitors. Behind the bamboo bar, Francis Long was dressed in a sharp black blazer and slacks. A portable television had been set-up on the bar. On the sofa, the British Attaché and his wife watched the screen with blank faces. On the same sofa, Barbara West was dressed in a fine cocktail dress - which, however, seemed to camouflage her against the frond-patterned upholstery. Barbara West asked: "Robert, have you seen Morgan?"

Robert Walker sat between Barbara West and the Greenes.

Albert Greene said: "Ah, there you are. I've been wanting to talk with you, Mr Walker."

Robert Walker replied first to Barbara West:

"He's at Silent Pete's place."

"What's he doing there?" Barbara West wanted to know.

"Same as you - watching television." Robert Walker observed: "That's a nice dress you're wearing, Barbara."

Elizabeth Greene spoke up: "Yes, isn't it? I've not seen you wearing it before, Barbara."

"I haven't worn it before. It's a . . .gift."

Albert Greene broke in with: "Must we talk about dresses? I was wanting to speak with you, Mr Walker, about-."

Robert Walker consented: "What do you have on your mind, Mr Greene?"

The two women relented.

"I'll tell you what I have on my mind, Mr Walker-."

"Aren't you having a drink, Mr Walker?" Elizabeth Greene enquired.

"I've already had a drink, Mrs Greene, thank you."

"At Silent Pete's, no doubt?" Barbara West said.

"No doubt," Robert Walker agreed.

"If I might just get a word in edge-ways," Albert Greene insisted.

"Why is it called Silent Pete's?" Elizabeth Greene asked.

"The landlord," Robert Walker explained, "hasn't spoken a word since the coup."

"The coup? Which coup?"

"There's no need to be alarmed, Liz," Albert Greene explained: "He means the change of government back in Seventy-Seven."

Mrs Greene said: "You mean, this gentleman hasn't uttered one word since Seventy Seven? Why ever not?"

"No one knows, Mrs Greene. The landlord hasn't been in a position to tell anyone."

Elizabeth Greene stared at Robert Walker.

"Listen here, Walker," Albert Greene said, "I'd rather you didn't pull my wife's leg."

"I wouldn't dream of pulling your wife's leg, Mr Greene."

"-?"

Barbara West smiled into the palm of her hand.

"I don't think it's all that funny," Albert Greene insisted.

"You said you wanted a word?" Robert Walker reminded the British Attaché. "If you're done now, I think I fancy a beer, after all."

"Listen here, Walker, I really must-."

"I'm listening, Mr Greene."

Barbara West's dark locks bounced around her shoulders.

The British Attaché said: "If you don't mind, Miss West-?"

"That's okay," Robert Walker said.

"All right then," Albert Greene continued: "here it is . . ."

"We've been watching Sea Chase," Elizabeth Greene remembered.

"Sea *Hunt*, dear," Albert Greene corrected his wife.

"Yes, that's what I said."

"I met him once," Barbara remarked. "A real gentleman."

"Who?" Mrs Greene wanted to know.

"Why, Lloyd Bridges," Barbara replied.

"Who's he?"

Albert Greene said: "He's the actor, darling, in the programme we were just watching."

"Oh, really? In Sea Chase, you mean? I didn't see him."

Over by the bay window, Robert Walker noticed a man by the telescope. It was the Italian expatriate, Mario Colon, who stared through the device at the night sky.

"Anyway," Robert Walker asked, "you were saying, Mr Greene?"

The British Attaché moved onto the edge of the sofa.

"Oh look," Elizabeth Greene said.

The chatter in the Marlin Room became subdued, then ceased. The parrot called No. 15 squawked - once. The television, this time in living colour, showed François Bellarmine half-way through a press conference at State House. A detached voice announced:

"Ladies and gentlemen, we apologise for the interruption . . . President Bellarmine . . ."

". . .And so I say to you, my fellow Bourbons, the multi-party system is not for us. In the short history of our island nation, this was the system that created deep divisions in our society: always the Red or the Blue, always, but no more. We are all now one people on one island.

"If we can liken our island to a patient in a hospital, then it was clear, back in Nineteen Seventy Seven. . .that this patient was deeply sick and in need of a cure. . .I must admit that I was the one to supply this cure in the way of some drastic action that same year.

"Since then, we have made real social progress under one system, for the benefit of all of the people, and not just the few, who seem to believe they have a natural right to achieve prosperity for themselves alone, while the majority of the people were left behind.

"I must tell you, then, that the rumours. . .that I am about to introduce a new system of government are entirely false. Our enemies have spread these rumours. Make no mistake: the rumour-mongers will be found and then . . . punished . . .under the law of our island nation."

François Bellarmine considered what he had said. At the State House press conference, no one else was in view. In the Marlin Room, only the slow churn of the fan disturbed the prolonged silence over the heads of the audience. The parrot performed a silent two-step on its perch.

Bellarmine, who seemed to look directly at the parrot, continued:

"I say this to you: as a measure of good faith. . ."

A member of the Marlin Room audience groaned.

"He's not for change," somebody out of sight remarked.

" . . . I am able to reaffirm, after many long consultations . . . that those who call themselves exiles, but in reality are Bourbons who have not found themselves willing to work with us in the task of nation-building, who have selfishly sought only to make money abroad - . These people who always seek an advantage over others . . ."

Bellarmine restrained himself from his customary tirade, and instead announced:

". . .are welcome to return to our island as long as their passports are valid."

François Bellarmime raised a well-manicured hand to his mouth, and coughed.

"*. . .These people are welcome if they are prepared to work with us and not against us. If they wish to return to make trouble, then the law shall deal with them as with any other criminal . . .*"

"Then he should arrest himself," someone suggested.

"*So, to conclude, let me say this: I have another cure to announce: we Bourbons must stop hating one another . . . and learn to love each other.*"

"You must be joking!" a heckler barked.

"He kint hear you, min."

"*The time for a national reconciliation . . .is perhaps . . .overdue. Now, I bid you goodnight. And long live the Bourbon Island People's Party!*"

François Bellarmine stared into the camera; he tried a smile, which did not work. The President of the Republic's image disappeared. The screen defaulted to: BIRTV.

"That's better," someone remarked.

Everyone started talking at once. A flood of orders from the thirsty viewers overwhelmed Francis Long. Only the Italian by the telescope paid no attention - except to the darkening horizon.

Barbara West's breast heaved; she ~~turned,~~ sighed, and turned her unfocused eyes on Robert Walker: "What was that you were saying?"

"I wasn't saying anything," Robert Walker said.

"Oh?"

Elizabeth Greene crossed and re-crossed her legs.

Albert Greene chose his moment: "Now, look here, Mr Walker, I've really got to pin you down on this one."

"Please, go ahead."

"I didn't meant to say this in front of the ladies, but I really must ask you not to venture up onto the plantations again. And this business on the John Savvy Show. We were all listening to it earlier, you know. Really, I've never heard such rot."

Elizabeth Greene interjected: "Well, you can speak for yourself, Alby. I for one enjoyed it very much."

"Well, I'm not speaking as myself, am I, Liz? I'm speaking in my official capacity as-."

"-But this is your evening-off, Alby."

"Yes, I know it is, but-."

"-Well, then?"

Barbara West asked: "How *did* the broadcast go, Robert?"

"You didn't hear the Johnny Savvy Show?"

"No, I missed it. I was, I think, *changing*."

"Well," Elizabeth Greene said, "I enjoyed it very much, Mr Walker. I thought you were very - *sensible*. I thought your remarks were - incisive."

"Why, thank you, Mrs Greene, but really I-?"

"-I didn't understand it," she interpolated, "but I can certainly say that I enjoyed it."

Albert Greene cast his eyes at the ceiling. "Oh God."

Barbara West's mind was elsewhere; she rose from the sofa, and wandered in the direction of the bookcase, where she studied some old black & white photographs.

"You needn't speak to Mr Walker like that, Alby."

"What I have to say is for Mr Walker's ears only."

"Well, in that case-." Elizabeth Greene stood up from the sofa, and joined Barbara West among the photographs and books.

Albert Greene said: "I cannot be more emphatic, Walker: after that business up on the plantation, you really must be much more careful. You're lucky to be alive."

Robert Walker did not pass any remark.

"This business of the treasure is a sensitive matter," Albert Greene persisted. "For example, I've just heard some news about those journalists who ended up in the harbour."

"Yes, Mr Greene, I've heard that story."

"My wife seems to find you a very interesting fellow, but that's only because she's bored."

Robert Walker looked over at the two women by the bookcase. "I should make something very clear, Mr Greene: I'm not looking for any treasure. Really, I'm not."

Elizabeth Greene reappeared: "D'you think you're onto it, Mr Walker?"

"I've just been telling your husband, Mrs Greene, that-."

"-I mean, it would be *quite* a find, wouldn't it?" Already, Elizabeth Greene had lost interest. She returned to the bookcase; one photograph in particular had caught the interest of the women. "Look, Alby, it's Lady Smythe-Smith!"

"Yes, dear, I'll have a look at her later."

Barbara West remarked: "The eyes are familiar. I've seen these eyes somewhere - only recently."

"But that," Elizabeth Greene explained, "is just not possible, Barbara. I mean, you being an American, and all - you probably don't realise that it's all a very long time ago-."

"-Realise what, Elizabeth?"

"*History*. . .Oh dear. The photograph is probably about fifty years' old."

Barbara West set the photograph on the bookcase, and stalked out of the Marlin Room. Elizabeth Greene turned her back on the lounge, and started to weep. On the sofa, Albert Greene turned on Robert Walker, and - through gritted teeth - whispered:

"Now, look here, Walker - I really must insist on your cooperation. The authorities have stated that you, a British subject, should not have been up there in the first place. There are certain military installations on the island."

"Harry Singh's General Store is hardly a military installation."

" -of which it is best to stay well clear. Especially near Sans Souci Bay."

"I was nowhere near Sans Souci Bay."

"I give you this information in the form of friendly advice, of course, but also in my capacity as Attaché. The old man - ah, the High Commissioner, I mean - is really quite upset about it. I shouldn't be telling you this, but these days he's upset by just about everything."

"Mrs Greene," Robert Walker observed by the bookcase, "looks upset, too."

"Yes, poor thing. She has this tendency to say the first thing that comes into her head. She's not a diplomat, you see?"

"She is a diplomat's wife, though."

"There is no need to be facetious, Walker," Albert Greene said. "Anyway, please be a good chap and do not go up to the plantations again. There's the question of your visa, you see."

"There's nothing wrong with my visa."

"Well, that depends on a number of factors."

Robert Walker studied Albert Greene's still youthful face. They were about the same age. Albert Greene, seasoned by the FO, had that unflappability which came with knowing your place.

Elizabeth Greene had reappeared. Her eyes were damp. She said:

"There's no need to speak to Mr Walker in that off-hand way, Albert. I'm sure Mr Walker can go wherever he likes. After all, this is a free c-." Mrs Greene bit her lip, and swallowed away her tears.

15

A VISITOR FROM BEYOND THE CROSSROADS

BEHIND THE TELESCOPE, the Italian star-gazer - Mario Colon - looked far over the dark horizon. Mrs and Mrs Greene had opted for an early night. Barbara West had disappeared. The other guests had settled down for a long evening of drink and talk. There was a lot to talk about; and, once Francis Long had regained control of the besieged bar and restocked, plenty more to drink. By the bookcase, Robert Walker studied the old photograph of Lady Smythe-Smith. Barbara West was right; there was definitely something about those eyes . . .

In the lobby, Morgan Beaumont had reappeared. The American entered the Marlin Room: he crossed the floor, and approached Robert Walker. Morgan Beaumont had changed into a light-tan suit, a slick silk shirt, and a big red kipper tie. Overall, he looked like someone else's idea of what a famous American journalist should look like.

"It's done," the American reported. Robert Walker set the photograph on the bookcase. "Ah, seen Barbara?" Beaumont added.

"She was here a while ago - with the Greenes."

"Where's she now?"

"I have no idea, Morgan. Maybe she's in her room."

"Yes, maybe. Who's, ah, that lady?"

"That is Lady Gwendolyn Smythe-Smith - the first Governor's wife."

"This all part of your research?"

"In a round-about way."

"What's on your mind?"

"The first Governor's wife is on my mind. She and Sir Godfrey were childless. Lady Gwendolyn, though, had an affair with a plantation owner. Sir Godfrey shot himself."

"Too bad."

"Not at all: he meant to do it. He's buried out there on the promontory."

Both men looked towards the bay window. The Italian turned away from the telescope, and made eyes across the room.

"Who's that guy?"

"That," Robert Walker said, "is Signor Mario Colon. Once upon a time, éminence gris of the Bellarmine regime. He's fallen out of favour." He looked at the American: "What's with the questions, Morgan? You know all this. You knew all this before I did. Trouvères? You broke the story, remember?"

"I don't know. I used to know," and Morgan Beaumont stared straight into the bookcase. "My mind's a blank. I was okay until about a week or so ago. I've been out walking around a lot. I don't know anything any more. What I need is a beer."

The two men approached the bamboo bar. Francis Long set up two glasses of BourBrew. They raised their glasses, but no further: from the big-ear of the lobby, the sound of boots echoed inside the Marlin Room. The chatter, smoking, and drinking ceased; the guests stood still, and waited. A voice from the lobby announced:

"YOU, MR SWANN, WILL SUBJECT YOURSELF TO A THO-ROUGH SEARCH!"

Chief Bugis followed through with a cane-splitting *CRaCK* over the surface of Mr Swann's reception desk.

Bugis screamed: "Ah! Too hard! Oh, bloody hell, man, you see what you've made me do now?"

The encounter brought meek expressions of despair from the guests, who, anyway, shuffled for a better view of the proceedings in the lobby.

Out of sight, the Chief seemed to be examining the split-ends of his cane.

"*I* made you break the cane?" Mr Swann's voice retorted. "How much does a stick like this cost? Less, even, than the special varnish on my desk. Now, to business: if you and your men are looking for the hornets' nest, then you know where to find it!"

"So, Mr Swann!" Chief Bugis shouted, "now, you joke!"

"Why, then, Chief Bugis, do you want to search me?"

"Not you - your hotel," one of the constables replied.

"You speak to me like this, sonny?"

The constable did not respond.

"We will not be made fun of, Mr Swann," Bugis insisted. "Here, now, leave your position there - and come with us!"

"You have no right," Mr Swann insisted, "to carry out a search for nothing."

"Nothing? Five hundred cases of the Blue Marlin beer is *nothing*? A cargo of beer!"

Mr Swann groaned: "I have told this Italian infidel not to come around here! We know about him, all right, but we know nothing about his cargo!"

By the telescope, Mario Colon flinched.

"You have no right. The authorities will see to this!"

"The authorities *are* seeing to this!" Chief Bugis screamed. "Who do you think I am, man? Some boy-scout dressed like this?"

Mr Swann chose not to reply. Chief Bugis, Mr Swann, and two special constables appeared through the archway. The boy, Charlie the Fish, hopped-in behind the oblong frame of Chief Bugis, and pulled a cheeky face at Mr Swann. The proprietor corrected his slightly rumpled suit. Chief Bugis' face was swollen big with anger. The crowd - in the Chief's eyes,

215

Mr Swann's despised clientele - started to fidget. A diplomat from the French Embassy chose to leave, changed his mind, and stayed put.

The Chief noticed: "I did not say move, did I? Stay still, everybody!" Chief Bugis, with a purple-lipped smile, added: "Now, no one is going anywhere just yet, please, please," and then paused to fix - one-by-one - every face there in his memory. As he did so, he swashed at invisible flies with the split ends of his rattan cane, with a final - *swat!* - into the palm of his hand.

Mr Swann winced, and straightened his tie.

Chief Bugis studied the frayed ends of the cane. He turned, gave the damaged cane to the boy, and said: "Hey! You there, Charlie! Get me my special one, boy!"

"Yes, Papa!"

"Don't say yes - get going!" and the Chief directed a boot at the back of the boy's shorts.

"Ahhg!"

The Chief howled with laughter.

The boy Charlie ran out of lounge, through the lobby, down the flight of steps, across Revolution Boulevard, and headed for the Victoria Road Police Station.

At the rear of the lounge, one of the guests managed an hysterical giggle. Chief Bugis - overreacting, Robert Walker thought - placed a fat hand on the butt of his side-arm.

"So, Mr Swann. This is a hotel for comedians, tonight? I can tell you some good jokes, too, if you please!"

Mr Swann ignored the outburst. The clientele stood together with the eyes of a herd on a predator.

Morgan Beaumont shifted his bulk from one foot to the other.

Chief Bugis watched everyone, except Mario Colon, who continued his observations through the telescope over the dark ocean.

"So," Bugis said, and puffed-up his jowls. "We have all the old familiar faces of the usual trouble-makers here tonight, haven't we, eh, Swanny?"

Mr Swann's face was tight with anger. He said:

"You call me this in front of my guests? You expect cooperation from me?"

Chief Bugis' uniform had been especially starched for this occasion: his boxlike shorts stood out - rigid - front and back; the rim of his big cap shone under the Marlin Room's lights; stockings had been pulled high-up over shaven legs (the eyebrows, too, had been plucked clean); the Sam Browne belt was in a state of high, Saturday-night polish. "Expect? I DEMAND cooperation!"

The Chief took off his cap: the extraordinary haircut was revealed. With his little fingernail, the policeman scratched at a place half-way along the parting, so that his eyelids drooped with pleasure.

An uncontrollable cackle of fear - it might have been the parrot, but it was not - erupted from the area of the bamboo bar. Then there was silence. Chief Bugis put on his cap, twisted it over his head, and flashed his eyes at the ensemble.

The boy Charlie returned from the Police Station, handed over a *sjambok** - and then dived - out of range - into the lobby. Sight of the implement brought groans from among the guests. The Chief test-swung the *sjambok*, but this time the rod was not, sensibly, swiped at his own hand.

"Now," Bugis said, "what are we here for?"

"You ask this?" Mr Swann lisped.

"We are only here for the beer," Chief Bugis declaimed, and sprung up-and-down on his heels. "Not one or two beers like Mr Beaumont or Mr Walker here - but a whole missing cargo of beer. "

He pointed the *sjambok* at the named men. The ensemble - happy that the Briton and the American should be sacrificed - relaxed.

An elated Chief Bugis said: "At last, two men who know when to keep quiet!"

Then the Chief, his authority boosted, swaggered towards the bamboo bar, where he swish-swashed the *sjambok*. "Now, you there - Francis Long - one glass of beer for the Chief! That's me! Chop-chop!"

A cack-handed Francis Long jumped-to, but broke the glass. The Chief shook his head. Then Francis Long managed to fill-up another, which he set - cold and frothy - in front of the policeman. The two special constables adopted positions either side of Mr Swann. Chief Bugis raised the beerglass to his head, and poured, without a gulp or a swallow, until the glass was empty. The guests, as they watched this feat, were both disgusted and impressed.

The Chief slammed the empty down onto the bar, and the glass shattered. Mr Swann made a move, but was restrained. The constables removed night-sticks from their belts. Francis Long stood away from the bar. The guests became unsettled; some emptied their own glasses while they had the chance.

Chief Bugis continued with his performance, all of which appeared to have been carefully thought-out before gradual enactment. "So, are you nervous, Francis Long?"

"No Chief, no."

---

* A short whip made from rhinoceros hide.

, Chief Bugis laughed. "No, Chief? No?" The Chief pointed at the pips on his epaulettes. "What do you think these are, man? Christmas decorations?"

"No, Chief, of course not."

The Chief rolled his *sjambok* along the edge of the bar. "So now, what we are looking for is not *one* beer, but three-hundred cases!"

"*Five* hundred cases," an Italian-accented voice advised.

"All right, five hundred! Now, Francis Long, I am going to ask you a simple question. . . Do you know the whereabouts of this cargo?"

Francis Long glanced sideways at the Italian by the telescope. Mario Colon swivelled the brass tube towards an object of interest - off-shore, say, by about a league.

The Chief specified: "Oh, no, Francis! You must answer this question without help from anyone!"

"No, Chief," Francis Long gulped.

"No, Chief? What you say, man?"

"I do not know of the . . . whereabouts of this beer." Francis Long, unable to bear the Chief's face any longer, looked down - behind the bar - at his own feet. The Chief seemed to take this as a hint.

"OKAY! " Chief Bugis ordered, "open up that hatch now!"

Francis Long fumbled with the hatch. The constables pushed-in behind the bar, and shoved Francis Long out of the way. Chief Bugis followed, and studied the floor space.

"Don't move, Francis! I'm watching you all the time!" The Chief pushed the brim of his cap back with the end of the *sjambok*.

Francis Long cringed in a corner of the bamboo bar.

"Now, now, what have we here . . ?"

After a pause, there was a steady, floorboard-pounding stampede out of the Marlin Room.

"NO! No. Let them all go! Except you two journalists-!" *shuffled*

Mr Swann side-stepped the onrush. A herd of customers charged through the lounge, into the lobby, down the steps onto Revolution Boulevard, and out into the night. Mr Swann grimaced as many hundreds of rupees' worth of business deserted the hotel.

Robert Walker and Morgan Beaumont held their ground.

Chief Bugis continued his investigation: "So, now, Francis Long, let us keep things simple, so you can understand. How about if I make a suggestion and then you follow things through nicely with no trouble, all right?"

"Whatever you say, Chief," Francis Long agreed.

Chief Bugis watched the bartender - in his eyes, an insect. "That's good, Francis. Perhaps you are not as stupid as you look."

The constables started to cackle, then shut themselves up.

"I can see we are going to make excellent progress," the Chief continued. "Now, how about us all having a good look in the cellar below?"

Francis Long blinked, then blinked again. "There's nothing down there, Chief."

The Chief looked at Mr Swann. The proprietor responded:

"This is accurate, Chief Bugis. You will find nothing much down there, except a few crates and barrels."

"Crates, you say? Barrels?"

"In fact-."

"- In fact? You talk to me about facts, Mr Swann? And you, Francis, just be a bloody good fellow and open up this cellar door here. Then we shall see about the facts!"

"All right, Francis, if you please!"

"Your men are standing on the trapdoor, Chief."

Chief Bugis barked at his men to stand aside.

Francis Long's face twitched; he stooped, and complied - and the trapdoor opened. Chef Bugis grinned:

"This a secret trapdoor, Mr Swann?"

"No, Chief Bugis, this is a very ordinary trapdoor."

The constables wielded night-sticks and torches. Chief Bugis directed them down into the cellar. Then the Chief followed his men into the dark cavity. Robert Walker watched, waited, and said nothing. The American tasted his beer; he smacked his lips, which distracted the Italian. Mario Colon turned away from the telescope, lit-up a cigarette, and sneered at Mr Swann.

Below-deck, crates were up-ended, glass splintered, corks exploded from gas-pressured bottles, and the contents of shelves crashed to the ground. After a long pause, Chief Bugis swore at his constables to turn on the lights. The search continued; after a series of knocks and thumps, and - a yelp - there was silence.

Below, and from the far-end of the cellar, the voice of Bugis shouted:

"Well, so there is nothing here, after all!"

The subterranean voice continued: "This means that you, Francis Long, and your bloody boss have hidden the cargo somewhere else! Well, don't you worry, we'll find it - and make you drink it! All of it!"

It was then that Francis Long acted: he kicked the trapdoor down-shut over the heads of the policemen. The Italian laughed until he coughed. Mr Swann stepped-in behind the bar, and pushed his nephew aside. Underground, Chief Bugis shouted: "OPENFF UFF!" Then, at his constables: "Bluffy fulls! The pfiffner hath espaathed!"

"De windf?" a constable suggested.

"Anf accidetnthf?" suggested the other.

Above deck, Mr Swann managed to pry-open the trapdoor. The three policemen, covered in cobwebs and dust, emerged.

Chief Bugis tried to speak, but he could not; his face seemed to swell by twice its normal size. "Aggghhhhh!" was all he could manage.

"The wind," Mr Swann explained. "A sudden draft."

Mario Colon spoke up: "That was no draft."

The constables kicked the trapdoor shut, and made a grab for Francis Long. The bartender was marched out from behind the bar and made to stand to attention.

Chief Bugis examined the state of his best uniform. He swashed the *sjambok* over the bartender's head, but seemed to miss. Francis Long fainted, and slumped between the arms of the constables.

"You hit him just then?" Mr Swann asked.

"He only thinks I hit him," the Chief explained. "It has the same effect on these simple fellows."

"This is all most regrettable," Mr Swann announced.

"Regrettable?" Chief Bugis screamed. "Regrettable?"

"What about my missing cargo?" Mario Colon wanted to know.

"Your cargo, Signor Colon? What about my uniform?"

Chief Bugis waved his *sjmbock* at the constables. "Under arrest. You, too, Mr Swann! Obstructing the course of, etcetera. In possession of, etcetera. Illegal aliens in your employ, etcetera!"

"Under arrest? How am to run hotel if I am under arrest?"

"Well, that is your business, Mr Swann, isn't it?"

The two constables dragged Francis Long out of the Marlin Room.

Mr Swann pleaded: "If you gentlemen would keep an eye on things in my absence?"

"Of course, Mr Swann," Morgan Beaumont agreed.

"Certainly, Mr Swann," Robert Walker said.

"I shall return very shortly."

The policeman laughed: "Shortly, he says! Ha! Ha! Ha!"

Mr Swann said: "As for you, Signor Colon, you are not welcome here. You will leave my hotel now!"

The Italian laughed: "You ask me to leave, Signor Swann, but it is you who are leaving!"

Chief Bugis escorted Mr Swann away from the hotel.

220

Part Four

Missing Cargo

PART FOUR

Missing Cargo

"Stand out of my light."
~ *Diogenese, who lived in a barrel, when Alexander asked what*
favour he might grant the cynic.

1

MISSING CARGO I

"I," MARIO COLON remarked, "have searched for missing cargo these many days and nights now. I suspect, at last, the trail becomes warmer."

The Italian slurped at the beer, which was of the Blue Marlin variety, the very same brand as the purported 'missing cargo'. He wiped away the froth that stuck to his long beard in the way of shaving foam. "Yes, much, much warmer."

Morgan Beaumont moved behind the bamboo bar, and closed the hatchway; he removed his jacket, and presented his salesman's kipper tie to the deserted Marlin Room. Robert Walker thought Beaumont looked as though he had tended bar - or worked in a nightclub - for years. The bird - No. 15 - seemed to be asleep on its perch.

"Pretty quiet for a Saturday night," the American observed. "Even so, Signor Colon, I was under the impression Mr Swann wanted you to leave the premises."

"You would speak to me like that? You know who I am?"

"I have a fair idea."

"I am a direct descendent of Dante Aligheri."

"Is that so? I'm impressed. I doubt, though, Mr Swann would be, so I'll have to ask you to-."

"-You Americans are always in such a hurry. All right, I say - I am on my way!" Mario Colon thrust his arms into the air. "I have - anyway - a midnight flight for Cape Town. But before that, there are matters to be discussed."

"I have nothing to discuss with you. I don't think Mr Walker here has anything to say, either."

"You're right; I'm going to call it a night, Morgan."

"Not so fast! You are Signor Walker? I heard you on the radio earlier."

"What about Francis?" Robert Walker asked the American.

"That's up to Mr Swann now," Beaumont said. "There's nothing to do but wait."

Robert Walker looked sideways at the trader, but said nothing.

"There's nothing you can do for him now," Mario Colon advised. "He is a criminal. . .What he gets is what he deserves. I know him from the old days. He is a bad man. What is he to you anyway?"

"Nothing," Robert Walker said.

"Nothing. Okay, so forget about him. There are more important things to discuss. Things that have gone missing. Like your treasure. Like my cargo!"

Robert Walker looked sideways at Colon. The Italian's unpressed, off-white shirt opened at the collar to show curly grey chest-hair. The face was broad, flat and leather-brown. The nose was nosey and seemed to point in various directions; black wires emerged from its nostrils. The beard sprouted from the face and mixed freely with the curly chest-hair. Yellow, splintered teeth filled a wide mouth; the breath did not smell of Blue Marlin beer or any other kind of beer. Aquamarine eyes watched out for any opportunity. Sun-bleached, wind-swept, white trousers reached the deck over sweat-darkened leather sandals. Hard toenails, unclipped for months, curled yellow over dark, hirsute feet. Robert Walker was sure this man knew things that no one should know, and had done things that-. "I think I'll call it a night, Morgan," he remarked.

"First, my friend, there is something to discuss."

Mario Colon's expression transformed itself into an unlikely, grandfatherly smile. Robert Walker almost believed it, too.

"You are the same Walker," Colon remarked. "I heard you on the radio today. We Italians know all about radio. It was an excellent programme - except for the bloody DJ!"

Robert Walker did not respond.

"How about another beer, Robert?" Morgan Beaumont asked.

"For me," the Italian responded, "another five hundred cases of the same."

Robert Walker said: "I'm sorry, Signor Colon, I know nothing about your missing cargo."

"I know something about your missing treasure. We could exchange information."

"You'll miss your flight."

The Italian glanced at the maritime chronometer behind the bar. "Time yet, Mr Walker."

"I don't have any information for exchange."

"Mario Colon," Mario Colon said, "always settles his bills; sometimes he settles other people's bills, too. And sometimes he pays off old debts, as well."

"Who are you threatening, Colon?" Beaumont asked.

"I am threatening no one, Mr Beaumont," the Italian replied. "Yet."

Robert Walker decided to stay a while. "I'll have that beer, Morgan."

"Right, you are," and Beaumont opened a bottle of Blue Marlin. Robert Walker counted-out the exact price in rupees.

"You usually drink this kind of beer, Mr Walker?"

"No, I usually drink the local brew."

"Then why are you drinking Blue Marlin? It is more expensive, no?"

"I don't know."

"You do not know?"

"No. For a change, maybe."

Mario Colon watched Robert Walker take a sip of the beer from Mauritius. Morgan Beaumont watched the Italian.

"I am an innocent businessman," Colon asserted. "All I am trying to do is make an honest profit. People say I am Cosa Nostra, but that is only because I am an Italian. You can see from my eyes that I am not Sicilian."

"I believe you," Beaumont said.

"You do? Well, this is all right, then."

"Fine."

"These same people don't know what they are talking about." The Italian glanced again at the maritime chronometer. "The people on the radio don't know what they're talking about. All the time chit-chat, chit-chat."

Beaumont advised: "You'd better get going now, Signor - or you'll miss your flight."

"Sure. Soon. First, I need to cover my losses - one way or another."

"I'll call a cab," Beaumont offered.

"No need. A taxi-cab is on the way."

"What people on the radio?" Robert Walker asked.

"You know. Savvy. That is the last time he will broadcast. He is a fool - like his dead cousin. He doesn't know what he's talking about. He should shut up. So should his special guests. They don't know what they're talking about, either."

"So much ill-will, Signor Colon," Robert Walker said, "and with such little reason."

"Well said," Beaumont applauded.

Mario Colon, over the rim of his beer glass, eyed Robert Walker. Then the Italian fixed the Briton's eye, and said: "Wilson told me about you."

"John Wilson?"

"Oh yes, Mr Walker," Mario Colon grinned. "Wilson told me you were looking for treasure."

"I specifically told Mr Wilson I was not looking for treasure."

Mario Colon set his depleted glass on the bar. "If you are looking, you will need to travel far and wide. Same as Colon. I have crossed an ocean, and end up here. In the end, I am not appreciated by my original sponsors. However, I am a diplomat - so I must be diplomatic. I am also" - he faced Robert Walker - "the Ambassador to this island of the Knights of Saint John of Jerusalem, Rhodes and Malta. You may address me as Your Excellency, if you so wish."

"Balony." (Beaumont.)

Robert Walker did not say anything. The Italian closed his eyes, and stroked at his beard. The American and the Briton regarded the Italian in silence. The ceiling fan *swish-swished* to cool an audience that had already departed. Parrot No.15 woke up, ran its beak through its feathers, and went back to sleep. After an interval, Mario Colon reached into a trouser pocket, and removed a document or booklet.

"In my official capacity, I am in a position to do you a very great favour."

"What do you have in mind, Signor Colon?"

"-For the right sum, of course. My diplomatic mission to this remote island has come to an end. . .unforeseen circumstances. Now, I am left to search the world for my missing cargo. The journey may never end. In between, I am prepared to be generous - cargo or no cargo. I might even die of thirst in my quest, which would be a very great irony, don't you think, Mr Walker?"

"For sure."

The American said: "We'll all die of thirst, waiting for Your Excellency to come to the point."

"All right, all right. So, I have here a passport entitling the bearer to enter all countries in the world - except Italy."

"Under the circumstances," Robert Walker advised, "perhaps you had better keep it for your own use."

The Italian turned on Robert Walker. "The document bestows, ah, the privileged bearer with full diplomatic immunity. I am prepared to issue this passport to either of you gentlemen . . .as a great favour . . .for a very special cash-price in US dollars."

"How much?" Beaumont asked.

"You are interested?"

"No, just curious."

"To be precise, I am seeking twenty thousand dollars - an exclusive, one-off deal for the right customer, who must also be a man of integrity."

"Well, that counts me out," Beaumont said.

"Me too," Robert Walker added.

"This is the last one," Colon said.

All of this seemed familiar to Robert Walker. A report had turned up at the Shoe Lane Agency some time during the late 1980s. A photograph had been attached to the report.

"Why are you looking at me like that?"

The man in the photograph had been this man, Signor Mario Colon. That was a decade ago, but the Italian was the same. The scam had been bogus passports under the aegis of the Order of the Knights of St. John. This passport in Colon's hand was, as the Italian claimed, probably the last such document. The Italian's eyes shifted, and then he returned the passport to his trouser pocket.

"Why are you looking at me like that, Mr Walker? The price is too high for you?"

"The document . . . is genuine, Signor Colon?"

"Genuine, you say? Of course it is genuine. If you cannot afford it, then you should have said so, and I would not have to waste my time. After all, you are only a journalist, and journalists are always short of money. Not all journalists, perhaps. How about you, Mr Beaumont?"

"No thanks. I belong to Uncle Sam-." The American hesitated: "Well, you know what I mean."

Robert Walker wondered how Colon, a crude opportunist, could have become the *éminence gris* of any regime. In the years prior to and after the coup, though, Bellarmine had likely sought out co-conspirators wherever he might find them. Fix this, Mario. Fix that, Mario. Arrange this-. Robert Walker, in that instant, could see a reflection of Jacques Savvy's betrayal in the pit of Colon's eye.

The Italian tried another angle: "Krugerands, then? I have Krugerands to sell for a good cash rate."

"Who the hell needs Krugerands?" Beaumont asserted.

"Everybody needs Krugerands."

"You keep them, then. You'll need them where you're going. Look, your flight-."

"-Is that clock working?"

"Sure it's working. "

"Then I have time."

The Italian, Robert Walker guessed, wanted to unload his assets on the island. The consignment of beer had gone missing, but everything else was up for sale.

Beaumont checked the chronometer: it was well after 22:00 hrs. He said: "How long is Mr Swann going to be? And the rest of the staff - where are they?"

"Maybe weeks, maybe months," Mario Colon said. "The rest of the staff are under arrest. The chef. The waitresses. There are many charges. As for Colon, I must soon leave this island - forever."

"You'll be greatly missed," Beaumont quipped.

The Italian turned to cross-examine Robert Walker: "John Wilson told me about you, Mr Walker."

"You've already said."

"Yes, I know."

"John Wilson is only interested in stamps."

"Yes - of course."

"You sold the stamp to him, Signor Colon? The stamp of the Fiery Cross?"

The Italian's chin jutted: "I cannot confirm nor deny this."

"If it's not true," Beaumont suggested, "then why not just deny it?"

"Is it real?"

"The treasure? Of course. You said so yourself on the radio."

"I meant the stamp."

"Of course it's real. . ." Mario Colon closed his eyes when he slapped his forehead. "I mean, I don't know. I don't know anything about stamps. I am a simple man. I don't know anything. John Wilson told me. Of course Mario likes to help people. Mario would like to help the consortium. If this is to be a European project, then an Italian must be involved."

"Consortium? What consortium?"

"Yes, I see you understand what I mean."

"Mr Wilson has gone out of his way to misunderstand me - for reasons of his own."

"I do not understand," Colon asserted. "I listened to the radio broadcast today. Johnny Savvy played those sentimental records-."

"-I never thought," Beaumont remarked, "I'd live to hear an Italian say a thing like that."

Mario Colon ignored the American. "On this same broadcast, Mr Walker, you said that you were looking for the treasure. That the consortium was-."

"No, I did not say that. I confirmed that I was *not* looking for the treasure. I said that I was interested in the story behind the treasure, even if it does not exist, for the purposes of my feature article only."

"If there is no treasure, then what - *what*, I ask you - is this consortium after? I must know this - for academic research only, you understand."

"Academic research?" Beaumont said. "You're kidding, right?"

"From an American," Colon snorted, "I have to expect comments of this kind. I am a businessman. I am interested in any academic research that can lead to an honest profit."

"I've heard enough of this," the American said.

Mario Colon shrugged: "If you help me, Mr Walker, then I'll help you. We are back-scratchers, yes?

"I'm not in a position to help you, Signor Colon."

"All right, then, we start off easy. If I help you with one clue only, then I think the consortium would - yes? - be most generous with he who renders such assistance. Am I right?"

"Consortium? Which consortium?"

"Ah, yes, which consortium indeed? I understand this game-play. I am a diplomat. Now, if I provide you with this clue, then you must also provide me with a clue, so I can find my cargo of beer."

"Are we still on that subject? I hadn't realised. Look, I do not know anything about your cargo, which is none of my business."

"All right, I believe you. Now, let me show you something. Let me show you how to turn academic research into a profitable enterprise. For certainly this must be the purpose of your journey to this island."

Mario Colon moved towards the bay window. The Italian took up a position behind the brass telescope.

"Over here, Mr Walker, if you please!"

Beaumont whispered: "This guy's gone loony-tune."

Robert Walker joined the Italian by the bay window. Mario Colon stooped to adjust the tripod, looked through the eyepiece, checked the alignment, and varied the depth-of-focus. The azimuth of the tube was set almost flat with sea-level.

"There, now - look!"

Robert Walker looked, and saw . . .a black disc.

"Well, what do you see. . .?"

Robert Walker stood up from the eyepiece: "Nothing."

Behind the bar, the American guffawed.

"Please, Signor Beaumont, this is no laughing matter," the Italian warned. "The Englishman Dunne surrendered his life for this knowledge. Now, Mr Walker, we must try again. Concentrate. Open you mind."

Robert Walker tried again: level with the brass tube, he fixed an eye against the optic. He concentrated; he opened his mind: the two attitudes worked against each other: Harry Stone looked back at him, and winked. Conny Trapp, naked to the waist, stepped out of the ocean, and smiled. . .Robert Walker did not see the coral beach, which glowed blue-white under the starlight. He did not watch the moonbeams that filled the Indian Ocean. Nor did he see the great container ship slip across the distant horizon; he did not see the black cone of the volcano, etched against the indigo sky; and he was unaware of the man in the *dacha*, with the woman at his side - François Bellarmine and his companion - who emerged from the *dacha*, and looked over the town of Port Bourbon. Robert Walker observed, and what he saw through the telescope was simple: an opaque black disc: he saw *nothing*.

"What do you see?" Mario Colon enquired.

Robert Walker's head spun; he stood up to report: "Nothing . . ."

"What is wrong with you? Why are you shaking like that? You are amazed by the sight of-."

". . . I don't see anything."

Again, Beaumont guffawed, and slurped at his glass of beer.

"You're trying to make a fool out of me?" Mario Colon asked. "Is that it?"

The American said: "He doesn't need to make a fool out of you, Signor Colon."

"Why? Because-? I am already-?"

Robert Walker interjected: "Look for yourself, Signor Colon. There is nothing there."

"You look like man who has seen *something*?"

"What's up, Robert?" the American joked: "Cock-eyed?"

Mario Colon said: "Millions of dollars are at stake, Signor Beaumont! Even an American should understand that much!"

"How about taking the lens-cap off!"

The Italian shouted: "Here! Let me look!" Once again, Mario Colon stooped before the instrument and made a very slight adjustment. "Now, now, let me see what we have . . .here. . . LOOK! Signor Walker - try again - about a league off-shore!"

Robert Walker pressed his right eye against the optic: this time, the focus shifted, and he saw a blue-grey disc . . .a ripple of dark water . . . a foaming flash of white surf, and then - nothing. . .but a jagged blackness, which rose out of the sea, about a league off-shore from Venus Beach. A strange green-blue luminosity surrounded the base of the rock, where the dark waters lapped at its craggy base. A shark's fin rose, and then dipped out of sight. . .Then, from the pinnacle of the rock, he observed a sharp, crystalline flash of crimson light - and then darkness.

Robert Walker stood up from the telescope. This time, the American did not pass any remark. The Italian asked:

"Yes? Yes?"

"Yes, I saw it . . .I saw something . . ."

"This is good. Now come with me," and Mario Colon led Robert Walker away from the telescope and back to the bamboo bar. He removed a document from another trouser pocket: it was a map, which he folded over the bar. The American drew closer.

"Now, gentlemen, we shall see what we shall see." Mario Colon glanced at the maritime chronometer; his face was streaked with perspiration.

Robert Walker recognised the map: it was similar to the chart he had bought and lost on the plantation; though it might be, perhaps, older.

He asked: "This map is real, Signor Colon?"

"Of course it is real! Men have paid in blood for this map!"

"All right, I was only asking."

Robert Walker, though drawn by the map, was careful to stand clear of Colon. Mario Colon, with a nicotine-yellowed forefinger, pointed at the map's legend, and said:

"Gentlemen, we have here a map made by the very hand of the infamous pirate - La Buse!"

2

DOG ROCK

ROBERT WALKER REMARKED: "A copy perhaps, and even then, the copy could be a fake, too."

Mario Colon insisted: "What do you mean by that? This is an original copy!"

"An original copy?" Beaumont asked. "What the hell does that mean?"

"Please, Signor Beaumont, patience."

"Where did you fi-?"

"-Now," Mario Colon continued: "we are dealing, over the space of more than two-hundred and fifty years, with a mind of spectacular resource and great cunning."

"Get on it with, Colon," Beaumont urged.

"Please, Signor Beaumont, let us show some respect for a great man - none other than Olivier le Vasseur! Now - look," and the Italian, with his hand, made circles over the south-west quadrant of the map. He thumped his fist on the map - "There!" - and pointed at an off-shore feature near Anse Venus. "This, this here, - Signor Walker, is the very rock we have been observing tonight!"

The Italian ran a fingernail over a block of annotation. "And these - these notes here - point to the location of the treasure."

"Why tell us?" the American wanted to know. "Why don't you put the map to some use yourself?"

"As you know, I have a flight to catch. Before then, to business." The Italian faced Robert Walker: "So, I have kept my promise. This is the clue. The one clue. The most important."

"Why do you say it's the most important clue?" Robert Walker asked. "Why is one clue more important than the others?"

"Good question, Signor Walker. So, now maybe I shall tell you."

"Yes, I'm listening."

The Italian looked around the lounge, which was deserted, and then at the parrot, which slept with one eye open.

"Yes, Signor Colon. . ?"

Colon hesitated: " . . .There are conditions . . ."

"Conditions? What conditions?"

"You expect me to give away a clue like this for nothing?"

"I don't expect anything, Signor Colon."

"You'll miss your flight," the American advised.

"All right, then, all right! I am prepared to sell this map to the consortium!"

From the lounge sofa, something slipped onto the floor.

"Who's there?" the Italian demanded.

"No one's there," Beaumont observed. "A cushion dropped, that's all."

"All right, then. Where was I?"

"You were talking about the map," Robert Walker said.

"Yes, the map, the map. I am prepared to sell this map to the consortium. In short, I am ready - to make this personal sacrifice - to sell this map to you - Signor Walker! - for a very special price!"

"-?"

"I know for a fact that you have lost your own copy of a much less reliable map! If you pay me, the consortium will reimburse you many times over!"

"-?"

"How much?" the American wanted to know.

"How much?"

"Yes, how much for the map? This map here."

"You are interested, Signor Beaumont?"

"No, just curious."

"The map is not for sale to curiosity seekers. This map has been bought and sold with blood many times over!"

"The ink looks fresh."

"The ink is not fresh, Signor Beaumont, "the ink is old - older than your United States of America! . . .Mr Walker, you are a serious man: I am prepared to sell this special map to the consortium, for a very modest sum. I do not want any percentages or any share at all of the treasure. What you do with the map is up to you."

Robert Walker looked at the Italian: "You keep talking about a consortium, Signor Colon, and I keep telling you: I don't know anything about any consortium."

"Not even the one that hired you?"

Robert Walker swallowed, and asked: "The provenance of this map? It belonged to Graham Dunne?"

"It did!"

"And this is why the paper is old but the some of the ink is fresh?"

"It is!"

Morgan Beaumont asked: "How did this guy Graham Dunne come by the map?"

"I do not know!"

"All right, how did you come by the map?"

"I cannot say!"

Robert Walker asked: "If Graham Dunne used this map, as you claim, then how far did he get with the clues?"

"All right, you ask; I will answer! Some people say he reached Clue Number Ten, after which he became very confused and was drunk most of the time, which of course did not help. The Englishman Dunne was at fault, not the map!" Mario Colon paused, and then said: "The Australian who is called Silent Pete - he told me that Dunne was delirious most of the time, and that he had so many clues inside his skull there was no sense to be had out of him - or the clues."

"The Australian told you this?" Beaumont asked.

"He did."

"Why, that cannot be so."

"Why not?"

"He is not called Silent Pete for nothing."

"All right - if it makes you happy - he spoke through an intermediary."

"Oh, he did?"

"He did! You doubt Colon's word? You are calling me a liar?"

Morgan Beaumont withheld his answer.

Robert Walker asked: "Are you saying, Signor Colon, that the rock out there is a clue in itself?"

"Maybe so, Signor Walker. I heard you on the radio. You said, why not go to straight to Clue Number Eleven? I thought, my God, this British gentleman has got a point! Why follow all twelve, when you can go straight to Clue Eleven or Twelve! Mr Graham Dunne spent ten years of his life going from One, Two, Three, and so on . . .It is crazy! And so, with my map and your tactic, we have an overall strategy."

The Italian glanced at the maritime chronometer. Then he checked his own wristwatch, which, he then remembered, had been confiscated by Customs, and anyway had been set for some other merdian.

"So, anyway, look -."

The three men studied the chart with fresh eyes.

" . . .This rock here . . .holds the clue . . .to Clue Number Eleven! If I had time, I would take up the quest myself, but I must very soon leave this island. You, Signor Walker, must buy this map - it is your professional duty - and then use the boat to reach the rock, where you will find, I am sure, the Clue Number Eleven! I only ask twenty thousand dollars in cash."

"-? A boat? You have a boat?"

"Of course. For fishing and things like that. There, down in the marina - it is the only vessel there at this time. . .I had almost forgotten about it. You know, it is small but it floats. You don't need a telescope to see it. Now, I must leave the island. You should take this boat and visit the rock. You have my permission. I shall include the boat with the price of the map: twenty thousand dollars!"

"I don't have that kind of money."

"Compared with the treasure, it is nothing! Your consortium can pay from their petty cash!"

"I've seen a map like this before, and it only cost me fifty rupees."

"You have the map here?"

"I lost it on the plantation."

"From Singh?"

"Well, yes."

"Those maps of his are no good. This one is real! Look-."

Again, the Italian turned to the map spread out over the bar.

"Look, read this here, Signor Walker!"

Robert Walker looked, and read: "Le Roche de la Chien. The Rock of the Dog. Dog Rock."

"I've seen it from the beach," Beaumont remarked. "It doesn't look much like any kind of a dog to me."

"Yes, and there is the mystery!" the Italian agreed. "So, why then, do we suppose this rock, which does not look like a dog, is named anyway for a dog? Look here," Colon added, "and see this writing . . ."

All three men leaned over the south-west quadrant of the map.

". . .By the hand of La Buse himself - in Latin, of course - so therefore I can read some of it as with Italian. The Englishman Dunne studied Latin and Greek as a public schoolboy, but as a man he was only an accountant. Good at counting, but not good at finding."

"Evidently," Beaumont said.

"Not good at translating, either. Look-."

The three men craned their necks over the map.

"Some of these clues read like they are upside down. Even so, they can be decrypted. If you forgive me, Signor Walker-. Time is running out on me, just as it ran out for La Buse and for Dunne."

Outside, the coastal breeze had dropped, and the night-time heat enveloped the hotel. The Italian sweated, and waited; a drop of moisture, predictably, ran off the end of his nose, and fell onto the edge of the map.

"You must decide now Signor Walker, or the special offer will expire by the strike of the clock."

Robert Walker waited, but clock did not yet strike.

"Signor Beaumont, there is something wrong with that clock?"

The American listened to the device: "I don't know; maybe it's stopped."

"You mean what - the clock is not showing the right time?"

"It's this heat; it must have affected the chronometer."

"You see? We must hurry! Signor Walker, put your eyes on these phrases here." The Italian pointed at a dense block of calligraphy.

"Where?"

"There. There!"

"Your finger is in the way."

The Italian grinned, and removed his hand.

"The consortium will be impressed, yes?"

"I don't know what you're talking about."

"John Wilson told me everything. You are under exclusive contract to the consortium. Maybe you don't know about it, but it's true. This is all free information. No charge. There is a German on this island who is watching you."

"You know about him, then?"

"Of course."

"Who is he?"

"I'm saying nothing more. I have already said too much. I must now go to the airport. If you please, you must decide-."

The American, in some attempt to delay the Italian, said:

"Here, let me see that!" Beaumont rotated the chart by 180°. He examined the calligraphy that annotated the landmark known as Dog Rock.

"Okay, okay, here it is . . ." Beaumont took a swallow of beer, and licked his lips. He leaned over the ancient parchment. The American's eyes travelled swiftly over each topographical detail - Mont Pomme d'Or, Venus Beach, Le Roche de la Chien - and the correlation for each of the various transcriptions from Latin into English. He looked up at Mario Colon, and said: "I think I can read Clue Number Eleven from here, if you don't mind, Signor Colon?"

"Please, proceed," the Italian said, but Colon had lost his smile.

Beaumont coughed, focused on the script, and read:

> *"And three times bites this dog from hell*
> *While one tail waves the Sign of the Cross. . ."*

"Morgan," Robert Walker interrupted, "I don't like the sound of this."

"Please, Robert, I'm trying to concentrate. You had your chance - and refused."

"Yes, Signor Walker," Colon said, "you had your chance, so please keep quiet while Signor Beaumont reads out the clue."

Beaumont glanced at the parrot (it seemed to listen), coughed again, and continued:

> *"The coker-nutt falls onto a deserted beach*
> *A fool's treasure to those who seek*
> *The Underworld's hound looks to the sky*
> *To the master with the bright blue eye . . ."*

Beaumont paused, coughed, and concluded:

"So the sun sweats down, on this mid-day noon
Until the golden apples fall ripe to the ground
There, an archer's bow stands by a lonely pool
Over the All-Seeing Eye-land
And there, the Fiery Cross, my friend,
Ye shall have found!"

"One thing is for sure."
"Yes, Mr Beaumont?" the Italian wanted to know.
"This guy was a lousy poet," Beaumont concluded.

3

HERR PAPIER-DRACHE

"IT CANNOT BE," Robert Walker realised. He looked at his hands; wet with perspiration, they had picked up ink from the map.

"He knows!" the Italian howled. "Mr Walker knows the meaning! You must tell Colon - now!"

"La Buse," Beaumont added, with a flourish, "the Year of Our Lord Seventeen Hundred and Thirty. . ."

Mario Colon reached for his beerglass, and guzzled away its dregs. The Italian, with froth on his moustache and tears in his eyes, said:

"After all these years! - the treasure has been found! - I have been like a blind man in a cave at night!

"If you please, Signor Walker, the meaning of this nonsense?"

"The meaning of nonsense? You ask for too much, Signor."

"You know the map is genuine: it is yours for the price stated."

"The Labours of Hercules," Robert Walker said. "Graham Dunne was right, all along. But there is no way of authenticating this map - unless by its direct use on the ground. A visit to the rock to begin with, and then-?"

"As I say, the boat is available." The Italian had become weary. "Take the boat . . . to the rock."

Beaumont remarked: "There is an aspect of all this that baffles me. If Dunne was right, and he had this map in his possession, then why did he fail in his endeavour?"

"Who knows?" Mario Colon said. "You can discuss this all night. I must go to Cape Town."

"Why Cape Town?"

"There, Signor Walker, my search for missing cargo will continue. Now, do we have an agreement?"

The American observed: "If what you suspect is true, then this guy Dunne should have skipped the clues - and gone straight to Number Eleven, and then onto Twelve, where he would have found . . ."

The Italian posed: "The Fiery Cross of Goa?"

"Maybe," Robert Walker said; "then again, he might have found - nothing."

"Nothing! Nothing, you say! Some clarity, if you please."

"Clarity? All right, Signor Colon: this map is . . .unreliable. . . It might also be a fake."

"What-? You say this to Colon?"

"I do. It is recorded that La Buse, as he was about to be hanged at Reunion island, threw his papers into the blood-thirsty crowd. I do not believe this could be the same map, or even a copy."

"I'll give you one hundred rupees for it," Beaumont interjected.

Robert Walker concluded: "This search is futile, Signor Colon. The result of at least one twisted mind, maybe more."

The Italian's faced tightened: "You say that La Buse had a twisted mind? Or Colon?"

"I say more than that: I say there are people on this island who knew Dunne was wasting his time, but who did not tell him. They watched him search, and they laughed. You mentioned John Wilson, Signor Colon. But there is also something John Wilson told *me*."

The Italian glanced at the chronometer. "What did he tell you?"

"He told me the only place you'd find the Fiery Cross is on the newly issued stamp of the republic."

Mario Colon's chest deflated.

"What this is really all about," Robert Walker speculated, "is tourism. Dunne's search for the Fiery Cross is being used to promote tourism, that is all; the more fools who look for the treasure, the better for the Bourbon Island Tourist Office."

The Italian's face appeared to turn inside-out. "There is no such organisation."

"Not yet."

"This is dangerous talk, Signor Walker. You realise what you are saying?"

"Mr Beaumont's offer for your map is reasonable. I'd be happy to double the offer. A souvenir of my visit, if you like."

"You what?" the American said.

"I do not like," the Italian replied. "I do not like - at all."

"All of this will be published in my feature article. If Roger Dupin were here, he would confirm my suspicions as facts."

The Italian became edgy. "Who, you say? Who?"

"It seems to me," Robert Walker stated, "that there are people making money out of stamps and maps, while Graham Dunne and Roger Dupin lie rotting in their graves."

"-You know nothing!" the Italian confirmed said. "Roger Dupin has no grave!"

"How do you know this, Signor Colon?"

The Italian's face reddened, and he gritted his teeth.

"Easy, easy," the American warned.

After a pause, Colon realised: "You two fellows are trying to delay my departure from this hotel? WHY?"

"I don't know. How about you, Morgan?"

pora

"Who, me? I am only a journalist: I don't know anything." Then, Robert Walker digressed: "Except that . . .Wilson said that this is the first time the Fiery Cross has ever appeared on a stamp of the republic. No one knows what the Cross looks like, because no one has, supposedly, seen the Cross for over two-and-a-half centuries - since it went missing. Unless of course, it had been found. The Cross has appeared on the stamp now - for a reason. It is a signal. For the outside world to see. Change is on its way. Again, I say tourism. Or p-."

Robert Walker realised what he was saying; he had said enough.

"You talk too much!" the Italian complained. "Why are you telling me this story? You are trying to delay me, Signor Walker? Why?"

"There is, of course, a general description of the Cross from the ship's manifest of the cargo, but that is all. About four feet tall, a solid gold staff, covered with rubies, which provided the Cross with its fiery appearance."

"Enough! Enough! If I miss my flight, you shall pay!"

"I believe someone is trying to develop tourism on this island."

"How," Beaumont wanted to know, "do we get from treasure to tourism?"

"Easy. By exploiting Graham Dunne."

Mario Colon's face was wax-like: in silence, he stared at the *swish-swash-swish* of the ceiling-fan. The Italian's features had melted.

Behind the bar, the telephone extension rang.

Beaumont answered: "Marlin Room."

"*Colon'sBeercargofMaputolocatedbyChiefBbugisandhismen.*"

"Is that so? Really? When? Where?"

"*TheItalian'scargomovedfrombondedwaregouseatheharbourbureacracyg onemadtoBourbonAirportreadynowinthecargoholdofthemidnightflgihtCapeT own Go!*"

"It is for me?" Colon asked. "My cargo has been found, Signor Beaumont?"

The American waved for the Italian to remain silent. Robert Walker, with his elbow, edged the map away from view

"Oh really? Right, then."

"*....Theevilbastardwillnothavetimetocheckcargoholdttoseeifbeerisonboard andfakesdocumentsalreadymadeoutforcollectionatcustoms.*"

"This message is for me," the Italian guessed. "Here, there, give me that telefon!" Colon lunged for the receiver, but the American flexed out of reach. "This is my private business," Colon protested.

Beaumont snapped the telephone over its receiver.

"Too late," the American reported. "They've signed-off for the night."

"-? On the telefon there: whom was it calling? Call them back, I say. Tell them this is Mario Colon who wishes to speak."

"There's no time."

All three men looked at the chronometer: it was, somehow, 11:30.

Colon demanded: "What was the message?"

"It was the airport."

"The airport? You take Colon for a fool? What was the message? Why are you smiling like that?"

"Your long journey begins, Signor Colon. This is why I smile."

"Well, then-?"

"The message: your cargo of beer has been found. It was mislocated, that is all, by the bureaucrats."

"Bureaucrats? Which bureaucrats?"

"It is on the midnight flight bound for Cape Town. The documentation is ready for collection at customs."

"WHAT! are you saying? This is impossible!"

"That's the message - and then they hung up."

"Let me speak to them also! Call them back!"

"I don't know the number. Anyway, there isn't time. Look-!" Beaumont pointed at the chronometer. "And," he added, "I think. . .it is . . . running . . . slow."

"WHAT?"

"Look," Beaumont observed, "your taxi has arrived, Signor Colon."

Robert Walker nudged the map out of sight.

A white Mercedes pulled-up outside the hotel with a rubber screech.

"My map! Where is my map?"

Robert Walker looked into the distance beyond the bay window.

"Mr Walker-!"

Outside, the taxi driver revved the engine, and *honk-honked*. On an upper floor of the hotel, a guest shouted for peace and quiet. The same hair-primping taxi-driver bounced on his driver's seat, and shouted: there was time, but only just, to catch the midnight flight for Cape Town.

Robert Walker passed a BIR200 note to the Italian. Mario Colon snatched the note. "You owe me, Mr Walker. You will pay or-."

The taxi driver *honked* and gunned the engine. Blue smoke crept over the balustrade and onto the veranda. The Italian spat before Robert Walker's feet.

"*Arrivederci!*" he shouted, then ran out of the lounge, through the lobby, and onto the road. Mario Colon jumped into the rear passenger seat, slammed the door, and snarled through the windscreen. The driver looked into his rear-view mirror, adjusted his oily *bouffant*, and rammed his foot onto the accelerator: the white Mercedes took off along Revolution Boulevard, and headed for the coastal road.

In the Marlin Room, the American said: "*Arrivederci* - and to hell with you, too, Signor Colon."

Robert Walker removed the map from under the beercloth. "This," he explained, "and the boat. You heard him say: I could take the boat, Morgan."

"I heard him say you could take the boat as far as the rock."

"Whose side are on, Morgan?"

"I don't know whose side I'm on. Whose side are you on?"

"All right, I'll use the boat to reach the rock." Then: "Was that really the airport on the telephone?"

"No, that was Mr Swann on the telephone," Beaumont grinned.

The American checked the maritime chronometer: "Colon is about to board the midnight flight for Cape Town, but he won't have time to check the cargo. When he arrives in Cape Town, it's my guess he'll find the cargo hold - well, empty. Mr Swann must have greased a few palms, including the Chief's."

"So, where's the missing cargo of beer?"

"I have no idea. Anyway," and the American threw down a cloth, "I've heard enough about that cargo. Where, though, is Mr Swann?"

Robert Walker looked across the lounge. One of the guests was seated in an armchair - beneath the great stuffed fish on the wall. This particular guest played a game of solitaire onto a glass coffee table. The straw hat had been set to one side. Robert Walker picked up the map, crossed the room, and spoke to the German for the first time:

"Herr Papier-Drache?"

The German looked up: "Ja?"

"Is this what you're looking for?"

"Ja." The German smiled: he indicated that Robert Walker should set the map on the table beside the playing cards.

Robert Walker said: "I see you've put your cards on the table, Herr Papier-Drache. Interpol?"

Herr Papier-Drache played a card. "Nein."

"Der Spiegel?"

He played another card. "Nein, nein."

"The consortium?"

"Ah, ja. Nein."

"Ja-Nein? Why is the consortium here on the island?"

The German shook his head - no, nein - he was not able to say.

"You're after tuna concessions, then? Licences for the EEZ?"

There was no response of any kind.

"The treasure?"

Again, there was no response.

Papier-Drache appeared off-balance; he played a card, which missed the table and hit the floor. The German ceased his card playing, and looked up from the armchair with pale-blue eyes, limp yellow hair, and features blotched by the sun, but he did not say anything.

"Maps? You're an antiquarian map dealer from Berlin? That's it, isn't it? There is no consortium."

Herr Papier-Drache would not say. He gathered up the cards, and put the deck into its packet.

"You've got to leave me alone. I can't get anything done with you following me all over the place. If this is what you want, take it, but you've got to stop following me around."

The German accepted the chart, and slipped it inside his jacket.

"Is it a deal?"

"Oh, ja."

Herr Papier-Drache lifted himself from the armchair, placed the straw hat on his head, and crossed the room to approach the perch. The parrot No. 15 was now alert.

Herr Papier-Drache reached into his pocket, and fed the bird a single nut. In Bavarian, he said: "*I'll say this, and no more: if you feed this budgie too many nuts, it might turn into a vulture - and bite off your hand!*"

"What he say, Robert?"

"I don't know. It sounded like a warning."

The German turned, doffed his straw hat at the lounge area in general, and departed.

"Look, he's left a card behind," Beaumont observed. "Maybe his business card."

Robert Walker picked up the card.

"What is it?"

"It's his business card, all right . . .it's a Joker.

"-?"

"The harlequin." Robert Walker slipped the card, for luck, into his breast pocket.

"Why'd you let him have the map?"

"I don't need it. I know where the rock is. I have the boat. Dog Rock points the way. But if it's the dog I think it is, it points three ways at the same time. "

"That map's worth twenty thousand dollars."

"Or ten dollars. It'll keep Papier-Drache off my back, anyway. I think I'll call it a night, Morgan."

"I'd better wait here until Mr Swann returns."

"You could be in for a long wait, Morgan."

"I don't think so. He said he'd be right over."

Footsteps moved - well-heeled, and in no particular hurry - onto the veranda and through the lobby. Mr Swann appeared through the archway.

"Thank you, gentlemen, for an excellent night's work - so far. The Italian, he has gone?"

"He's gone, all right," Beaumont grinned.

Robert Walker asked: "Francis, he is all right?"

"He is, Mr Walker, more or less. But he won't be released for another hour or so. Chief Bugis feels he must make an example of my nephew."

Robert Walker said: "It's been a long night, Mr Swann. I was just about to retire."

Mr Swann said: "The night, Mr Walker, is not yet over."

4

MISSING CARGO II

THERE WERE NO witnesses. Mr Swann's hand-picked team set to work.

The hotelier acted as director of operations. Morgan Beaumont was sent to the kitchen, where he found Sami the chef and Danielle the waitress stationed by the dumb-waiter. The waitress from Paris, Bebe, was sent to wake up George. The gardener usually did not work by night; but this night he was required to deploy two luggage trolleys between the kitchen, through the dining room, along the corridor into the lobby, and then into the Marlin Room, and down - through the trapdoor behind the bamboo bar - into the cellar.

The group by the dumb waiter could only guess as to nature of the 'goods' to be shifted. There was a rumble of ropes, pulleys and weights, and the first batch arrived. . .

Sami the chef opened the dumb waiter.

Inside, the first three cases of Blue Marlin Beer had arrived.

Beaumont and Danielle loaded the cases onto the trolleys. Then George and Sami, working in relay, trundled the laden trolleys along the chosen route to the cellar. There was no other way. They went unobserved, except by the parrot, No.15, who watched and seemed to record the proceedings, move-by-move, box-by-box. This worried the gardener and the chef, but they had their orders, although, at one point in their relay, a whisper was exchanged . . . something about . . . "No. 16."

Robert Walker and Mr Swann fed the process from above. They had climbed the great staircase together, where they had reached the fourth floor and once more passed through the linen closet, and made their way up - as before - onto the observation deck. Beneath the cupola, the entire space was taken up by an array of cases. The solid wall of cases bore the same Trade Mark: BLUE MARLIN.

These, Mr Swann admitted, represented Mario Colon's entire missing cargo - five hundred cases - all the way from Mauritius. The presence of the hornets' nest, occluded by the shipment, was discernable only by a contented hu*mmmm*.

At Mr Swann's direction, Robert Walker conveyed the cases from the observation deck, down through the linen cupboard, and - three-by-three - into the dumb waiter, whereby each batch was lowered to the kitchen.

All the while, Mr Swann watched, and smoked from his packet of 555 State Express. The hotelier's lips moved in a silent count of the boxes. The Italian's cargo was on the move.

After an hour, a good third of the observation deck had been cleared, and Mr Swann signalled for Robert Walker to rest.

Robert Walker fought for breath, and asked: "What . . .are . . .you . . .doing, Mr Swann?"

"I am on look-out for the Chief and his constables. When Francis is released, you can be sure they will all be headed this way."

Behind the cases of beer, the hornets' nest went hhh*hmmmm*.

"Also, I must ensure these creatures stay asleep with the smoke."

Robert Walker gasped: "Okay . . .okay." His head spun; his clothes stuck to his frame; his legs and arms had turned to jelly, and his spine creaked.

"All right, Mr Walker, nearly there now."

Robert Walker reached for the next case: the chimpanzee gargoyle stared back at him. "Ah!"

"Please, Mr Walker," Mr Swann advised, " we must have quiet."

"Yes, yes, of course, Mr Swann." He shifted the case, then dragged it over the observation deck. Over the roofs of Port Bourbon, the sculpture of Roger Dupin seemed to gesticulate at the slopes of the mountain.

The proprietor wiped a tear from his eye. As he smoked, he appeared to laugh. The joke was a good one, and so was the plan. The 'missing' cargo had been secured, stowed, and re-stowed. Mr Swann had already invited the Chief and his constables to inspect the cupola, the home of the hornets. That had been risky, but the Chief - with fear in his heart - had opted instead for a spot-check on the cellar. In the morning, should the Chief send his constables up onto the roof, they would find only the angry hornets' nest.

Robert Walker, in admiration of the plan, found the strength to continue. Again, he lunged at the nearest case, brought it down into the linen cupboard, and shoved it into the dumb-waiter along with another two cases. Then he lowered the batch to the kitchen with a *squeek-squeek-squeek* of the pulleys.

After another hour, Robert Walker's eyelids were closing and his legs had started to buckle. Mr Swann, who allowed himself one cigarette a day, had smoked the whole packet, and had become drowsy, too.

On the fifth deck of the hotel, the two men were jolted awake by a night-splitting scream from the direction of the Victoria Road Police Station. There could be no doubt that Chief Bugis and his special constables were also working overtime. The Chief, then, wanted some sport prior to Francis Long's release. A dead-blank look from Mr Swann implied these were fake screams made only to frighten people. Robert Walker was not so sure.

"Almost there, Mr Walker. Look, the hornets' nest: it is quiet now, but we should not wait for the sun to come up."

"If ever the suns comes up, Mr Swann," Robert Walker remarked.

5

DR MOBUTO

BY THREE O'CLOCK in the morning, the observation deck had been cleared, and the cargo stowed at the lowest level of the hotel.

The cellar trapdoor was closed, and the Marlin Room secured. Mr Swann congratulated his team and, armed with the abacus, the ledger and a pencil, went to bed. The staff returned to their separate chambers. The American climbed the staircase to reach the fourth floor, and found the Presidential Suite. Morgan Beaumont closed the door, and was not seen again for days.

Robert Walker struggled against the fatigue, and with dead man's feet made his way out onto the veranda. He needed air, plenty of air, more than was available in the room under the stairs. He positioned himself on a long bench; he was too tired to sleep, but he could rest a while. . . He tasted the night air. Resin, from high-up. A smell of conifers was on the wind. Beyond the crossroads, the Police Station was at high alert. An emergency lamp shone with a cold blue light. Francis Long's lengthy interrogation was not yet over, although- . . .In one of the holding cells, the Chief barked, and the lights were subdued. Francis Long was allowed to sleep. Outside the block, the constables appeared with bicycles, and went home in different directions. One light remained: the Chief's light, which never went out. The Bamboo Mill said that Bugis never slept, because the policemen's conscience, if he had one, would not allow him to sleep as a result of all the beatings and tortures that had been administered over the years.

Instead, the Chief read comics far into the night and early morning, so when he at last became sleepy - it was time to start work. The comics, imported from America, were routinely confiscated from the newsagent up the road - *Batman, Superman* - which the Chief read by the yellow light of his anglepoise lamp. The Chief's favourite, though, was not any of the super-heroes, but a comic by the name of *Sad Sack*. The Chief loved this comic because Sad Sack, an ordinary 'dog-face' private in the US Army, was always pulling KP duty. The Chief, it was said, liked to shout orders at Sad Sack - just like the Sgt.

Robert Walker, from the bench on the veranda, watched the Police Station for a while. Soon, he thought, Chief Bugis would continue his investigation into Mario Colon's missing cargo. Mr Swann's masterplan, though, had implicated the entire staff of the hotel and at least two of the guests. . . As for Mr Swann's purpose, this had to be more sublime than grand larceny. Vengeance, perhaps, on behalf of the mothers of Port

Bourbon. Colon must be made to suffer, and Mr Swann had found a way. In the meantime, the Italian's long voyage had begun.

Robert Walker looked up from the veranda at the slopes of Mont Pomme d'Or. The jet-black cone - a mere cardboard cut-out, then - was set against the sky, yet darker than the night, and surrounded by the constellations of the Southern sky.

The world revolved on its great, invisible axis. . .

Robert Walker was aware that sleep approached. From a distance, something else approached. He should, he knew, make a retreat for his room under the stairs, but his legs had seized-up from shifting the cargo. Soon, he was flat on his back, stretched out along the length of the bench, and looked up at the portico. His eyelids closed and opened again; he was vaguely aware of some hotel rule: guests shall not sleep on the veranda under any circumstances. Under *any* circumstances? Then, the seconds stretched into minutes, and he had almost forgotten about the rule. Rule? Which rule? His eyes closed on him again, and he listened. The nightly sounds of the hotel were intermittent: as anomalous creak of a floorboard; a disturbed groan from a sleeper upstairs; a *glug-glug* from a tube behind the bar inside; the orchestra of the tropics, which presented a cacophonous wall of insect-sound, settled down to a creak-*creek* of a lone cricket; and then this, too, ceased, the victim of some merciless rodent beneath the veranda's planks. Something approached . . .

Out on the street, a giant frog - doomed from the start - approached the crossroads, leap-by-leap, in search of water. The creature was headed in the wrong direction. Robert Walker, with the hard bench at the back of his head, waited for the sweat to evaporate from his face, to leave only invisible salt. Then, there was a strange, wispy sense of feathers, which he knew to be black - but the feathers of evaporation were not black, they were white salt crystals. He opened his eyes: the fear in his throat tried to make a scream, but the sound would not come, for he had no voice. Face-to-face, a feathered man looked down, over the bench, so that the bulging black eyes stared into his own. A steel-wire beard surrounded black-red lips, which opened to reveal thick white teeth and an orange tongue. He struggled, but could not - it was impossible - move off the bench. Then, then . . .the feathered man's cheeks puffed-up. Robert Walker tried to twist off the bench. It was no good; his legs were paralysed; and the bench had stuck to his spine. The rule, the rule . . .The guests shall not - *must notttttt!* - spend the night on the veranda. Again, he closed his eyes, and opened them, but the feathered man hovered over the bench. Then the feathered man spoke:

"Dr Mobutu will make you fly."

Robert Walker's arms were free: he reached for - and grabbed - the feathered man's neck. The strength returned to his hands, so he squeezed:

the feathered man's cheeks puffed and puffed - each eye rolled (clockwise, anticlockwise) in its socket - and then the whole puffed-up face exploded. A breath from hell escaped through the bearded orifice. Herbs, garlic, the East wind from the Spice Islands, these were only to lull; and then, an odour of something unspeakable - the pit, the noisome gunge of - - -. A thick cloud of white powder engulfed Robert Walker. The powder expanded until it filled the volume of the portico. He retched; he fought for clean, pure air. Robert Walker released the muscular neck, and the feathered man, with a choke-choke, seemed to take flight up inside the portico. The plume of white power blinded Robert Walker. He rolled off the bench, and fell onto the deck with a bump. He turned on his knees, wiped away the powder from his eyes, and stood to his feet. Through one streaming eye, he was sure the feathered attacker had taken flight, and disappeared.

6

ROGER DUPIN

AGAIN, THERE WERE no witnesses to the encounter, except for the giant forg - no, frog - which leapt again, and lumbered towards its death beyond the crossroads. Robert Walker's lips and tongue were so numb, he could not shout for HELP! So, arms outstretched, with his face caked in the white powder, he lurched back into the lobby, and then - half-blinded - found his way along the corridor towards the room under the stairs.

By the time he had gained access to the cabin, the powder was at work on his mind. He thought he could hear the thirsty frog out on the crossroads: *Help! help! help! Which way to the pond? Anything for a drink of pond water, Mr Walkeeeeeeeer! Arrrrrrrrrpp! Bloody good stuff, too, if you can get it - duty free.* But what is this stuff? What is this powdery residue from hell? His rational mind, barely intact, knew it was a concoction of the feathered man, who must, then, be a witch doctor, thrown up this night from the bowels of the island. That damned frog is probably his pet - a pet spy. Beware those who sleep on the veranda at night. Beware! That is an hotel rule. This is a rule of the hotel. A rule, to rule. Do not, not. . . ignore the hotel's rules. Ignore them at your . . . Dr Mobutu's prescription? He must wash it off. Now! He looked: where is the water? He had not turned on the light, and yet he could see in the dark. He had not stooped, but he had not knocked his head on the sloping interior ceiling. A thump on the head at this time of night is always welcome. Knock some . . .sense into you, Robert-. What is your name, anyway? He turned, and turned again: there was the shaving mirror, above the washbasin. He stepped forwards, and looked into the mirror: he jumped back from the reflection. A white-faced ghost walks this hotel at night, Mr Swann. AAAAAArrrrgggggh! This cannot be, sir, for all the rooms are FULLY EXORCISED - it says so in the brochure. The brochure? What bloody brochure?

Robert Walker tried again, and looked into the shaving mirror: this time, dark eyes, which were not his, stared out from the mirror. . . the eyes of - oh no - the carpenter, Roger Dupin. This is Roger Dupin here, paying a friendly visit. Robert Walker, his mouth open, screamed but there was no sound. No sound . . ? No sound here, old boy, not in this place, he heard John Wilson say. I mean, for this price, what do you expect? Oh no, there is no such thing as - this is impossible. There is no need to be frightened, Mr Walker, you are in my realm now. He looked: the carpenter's face was a happy one, crinkled about the eyes with much laughter in his time, for this was a man who had pursued his desires while on Earth. That all sounds very well, but what does it all mean? These are the eyes of someone who knows something worth knowing. Listen-. Robert Walker watched the image in the shaving mirror: the lips moved, and told secrets that had to be told.

"What? What? I can't hear you, Roger."

The dead man mouthed words, but Robert Walker could not hear, which was reasonable, for how could you hear the words of a dead man? You think this is a madhouse? You ain't seen nothing yet! All right, then: learn to lip-read, and quick. . .Yes, yes, there is something there, mostly words without meaning, but there are a few. . .words without sound . . . but about that Dog . . .

"The dog? What dawwwwwg?"

Robert Walker could hardly speak; his whole face was numb from the narcotic. He thrust his head into the shower capsule, and pulled the chain. . .He watched: the mist turned into a dream of water, and flowed - the dreams of men and women - down into the open plughole, and out to sea. When he looked into the mirror again, he saw only his own, tired, wet - but cleansed - face. It was his face, his own face, not Dr Mobuto's. . . Enough of all this gibberish; he was falling asleep after a very, very long day - that was all - and he was overtired. He yanked at the dangling sash, and the big, comfortable, welcoming bed slipped into place, a last refuge against this long night. His hands would not let him undress, so he fell onto the bed as he was: the timber-springs bounced, accepted his weight, and settled. . . In sleep, he found peace, but not for long . . .The last vestige of the powder worked its way up his nostrils, and into his brain. Once there, then what next? The sleeping mind of the automaton works on the powder as much as the powder works on the sleeping mind. A snuff from Zanzibar. . .That damned witch doctor, Dr Mobuto, how Robert Walker looked forward to their next encounter. Fear? He would find a way.

In the night of the cabin, a while before dawn, a voice spoke: Robert? Robert? I say, Robert, are you there, old boy?

"Is that you, Wilson?" Robert Walker asked in his sleep.

It's me, but it's not John Wilson; I've only borrowed his voice so to speak.

Robert Walker stiffened against the sponge-pillow:

"Who speaks?"

Do not be frightened, Robert. This is Roger Dupin. You know me. My sister, she's in love with you. Your are a foreigner, and you were wounded. An unbeatable recipe for a woman's heart, my friend. Tiger pills from Harry Singh? Tiger, tiger, you can forget about the pills - I've tried them.

"Sylvia? She is? Where is she?"

As always, you ask questions of the dead. One-way traffic, as always. At this early morning hour, she is collating the latest edition.

"The latest edition? Of what?"

Why, *The Black Turtle!*, of course. She is the editor of that creature! "Ah. A woman of many talents, your sister. But what would Conny say? I'm to leave the women alone. I'm to stay out of politics."

Then find her - find her if you can - but do not look for her.

"More riddles? What were you trying to tell - before? About the Dog? You see? There you go again with your questions.

"You started this interview, Mr Dupin, not me. I am asleep - or trying to sleep - but my face is numb."

Your face is numb? You should feel mine!

"Who is this Dr Mobuto?"

He is back on the island, then? Stay away from Dr Mobuto, Robert; or he'll do for you what he did for me.

"What did he do to you?"

Is was Bellamine's bidding, of course. The Italian played his part, too. Betrayal is his speciality. Mobuto performed the deed, with Dr Marigold's help. . .More than that, I cannot say. Ask my sister, Sylvia. She knows everything; she knows . . .what happened to me.

"Who is Herr Papier-Drache?"

I do not know him, but there is something about that name. . .you should check with the German dictionary in the morning; you will find it there on the shelf. But I'm sure it means . . . Paper Bird.

"Paper bird? But that is the same as . . ." The delirium worked its way through Robert Walker's skull, but then the answer unfolded: "That means Kite. A paper bird is a kite. Herr Paper Bird is . . .Mr Kite!"

Now who speaks of riddles?

"Never mind; he's my shadow, but one. . .who casts a shadow from the sky. A projector. . .for the consortium and the CIA both - or not. A member, perhaps, of the emergent EU intelligence community. But that cannot be right! Mr who? Herr - who? Yes, but of course. As I deduced earlier: an antiquarian map collector from Berlin. But is - as someone suggested - Mr Kite a potential ally?"

The consortium, Robert?

"The consortium that's looking for the treasure."

The treasure? But-? The treasure is-.

The voice of Roger Dupin became faint, and added only. . .*Three ways looks this hound from hell.*

Robert Walker woke up, sweating: he stared into the deep recesses of the cabin, but heard and saw nothing, except, perhaps, for a grey shadow - there - once again, in the shaving mirror. He had been talking, then, to shadows. What had the carpenter been trying to tell him about the treasure?

He slumped back on the bed; its structure bounced, he knocked his head against the twelve symbols of the headrest, and he was unconscious once more.

The effects of Dr Mobuto's powder had not yet dissipated.

Then, although his eyes were closed, he was granted a vision of the Fiery Cross of Goa - so that it illuminated the cabin with its rose-tinted aura. The heavy gold staff, encrusted with rubies, blazed before his eyes, hypnotic, but taunting the searcher. . .who was Graham Dunne, while La Buse laughed at the man from Essex, who stood, the vision now revealed, on the coral sands of Venus Beach, and wept, and stared, not at some obscure clue, but up, up, up at the rim of the volcano, which had to be, Dunne knew, the Garden of the Golden Apples, Mont Pomme d'Or - the end of Hercules' great voyage. Then Dunne kicked at the sand, and pulled at his thinning flaxen hair, and shouted at the sky, but Robert Walker could not hear the words, for now the laughter was not that of La Buse, but . . .the man in the dacha; he who rules and looks over the island and the shoals beyond.

Robert Walker reached for a torchlight on the bookshelf: he turned its beam onto the penultimate symbol of the headrest. The Eleventh Symbol showed a three-headed dog, which had to be Cerberus, the hound, which guards the entrance to the underworld. The beast looked three ways, but the middle-way was in the direction of the Twelfth Symbol, which had been left - or cut-out - as a blank, circular tablet, unfinished. . .The gateway to the underworld, he guessed, had to be mouth of the volcano, and the lush slopes of Mont Pomme d'Or... formed the Garden of the Golden Apples.

Robert Walker turned off the torchlight, and listened. In the shaving mirror, he saw the same grey face. The lips of the dead man moved, but said nothing. A question was needed, a good one:

"How do you know all this, Roger?"

I know, I know; I had to die to find out, or I found out and then I had to die; but before I died I carved the monkey. You see, Mr Walker, it *is* possible to redeem oneself, but you have to die for it!

"-? The carving? It is a monkey, then, and not a chimpanzee?"

It is indeed a monkey. I carved it in a hurry. A glancing blow with my chisel took off its tail, so it is a monkey without a tail.

"And a tale without an end, Roger!"

Well, I am not sure I should tell you.

"TELL ME WHAT?"

Ah, so you would try to trick old Roger Dupin! Well, I did not have a chance to grow old; my children remain unborn, my sister remains unwed, my carvings remain uncarved, but for the monkey; my stories remain untold, except for the one that I might now tell only to you. Quick, the dawn approaches!

"Well . . .?"

A groan of despair and heartache filled the cabin.

Robert Walker flinched, and the bed bounced. The effects of the powder had not yet waned: in the shaving mirror, a grey face looked out at Robert Walker. The eyes of Roger Dupin opened, but his eyes were empty. The lips moved:

Now, listen to what I have to tell you. You are not you; you are you.

"I don't understand."

Only Sylvia Dupin will love you until the day you die.

"On which day will I die?"

Do not ask me that. That is the one question-. Anyway, no conditions. Whether you fail or succeed in your mission, her love is like a continent. Also, she is a most beautiful woman, don't you think?

"I have only seen her twice, but I think I understand. Yes, Sylvia, a woman of many faces, but one face for the man of her heart."

This is good. There is hope for you yet. This means that you and I are brothers, and only brothers may confide, where no friend is to be trusted.

"More wisdom from the beyond?"

Yes, but enough of the jokes. Now, listen, Robert, to what I have to say. My life was taken from me. Bellarmine and his agents are murderers without conscience. I was drowned on the Shoals of Paradise, where I was cut into pieces. After the sharp coral, even the little fishes had a go. A thousand cuts for the carpenter. A thousand bites from the fishes. They took me in their boat. I did not come back. They said it was an accident, but it was no accident. The truth is what got me killed. It is the one thing that got me killed. I knew, you see, that poor Graham Dunne chased only clouds and shadows, but I should not have known. This is the secret that financed a revolution. Look to the map - there is the clue for all to see.

"You mean, the map is real?"

The map is as real as you or me!

"-? But I gave the map to Herr Papier-Drache - Mr Kite!"

You are with the consortium, Robert?

"No - I mean, I don't know. I don't think so."

Well, what does it matter? The consortium will not find the treasure. The map leads the way, but it is too late. The three-headed dog looks to the sky. His master with the bright blue eye? That is the extinct volcano, below its rim or eyelid, there is an archer's bow - a tree - but the tree is no longer there. In the days of La Buse, may be so! And so, along came a man who wanted to build a dacha to match his lust for power. And there, in the foundations, there was an enormous old tree-stump, and inside the ancient wood remains there was-.

"- The treasure?"

Yes, it was by accident that Bellarmine built his *dacha* on top of the treasure!

"Incredible luck!"

So, you see, the treasure buried in Seventeen Twenty Five was used to finance a coup in Nineteen Seventy Seven? La Buse - if only he knew it! - financed a revolution over two and a half centuries after he was hanged.

"And for this knowledge, you were-?"

No, no - not quite.

"Tourism, then. I was right! For tourism to thrive, the treasure must never be found. Tourism is the real treasure. Millions of rupees every year: a treasure, renewable - there's the cache!"

Now, at last! At last! I can rest in peace! My sister knows the how, but not the why. You must tell her. She will print it in *The Black Turtle!* and the people will turn against Bellarmine!

"There is something missing. Something is not right-."

Yes, yes, so beware, for your consortium, which searches for the Fiery Cross, is really after Bellarmine himself - which you, Robert, had already guessed.

"I had? Yes, I suppose so . . which means that I-."

Goodnight, Robert Walker, and may you sleep well this night - what is left of it. Quick, the dawn approaches! I go now, to rest in Limuria!

Goodnight to you, too, Roger Dupin, though it is nearly morning; for now it has been told, and may you rest in peace, forever.

7

BISHOP CHIN'S QUARANTINE

WORLDLY SUCCESS, THE bishop maintained, brings its own special kind of failure.

David Chin's sermon was among the most popular, widely admired, closely observed and detested (by the BIPP) occasions in the life of Port Bourbon.

The BIPP had suppressed free expression for so long that debate, argument or innovation of any kind had become fugitives to the minds of the islanders. The bishop's words were, therefore, monitored by the state apparatus, not for their spiritual content, but for signs of dissent. In the pre-coup days, the sermons were accepted as the tedious ramblings of a cleric; in the days of Bellarmine, the ritual message to the flock was heard as a speech. The sermon, then, had become more than a homily; it was an event, an entertainment, and, for the devout, the serious business of reflection - on religion and politics, and football (*see below*). For many islanders, the sermon was better than anything on BIRTV - except for *Sea Hunt* - and more provocative even than Bellarmine's own speeches about 'La Revolution'. David Chin, it was said, would make a better DJ than Johnny Savvy, and the *Echo of the Island*, which the priest edited, was regarded as superior to both the underground *The Black Turtle!* and the exiled *Bourbon Island Star.* The Bamboo Mill asserted that these publications did not really stand for anything, except against each another; and Johnny Savvy, as a DJ, stood for nobody but Johnny Savvy.

In contrast, the bishop was always 'on-message': God could make a man or a woman great, but He might also cast them low again - at a whim.

In response, the regime - sensitive to criticism direct or implied - had resorted to blunt ultimatum: the doors of the Magdalene Church would be closed, unless the priest stayed out of politics. The threat had been heard in Rome. The Pope, who was a busy man with so much sin and hate in the world, had been forced to respond: the saying of Mass, even on the remote Indian Ocean island, the pontiff declared, must not be interfered with by the secular authority. The epistle had not invited a reply. François Bellarmine desisted, and the bishop had - so far - gone unmolested. As almost everyone knew, the dictator as a young man had been refused Holy Orders - on 'the ground of temperament' - which did not mean anything, necessarily, except that Bellarmine was perhaps loath to escalate the battle of wills, between politician and cleric, church and state, and - for those prone to hysteria - good and evil.

It was generally accepted, even among the diplomatic community, that the bishop was a man of great moral fibre, who would certainly be destroyed, while other men of acknowledged stature had accepted money or favour - such as an import tariff monopoly on a staple - and advancement in the one-party system.

The bishop said that he, too, belonged to a one-party system: the Catholic Church, which stood firm against Godless Marxists like the BIPP, who sought only power.

David Chin, besides his moral fibres, was also noted for his diverse interests. As a bachelor, whose family was his parish, he had cultivated these interests over four decades: as an accomplished cook; a connoisseur of fine wines (an interest he shared with his tormentor); a world-renowned authority on orchids; an amateur ornithologist; a gardener; a student of the Socotra-Chagos shell-fish and the island's insects (the BIPP bureaucrats, somebody once joked); an occasional rod-fisherman, who was capable of a mighty cast from the promontory; and a preacher or orator, whose ability, though, followed the tides: it was either in or out.

On this Sunday, the tide - which lashed at the rocks outside the church - was high:

"Why do we behave as spectators in this life," David Chin said from the raised granite pulpit, "instead of active participants? Is life a football game, where we watch a few others play?"

In the farthermost pew by the doorway, Morgan Beaumont watched heads turn among the congregation. Does he expect us to answer? We *are* spectators, aren't we? A fair number of the parishioners, though, could guess which way this sermon was headed. The bishop paused with a frown at his notes, and continued:

"Life, being a gift from God, is neither mean nor trivial; and nor again is it something to be despised, since God is not like that, and He does not deal in trivialities. These are the mean characteristics of Man, not God . . . Anxiety, fear, self-loathing, the hate of others, leading to - to who knows what? - perhaps misanthropy on a global scale, which will bring its own rewards as States collide, just as cynicism brings its own rewards, being few and unnameable."

The congregation became restless. What was the bishop talking about?

"Let us hear no more about cynicism, then. We have these obstacles so that we may overcome them. Without mountains to climb, there can be no mountaineers, and no view from the top. Without God, there can be no love; and without God there can be no Man, and without God, Man is nothing. "

Morgan Beaumont, who was tired after a long, long walk the day before, listened to David Chin's words. On the side of his face, he could feel the fresh breeze blowing-in off the Indian Ocean. The wind moved over the promontory, across the expansive gardens, and then passed - through the open portals of the church - along the aisle as far as the altar.

Morgan Beaumont thought about his wife, who was not real, the children they never had, and of the career that had been manufactured for him, but he could not yet recall the details of his former life as a doorman in a nightclub. His current worldwide, door-opening reputation was real enough, which was some compensation. But he was only a stooge, for Barbara West, though, and - now that he thought of it - her predecessors. Secretaries all; spooks all of them. . .A danger to journalists everywhere, but the Agency did not care; journalism was not the Agency's business. It had been in that same Dallas nightclub, for sure, that the Agency had recruited him, and then remade him in its own image. Now, it was all over, and he wanted to forget about the whole long episode. Soon, though, they would send an assassin to silence him - one, perhaps, had already been despatched in the guise of a tourist visiting the island - suntan lotion, dark glasses - but this would be no ordinary tourist. As he listened to Bishop Chin's words, he knew it did not matter who he had been, or who he was, or what he might do next - or not. In that respect, he was no different from anyone else - except. . .If he had been programmed, then the program had started to unravel: for no good reason, all that mattered now was that he complete a circuit of the island's shores. After that - peace. As for Miss Barbara West-.

"-Beauty," the bishop was saying, "the eye can see, but beware the beholder. Beauty does not last. . .only virtue lasts. Cultivate virtue, this is the real beauty on Earth."

In the same pew, a plain, wall-eyed woman exchanged glances with the American. The bishop's words echoed inside Morgan Beaumont's head. . . He had been programmed - somewhere around 1963. He was 'a spook'. He was a spook's spook. He was a member of the Cold War's living dead. He knew that much, and no more. Morgan Beaumont looked along the aisle, over the heads of the many islanders, toward the pulpit. Bishop Chin took a breath from the ocean breeze, and said:

"This Sunday, I wish to talk to you all concerning a few fundamental matters. . .the facts of life, if you like, but not as you, my people, would know them."

David Chin's ears were alive to whispers and giggles among the congregation. The priest's deep-blue eyes moved under his dark eyebrows. He raised a vestment-clad arm, and coughed into his fist. Along the aisle, there were other coughs of support. He continued:

"There is a great mystery at the heart of our very existence. The justification for our being here in this world is to explore that mystery; this, and this alone, is our purpose. Those who deny this mystery, and live only for gratification of the flesh and the senses, mines the purest form of Fool's Gold.

"We need, I think, an example . . ."

"Here it comes," Morgan Beaumont whispered. The wall-eyed woman studied the American, then turned away.

"There is a country where . . .the government's political philosophy has been supplanted by state gangsterism; its economic policy has been substituted with corruption."

In the front pew, a cabinet minister was infuriated. Bishop Chin realised he had said enough for one sermon, and made the Sign of the Cross.

So did the congregation. A young woman groaned, and went into a faint. A couple of adolescent males in Sunday-best suits, escorted the girl along the aisle and out of the church. Outside, the girl was quickly revived; threesome linked arms, and carried on into town. Inside, the cabinet minister's face had turned a sweaty grey; his wife scolded, and passed a hanky. An irritable child kicked at his mother's shins; then the husband shuffled his family away down the aisle.

"You have no right, Bishop Chin!" the minister spoke up. "Politics is none of your concern."

The priest glanced down at the pews: "Anything that affects the spiritual well-being of the people is my concern. That is the end of my sermon. God go with you all."

A dark wave of protest moved over the congregation, while a few agreed with the priest's words. A woman stood up, and fainted into the aisle. A stevedore raised her limp body, and carried her - with the help of a plantation worker - into the vestry.

The bishop might have finished his sermon, but he remained in the pulpit. David Chin looked directly at the cabinet minister and his wife. The couple, he seemed to recall, had owned a sweetshop in Port Bourbon prior to the Bellarmine coup.

Fear moved among the pews. A young woman developed hiccups. In general, the congregation started to cough, splutter, and fidget. Panic started to build. At the rear of the church, a young couple stood up, and ran outside - into the gardens. Then the cabinet minister rose, and dragged his overdressed wife from her pew. She resisted, and then complied: together, they marched with stony faces out of the church, and were then bundled - by a pair of androgynous Party-workers - into a waiting limousine. A government chauffeur slammed doors; the engine started, tyres crunched over gravel, and the vehicle sped away.

Bishop David Chin seemed unable to leave the pulpit. The sweat ran from his face, and dripped onto the Holy Book.

"What is he waiting for?" someone whispered.

An altar boy had visibly wet himself. He got up - genuflected - and, with his head hung low, removed himself from the altar.

In the pulpit, the bishop wiped his face with an oversize handkerchief. Among the congregation, a break-away group formed near the vestry, and trundled along the aisle. They reached the baptismal fount, where they stopped, turned, and then retreated.

Morgan Beaumont had seen the soldiers approach from the direction of the promontory. Now, they blocked the doorway. The congregation made a series of exclamations, then assumed silence. The older soldier dipped a hand into the holy water, grinned, and blessed himself.

"Shame!" an old man volunteered.

In silence, the soldiers march steadily along the aisle towards the pulpit. The younger of the soldiers reached for, and unflapped, his holster. After a few paces, he withdrew an automatic weapon. In the rows of pews, the congregation quaked. Among the men, a few showed anger. One woman with pearl earrings readied her handbag, but was persuaded by her husband to relent. On the breeze from the promontory, the khaki-clad men brought with them a smell sour toddy and tobacco.

In the front ranks of pews, a young wife sobbed against her husband's shoulder. The young husband offered comfort, and looked up at the bishop for guidance. The bishop said:

"You would bring guns in here?"

The soldiers made a rush for the pulpit. The clomp of boots echoed among the rafters of the Magdalene. A middle-aged man - known as brave but stupid - made a dive for the soldiers, and was kicked unconscious. A loose tooth skittered across the granite floor, and disappeared from view. A woman shrieked, and fainted into the arms of another woman, who collapsed - with three others - along the length of the bench. The soldiers laughed, then assaulted the bishop. A powerful David Chin fought back, and almost rebuffed the attack. After a struggle, the bishop was dislodged from his pulpit.

The priest thrust his arms at the rafters. "I'll come in peace," he said. "Please do not hurt anyone else."

An odd-seeming fellow from the plantation cheered the priest, but no one else would intervene.

"Who was that?" the corporal wanted to know.

"Not me," the odd-bod fellow said.

"He's crazy. Leave him," the sergeant told the corporal. The sergeant pushed the priest along the aisle. "Move, monsignor!"

The bishop recognised the futility of his plight. The sermon was over. David Chin's career was finished. Exile beckoned - in some far away place. There, too, he would tend a garden. The congregation watched and waited for the soldiers to return to their barracks. Among the women, tears flowed; a few choked back their fear; a child wailed (thirsty); and a group of the older men shook their heads to no avail (if only they were twenty years' younger).

The priest and the soldiers had processed almost to the end of the aisle.

Morgan Beaumont knew what he had to do: he stepped into the aisle, and blocked their passage.

"You there! Out of the way!" the sergeant barked.

"Who me?" the American asked.

"Please, Mr Beaumont, it is no good," David Chin pleaded.

The younger soldier stepped forward, and raised his automatic pistol level with the American's head.

"You are tourist, man?" the sergeant asked.

"If you like."

Angered, the corporal pressed the barrel against the American's temple. Morgan Beaumont could feel the cold, hard steel against his flesh and bone. Beaumont turned - ever so slightly - and looked into the eyes of the younger soldier.

"Where are you going, Mr Beaumont?" the sergeant asked.

"That's depends on your corporal, sergeant."

Beaumont waited: a spasm of the soldier's finger would, he realised, send him into infinity. A sense of nausea formed somewhere behind the bridge of his nose. Beaumont looked straight ahead. An anaemic looking man with a too-tight collar keeled over the back of a pew. A youth, a few pews' distant, lost his breakfast into an open prayerbook. The sergeant and the corporal laughed. Beaumont felt the cool barrel shift against his skin. There were groans among the pews. The eyes of the congregation waited to see what would happen when the trigger was pulled. Real American brains or the empty head of a mannekin? The corporal's gun-hand started to tremble. The sergeant saw, and asked:

"If you're a tourist, Mr Beaumont, you should do what tourists do."

"Good idea."

"What are you going to do?"

The corporal's knees quaked until he had to remove the barrel from the American's skull. The young soldier's face turned yellow and then green.

Morgan Beaumont found that his breath, though shallow, was still there; so he said: "I was going to walk around your island. Follow the coast until-."

The sergeant pushed David Chin one step ahead. The sergeant grinned: "I have done this. On our manoeuvres. You must do it also."

The corporal, who held his stomach, looked from the American to the sergeant. He returned the weapon to its holster.

"Don't come back until you're done. Okay, Mr Beaumont?"

"Okay. When do I start?"

"You start right away after we are out of here. Don't go into town. Just strike out along the coast there. If I catch you going into town for supplies, you can join the priest here in the glasshouse. Have a nice journey. And don't come back until you're done. I expect a full report when your mission has been accomplished." The sergeant gargled with laughter. "Understood?"

"I understand, sergeant."

David Chin's face showed that he understood something extraordinary had happened. The doors of the Magdalene would be closed, but - before then - something very unusual - for which he had waited all his clerical life - had transpired.

The sergeant pushed David Chin outside - into the intense sunlight.

8

VODKA ON THE VERANDA

THE ISLAND ENTERED the doldrums, and the ambient temperature soared. The British High Commission hosted the weekly meeting of diplomats on the veranda of the Marina Hotel. Albert Greene, the Attaché, stood in for Mr Browne, OBE, who did not, these days, attend his own receptions. His deputy would neither confirm nor deny the rumours of Mr Browne's imminent departure for England, and early retirement - to Budleigh Salterton in Devon. An agency intercept reported that 'Badger Browne' - to his intimates - had not been his usual-self after the abortive counter-coup of Alfonse Trouvères. On the Bamboo Mill, one rumour persisted: Browne had got wind of the planned coup, and had betrayed the French mercenary to the Bellarmine regime. The High Commissioner, wracked by guilt, had confined himself to the British compound's garden with a bottle of Gordon's for company. It was all only hearsay, the official channel maintained - idle gossip - and nothing more - the chit-chat of the tropics.

"He's with this fellow called Gordon, then?" a voice outside asked.
"I am unable to comment on that," another voice replied.
Francis Long drew aside the articulated screens. In this way, he could monitor the diplomats from his position behind the bamboo bar. As at an auction, whenever a drink was required, the diplomats would raise a finger, wink an eye, twist a neck, or cough into a closed fist - which was often.
The heat inside Robert Walker's cabin had become unendurable. He made his way to the Marlin Room lounge, and signalled Francis Long for a very cold beer. Then he seated himself in an armchair, and spread his set of onionskins over the glass surface of a coffee table. Under the ceiling-fan, the onionskins fluttered while he tried to make sense of his notes. The feature article had been outlined in its bare bones, but it had not yet been written, so it could not yet be typed-up for submission. The title-page seemed to taunt him from the glass surface: 'The Terminal Odyssey of Graham Dunne'. Progress on the article had been abysmal, and the deadline of 5th September 1991 drew nearer. Bureaucracy had delayed a fairly straight-forward off-shore trip. The permit (which anyway had been confiscated by Chief Bugis) was a 'dry land' permit, unless Robert Walker could argue that Le Chien de la Roche - or Dog Rock - was dry land, with a short passage over water. There were complications, too, over ownership of the Italian's boat, which he had attempted to sequester for the short journey. Harry Singh, who claimed sole-broker status on the boat's use or

disposal, was having none of it, and had since become evasive - which meant no boat trip, not yet.

Robert Walker reached for a stray copy of *The Times*. The headline of 26th August 1991 read:

Soviet Union begins to fall apart

The headline had escaped the censor's scissors. Robert Walker looked at the five words until his eyes became unfocused. The world of Harry Stone was being made and unmade. This was the end, at last: the end of the Cold War, the unimaginable, which no one - not even this agency or that agency - had predicted.

Robert Walker wiped a deep film of accumulated sweat from his face. What would Uncle Sam - on battle-alert for decades - do now? The Russian Bear was dead or, more probably, in for a long hibernation, so new dangers would have to be found, while the American Eagle looked elsewhere for reassurance that it actually existed.

Robert Walker looked up: it was Francis Long, who set a cold glass of beer on the glass table. The bartender whispered:

"When do we go out on the boat, Mr Walker?"

"Soon, Francis. We'll go out to the rock - soon."

"You wouldn't go without me?"

"No, but it looks like we'll need Harry Singh's permission."

"I don't have enough money yet," Francis Long said.

On the veranda, heads turned.

'We'll tell him we're taking it out on a test-run as suggested by the owner. Singh owes me a favour," Robert Walker explained (recalling the haircut). "We could make him an offer. . . or we'll offer him the commission he would otherwise have had if-."

In the lobby, the sound of juvenile footsteps ran out of the hotel and into the street.

Francis Long went to investigate. He saw the boy, Charlie the Fish, heading for the Victoria Road Police Station. In the lounge, he reported:

"It's that boy spy. He heard everything."

"Well," Robert Walker supposed, "maybe he won't understand what he heard."

Francis Long reasoned: "I don't believe it. He'll tell the Chief what he heard, even if he doesn't understand it."

A voice from the veranda asked: "I say, is anyone there?"

Francis Long jumped-to: "Yes, Mr Greene? "

"Same again, if you please, Francis - there's a good chap. We could all die of thirst out here. Can't have that, can we? "

"Yes, Mr Greene. I mean, no Mr Greene."

The voice on the veranda observed: "That you there, Mr Walker?"

"Yes, it's me, Mr Greene."

"Didn't see you. Not spying on us, are you?"

"No, of course not, Mr Greene. Just reviewing my notes."

"I was only joking, Mr Walker."

"Joking, Mr Greene?"

"No hard feelings, eh? About the other week, I mean. Only doing my - well, you know. Why don't you give the notes a rest? Come over and meet Their Excellencies."

Robert Walker did not see how he could refuse. He rose from the armchair, and abandoned his notes to the glass table. He passed through the articulated screen, and stepped-out onto the veranda.

"Ah, there you are, Mr Walker," Greene observed. "I was just telling Their Excellencies about that witch doctor fellow."

Robert Walker exchanged smiles with the other diplomats - both of whom, he saw, were very much senior to Greene - but he did not take a seat, and he did not say anything. Outside, he crossed the veranda - rested an arm against the parapet rail - and looked beyond the crossroads.

"The story goes," Greene was saying, "that the fellow was despatched East to Zanzibar by Julius Nyerere himself."

"That's a great story, Al," the US Ambassador said, "but to what extent is it true?"

"Degrees of truth?" Albert Greene, the Oxbridge man, asked.

"Degrees of truth, as you like," said the cigar-puffing Harvard-man, who had also been a McNamara-man at Ford. "This is our business. I have heard it reported that Bellarmine himself requested the services of a witch doctor from Nyerere. Uncle Julius found just the man, whom he wanted to expel anyway as an undesirable, from Zanzibar - still to close to home - where he, the witch doctor, that is - had been in hiding. Bellarmine's request, if true, was timely."

"The result is the same," the Soviet Ambassador said. A Gorbachev-man, the Russian had thought deeply at the Academy of Sciences, before a stint at the Ministry of Agriculture, and then the Foreign Ministry. "We have here on this island a being from Africa whose very presence is an insult to the Soviet mission to this republic. Our friend Bellarmine is ill-advised. For how long have these islanders been prisoners of their own superstitions? "

"You believe in witch doctors, then?" Albert Greene asked.

"Mr Greene, I recognise that there are men who would call themselves witch doctors, who have a powerful influence in many distant communities. It is not for me to believe or not believe; these men believe in themselves, and so that is enough."

"There are some," the American teased, "who would regard Bishop Chin of the Diocese of Bourbon as a witch doctor, too. Viktor here is one of them," and he arched his head at the Russian.

Since none of the diplomats was a Catholic, it was only Francis Long who flinched, unobserved, behind the bamboo bar. Robert Walker, for his part, tried not to think about that night under this same portico.

"It is the same," the Soviet Ambassador, who had perhaps consumed too much vodka, shrugged.

"The same?" Albert Greene, on this third gin and tonic posed. "I wonder how the good bishop would react to being compared with the likes of a witch doctor?"

"I did not make the comparison," the Russian said: "Ambassador Cody did."

Ambassador Cody balked; he knew he had made the remark, but he did not want the Russian saying so, who anyway continued:

"The Church of Rome is a power on this island, Mr Greene, on that we can agree. We should therefore limit our remarks. But there are older forces from the mainland at work on these islanders. The dark forces of Africa, you could say. If you wanted to be careless, you could say that history starts there; one day it may end there."

William Cody chewed on his cigar; he did not much like the sound of that, either. Viktor Chomsky laughed: "Yes, by all means, let us be careless! We may never get another chance."

"Apocalyptic visions, Viktor?" William Cody puffed. The Russian, he knew, was not as careless as he pretended.

"When it comes, it will not be as we think," the Russian brooded; his chin rested almost on his chest. He wore a very expensive, Milan-tailored suit of dark-blue. "I say again: our friend is ill advised."

"Well, you're the one who advises him, Viktor," William Cody laughed, and blasted a plume of blue cigar smoke over the Russian's head.

"Let it be said," Viktor Chomsky coughed, irritated by the unwanted smoke from Havana, "that François Bellarmine does not always take my advice. We are open for once. We talk, so let us talk. In the States, straight-talk?"

Cody provided a blank smirk.

The Russian embellished: "In England, a frank and candid exchange of views?"

Greene provided a wan smile.

William Cody asked: " . . .and in Russia?"

"In Russia - silence," Viktor Chomsky uttered below his breath. "Like the Siberian winter in Yakutsk. Now, we have glasnost and also perestroika. In the spirit of these new things, and since this is my last day on this island, we talk. I go back to Moscow tomorrow - on Aeroflot!"

"If it arrives," Cody quipped.

"It will arrive. It has no choice."

Inside the Marlin Room, the parrot squawked.

The Russian became gloomy: "One of these days, someone is going to shoot that bird. A Russian bird of this kind would not be tolerated."

The other diplomats were stunned by the low quality of their intelligence gathering. News of Chomsky's imminent departure - from Chomsky himself - had come as more than a surprise to the two Western diplomats. Albert Greene looked over the parapet and onto Revolution Boulevard, while William Cody found, suddenly, that his seat had become uncomfortable. He moved, and the bamboo structure creaked.

Robert Walker turned, but stayed where he was, with one hand on the parapet. The Russian and the American seemed oblivious of his presence. The Russian Ambassador, enjoying the silence, watched nothing. Neither Cody nor Greene could ask what they wanted to ask. Albert Greene sought a distraction: "I understand. . .President Bellarmine rarely takes anyone's counsel but his own . . .Some - not us, of course - have referred to his increasingly erratic behaviour."

The Russian laughed. "Erratic, you say? I had not noticed. You agree, Ambassador Cody?" Viktor Chomsky asked.

"I am not at liberty-."

"I know, I know," Chomsky interrupted: "you are not at liberty to comment on this matter at this time. It is the same: the language of the State Department; I shall go to my grave with this in my ears."

Ambassador William Cody puffed blue smoke up into the portico, and allowed his thoughts to drift elsewhere. Annoyed, Viktor Chomsky continued:

"I am given to understand he has spoken to hardly anyone these few weeks; that he is preoccupied by, by-."

"Well?" Cody asked.

"Well, you know, other matters, shall we say? For instance - to be less than diplomatic - the softening influence of the blue-eyed beauty from America. A covert employee, we believe, of the American Embassy here on the island, assigned to take photographs of our excellent Soviet naval base facilities at Sans Souci Bay."

"Absolutely not," Cody puffed. "Categorically, no."

Albert Greene became unsettled; he said: "Mr Walker, if you don't mind-?"

"-Let him stay," the Russian insisted.

"Yeah, let him stay," the American agreed.

Viktor Chomsky smiled, and shrugged. "This is the famous, how do you say? - honey trap? - from the early days."

Robert Walker edged slightly along the parapet.

"You say categorically, no, " Chomsky smirked. "It is true, then."

Disturbed, Greene asked: "Am I to understand, gentlemen, that you are referring to Miss-."

"-That's enough, Al," William Cody warned. "Anyway, you were talking about witch doctors."

Albert Greene gulped: "Yes, so I was." The British Attaché looked up: "What about you, Mr Walker? Know anything on the subject of shamans?"

"Well, Mr Greene, I myself have encountered . . .the gentleman to whom you refer."

"Gentleman? Which gentleman?"

"Your shaman, as you call him. The witch doctor."

The Russian laughed: "The witch doctor is a gentleman?

Cody, as he chuckled, blew cigar smoke across the veranda.

"Doctor Mobuto is his name."

Albert Greene set his gin and tonic on the table. "You have? Surely not?"

Francis Long looked, open-mouthed, at the guests on the veranda. Under the portico, the three diplomats stared at Robert Walker, who said nothing more. An off-balance Albert Greene asked:

"You *are* joking, Mr Walker?"

"No, Mr Greene. I don't do jokes."

"You don't? Well, then, I don't know what to say."

"I wish I *were* joking, Mr Greene. I was out here - on this same veranda - several nights' ago. It was quite late - past midnight, anyway."

"Oh really? And what were you doing out here at that time of night?"

"I couldn't sleep, so I came out here for some fresh air. I sat down - on that bench over there - and unintentionally dropped-off."

"I thought you said you couldn't sleep?"

"When I awoke, the gentleman in question stood over me. He was wearing a suit of feathers - of some kind."

In the Marlin Room, Francis Long found work to do: he located a niche closet crammed with old liqueurs from the pre-Revolutionary days.

"You haven't mentioned this before," Greene said.

"I didn't think anyone would believe me."

"You're right," Cody chuckled.

The Russian Ambassador said: "Let him speak, let him speak."

Albert Greene asked: "Did anyone else see this . . .fellow?"

"I don't believe so. There was only-. I mean, there was no one else around at the time. And I haven't mentioned it to anyone until now."

"This is absurd," Greene decided.

"You brought the subject up, Mr Greene," Robert Walker replied.

"Well, I know; but I-. I didn't think that-."

The US Ambassador blew a plume of blue cigar smoke in the direction of the British Attaché, who coughed:

"What - ah, arg - were you doing up so late?"

"I told you: nothing. I couldn't sleep."

"It was the imagination," Chomsky explained with a half-yawn. "This island does strange things to the mind. It is a scientific matter."

Robert Walker said: "The ambassador may be right about the manifestation being a scientific matter."

"Ah, so you admit it was a manifestation?"

"The manifestation was real enough. And, only moments' ago, this group was discussing the individual in question as a real man - not imaginary."

"By reputation," Greene, the Oxbridge-man insisted. "Possibly, therefore, mythic."

"Either way, I've seen him. Dr Mobuto is his name."

William Cody enquired: "How do you know that, Mr Walker?"

"The name sounds familiar," the Russian admitted.

Robert Walker explained: "He told me his name, and then-."

"- and then what, Mr Walker?" Greene prompted.

"Well, he stood there, and when I tried to move, he blasted me with some kind of white powder: I was quite powerless."

Albert Greene could not quite comprehend. "I made a polite enquiry, Mr Walker, and you reply by coming up with this ludicrous story."

A suspicious Ambassador Cody asked: "What kind of powder?"

"I don't know."

"Talcum powder?" Greene suggested.

"I doubt it, Mr Greene. And it wasn't a sherbet fountain, either."

"-? You're making fun of me, Mr Walker."

"Sherbet fountain?" the Russian asked. "What is this thing?"

"I have no idea as to the exact nature of the powder. A narcotic of some kind, though."

The American probed: "You know anything about narcotics, Mr Walker?"

"Nothing, ambassador."

"He doesn't," Greene advised.

The Russian asked: "You were blasted by this powder, you say?"

"Yes, ambassador."

"A weapon of some sort. It is being tested on innocent civilians."

Albert Greene saw scope for serious conflict; he said: "As long as you are . . .safe, Mr Walker, that's the main thing - the important thing. Please, be seated," Greene motioned, "and let us say no more about it for now."

Robert Walker aimed for, and sat, in the fourth chair: although unoccupied by High Commissioner Browne, the place was maintained for protocol between the American and the Russian.

"Yes, yes," the Russian agreed, "let us say no more about it for now. It is more interesting to talk about the blue-eyed American beauty, is it not, than the man with feathers from Zanzibar?"

A deep-seated Cody said: ". . .I thought we'd finished with that subject, Viktor."

An edge-of-seat Chomsky replied: "No, William, we've just started."

Robert Walker said: "I sit, but do not presume to occupy Mr Browne's place."

"Excellent, Mr Walker!" the Russian said.

"Very good," Greene confirmed.

The US Ambassador said nothing.

In the Marlin Room, Francis Long emerged from the liqueur cabinet. Albert Greene saw the bartender, and raised a limp forefinger: "Same again, Francis, - and whatever Mr Walker's having."

"Yes, Mr Greene."

In no time, Francis Long had prepared a fresh round of drinks, which he placed on a tray, and ferried out to the veranda.

"Put that on our usual cheque - that's a good fellow."

"Yes, Mr Greene."

Once he had set up the drinks, Francis Long retreated to the bamboo bar.

"So, the beautiful American lady?" Chomsky continued. "This time, with real brains. Berkeley College? Harvard Law School? Now, working as a mere secretary to a journalist who has disappeared off the face of the earth!"

"You must mean Morgan Beaumont, ambassador," Greene said. "I don't think he's disappeared, exactly. I believe he's gone for a long walk, that's all. A very long walk."

"You believe what you want," the Russian said. "I believe he has disappeared. You English say long walk when you mean disappeared."

"I don't mean to contradict you, sir, but-."

"-*Nyet* and again *nyet*, Mr Greene!"

Albert Greene pouted, and sucked the edge of his gin & tonic.

"If ever," Chomsky bayoneted, "you are promoted to the full rank of high commissioner, only then may you contradict me. And even then- . . ."

Ambassador Cody leant back, and grinned at the sky. Robert Walker turned, and looked beyond the crossroads. Port Bourbon seemed abandoned: there was no indication of movement at the Police Station, the BourBrew bottling plant was at a standstill, and there was no sound of any commercial activity from the direction of the harbour.

"I do beg your, ah, pardon, Your Excellency," Greene managed to say.

"Of course you do, Mr Greene. And so does your High Commissioner Browne, who is also nowhere to be seen, except perhaps in his dried-up garden. All you Englishmen with your different colours for names - and still you cannot be seen, ha, ha! You can tell your Mr White back in Whitehall the same thing, ha, ha."

Viktor Chomsky was entertained by his own joke. Buoyed by his wit, the Russian signalled code at Francis Long for more vodka with fresh-sliced cucumber.

"I fail to see-" Albert Greene started. "I mean, High Commissioner Browne has not been well of recent. It is a familiar pattern among long-serving senior civil servants in the region."

"Only, it seems, among British ones," Chomsky probed.

"But not you, Al," Cody quipped. "Yet."

"That may well be, Ambassador Chomsky. And, no, not me, Ambassador Cody. Yet. . .Perhaps, as has already been intimated, I am not senior enough," Greene pouted.

"And the cause?" someone asked.

"Well, torpor, I suppose."

"Torpor? Torpor?" the Russian parroted. "This is *what* exactly?"

"In my own country, Alaska anyway," Cody reported: "Cabin Fever."

Francis Long arrived with Chomsky's vodka and cucumber; he set these items on the table along with a white 'Marina Hotel' tissue, and then returned to the bamboo bar. Out of habit, the Russian checked the tissue for any hidden messages. The American smiled, and chewed on his cigar.

"Ah, let us not speak of Alaska, William. This is really Russia. East and West - it is the same. Time stands still at that place in the middle. The Diomedes. Ours is Ostrov Ratmanova. Big Diomede. The Americans have Little Diomede."

William Cody frowned; the Russian folded a slice of cucumber, ate it, and chased it with a swish of vodka. Then:

"I understand. We have this same thing in Siberia. The Russian winter is long; it can do strange things to a man's sense of identity. I myself-. Hum, not now. If the mind is weak to begin with, then . . .Hum." The Russian's face shone with sweat and the cool heat of the vodka. With the same forefinger, he made circles over his head to indicate insanity. He smacked his lips with satisfaction, and continued:

"Torpor, then. I understand. It is the same. You Englishmen are always suffering from the torpor?" The Russian glanced somewhere between Robert Walker and Albert Greene, who explained:

"It all started a long time ago, you see-. What I'm saying is, Mr Browne is hardly the first to-. Even the first governor of this island suffered the symptoms - in, I'm afraid to say, the extreme."

Robert Walker spoke up: "Smythe-Smith. You must mean Sir Godfrey Smythe-Smith?"

Albert Greene looked at the deck. "Yes, Mr Walker," he said, "I do believe that *was* his name."

"This man suffered from the torpor?" the Russian asked.

"Indeed he did," Greene said.

"His wife was called Gwendolyne," Robert Walker related. "Or Gertrude. You may have heard the story."

The Russian remarked: "Gwendolyne? This is the strangest name for a woman I have ever heard in my life." Chomsky furrowed his dark eyebrows to say: "I would not give this name even to a dog or a horse. She suffered from the torpor, too?"

"Not her, her husband," Robert Walker replied. "With her, it was quite the opposite - in a way."

"-?"

"It could be argued, though," Robert Walker continued, "that - through her actions - she contributed to the general decay of Sir Godfrey's state of mind."

"Intriguing," the Russian said.

"Really, Mr Walker," Greene insisted, "do we have to recount the whole sordid episode? It was all a very long time ago."

"Well, you brought it up, Mr Greene."

"Sordid?" the Russian asked.

Albert Greene replied: "Well, I didn't mean to bring it up." The British Attaché's face had become moist. "I know you're a journalist, and all of that, but do you really have to go around digging things up?"

Ambassador Cody spoke up: "Come on, Al, Mr Walker's got his job to do."

"I don't see how."

The Russian agreed: "I'd like to hear what our guest has to say on the subject."

"Guest? Oh yes, I see what you mean."

The Russian said to the American: "He sees what I mean, William."

Robert Walker spoke to Greene: "You're right, it was all a long time ago - and, besides, the woman is dead. Or not, as the case may be."

Albert Greene sat bolt-upright: "Or not? What do you mean by that, Mr Walker?"

"Go on, Mr Walker," the Russian prompted.

Albert Greene, out-voted and outranked, said nothing.

"Well," Robert Walker continued, "it seems that Gwendolyne Smythe-Smith was a woman of some passion, who of course - in this isolated place - craved attention."

"It's the heat," Cody put in.

"Speculation," Greene mumbled. "No proof."

Robert Walker took a sip of his beer, and continued: "Oh, there's proof, all right."

"Passion?" the Russian asked. "What do you mean by this, Mr Walker?"

"Well, Ambassador Chomsky, her husband was, it appears, unable to satisfy her emotional needs. After all, he had a substantial administrative workload, and was preoccupied most of the time as governor of this island."

Albert Greene said: "If you don't mind, Mr Walker, getting to the, ah, point."

"I *am* getting to the point, Mr Greene. Anyway, over time, Lady Gwendolyne or Gertrude formed a grudge - close to her heart - and set out to ruin her husband's career by seeking solace . . .in the arms of a plantation owner from France."

Albert Greene's face had reddened; he said: "You're making this up, Mr Walker."

"You look like you need a drink, Al," Cody advised.

"First, we have to endure a story about a man in feathers, and now this story about Lady G. on the plantation. Really, I must ask you to show some restraint."

"Al, Al," Ambassador Cody reasoned, "all of this was maybe fifty years ago. You're acting like it was yesterday. What harm can it do? Let Mr Walker proceed with his, ah, yarn."

"Well, I've warned you," Albert Greene said, and cradled his gin and tonic.

Robert Walker explained: "This, Ambassador Cody, is no yarn . . .Even in the rare moments when Sir Godfrey was off duty, he would get so drunk on the local toddy that he wouldn't be much good to her - or himself."

"Really, Mr Walker, this is outrageous!" Greene spluttered. "You're making allusions."

"Allusions, Mr Greene? Which allusions?"

"You journalists are all too clever for your own good."

Ambassador Chomsky chimed: "And all of this that you describe, Mr Walker. It is the same as the torpor?"

Albert Greene cast his eyes along the portico, saying, "Perhaps it is Mr Walker who suffers from torpor."

Robert Walker ignored Greene, and explained: "A combination of factors, ambassador. Torpor, for one. Guilt, perhaps. The effects of the local toddy, for sure . . .All combined with jealously and of course remorse. In the end, Lady Gwendolyne spent more time on the plantation than she did here. This hotel was, of course, the governor's official residence at the time. Sir Godfrey took his life in this very building - in what is now the Presidential Suite."

"This is amazing," the Russian said.

"That's one hell of a story," the American said.

"It's not over yet, Ambassador Cody."

Albert Greene, who had his eyes tight-shut, opened them: "I think that will do for now, Mr Walker. I am sure Their Excellencies do not want to listen to this kind of thing."

"Then, I have nothing more to say."

Greene showed relief. "Good," he said.

"I have a question?" Cody asked.

Greene, who had relaxed, again stiffened. "Oh God."

William Cody said. "I've seen Sir Godfrey's grave - somewhere along the coast. But his wife, she is not buried at his side. So, Mr Walker, what ever happened to Lady Gwen?"

Albert Greene groaned, then drained his glass with a clink-chink to show marooned ice-cubes. They melted, fast.

Robert Walker replied: "Well, after a while . . .with Sir Godfrey in his grave, she led a life of unfettered freedom. She became heavy, as they say, with child-."

"You mean this plantation fellow?"

"I do. As far as I can make out, she decided on a discrete - ironically - course of action: she travelled with her plantation owner to Paris, where she gave birth to-."

"-How do you know all this, Mr Walker?" Greene asked.

"Research. I pieced it all together, I suppose."

"You suppose a great deal," Greene complained.

Robert Walker guessed that Albert Greene was concerned, not about Lady G., but about his wife, Elizabeth.

William Cody said: "I have a second question."

"Yes, Ambassador?"

"You'll regret it, Ambassador Cody," Greene advised.

"What, ah, was the name of this plantation owner from Paris?"

"I believe his name was . . . Jean-Paul."

"Jean Paul? Jean-Paul who?"

" Jean-Paul Bellarmine."

There was no sound on the veranda. In the Marlin Room, the fan seemed to whirrrrrr-*whir-whir* out of control. The parrot had its beak stuck firmly into the water fount at its feet. Francis Long had disappeared.

Albert Greene spoke first: "Are you really expecting us to believe, Mr Walker . . .that - that President Bellarmine is. . .the bastard son of this woman and a planter from France?"

"You said that, Mr Greene, not me," Robert Walker said. "I would, perhaps, put it more diplomatically."

"Well, I really don't know what to say. Except-. Do you think he knows? You mean, all these years - the fellow's half-British. That he's one of us?"

"Half one-of-us," Robert Walker corrected. "Also, half French."

After an interval, William Cody said to Greene: "You were right, Al, I *am* regretting I asked."

The British Attaché replied: "These are, of course, just stories, Ambassador Cody. There's no need to take them too seriously."

"Well, it's one hell of a story, anyway," Cody decided.

Viktor Chomsky fiddled with a slice of cucumber, and said: "I am thinking that history has this tendency to repeat itself, though this time not quite in the same way. Fifty years' later. There is a pattern in everything, but you must stand back at the appropriate distance to see anything. Determinism. The balance of probabilities leads this way or that way, but usually this way. It is the same with our own profession. I drink too much vodka today, but then why not? My time draws near. I talk. You talk, too."

"How do you mean, Ambassador?" Greene asked.

"You speak of allusions, Mr Greene. Here is one allusion for you. Just like the English woman and the French plantation owner. This time, the American beauty and the master of this island? An alliance? A strange match, for sure."

"I'm afraid I am unable to comment," the British Attaché said.

"Do not be afraid, Mr Greene," Chomsky said.

William Cody responded: "Viktor, there is absolutely no merit in your remarks."

"So, this means it is true."

"Absolutely not."

"You say absolutely when you mean relatively. You said so earlier: degrees of truth: that means relative."

"Did I say that?" the American said through a fog of cigar smoke.

Robert Walker's face changed.

Albert Greene noticed, and said: "You see what you've started, Mr Walker?"

"The woman," Chomsky chanced, "she is CIA, of course. The famous American journalist - a buffon -."

"A buffoon, you must mean, ambassador, " Greene suggested.

"I mean buffon. He is only a cover for her secretarial duties. In this way, too, our friend is ill-advised. He does not know, either way." Then, to the British Attaché:

"You have information?"

"I do not have any information."

"Then, why do we have these receptions every week? For no reason, eh?"

"That's right, ambassador, for no reason. A purely social function."

"I know all about the social functions. The honey trap, for sure."

"I don't know what you mean, ambassador."

"Your wife. She is a friend of the American woman?"

"I'd rather you didn't bring Liz into this."

"She knows. Ask her. Gossip. Chitty-chat."

Albert Greene grew bold: "I have no idea what you're talking about."

"Your wife knows all about it."

"How do you know, Ambassador Chomsky," Green gulped, "what my wife knows?"

"I'm afraid I am unable to comment," the Russian mocked. "I say this: the American woman charms our comrade."

"Wild speculation, Viktor," William Cody said. "You deserve a rest. When you get back to Moscow, I mean. You've been on this island for too long."

"You think I have this same torpor?" the Russian asked.

"I do."

"Then the torpor has made me say all of these crazy things."

Albert Greene looked hopeful.

"I say these things because the heat is in my head - just like Sir Godfrey. I apologise to our host, who is not here, and to you, Mr Greene, and to Mrs Greene also. . ."

"I understand, ambassador." Albert Greene smiled. It was Greene, though, whose judgement had become unsound, when he said: "Good. Perhaps, Mr Walker, you could assure Their Excellencies that there is no truth whatsoever in these stories."

"About Miss West-? I've met her once or twice in the presence of yourself and Mrs Greene, that is all. I cannot comment on-."

Albert Greene realised his blunder: "I didn't mean that story," he said. "I meant the one about Lady G and-."

Viktor Chomsky intervened: "-So, Mr Robert Walker, you are acquainted with Miss Barbara West?"

"I am acquainted with her employer, Mr Beaumont. He is very well known in my profession."

"Your profession?

"The world of journalism, I meant."

"Yes, I thought that is what you meant, Mr Walker."

Albert Greene studied the distance between Robert Walker and Viktor Chomsky.

Robert Walker saw that the Russian required discreet elaboration: "Miss West's private affairs are none of my business. If anything, I've formed the impression that she's dedicated to her work - with very little interest in anything else."

"Yes, that's more or less what Liz said," Albert Greene confirmed.

The Russian ambassador slurped at the vodka, and said:

"Dedicated to her work, you say? In the same way a courtesan is dedicated to her work?"

Cody turned away; Greene squirmed in his chair, and said:

"Really, Ambassador Chomsky, I don't know what to make of that remark. Miss West strikes me as being a very nice young woman."

"Don't let your wife hear you say that, Al," Cody jibed.

Chomsky said: "Yah, of course she is! That is why our comrade's mind is not so much on politics these days. The well being of his people is not uppermost in his mind. In only a few weeks, he has developed what we may call 'a personal life' - as this thing is called in the West. When I see such a process, I wonder to myself - what is going on around here?"

Robert Walker wanted to get up from his seat, leap over the parapet, and escape along Revolution Boulevard.

Albert Greene helped himself to a fresh gin & tonic; he had, though, already had too much. He said: "On a general point-. I mean,-. The old man - High Commissioner Browne, I mean - made a similar remark. Something about-."

"What on earth are you talking about, Al?" Cody asked.

Greene looked at Robert Walker for support: "Surely you've heard the same thing, Mr Walker?"

"Heard what thing?"

"This is amazing," the Russian said. "First you deny, then you-."

"-This is ridiculous," the American countered. "Are you really expecting us to believe that a US citizen is engaged in-?" William Cody removed the cigar from his mouth: "No, no, no - I just will not have it. I won't hear of it . . . These, Mr Greene," the American added, "are very serious allegations. Clarify. Are we talking about fifty years ago - or now?"

"Please, ambassador, I have made no accusations. I may have gotten the two stories mixed up, that's all."

The Russian showed disappointment. "It is not true, then?"

"It was just conversation, that's all."

"Conversation?" the Russian asked.

"That's it, just a rumour, perhaps. Island talk. Mischievous non-sense, really, that's all."

The gin had eroded Albert Greene's judgement beyond retreat. The Russian Ambassador seized on the *faux pas*: "Mischievous nonsense? From High Commissioner Browne himself, who you call 'the old man?' - or 'the Badger'. I don't believe it."

"Did I say that?" Greene gulped.

"Yes, you did, Al," Cody confirmed.

"Yes, I suppose I did, really, didn't I?"

"So," the Russian said, "the High Commissioner, who sits in his garden compound, who looks up at the sky, he does not miss much. So how does *he* know?"

"Well, I suppose. . .President Bellarmine must have passed some remark on the subject. I don't know, really. I'm not privvy to-. Please, forget I said anything."

William Cody reminded Greene: "Bellarmine speaks with no one these days, you know that, Al. . . He does not, as you know, speak with any of us."

"And if he speaks to no one," Chomsky continued with Muscovite logic, "then how does Mr Browne know? And Mr Browne, we know, is also a man who speaks to no one. So, how is it that these two men who never speak to anyone suddenly become very friendly by telling each other stories?"

Albert Greene sighed, and said: "Well, you have me there," he confessed. "All I can say is. . .the High Commissioner is not at the top of his form these days."

"This torpor again?"

"Yes, that's it - the torpor! He must have imagined the story; he's not, ah, been well just lately. Look, can't we forget about the whole thing? I would not want to be the cause of any grief or any kind of - you know. I don't want any trouble arising from what is probably only gossip anyway."

"I heard he was bitten by a snake."

"Who was bitten by a snake?"

"Mr Browne."

"I heard that rumour, too," Cody puffed, "but I didn't want to say anything."

"Your Excellencies, please," Greene pleaded, "there are no snakes on this island."

"Is that so?" the Russian said. "In that case, what is it that has bitten the High Commissioner?"

"He hasn't been bitten by anything," Greene said.

"He has been bitten by the torpor," Chomsky said, and took a fair swallow of the vodka. "I have said it before: all of you British people are being bitten by torpor. Your own Mrs Greene; I have seen it in her eyes."

"Please, ambassador," Albert Greene protested. "Let us leave Mrs Greene out of this: she misses her home dreadfully, that is all."

"Ah yes," Chomsky hummed, and his grey eyes became moist, "the *homeland*."

On the veranda, the silence was complete. Viktor Chomsky had succumbed to a deep, Siberian quietude in the depths of winter; soon, the short summer would arrive, and he would make the trip to Sakhalin Island. William Cody, by some whim of his ancestors, puffed smoke up into the portico, and had a vision: a million bison streamed over the prairie, kicked-up great clouds of dust until no bison was seen, and then, as the hooves of the beasts made thunder, all had passed into history. Albert Greene stared into his glass of gin, where he saw the dome of St Paul's, with its silhouette against London's evening skyline. He was on his way, along Fleet Street, to the Olde Cheddar Cheese, where Liz would soon join him for a half-pint of bitter.

Robert Walker watched the three diplomats for a while. The island had ground down each man in his own way. Then, he asked:

"Homesick, Mr Greene?"

"Yes and no, Mr Walker. Mrs Greene, yes. It's hard for a man to make his mark in England these days."

"That's true. I suppose."

"You would know, Mr Walker? A hack from Fleet Street - lost to the world? Washing other people's laundry in public, that sort of thing?"

Robert Walker watched the corners of Greene's mouth and eyes for signs of spite, but he saw only indifference - this man's worst enemy.

"Homesick?" William Cody quipped. "Sounds more like you're sick of home, Al."

Viktor Chomsky, who chuckled, was already back in the USSR.

Robert Walker looked over the balcony in the direction of the Police Station, where the arrivals and departures of some investigation was in progress.

"Mr Walker?"

Robert Walker turned, and discerned his own, featureless reflection in the Russian's grey eyes.

"We speak, so let us speak, Mr Walker. If I may ask - in a gentlemanly way - your reason for being on this island?"

"You heard it from Mr Greene, ambassador. A Fleet Street hack. Research."

"Hack? Hack?" the Russian seemed to cough. "Research, you say? What kind of research?"

Albert Greene narrowed his eyes. He, the British Attaché, would speak on behalf of his fellow national: "Mr Walker is researching the Dunne case. An article. Human interest - that sort of thing. His agency, you know, has-. "

"-Agency, you say?" Chomsky probed.

"News agency," Albert Greene said. "A feature article for syndication. Women's magazines, that kind of thing. I am right, Mr Walker?"

"That's correct, Mr Greene, but not just women's magazines."

"Not, of course not - I was only using that as an example for the ambassador's - ah - enlightenment."

Viktor Chomsky did not know which way to look.

William Cody puff-puffed: "You must mean Graham Dunne, the treasure hunter?"

"That's him, yes," Robert Walker confirmed.

"We picked-up the transmission," the American said. "Ah, your broadcast. On the radio, I mean."

"You all may have heard. I was asleep. Jet-lag, maybe."

"Yes, it was all very interesting - in its way," Greene mused.

In a more general way, William Cody asked: "What do you suppose, Viktor, to be going on?"

"I cannot say. And again, I must go back to Moscow." Chomsky looked at Robert Walker with deep regret in his grey eyes. "I must go back to the embassy soon and pack my bags. I am not sure that I shall miss this island."

After a while, Chomsky said:

"You will forgive me, Mr Walker? The situation is very . . .at home. I am tense. Tense, that is it, and maybe I have the torpor as well."

"I understand, ambassador."

The USSR was falling apart. *The Times* said so - so it had to be true. Albert Greene was ill-at-ease; it was obvious he wanted the reception over with and out of the way. Badger Browne would have to be told about Chomsky's departure. London would have to be told about-. He would have to tell Liz first, then she could deal with the Badger in the garden. One day, then, Greene would end up like Browne, but only after a well-earned promotion. You had to grow in to a job like that, slowly. The US Ambassador asked:

"Something on your mind, Al?"

Albert Greene could not say what was on his mind, so he said:

"That was a very bad business with Bishop Chin, don't you think?"

The two ambassadors would not comment.

"I understand," Greene continued, "that the bishop and Bellarmine had one of their card-playing sessions recently. Lots of brandy and cigars, that kind of thing."

William Cody picked up his cigar from the edge of the ashtray.

"You mean," Chomsky said, "that our friend still has time for playing cards?"

The British Attaché ran a hand through his sandy hair, which revealed early flecks of grey. "No, I mean he has the bishop under detention. London is not happy about it. Not happy at all. I meant to discuss it with you earlier, but we were talking about Dr Mobuto and Sir Godfrey instead." Greene cast a baleful eye at Robert Walker. Again, the other diplomats would not or could not comment.

Beyond the veranda of the Marina Hotel, the whole world seemed to hesitate, while some great, distant event to took place. A lone cyclist moved along Revolution Boulevard; he pedalled, with a Huntley & Palmers biscuit-tin tied behind the saddle, and in an unsteady, sluggish motion passed the hotel. In the Marlin Room, Francis Long stood without movement; the bartender's eyes were open, but saw nothing. The doldrums had settled over the island. In the middle of the road, the cyclist appeared to balance without forward movement. In the distance, a dog barked itself hoarse. Then, the bicycle started moving again, and travelled - at improbable speed - out of town, and up into into foothills. Behind the bar, Francis Long awoke with a faint smile on his face, and polished a glass.

"Something has happened," Robert Walker said.

Greene responded: "Something? You could be a little more specific, Mr Walker."

"No, I cannot."

"He's right," Chomsky agreed. "Something has happened. Not here on this island. Far away in some other country. I think, my own."

The four men looked at each other.

Chomsky wanted to change the subject: "Mr Walker, tell me about Mr Dunne. Please, talk now."

"Do we really have to go into that again," Greene complained.

"I insist."

"It's all old hat, isn't it?"

"It is not old hat, as you put it, Mr Greene. This Mr Dunne fellow, he never found anything, did he, Mr Walker?"

"No, he didn't - except for a few clues."

"Then it's not over yet," the Russian decided.

"Well," Albert Greene intervened, "Mr Walker's had a jolly good look at the subject, and there's nothing to it - isn't that right, Mr Walker? I mean, you've just about run out of time, haven't you? Time to go back to London, isn't it?"

"Almost," Robert Walker said.

"Thought so," Greene said. "Anyway, you must have finished the piece by now, haven't you?"

"I've made some notes," Robert Walker confessed.

"Notes? *Notes?*"

"Yes, notes. I'll need to write it all up in the next day or so. There's one or two missing strands."

The three diplomats were unimpressed.

Albert Greene ventured: "Wild Geese come to mind, Mr Walker."

"Wild Geese?" Cody asked. "You mean mercenaries?"

"I do not mean mercenaries, ambassador. I mean real geese. Mr Walker knows what I mean."

Chomsky asked: "There are wild geese on this island?"

"Not those kind of wild geese, ambassador."

"Which kind?"

Robert Walker explained: "Mr Greene implies that my efforts are futile, ambassador. In England, this is known as a Wild Goose Chase."

"Ah, yes, we have this in Russia also. Very good sport."

"-?"

"Mr Walker, as I was saying . . ."

"Yes, Mr Greene-?"

"I was trying to establish when, exactly, you would be travelling."

"You sound like you're trying to get me off the island, Mr Greene."

"I foresee-. Well, never mind what I forsee. Please don't take this the wrong way. But I'm anxious you do not overstay the limit of your visa."

The American, William Cody, and the Russian, Viktor Chomsky, stared at Albert Greene as though their host had become irrational.

In the lobby, Mr Swann appeared in an impressive light-blue day-suit. The hotelier snapped fingers at Francis Long, who dropped what he was doing, and joined his uncle in the lobby. Mr Swann, on urgent hotel business, pressed Francis Long into service, and the two men ascended the great staircase.

On the veranda: "Really, Mr Greene," Robert Walker explained, "there will be no difficulty. I don't want to stay here any longer than I have to. I have no plans on this island beyond my copy deadline - which approaches."

"Well, as long as we - understand each other," Greene said. "I don't mean to sound unfriendly, but there it is."

"No, of course not."

Then the British Attaché had an idea: "Look, Walker, if it'll help speed things up a bit-."

"Yes-?"

"I'll get Liz to type your script up for you. How about that? She's excellent. Cheltenham Ladies College, don't you know."

"I've heard of Cheltenham," the Russian remarked.

"I'm sure you have, ambassador. . . Now, Mr Walker, if I might have your attention."

"I'm listening, Mr Greene."

"Just feed Liz the script - page by page - and she'll type it up. I'm commercial attaché here, so you could argue that it's all part of the job. More than that, we can can fax the article from the British compound direct to your editors. That way, you can meet your deadline - and leave the island." Albert Greene set the gin & tonic down firmly onto the table, and rested back into his chair. "There, I can't say fairer than that, can I?"

"So," the Russian said to the American, "the British stick together, after all, eh?"

Cody grinned, and chomped on his cigar: "Sure."

Robert Walker replied: "I wouldn't want to put Mrs Greene to any trouble."

"No trouble at all," Greene said.

"Well, that's very good of you, Mr Greene. I accept. I'll feed the pages to you when they're ready."

"To Liz."

"There's no need to mention this to High Commissioner Browne, is there? I wouldn't want to get your wife into any trouble."

"Agreed," Greene said. "Liz needs something to - you know - keep her mind occupied."

"The English," the Russian remarked to the American, "are a very strange people. The word, I think - also strange - is *convivial*."

"Well," Cody cigar-puffed, "you'll get no argument from me on that one, Viktor."

The Russian eased back in his chair. "You must allow me some fun, William."

"I've never known you to be interested in having fun, Viktor," the American said.

"This is my last day - my last hour - on the island. There will be no time for such talk when I get back to Moscow."

Albert Greene, who played with his MCC tie, seemed to have lost interest in the conversation. "Anyway," Greene was saying, "let's clear the decks, and then we can forget about the whole thing. We must think of the future, not the past."

"I concur," Cody said.

"That is because," Chomsky said to Cody, "you have no past, William."

"And you have no future, Viktor."

The Russian shrugged: "We are both wrong, of course."

"My sentiment, exactly, ambassador," Greene rambled. "The sooner we can forget about the treasure-."

"-!"

"-?"

"- the better. Have done with it, Mr Walker, that's what I say. Where do you suppose your editors will send you next?"

"I really have no idea."

Albert Greene frowned, in the way of the Russian, and said: "There is one thing that's worrying me, Mr Walker."

"I'll get started right away."

"No, I mean . . .I understand you and the bartender are planning a boat trip to that off-shore rock." Greene narrowed his eyes. "I really don't think you have time for that kind of thing, you know. I really don't."

Robert Walker regarded each diplomat in turn.

"Well, any comment . .?"

"Is - this . . . true, Mr Walker?" William Cody asked between puffs.

"It depends."

"You're in the wrong game, Mr Walker," the American said.

"Ambassador Cody means," Greene guessed, "that you ought to be a diplomat."

"But you wouldn't agree, Mr Greene?"

"No, I would not, Mr Walker. I have only offered to assist you with your article so that you may leave this island without further incident. Now, it transpires, you are off on some mad treasure hunt."

"If it's any consolation, Mr Greene, I'm not looking for any treasure. I don't believe there *is* any treasure to be found, not any more."

"Then why, Mr Walker, are you planning a journey to the off-shore rock?"

"For verification purposes."

"Verification?" Greene almost snapped. "Of what?"

"If the treasure of La Buse was ever on this island then there should be a clue intact on that rock. Clue Number Eleven. The dog Cerberus, who guards the way to the underworld. That will complete my article."

"This is insane," Albert Greene said, and fumbled again with his MCC tie. "I'll wager - a thousand pounds - you won't find anything on that rock except seaweed and limpets."

William Cody, who had reached the end of his cigar, leaned forward, and said: "Did I hear something there about a wager, gentlemen?"

"I accept the wager," Robert Walker said.

Albert Greene loosened-off his MCC tie, and explained: "Really, Mr Walker, a figure of speech. I didn't mean to-. Surely you're not going to hold me to-? You *are*, aren't you?" Greene face's blanched: "Liz'll kill me."

"I heard him," Chomsky confirmed, "one thousand of your English pounds for the dog Cerberus."

"What are you worried about, Al? If you believe there's nothing on that rock, and there's nothing on that on rock, then what have you got to lose?"

"Yes, you're quiet right, Ambassador Cody. I-. Listen here, Walker, you've got to promise me that once you've been to that rock and written up your damned article then you're going to leave this island. And don't say a word to Liz about it. "

"Agreed."

"You're good for the money, then?"

"I can get it."

"Well, that's good, because there's nothing on that rock - and you're going to lose!"

"Take it easy, Al."

"Yes, take it easy, Mr Greene," the Russian agreed.

Robert Walker asked: "And you'll have the article typed-up and faxed - no matter which way the wager goes?"

Greene looked as though the MCC tie had hanged him. "Of course, you have my word as a gentleman - before Their Excellencies!"

William Cody looked doubtful: "You two had better shake hands on this," he advised.

Robert Walker felt the British Attache's hand: it was damp, and shook without being shook.

"So, gentleman," the Russian Ambassador said. "This will make a good story to tell when I get back to Moscow."

As the Britons parted hands, William Cody looked up from his seat, and said:

"My God, Chief Bugis! I hope you have an explanation for this intrusion!"

*

AFTER ROBERT WALKER had been taken away, Albert Greene continued:

"Well, it looks as though my wager is safe for the time being." Then: "Francis, where are you? Francis: refreshments for Their Excellencies, if you please!"

9

CHIEF BUGIS IN PARADISE

"YOU CALL THIS journalism? I call this rubbish! Look, I will prove it to you! See?":

Chief Bugis crumpled-up the onionskin into a fat fist, and tossed the ball of crushed paper into the wastepaper basket of the Victoria Road Police Station.

"There!":

Robert Walker watched, through the bars of the holding cell, as the missile found its target with ease. In the form of Chief Bugis, he had found a critic worthy of Harry Stone himself. The Chief returned to his desk, where he studied a well-thumbed copy of *Sad Sack* among his more important papers.

"There is more proper journalism," the Chief alleged, "in the charge-sheet I myself have written for your case."

"My case? Why are you keeping me here? What are the charges?"

"I've already told you, Mr Walker: you are under suspicion."

"Under suspicion? Of what? You can't keep me here. I'll speak with-."

"-The British Attaché?" The policeman - who revealed orange-coated teeth, gums, and tongue - creased-up with canned-laughter.

"You can't keep me here!"

The Chief rolled his eyes. "Oh no? Then who is that man behind those bars there? The Invisible Man maybe?" Again, the Chief howled with laughter, until he grunted and snorted.

"Under suspicion of what?"

"Under suspicion of writing an article, maybe? Haahahahahah-ahaha!"

Chief Bugis wiped tears from his face; he lifted the copy of *Sad Sack*, and tossed the comic to one side. "Haaarararaghaha!"

The raucous hyena-laughter brought in a constable from the office. "Get out! Get out!" the Chief demanded, and the assistant fled in a flurry of dockets and paper clips.

There was, Robert Walker had to acknowledge, some truth in the policeman's words. After almost a fortnight in Dupin's cabin, he had achieved very little except for a bird's nest of stray notes, clues, and speculations - which one of the constables had been diligent enough to recover from the Marlin Room 'for evidence'.

"I'll need my notes."

"Here, I'll give you your bloody notes, man!" The Chief whistled: "Hey, you hear that, constable?"

A voice replied from the office: "Yah, Chief?"

"Yah, Chief? Bring those skins in here!"

The constable brought Robert Walker's notes. The Chief accepted the wad, and added: "Now, get out!" and the constable vanished.

Chief Bugis rubbed, sniffed and shuffled the onionskins, and then fanned his bloated face with the wad. "Clues . . ?" he asked.

"Notes, not clues. I'll need the notes to write it all up."

"Then why didn't you say so, Mr Walker?"

"I wasn't sure I was going to cooperate."

The Chief stood up from his desk. "You sure now?"

Robert Walker stayed where he was on the edge of the bunk bed (wood, no sharp edges), and said: "Yes, I'm sure."

"Well, that is very good, Mr Walker." The Chief rolled-up the onionskins, and passed the tube of notes between the bars of the cell. "Because the only way you're going to get out of here is by writing the article."

Robert Walker accepted the notes, then said: "I would like to speak with the British High Commissioner."

"Impossible!"

"Why is it impossible?"

The Chief grinned: "Mr Browne's predicament is worse than your own. His Excellency has returned to England. He has retired to a special home in some bloody place called Salty Budlerton, by the coast. Stones, no sand. Very nice, too."

"- *Budleigh Salterton*?"

"In the kind of place where he resides, it does not matter." The Chief had a big, false teardrop in his eye. "There, he will have lots of cups of tea, put his feet up many times, and have a good, long rest by the sea."

"Then I-. I demand to see his replacement."

The policeman tipped his great head back, and laughed. "You mean Acting High Commissioner Greene?" Chief Bugis blinked his long-lashed eyes. "A bad conscience, it seems, along with too much bloody gin and tonic."

"You would know, Chief Bugis, about matters of conscience?"

"Personal insults mean nothing to me, Mr Walker. Now, why don't you be a bloody good fellow - and GET ON WITH YOUR BLOODY WORK!" . . . The Chief smiled, and added in a tiny voice: "There's a good chap now."

"Why?" Robert Walker asked.

"You're asking questions, Mr Walker?"

"It's my job to ask questions."

"Don't be so stupid, man. Now, be a good fellow, and get on with your work."

Robert Walker looked at his left wrist, but his watch had gone. "All right. But what date is it today? I have a deadline to meet."

"Yes, my deadline!"

"This is the third of September, Mr Walker. I think. Maybe it's the fourth. I had a saucy calendar here, but it's been stolen."

"The third! The fourth?" Robert Walker stood up, and grabbed at the cell-bars. "I've got to get out here!"

"That's what they all say."

"-Please, Chief Bugis, I'll-."

"You must be joking! You sit back down there, Mr Walker, and behave yourself! Perhaps an in-depth strip search might suit you - every fifteen minutes, say?" The Chief returned to his desk, where he attacked a nest of paperwork.

Robert Walker understood: he slumped onto the bunk, with his head reeling, and tried to work out where he had lost the time. Ever since that night under the portico, his sense of time had been distorted. Dr Mobuto's potions were to blame. How long, though, had he been held captive inside this cellblock? Then, he recalled the headline in *The Times*-? But, he realised, a day or so late - no doubt. On the holding cell wall, the clock's hands moved anticlockwise, and the present time did not make any sense. On the opposite wall, President Bellarmine's steady gaze looked over any prisoner held in this same cell. Chief Bugis scratched at his back. In a lazy mood, he was ready with a policeman's prognosis:

"Your mind has been affected, Mr Walker, by your time on the island. I understand these things, believe me. If you persist in these delusions, however, I shall have to move you to more secure accommodation - at the special hospital. Dr Marigold is very good at this kind of . . .treatment."

"Dr Marigold? That won't be necessary, Chief Bugis." Then Robert Walker remembered something. . .about Elizabeth Greene:

"Then, I - request - an interview with Acting High Commissioner Greene. Most urgent."

"You do? Why, Mr Walker?"

"Why? I'll tell you why. . I must meet the deadline. Not your deadline, my editor's deadline. His wife - Mrs Greene -."

The Chief rolled his eyes: "Oh yes? Nice legs, shame about the face."

"She has agreed to type-up the article. I'm to feed it to her sheet by sheet. It's already been set up."

Chief Bugis insisted: "One of my constables can type this up - as you say, sheet by sheet, also."

"Too slow. Mrs Greene is very, very fast - and accurate."

The Chief looked doubtful; he narrowed his eyebrows, which had been plucked almost invisible. Robert Walker was sure that Mrs Greene, when she plucked-out her eyebrows, painted them on again.

"All right, Mr Walker, my constables can type - more like hunt and punch - but maybe you're right. We shall see we what we can do. Now, no more talk. First things first! Get on with your work!"

Robert Walker had been provided with a yellow plastic *Bic* (an acceptable risk against a pencil shaft); so he scratched at a fresh onionskin. Chief Bugis watched his prisoner for a while, then reached for the telephone extension: there was no answer. The policeman rattled the receiver. Robert Walker said:

"I can't concentrate while your carrying on like that, Chief Bugis."

The Chief jumped to his feet, seized the *sjambok* from its special hook on the wall, and crossed the floor of the holding cell. He drubbed the whip along the bars of Robert Walker's cage. "THERE! You can concentrate with that? NOW, try again!" Chief Bugis screamed. "You really must try much, much harder, Mr Walker!"

Robert Walker set to work. Chief Bugis replaced the *sjambok* on its hook, and returned to his desk. The policeman's in-tray overflowed, while the out-tray was almost empty. As he studied the various charge-sheets, Bugis emitted a grunt, groan, and - once - a peep. Outside, late afternoon approached, although the clock on the wall indicated midnight or midday. Over the desk, the Chief activated an anglepoise lamp. In the holding cell, the strip-lights flickered into life, and settled down to a steady buzz. Robert Walker stared at the uppermost onionskin - its surface dazzled at 100Hz flicker - and tried to focus on what he had written. His brain - a wallnut - had become shrivelled by a lack of moisture, nutrition and sleep. Over the years, the Chief and his men had, no doubt, developed and refined their own methods. Mind-control drugs? Sleep deprivation? Disorientation?

In a stupor, he guessed what he otherwise would not have guessed: that the Chief of Police had an agenda: retirement, not on a policeman's pension, but on a cache of gold and rubies.

Robert Walker spoke up: "Why do you want the article?"

The Chief was dreaming of naked women and gold bullion. Asleep with his eyes open, he replied in a strangely mellifluous voice:

"There are many superstitious circumstances."

"Suspicious, you mean?"

"What does it matter?" the Chief gargled.

The policeman's eyes were fixed on the walls of the holding cell. Robert Walker followed Bugis' gaze. The prisoners' *graffiti* included an octopus with more than eight arms, a snake swallowing its own tail, and a tiny Fiery Cross of Goa - sparkling, in this depiction, with rays of long-dried blood. The Chief of Police, he guessed, had issued standing orders: the cell walls were not to be scrubbed of any possible clues, ever. If not treasure, then:

"What are you looking for?" Robert Walker asked.

"The missing cargo," the Chief almost sung. "You know where it is?"

"What cargo?"

"The Italian's cargo of beer," the Chief, in a trance, explained.

"No," Robert Walker replied.

"You had a hand in its disposal? It's hidden somewhere inside the Marina Hotel. Tell me where, and you shall receive good treatment."

"I don't know anything about it."

The Chief had hypnotised himself with the anglepoise lamp. "An Englishman should always tell the truth."

"Who told you that?"

"Graham Dunne told me."

"Graham Dunne is dead, Chief Bugis. The truth killed him."

The policeman rested a while, then asked: "You must tell me the truth. Mr Swann is the mastermind behind this whole plan. You must confirm this. You owe him no loyalty. While you are in jail, he is having a good laugh and lives in comfort."

The Chief was in a deep trance.

"Is that all I'm here for? Missing cargo? A cargo that may never have existed in the first place?"

The dreamworld of Chief Bugis shattered; he woke up, and asked:

"Did I say anything?"

"Yes, you said I'd been here long enough, and that I could go back to the hotel."

The Chief grinned: "I say that?"

"Of course."

The Chief yawned: "I don't think I said that; it doesn't sound like something I'd say, Mr Walker."

"No. No, you didn't say anything like that. But you did say-."

"There, there - you can tell the truth when you try ever, ever so hard, you see? It is easy-peasy."

"Yes."

A cockroach scuttled out from under the bunk, and across the floor. Chief Bugis crushed the creature under his heel, and kicked the carcass aside.

"Now, next subject." The Chief lifted a pencil and dawdled at a piece of paper. "Who are the members of the consortium?"

"What consortium?"

"You are a member of the consortium! What are the true objectives of this group?"

"I don't know anything about any consortium!"

"Then why are you looking for the treasure?"

"I'm not looking for any treasure!"

The Chief had become volatile: "You have an invalid treasure permit!"

"You confiscated the permit on the day of my arrival. It is, I believe, valid."

"It is not valid: it is for dry land searches only. You, on the other hand, are planning a trip to the Rock of the Dog to find clues. I know this to be true."

"How can I be planning a trip when I am locked up here?"

The Chief's dark features changed to include a charming smile: "This is very true, Mr Walker. How, indeed, could you?"

"Well,-?"

"The permit, of course," the Chief added, "can always be upgraded to include a maritime search - if ever, you know, you were to embark on such a voyage." The Chief took on an urbane air: "I am dedicated to my work. Always. A police escort might therefore also be provided - for a consideration."

"That is an example of your dedication to duty?"

"You, Mr Walker, have not yet seen such an example."

"I've told you, Chief Bugis, the only voyage I intend making is the one that takes me off this island-!"

"Ten thousand rupees is all," the Chief offered, reasonably, but the pits of his eyes had turned white. After a massive mood-swing, the Chief called for - tea: "TEA!" and waited until it arrived. A constable appeared from the office, and handed the Chief a big mug. The brand name "Boh Tea" stood out in red lettering against the white mug.

Robert Walker could feel moisture in his eyes and he tasted . . .salt. The Chief of Police slurped at the powerful hot brew.

"You see, Mr Walker, how I can drink boiling water?"

The Chief closed his eyes as he sipped, and - with the flick of a finger - dismissed the constable.

"Ah, that is better . . .One of these days, I shall retire, Mr Walker. Now, where do you suppose is the cargo?"

"The cargo of beer?"

"Yes, yes, yes."

"Well, I don't know - but if you, Chief Bugis, were going to hide such a cargo-."

"Yes, yes-?"

"-then were would *you* hide it?"

The Chief set the Boh Tea mug on his desk, and considered the matter. "Where indeed?" the policeman mumbled.

"Who knows?" Robert Walker chanced. "The cargo might well be in Cape Town as we speak."

"You are suggesting," Chief Bugis deduced, "that the Italian has stolen his own beer?"

Chief Bugis fluttered his long eyelashes, and with an almost feminine voice whispered: "Mr Swann is the culprit, Mr Walker. A capitalist without conscience. A policeman's instinct. Something you would not understand. But there is no crime unless I can locate the beer inside Mr Swann's hotel. . . However, on reflection, discovery of a single bottle of the missing Blue Marlin might be adequate."

"-?"

"Once I have accomplished that, I have my man. Tell me this to be true, Mr Walker, and I will let you out of this place right now. Then you can drink all the beer you like, stolen or not - I do not care. We can also find you more pleasant accommodation in which to finish your article with a beautiful woman - not Mrs Greene - to assist you. And, when you are done, you are done, and you are free to leave the island for good! All you have to do is come with me to the hotel right now, and point the finger at Mr Jeff-bloody-Swann, and I will have his guts for garters. It is easy, see?"

It had been a long time since Robert Walker had heard the expression. Guts & Garters. Boh Tea & Treachery, which came as easy as breathing to Chief Bugis. Once again, the Chief got to his feet, and removed the *sjambok* from its hook on the wall. Then, with a twirl of the whip, he approached the cell, and stroked the *sjambok* across the bars.

"I must have something from you, Mr Walker!"

"I can't help you, Chief," Robert Walker swallowed. "That's all there is to it. I don't know where the cargo is located, and that's the truth."

Chief Bugis erupted in a bout of multilingual swearing.

The constable from the office reappeared: "More tea, Chief?"

Chief swiped at the man: "GET OUT!"

When Bugis' temper had subsided, Robert Walker repeated:

"I really must insist on seeing Acting High Commissioner Greene, Chief Bugis."

"Oh really, really? Insist, do you? Okay, yes sir, yes sir, three bags full, Mr Walker!"

In a deep sulk, the Chief stomped towards his duty desk. Once again, he returned the *sjambok* to its hook. Once again, he lifted the 'phone, and redialled the number. On this occasion, there was an answer. The Chief spoke in a bizarre imitation of a civil service accent: "Oh really? No one there? Then, where? No one knows? Oh dear. Mrs Greene? Yes, if you would, please. Yes, I'll hold."

The Chief waited on the end of the line, and - to taunt Robert Walker - wrapped the flex around his neck, and stuck-out his orange tongue. Death by strangulation - the garrotte - the preferred method of the State.

Robert Walker despaired of the hefty wager he had placed with Albert Greene. The British Attaché was, then, incommunicado, and - potentially -

a thousand pounds the richer, while this prisoner was unable make the trip to the Rock of the Dog or Dog Rock.

Chief Bugis responded: "Mrs Greene? Yes, Mrs Greene. I understand you have volunteered to assist Mr Walker? You didn't volunteer. Your husband volunteered for you? I see. Yes, that'll do perfectly. Jolly good. No, I'll have the pages despatched by a constable on a bicycle. Who, me? Well, I'm helping out also. Where is Mr Walker? He's at his usual accommodation. Oh yes. No, he must not be interrupted. Thank you, Mrs Greene. The Bourbon Island Police Force always tries to be of service. Jolly good. Thank you, Mrs Greene."

Chief Bugis slammed the 'phone down: a shard of Bakelite shot out from the base of the receiver, and ricocheted off the wall.

The policeman's gamely plucked eyebrows jumped. In the accent of a mandarin, he reported: "There is no need for undue anxiety, Mr Walker. I have complied with your request. Mr Greene's whereabouts are unknown. They will find him in due course and send him here. As you are not cooperating with our investigation, you will likely be deported anyway - but not until you have kept your appointment."

"What appointment? Who with?"

"No more questions! Now, back to work!"

Robert Walker stewed in the heat of the cell. He continued with the scrawl over the onionskins. After a while, he discovered there was, after all, not all that much left to do, and the "The Terminal Odyssey of Graham Dunne" would be completed. Robert Walker saw Harry Stone's promised bonus (£1? £1,000?) appear and then disappear, in a wink, before his eyes. What, though, was Albert Greene doing that he could not be located? The social-round, as the new High Commissioner (Acting)?

Robert Walker signalled Chief Bugis, and passed only the first onionskin through the bars of the cell. The policeman returned to his desk, and scanned the page for evidence. Robert Walker paused, and watched Bugis. At one side of the Chief's desk, a row of hooks supported: various sets of keys, a malacca cane (with split end), a long shoe-horn, a back-scratcher with an ornamental clawed hand, and a beer-bottle opener; and, as a centrepiece, the splendid *sjambok* or rhinoceros whip.

The Chief spoke up: "This is really much better, Mr Walker," and continued reading. The hypnotic anglepoise lamp had been clamped onto the desk. On the wall, above the desk, there was a short shelf, which held a small, electric swivel-fan, which buzzed, and cooled - and did not reach beyond - the Chief's face in 5-second sweeps. A cork noticeboard was affixed to the wall. On this, the Chief had pinned holiday postcards - Mauritius, Seychelles, and Moscow - alongside mugshots of dangerous-looking criminals. In this way, a postcard of Big Ben appeared beside a double mug-shot of an individual with the blank eyes of the condemned.

The Eiffel Tower played adjacent host to an official photograph of - limp in death - a hanged man. Chief Bugis glanced up, and Robert Walker looked away. When the Chief turned back to the skin, Robert Walker saw that the cork noticeboard also held a poster for: WANTED FOR TREASON - Alfonse Trouvères - REWARD of BIR1,000,000.

Robert Walker's vision doubled. In the swelter of the cell, he stretched onto the hard bunk, and - with his back lodged against the wall - continued with the article. The rancid smell of the wafer-thin matress pervaded the cell. Then the yellow *Bic* - with the sweat - slipped through his fingers. The sweat was in his eyes, too, so that he could barely read what he had written. Above the holding area, the harsh striplight seemed to burn its way into his skull. The onionkins had become ionised. He could not stand it any more. A fast, running dash into the cell-wall might end it all, but probably he would only hospitalise himself - again - and there was no room, anyway, to build up any real momentum. The handle from a cloth-covered bucket had been removed. In this way, since the electric light-fixture was out of reach, the means of any permanent escape were denied the prisoners of this cell. He might stab himself with the *Bic*, but that would never do for an employee of the Shoe Lane Agency. Not good headlines: Journalist Stabs Self with *Bic*. It would, anyway, crumple into his chest and shatter, as Bugis well knew. He thought about Conny Trapp, and desisted. A shame he had not got to know her. Now, it was too late. She was in Blackfriars. A shame. . .

He was falling asleep.

"WAKE UP, MR WALKER!"

It was no good, though. Good night, Chief Bugis, and sweet dreams. The cell-floor seemed to open up, ready to swallow him up and away.

"OKAY! DINNER TIME!"

He fought of sleep, and awoke.

"Where do you think you're going, Mr Walker?"

"I'm not going anywhere."

Chief Bugis said: "I saw you - you were going off to the Land of Nod."

"Nod? I don't know Nod."

"WAKE UP!"

Chief Bugis coughed, and spat dark-red liquid into a concealed vessel under his desk. "What are you doing there, my good fellow?"

Robert Walker eyed Bugis through the cell-bars. "Thinking."

"Thinking? You don't need to think, man. Too much thinking! Not enough scribbling. Now, get on with it!"

"You said something about dinner time?"

"My dinner time, not yours," the Chief grinned.

Robert Walker started on a fresh onionskin. He finished the sheet in no time, and held it up for the Chief's attention. The policeman crossed the floor, and grabbed the onionskin, which he then read on his way back to the desk. He turned:

"What's this got to do with the treasure?"

"You'll see soon enough."

"COPY!"

The constable appeared: "We've run out of coffee, Chief."

"Not coffee, FOOL!" the Chief screamed. "Here, take this sheet - and this first sheet here - and cycle over to the British compound. Hand over to Mrs Greene only. Understand?"

"I understand, Chief." The constable ambled away.

"MOVE, I SAY!"

, The constable ran - out of the general police block, mounted his bicycle, and pedalled-off in the direction of the British compound.

Somehow, it was mid-day outside. On the wall, the hands of the clock swept out arcs in the normal direction, but at . . .high-speed. The Chief's uniform showed dark-wet under the arms. He took off his cap, and revealed a close-cut, well-oiled head. For no reason, a parting ran severely down the middle. The skull looked partly cleaved. Robert Walker was sure the Chief wore some kind of perfume; and - more alarming - the policeman's stubby fingernails had been varnished with a cochineal-coloured lacquer. The Chief moved closer, and pushed his fat face between two cell-bars:

"Progress?" Then Bugis reached into the cell, and snatched away the most recent onionskin. Robert Walker thought to grab the Chief by the head, but - while he might have seized a firearm - the keys to the cell were well out of reach on the row of hooks.

"This part," the Chief read, "this is true? About the hanky-panky on the plantation?"

"Yes," Robert Walker confirmed, "I believe it is."

"And what has all this got to do with La Buse?"

"Nothing."

"Then why are you wasting my time?"

"It is all inter-connected, Chief Bugis."

The policeman sighed: "Yes, I know, Mr Walker. Everything is interconnected on this island." Then: "COPY!"

The constable reappeared, and - once again - relayed the sheet to the British compound.

"Why are you doing this?"

"Be a good chap, Mr Walker, and shut up. Concentrate, apply yourself. Next sheet, if you please."

"Soon, Chief Bugis, very soon."

The Chief's eyebrows, by this stage, were raised almost up to his oiled-hairline. "That is good. I am looking forward to the part about the Englishman. I knew him, you know."

"Graham Dunne? So I believe."

"What do you mean by that? You are implying something?"

"That's the next part, Chief Bugis."

"All right, then, get on with it! The Chief turned away. "Time is very short!" The policeman looked up at the wall-clock, which did not make any sense. He swore under his breath, and referred instead to his own wristwatch. The policeman sat at his desk, and waited. After a while, the Chief's eyelids had almost closed.

"Why are you doing this, Chief Bugis? Why?"

The Chief's eyes remained half-closed: "Nice legs," he murmured. "Mrs Greene has very nice legs. Shame about the . . ." The Chief had fallen asleep; he dreamed, then, of Mrs Greene. That, Robert Walker, thought, was unlikely, so how much had she offered the Chief of Police? Why else would the policeman allow Mrs Greene to transmit pages out of the country. In his sleep, Bugis mumbled: "One thousand pounds equals . . .about ten thousand rupees. . . "

The Chief awoke, and rose from his desk: "Time for curry. Back soon. In my absence, you work hard, Mr Walker!"

The Chief departed, and no constable took his place. Robert Walker's stomach lurched with hunger; his throat felt of sandpaper. Out of nowhere, he had a vision of a Ploughman's Lunch and a pint of draught Bass.

Robert Walker had, though, made progress where none had been made.

"Mr Walker?" someone whispered. "Mr Walker, you are asleep?"

"I am asleep. I am. Who's there? Is that you, Chief Bugis?"

Robert Walker tried to open his heavy-lidded eyes, and failed.

"Mr Walker. There is very little time. I believe you have made a discovery of some personal interest to me. Is this true?"

"Personal interest? There is no personal interest on this island. There is only the collective."

"This is no time for dialectics, Mr Walker."

Robert Walker, when he opened his eyes, was staring at the portrait of François Bellarmine. He, and he alone, occupied the holding cell. He had slept, where sleep was impossible, and the fluorescent strip-light burned on and on and on. . . Footsteps moved from nowhere - across the holding cell floor - to nowhere.

"You know something?" the man asked. "About the American woman?"

"A little. Not much. She has a mind of her own. By the way, am I asleep or is this conversation real?"

Robert Walker encrypted the next onionskin to read:

Mario Colon, former bagman for the regime, now in Cape Town. Recommend arrest for complicity in the murder of exiled resistance leader Jacques Savvy (Paris, 1984). Bellarmine' s direct order, for sure. Actual assassin remains unknown. Bourbon Island current situation: Russians to withdraw as situation in Moscow deteriorates. As yet, unsure of naval facility status at Sans Souci Bay . . . Bellarmine losing will to rule, if not grip on power. Appears to have been persuaded by a high-level US operative (female) to retire from politics and leave the island. Discovery: Bellarmine has elderly mother living in Paris. Mrs G. Bellarmine, formerly known on this island by married name of Lady G. Smythe-Smith - leverage potential clear. . . Local militia out of control, but poses no real threat. No leader likely to emerge. Recommend now safe for Anthony Montainge to return via Diego Garcia. Transfer bonus to London account as agreed. . .Message terminates.

Robert Walker returned from the semi- to the conscious state, where he was thirsty and hungry.

Chief Bugis returned from his curry bout: his paunch bulged through his uniform; and sweat ran from his scalp, face and torso.

"Phew! What the *hell* are you doing, Mr Walker? You British are lazy blokes nowadays. All finished? Let me see what you have there, then."

"I'm dying of thirst, Chief Bugis. And I'm hungry."

"Anybody there?" asked a voice from the next-door office.

The Chief turned on his heels: "Someone following me there? Come on, show your face!"

After a pause, Harry Singh stepped into the holding cell area. The merchant wore his trademark white shirt and slacks, and bore - with a strap around his shoulder - a portable box-unit or chest of some kind.

"Mr Singh?" the Chief observed. "You've taken a wrong turn somewhere, I think?"

"Why, Chief Bugis, good evening to you! What strange weather we are having the days. Rain is predicted from the north."

"Rain? At this time of year?" the Chief blinked. "What are you talking about? You come in here to talk about the weather? Who admitted you?"

"Why, the nice constable, for my usual weekly visit. Your haircut, Chief?"

"I've had my bloody haircut this week, Mr Singh, as you well know."

"All right, haircuts all-round for the prisoners?"

Robert Walker saw his chance, and took it: he stood up, with the last of the onionskins:

"Chief Bugis! If you please? An urgent matter. The task is-."

"-You have finished?" The Chief had a vision, not of onionskins, but luxury retirement funds. The policeman made a grab at the papers; while, to the merchant, he said: "You stay there!"

Robert Walker explained: "I've almost finished! Mrs Greene should continue with these while -."

The Chief rifled through the papers. "Almost, you say? Always almost! How much more?"

"-A few more pages is all."

Harry Singh spoke up: "Oh, really Chief Bugis, why do you have a nice gentleman like Mr Walker in your jail?"

Chief Bugis warned: "Do I come to your general store asking questions, Mr Singh?"

"Well - yes - occasionally you do."

"Police business. What about your business here?"

"A nice shave for the prisoner?" Singh suggested.

"Oh no. No. Don't let him near me," Robert Walker pleaded. "It's too dangerous."

"Keep quiet, Mr Walker!" Chief Bugis snarled. "If I decide you are to be shaved, then you shall have a bloody shave!"

"The prisoner," Singh goaded, "must look his best for-."

"-Yes, yes, yes," Chief Bugis said. "You know everything, eh, Mr Singh?"

"Not everything," the merchant said.

"Then damn near everything?"

"Well," Singh said.

"Then how about this: the prisoner does not have money for a shave."

"I shall submit an invoice to Mr Swann at the Marina Hotel for the amount."

The Chief looked edgy, but he said: "Bring the box!"

"Of course."

The Chief set the onionskins aside; then, he motioned for the merchant to present the box for inspection. The policeman opened the portable barbershop: he checked the mirror set into the lid, the tonsorial equipment, and the various lotions and creams. Harry Singh watched the policeman's lacquered fingernails, but he did not pass any remark.

Chief Bugis picked up a bottle of spirits: "What's this?"

"It's yours," the merchant said. "A free sample."

"You would try and bribe me, Mr Singh?"

"A man of your integrity, Chief Bugis? Never!" The merchant, who said this with a dead-pan expression, added: "On the other hand-?"

"-That's all right, Mr Singh: I'll test the lotion for you, and let you know if it is any good."

"As you wish, Chief," Singh said.

"All right, Mr Singh, you may proceed. But no funny business."

"No funny business, Chief Bugis, never," the merchant agreed.

Robert Walker peered through the bars of the cell. The Chief read the latest batch of onionskins. Harry Singh waited, then asked: "You're not going to open up, Chief?"

The Chief looked up: "Open up? Open what up?"

"Why, the cell."

"You're joking, Mr Singh!"

"Is the prisoner dangerous? I am expected to provide a shave *through* the bars?"

"You are!"

"I don't want a shaved," Robert Walker said.

Chief Bugis asked: "It is possible, Mr Singh?"

"It is possible," the merchant said, "but I might, by accident, you know, cut the gentleman's-."

"-Very well, Mr Singh!" The Chief grabbed the keys. "You, Mr Walker, will prepare yourself to be shaved. Stand back! Stand back!"

The policeman opened the cell. Harry Singh, with his portable barbershop, entered. "We meet again, Mr Walker?"

"Shaving only, if you please, Mr Singh. No chit-chat," Bugis insisted.

The Chief re-locked the cell. "There!" he said. "Now, Mr Singh, how do you propose to leave?" The policeman howled with laughter, and returned to his desk.

Then: "COPY!" The constable reappeared, collected the next sheet, and disappeared, while the Chief worked his way through the rest of the batch.

"That's it, Mr Walker," Singh was saying, "make yourself comfortable."

"No talking!" Chief Bugis shouted. "Only shaving!"

In the passing of a half-minute, Harry Singh had unfolded a tripod, and set up his portable barber's kit: basin, hot water from a thermos, brushes, lotions, and - on the inside lid - a mirror.

Robert Walker looked at his reflection: the tired, hungry, thirsty, prisoner was lathered, ready for the shave. Harry Singh whispered:

"Do not look so worried, Mr Walker. This is old-fashioned equipment. No electric clippers. Now, a good shave, so please stay still. No sudden movements, if you please."

"NO WHISPERING!"

On the edge of the bunk, Robert Walker remembered that day on the plantation, the general store, and - around the barbershop mirror - the pastoral scene with kohl-eyed maidens. A couple of spontaneous tears welled-up, and stung the corners of his eyes.

By some act of ventriloquism, Harry Singh asked: "I am hurting you?"

"No, Mr Singh."

"Good, now look into the mirror."

Robert Walker's throat choked with emotion. The merchant had worked a miracle on his appearance: he was not a prisoner any more; he was - a *boulevardier*! - once again. Then, with a deft movement, Harry Singh pulled the mirror away slightly: a second miracle revealed - behind the mirror, pasted into the lid - a message:

I AM AWARE OF YOUR PROPOSAL:
THE BOAT IS YOURS - OUTRIGHT - WITH PAPERS - FOR THE
EQUIVALENT OF MY COMMISSION: BIR15,000 x 12.5% = 1,875
RUPEES
VERY GOOD PRICE
NO QUESTIONS ASKED
NOD YOUR HEAD IF YOU AGREE.
(This shave is free of charge.)

Robert Walker's chest heaved with unwanted laughter. As instructed, though, he nodded his head, while moisture streamed down his face.

"Stay still now, please, Mr Walker. No laughing." When the merchant pushed the mirror back into place, the reflection was that of Harry Singh's own broad grin.

"Any extras, sir?

"No thank you, Mr Singh. I don't think I'll be needing anything like that in here, do you?"

"You're quite right, Mr Walker. How foolish of me. Lotions?"

"Yes, I'll try some of that stuff." Robert Walker pointed at a bottle of emerald green liquid.

"That, Mr Walker, is not 'stuff'. It is the finest hair lotion - imported direct from Bombay."

"All right, that'll do.'

"My own choice," Singh said. The merchant splashed lotion over his hands, and then patted Robert Walker's scalp and face. The scent from Bombay - a kind of sub-Continental Bay Rum - had soon overwhelmed the holding cell area. Chief Bugis sniffed at the perfumed air, but he did not seem to mind; then, the policeman, with his eyes open wide, stared and stared at the latest onionskin

Harry Singh, with a comb, worked Robert Walker's hair into a respectable quiff. "There, now you look like a proper English gentleman."

"He may look like an Englishman, Mr Singh," the Chief broke his silence, "but he smells like something else." The policeman snorted, and spat red liquid into the vessel under the desk. The merchant packed-up the various components of his portable barber's kit. The rancid smell of the mattress had, for now, retreated.

"You'll see, Mr Walker," the merchant was saying, "when you get out of here, the ladies won't be able to resist."

"Ladies? Eh, what? Who said anything about anyone getting out of here, Mr Singh?" The Chief stood up from his desk, then held out - and jangled - the bunch of keys.

"You see, Mr Walker?" Harry Singh observed: "Our Chief of Police likes to have his little joke occasionally."

After an interval, the Chief opened-up the cell, and released the merchant.

"BACK TO WORK, MR WALKER"

Refreshed, Robert Walker continued: word-for-word, he wrote down Clue Number 11. That much alone would please Chief Bugis.

"All right," the policeman said. "You may go now, Mr Singh."

"A token of my appreciation, Chief Bugis," and Harry Singh offered a special packet.

"-! Why, you cheeky fellow! You think I need these things?"

"It's only a sample, Chief Bugis!"

"Well, you've got the wrong man, Mr Singh! GO NOW!"

The merchant departed: on his way out, he seemed to encounter someone known to him.

"No more distractions!" Bugis howled. "The next man who comes in here will be shot!"

It was Francis Long, who arrived with a large, covered tray.

"What the hell is this? You think this is some kind of hotel?"

"Compliments of Mr Swann," Francis Long announced.

The bartender tried a smile, which collapsed. Chief Bugis' eyes radiated nothing but contempt. Then: Francis Long whipped away the cloth from the tray. A revolver? A blade? No, it was-.

The Chief's face became charitable and forgiving. "Ahhhh, well - in that case, Francis, I am sure we can make an exception."

"Good afternoon, Mr Walker."

"SHUT UP! Do not address the prisoner!"

"Not for you, Chief. For the prisoner."

"Eh? You say what, man?"

"Lunch for Mr Walker."

The Chief glanced at the *sjambok,* which hung from its hook, and then at the clock, which made no sense:

"You call this lunchtime?"

Francis Long explained: "All the clocks in Port Bourbon have gone crazy. I'm only following my orders, Chief."

The Chief's face changed, and snarled: "I don't care about your bloody orders, man."

"Everyone at the hotel is celebrating."

"Celebrating? What are you talking about, you bloody fool?"

"There's something for your attention, Chief. Inside the glass there. See?"

The Chief inspected the tray: he slotted two fingers into an empty wineglass, which held a tissue. Inside the tissue, a thick roll of paper had been bound by an elastic band. Chief Bugis removed the roll, which he stuffed into a button-down shirt pocket. There was enough cash in the roll to make the Chief say, "All right. What have you got there?"

"From Sami's kitchen."

"That Mauritian couldn't boil an egg," Bugis laughed.

"No eggs here, Chief, except in the mayonnaise."

"Except for the mayonnaise," the Chef mocked, and curled his eyes at the bartender.

Francis Long reported: "Lobster. Cold white wine: Pouilly-Fuissé, Nineteen Eighty-Six. A light salad tossed in olive oil. That's all, Chief."

"That's all?" the Chief mocked. "All right, go ahead. But no talk. Not one word."

Robert Walker chose to stand: "I've finished another page, Chief Bugis!"

"You have? Excellent, Mr Walker! Gimme!"

The policeman thrust an arm through the cell-bars, and snatched the offering. Francis Long was made to wait his turn. The policeman read the latest skin with special interest:

"This is really quite extraordinary, Mr Walker. This is much, much better than that first rubbish. The dog points the way, then?" The Chief stared at Robert Walker: "You think this is true? The rock off-shore there - La Roche de la Chien?"

"I'm almost sure it's there," Robert Walker explained. "But there's no way of confirming that, unless-." He glanced at Francis Long. "I had been planning a boat-trip this afternoon."

"There are sharks out there," the Chief warned. "They especially like the taste of Englishmen with white legs."

"Well, I'll never know, will I, Chief Bugis? I am in here, and the rock - and the sharks - are out there."

Chief Bugis had his eyes on the bartender: "You mind your own business, Francis. Okay?"

Francis Long played dumb; not one word, he had already been told.

"That place is bad luck," the Chief went on.

"Why? Because of the sharks?"

"No one knows, but know one will go out here. And I mean no one. Not even a fool would go out here." The policeman glanced at Francis Long, who stood there - like the rock itself - with the tray in his hands. The tray had begun to shake. The bartender sweated, and waited. . .

"That's why," Robert Walker guessed, "no one has found the clue. It's still there. . . The clue itself might be valuable."

Chief Bugis blinked his long eyelashes. "Valuable? Like the treasure?"

"No, not like the treasure. Of lesser value, but still valuable as an artefact."

"An artefact?"

"Yes. The artefact of Cerberus. The three-headead dog. Jade, maybe."

The Chief's face had become a map of clues pointing in all directions. "How come this fellow Graham Dunne," the Chief asked, "did not find this bloody dog with three heads?"

Robert Walker, who was not sure, guessed:

"I believe Dunne reached as far as Clue Number Ten. This dog on the rock is Clue Number Eleven."

Francis Long's arms ached; he pleaded: "Please, Chief?"

"YOU SHUT UP, FRANCIS."

Robert Walker stood away from the cell-bars.

"Can you believe it, Mr Walker?" the Chief posed. "That a clever man like Mr Swann could have a nephew who is so bloody stupid? I have my suspicions, you know, about them being related."

Robert Walker did not respond.

"So," the Chief summed-up, "this fellow Dunne reached Clue Number Ten - and then he went crazy?"

"So I understand. Crazy. Broke. Drunk."

"Yes, yes," Bugis recalled. "Most infortunate. These English fellows don't know when to give up, eh, what?"

"It seems that Dunne never reached the rock. So, I believe that he who takes a boat to the rock will find Clue Number Eleven."

"Why are you staring at Francis like that, Mr Walker?"

"I'm starved. I haven't eaten for-."

"Okay, okay, Mr Walker! As a reward for you excellent progress, you can have your bloody lobster and wine. Then you must finish your last couple of pages. . ." - the Chief checked the wall-clock, which showed exactly 15:30 - "by Sixteen-Thirty at the latest. In the meantime, after I have a made a few notes, I shall despatch this to Mrs Greene." Chief Bugis returned to his desk, where he transcribed notes for his own reference.

"Chief Bugis?"

The chief was lost in his transcriptions.

"If you would open up, please, Chief?"

"Open up? Oh no. If I open up, Francis, you go inside to stay this time."

The Chief turned his back on the holding cell area.

Francis Long was left holding the tray.

Robert Walker had an idea: he signalled for Francis Long to pass the contents of the tray - item by item - through the bars of the cell. Francis Long understood, and took the lobster, whole, and passed it - so that its claws did not catch - through the bars. The Chief grinned at the procedure, and returned to his work. Next: the chilled bottle of white burgundy, which, with a slight twist, Francis Long was able to push between the bars; then the glass, and then the salad - which was more complicated - then the mayonnaise sauce, the condiments, cutlery (plastic) and a napkin. Then, finally, the tray itself, which - in the vertical - was easy to slide through the bars. Robert Walker re-assembled the lunch more or less as it had been presented.

Francis Long departed, without another word, then slipped away from the general police block.

It was exactly 15:30 for a long time.

Robert Walker wrapped the napkin about his neck, and set to work on the lobster, the salad, and the wine. Under these circumstances, the mayonnaise was exceptional. The white burgundy - the cork had been loosened-off - was outstanding. . .After the shave, the lunch and the wine, he was ready to complete the article. Chief Bugis shook his head with approval, and then shouted: "COPY!"

The constable, who by now had built up a steady sweat, reappeared, collected the sheet, and again set off for the British compound.

Chief Bugis shouted: "NOW, IS THERE ANYONE ELSE OUT THERE WHO WANTS TO COME IN HERE AND CAUSE TROUBLE?"

The uncertain head of Albert Greene showed itself:

"Yes, ah - as it happens, Chief Bugis, *I, ah,* DO." Albert Greene, High Commissioner (Acting), stepped into the holding-cell area, where he fiddled with his MCC tie. He looked as though he was dressed for a cocktail reception.

Chief Bugis stated: "High Commissioner Greene? It is you?"

"Acting," Greene said. "Yes, I know it's me."

"Acting? Acting? Who cares about Acting? Acting is the same as Being. Congratulations are in order. Please, come in - we have one of your fellow countrymen staying with us as a very special guest," and Bugis displayed his widest grin.

"Ah, yes, Chef Bugis, that's what I - sort of - wanted to see you about."

Albert Greene turned to face the cell, and his face fell. "Well, Mr Walker, it looks like you're being very well looked after."

Robert Walker did not say anything.

The Chief shrugged, and returned to his notes.

Albert Greene peered through the cell-bars. "I fail to understand-?"

Robert Walker sucked on a claw of lobster, to which, until today, he had not been at all partial. "That about sums up your policy, Mr Greene. Indifference."

"There's no need to be offensive, Mr Walker, really."

"You having a tiff there, gentlemen?" the Chief enquired.

"It's all right, Chief Bugis," Greene said, "just a quiet word with Mr Walker. If you don't mind."

"Don't mind me," Bugis replied, "I'm only the Chief of Police. As for a quiet word - not too quiet, if you please."

Albert Greene clasped the bars with both hands.

"Can I offer you a glass of burgundy, Mr Greene? It really is excellent."

"No thank you, Mr Walker. We're having a little get-together at the Marina Hotel."

"I wouldn't want to interrupt your social life, Mr Greene."

Chief Bugis spoke from the desk: "I can let you go into the cell - if you like, High Commissioner. No problem for a big shot like you."

"That won't be necessary, Chief Bugis, thank you." Then, to the prisoner:

"This place stinks of-."

"-Human beings? Yes, I know, Mr Greene. But I would say it smells mostly of - *fear*."

"Enough of that kind of talk," Chief Bugis warned.

"Yes, I see what you mean." Greene studied the confined space, and the *graffiti* on the cell-wall. "And yet, if you don't mind me saying so, you do seem to be fairly well appointed. The prison food looks rather - fine - ah, exceptional, really. And-."

"-Yes?"

" . . .There's some other smell, more pleasant."

"Yes, the barber was here. A lotion direct from Bombay, I am told. You should try it."

"Oh really? Yes, I might do that."

"How can I help you?"

"Well, I was trying to help *you*, Mr Walker, but there doesn't seem to be much we at the British High Commission can do just now."

"-So, why are you here?"

"To let you, ah, know that . . ."

" . . . there's nothing you can do?"

"It does seem that the police" - Green coughed - "have some rather serious charges against you."

"Well, I'm checking out of here by four-thirty. Just as soon as Mrs Greene has finished the typing."

"You are? She-? Oh really? She said she wanted to be left alone, but I hadn't realised why. I hadn't realised that-?" Albert Greene turned: "Have you got anything to do with this, Chief Bugis?"

"I don't know what your talking about, High Commissioner. And by the way, visiting time is almost over. There is much work to do around here."

"I see. Very well, then-. ."

Robert Walker stipulated: "You promised about the fax. You'll have to tell her where to send it - to my editors, I mean. There's the deadline, you see."

"It's none of your business, Mr Walker, but - you see - my wife is not speaking to me."

Chief Bugis pretended not to listen.

"Pass the instruction to her; she'll speak to you, all right."

"She will? Do you think?" Albert Greene's eyes, for the first time, met those of Robert Walker, who said: "The Shoe Lane Agency "

"The Shoe Lane Agency? Oh my God, you're-? I should have known." Albert Greene, realising why Robert Walker was on the island, shut his eyes. Quickly, he reopened them, and said: "While I'm here, I wanted to ask you, Mr Walker, about our wager."

"What wager is this?" Chief Bugis had crept up behind Greene.

Albert Greene took a step away from the policeman. "I was just saying to Mr Walker-."

"Something suspicious here," Chief Bugis discerned. "What is this talk about the fax?"

"The facts, Chief Bugis, the FACTS - are this: as long as Mr Walker is here in your custody, we might as well cancel our wager. I mean, there's not much chance that-."

"Wager? What wager is this? Explain."

"Well, Chief Bugis, I rather foolishly placed a wager with Mr Walker that he would find no such canine artefact on that off-shore rock."

"You did? You don't think there is anything there?" the Chief asked.

"No, I don't, Chief Bugis. I think the whole notion is ridiculous. If you ask me, it's nothing more than a cheap publicity stunt to promote magazine sales."

"Then, why do you say the wager is foolish," the policeman enquired, "when you are so sure of winning, Mr Greene?"

Robert Walker continued his lunch of lobster and white burgundy. A lunch, he thought, that he would remember for a long time to come.

10

UP AT THE DACHA

THE POLICEMAN'S DREAM of a wealthy retirement went up in a puff of François Bellarmine's cigar smoke.

Chief Bugis had read the completed article, page-by-page, which had since been typed-up by Elizabeth Greene and transmitted from the British compound. The Bamboo Mill re-broadcast the news - for anyone who was listening - in its own way. The treasure of ʿLa Buse' was no more; the hoard of gold and silver had been used to finance the coup of 1977. Graham Dunne had spent a decade in search of clues that led nowhere, except to Silent Pete's, and then to the grave on the promontory. As for the Fiery Cross of Goa, it was probably - and who could say for sure? - in the hands of the President of the Republic, the Kite/Papier-Drache consortium, the bottom of the ocean - or, most probable of all - broken up for portable cash a quarter of a millennium ago. (The Bamboo Mill did not yet know that the consortium was really after François Bellarmine.)

Chief Bugis, overwhelmed by these revelations, had taken Bellarmine's portrait from the wall, and - in a rage - smashed the image onto the floor of the holding cell. A bastard child, then, of Gwendolyne Smythe-Smith and Jean-Paul Bellarmine - the plantation owner. So the son had, after the coup, stolen his own father's land. The kleptomaniac François Bellarmine had stolen his *own* land! In a deluge of tears and manic laughter, Chief Bugis released the prisoner at the real-time of 17:30 hrs - on schedule.

After three days in jail - at a guess - Robert Walker had lost track of the diurnal cycle of the external world, and his visa was about to expire.

The sun had already started to slip over the horizon.

Outside the Victoria Road Police Station, the white Mercedes-Benz waited for a fare. Robert Walker aimed for the Marina Hotel beyond the crossroads. The hair-primping taxi driver checked his bouffant in the rear-view mirror, and shouted: "This way, Mr Walker!"

"No thanks; I'm only going back to the hotel - over there!"

"Chief Bugis insists I take you, man! I'll get into trouble, man! I'll lose my licence." The taxi driver seemed to grin at the prospect.

Robert Walker hesitated - so short a distance? - and opened a rear passenger door of the taxi. A burst of laughter came from the veranda of the Marina Hotel. The taxi driver *honk-honked*: "Please, Mr Walker, I have my instructions!"

A ray of sunlight gave sheen to the man's bouffant.

Robert Walker climbed into the taxi. The driver had a leopard-skin steering wheel. At its hub, a girl's photograph had been pasted over a wedge made up of similar snapshots - though probably not of the same girl. The taxi driver turned, and grinned: "You okay, Mr Walker?"

"I'm okay; let's get going - or I'll miss the party."

The driver sniffed, and detected Harry Singh's lotion from Bombay. In the rear-view, the driver showed excellent white teeth, reddened around the gums by the chewing of betel-nut. He wore a fancy oyster-white shirt, and displayed a gold medallion at his chest.

"You have been to the barber, Mr Walker?" the driver observed.

"The barber has been to me," Robert Walker replied. "Now, what are we waiting for?"

"Why? You must tell me your destination, Mr Walker!"

The driver swivelled the ignition-key; the engine purred.

"I have a choice?"

"Of course you have a choice," the driver said. "What kind of taxi service do you think I operate?"

"I'm not sure. All right, take me to the Marina Hotel."

"Right away, Mr Walker!"

The driver reached for the meter, and slapped a lever. Then, with ease, he accelerated the taxi - away from the hotel - along Victoria Street.

"The scenic route, Mr Walker."

Ready to object, Robert Walker instead relented: "I should have known."

At a cruise, a steady breeze warmed his face. After three days and nights, fresh air. "Air-conditioning," the driver explained, but then - after rapid hand movements - automatic windows rose, clicked into place, and the vehicle was sealed. A screen shot up from nowhere, and so passenger was closed-off from driver by a transparent barrier. Robert Walker knew what he had already guessed: that this was a BIPP taxi. The driver flicked an intercom switch: "Take it easy! Enjoy the ride!" The driver threw his *bouffant*-head back, and laughed.

What was so funny? What was so-. The internal temperature escalated. So did the fare indicated by the meter, which was already in excess of one hundred rupees, and climbing.

As the taxi cruised at speed up Victoria Street, it passed the BIRTV station, where the sign showed, 'The Voice of the Island'. Robert Walker asked through the screen or via the intercom or both:

"We're not going to the Marina, then?"

"Big party tonight," the taxi driver said; he laughed, and flicked at a stray lock of hair. "You're my last fare. After that, I'm going to the party, too."

"Your last fare? Of the day, you mean?"

"Oh no, you're my last fare - ever! You think I want to be a bloody taxi driver, man?"

"Then, aren't we going in the wrong direction?"

"I'm going in the wrong direction. You're going in the right direction."

"Where are you taking me?" Robert Walker demanded.

The taxi driver glanced into the rear-view; his eyes were wet from laughter. "You'd better sit back and enjoy the ride, Mr Walker. You wouldn't want me to say anything you don't really want to hear, would you?"

The white Mercedes reached the outskirts of Port Bourbon, where Victoria Street gave way to a dusty track, which wound upwards into the foothills.

"The . . .destination . . .is all I - ask." Robert Walker bounced over the luxury leather seat.

The taxi driver pointed: "THERE!"

Robert Walker slunk back into the seat, and looked - from under the windscreen's sun visor - at the towering rim of Mont Pomme d'Or.

"And where is that?"

"That, Mr Walker, is the gateway to hell! HA-HA-HAAAG!"

Behind the leopard-skin wheel, the taxi-driver became frantic. Robert Walker was tossed across the grey leather seat and back again. The vehicle climbed up the dirt track, and seemed to race against the elongated shadows cast by the sinking sun. A wavering, craggy ridge pointed the way above the eastern plantations, and eventually the vehicle found its way onto a plateau. Out of an ocean-facing windscreen, a glimpse of Port Bourbon below: the church, the harbour, and then the landscape turned inwards against a long, lush ripple of green and yellow until the dirt-track entered a vegetation belt at this altitude. Robert Walker's heart pumped until blood was ready to spout. Then, he managed to focus his sweat-blurred vision on a shiny door-handle, but he knew, without trying, that the doors were power-locked. As the taxi headed for the island's summit, he spread his arms to steady himself against the swerving, dipping motion. The driver noticed, and laughed: "That's the spirit, Mr Walker!" and then kept his eyes on the track ahead, which narrowed, and darkened as the twisted foliage thickened into a canopy.

Robert Walker watched the meter: the rupees clocked-up at an alarming rate, and the fare now stood at over one thousand rupees. The driver swerved to avoid a great mound of rubble from a recent landslide.

"Close one!" the driver howled. Behind the Mercedes, the dust in its wake turned from yellow, to red, and then from black to grey, and then blue. The driver pressed a button that activated water-jets and wipers, and soon the windscreen was smeared with a cobalt-blue gunge of volcanic mud.

Robert Walker's mouth vented words without sound, and he was thrust back into the seat. The taxi climbed along another ridge, which snaked onto yet another, higher plateau. After a long interval, the vehicle passed along an abyss, and then plunged into a clearing, where there were giant conifers, rocks, huge boulders, and - just visible above the tree-belt - the grey, wind-torn rim of Mont Pomme d'Or. As the sun fell below the Indian Ocean, a jagged play of shadows leapt and danced around the *massif* of the summit.

"There - Mr Walker - is your destination!" and the taxi braked to an abrupt halt. In the rear-view mirror, the driver fixed any disturbance to his bouffant hair-do, and smiled. Robert Walker reached for the door-handle - and it opened. The driver looked knowingly at his passenger:

"You have been with Chief Bugis for too long, Mr Walker. You were free to leave any time."

Robert Walker stepped out of the vehicle and onto the floor of the rocky plateau. He lost his balance, and grabbed at the great trunk of the nearest conifer.

"Easy now," the driver advised, and wound-down his window. "You think you're dizzy now - wait until you see the fare. Look!"

Robert Walker peered into the taxi: the fare on the meter stood at over 10,000 rupees. "One way only!" the driver cackled. "I can't take you back to Port Bourbon unless you pay up."

"To hell with you!" Robert Walker instructed the driver.

"Not me," said the breathless driver: "YOU!" and pointed at the wind-torn crater. Robert Walker followed the man's - manicured - finger. The dacha was set in a field of giant boulders on the edge of a cliff, which overlooked a dark forest of conifers. The air here had an ancient smell, of minerals and resin from the trees, and the ocean air, and-.

"I'll wait here for you, Mr Walker, don't you worry!"

Robert Walker made awkward steps towards the dacha. Already, the taxi driver had re-started the engine: then, he made an efficient, rock-crunching, three-point turn, and started away down the slope of the track. The mud-splattered Mercedes - with a *honk-honk* against the wind - had gone. Over the far-way African mainland, the sun dipped, and the conifer-shrouded plateau was engulfed by darkness.

Spotlights illuminated the dacha set among the nest of boulders. A catwalk ran along the perimeter of the construction. Uniformed guards with sub-machine guns appeared - North Koreans? - and marched out of sight along the catwalk. One of the guards waited, and - aware that a taxi-passenger had alighted - waved for Robert Walker to approach the installation. Robert Walker, before obeying, turned and looked far-out over the ocean wilderness. On a distant ship, the mast- and bridge-lights sparkled and winked. Inland, far down below, the track wound through the vegetation belt, the plantation, and - beyond - the dirt-track in the foothills. The lights of Port Bourbon had started to appear, and ignited - from East to

West - until the whole town stood out against the coastline. A drunken party at the island's power station, too?

The guard shouted from the catwalk. Robert Walker turned his back on the ocean, and started through the high conifers in the direction of the dacha. He reached the base of a short flight of aluminium steps. It was almost night. Somewhere nearby, but not too close to presidential ears, a generator-set coughed, spluttered, and then fed the dacha with electricity. Overhead, a cable buzzed, and a satellite dish swivelled at the sky. Another set of lights came to life around a get-away helipad. The guard stared down from the catwalk. Robert Walker looked up the flight of steps into the barrel of a sub-machine gun. The weapon, though Russian, was real. The Korean waved for this visitor to climb the super-alloy steps. Robert Walker, still unbalanced from the taxi-ride, grabbed the cool handrails, and mounted the steps until he reached catwalk-level. There, he stared into the guard's dark, unblinking eyes, but he knew, by now, not to say anything. Five more North Korean guards appeared with Soviet-made rifles held in front of their ill-fed, badly uniformed chests. In tight formation, they moved in a slow-trot from one end of a balcony to another. The first guard and Robert Walker were invisible to their intentions, if they had any. The five automata - Robert Walker remembered the Great Leader's fiftieth birthday present to Bellarmine - disappeared around the far side of the dacha. A breeze seemed to come in off the ocean, and blow the half-starved Koreans, one-by-one, off the balcony.

Robert Walker looked, above the dacha, at the enormous wind-shedding cone of the crater. At that same interval, the man in the moon appeared, full of face, and rose over the Indian Ocean until he looked down into the eye of the extinct volcano. Robert Walker, struck by the moon, felt the earth wobble beneath his feet, but it was - "ARRG*gh!*" the first guard who had kicked at his shins. Then the Korean sniffed with disgust - the lotion from Bombay - at this decadent Westerner. The guard, affronted by this non-military perfume, provided an angry shove, and Robert Walker fell sideways through a steel-grey security door.

He was inside the dacha.

Someone, caught-out by the sudden entry, hid behind the grey steel door. Robert Walker saw the white-sleeve of a laboratory coat. A hand fumbled, reached for a pocket, and managed to conceal a glass-and-metal object. Robert Walker moved into the circular corridor, pushed aside the security door, and found-.

"Dr Marigold, is that you?"

A plump man in late middle-age, with silver hair that had once been yellow, and a grey-pink face, stepped into view. Outside on the catwalk, the soldier grunted, more or less satisfied, and went the way of his compatriots - over the side.

"What are you doing here, Dr-?"

"So, you've arrived at last, Mr Walker?" Dr Marigold, who might have been embarrassed, but was not, secured the grey steel door. "I suppose you're wondering why I was behind this door here?"

Robert Walker found his breath: "Yes, I suppose I was."

Dr Marigold, who seemed detached from reality, adjusted his steel-rimmed spectacles, such that his amused - but not amusing - brown eyes looked straight through his former patient at the military strip-lights along the corridor. Robert Walker recognised the man's detachment, and asked:

"Why, Dr Marigold, have you brought me to this place?"

"I? Oh no, you misunderstand, Mr Walker. It is not I who have brought you to this place. In a way, you brought yourself here."

"No, I was *brought* here by a taxi driver in a white Mercedes. Quite a hefty fare, too."

"Against your will?"

"Not exactly, no."

"So," Dr Marigold observed, "you seem to have recovered from your injuries since I saw you at the Infirmary. A most unfortunate incident. You should be more careful."

"More careful? I'll try, Dr Marigold. I have a few bruises on the shins, that's all."

"From the encounter on the plantation?"

"No, from the North Korean guard outside this door."

Dr Marigold smiled: "There are no North Koreans around here, Mr Walker. Really, you must get a grip on yourself." The doctor sniffed: "And you've had a shave?"

"I've recovered from that, too."

"But, more than that, you look remarkably well-rested for a man in your situation."

"I am - thanks to Chief Bugis. But what *is*, ah, my situation?"

"Hmm-hmm. Ask me again later. Please, Mr Walker, we are expected," and the doctor started along the low-ceilinged corridor, with his hands thrust deeply into his laboratory-coat pockets. Robert Walker was sure Marigold had planned to thrust a syringe into his arm, and allowed the doctor to lead the way. This was the man, he recalled, the same Dr Maxwell Marigold, who was said to have done many questionable things during his long medical career, and had distinguished himself - in the eyes of Bellarmine - by prescribing fear-suppressing, coup-night pep-pills for the insurgents all those years ago. This simple prescription, along with a few special errands, had been enough to earn Dr Max seniority in the BIPP regime. Those days, though, were long behind the medical man. As was Robert Walker:

"I heard you'd left the island - in a hurry."

"Oh no, Mr Walker." The doctor glanced backwards over a sloping, white-coated shoulder. "I am very much on the island - as you can see - there being so much always to do."

"Are we alone here?"

"No, we are not alone. Please, Mr Walker, this way," and Dr Marigold showed the way into the central, domed area of the dacha, from which more corridors radiated into various ante-rooms. At the southern sector of the dome, a great balcony opened over the ocean. A telescope pointed at an angle-of-dip towards Port Bourbon. Outside, the moon continued along its locus over a tranquil evening, and deep-night approached from the east. Across the floor-area under the dome, crates and packing cases were ready for transhipment. One case, reaching as high as Robert Walker's solar plexus, focused his attention: it was set apart from the other cases, which were strewn in a more haphazard way around the dacha

A young woman in a nurse's uniform, with her back to the room, worked at a dispensary. An assistant to Dr Marigold, he supposed, although they were a long way from the Infirmary. She prepared vails of medication, but she did not speak, show her face, or offer any acknowledgement. Then, by the far side of the balcony, Robert Walker became aware of a dark-haired man seated in a fan-backed bamboo chair. The man was dressed in a safari suit, and smoked a cigar. It was François Bellarmine - not a photograph - but the real President of the Republic - himself.

A gust of wind bounced over the balcony, and wafted cigar smoke into the central domed area. François Bellarmine, distracted from his thoughts, stood up from the bamboo chair, and moved into the lounge. "Ah, Dr Marigold - Max - I see you have found our guest."

"Outside, sir, with one of the guards."

"That's not quite true," Robert Walker spoke up: "it was I who found the good doctor - lurking behind a door."

"Lurking? Really? He becomes eccentric. Too much of his own medication, perhaps. Complacency - he grows a soft underbelly. "

An irate Dr Marigold fumbled in his pockets, and almost jabbed himself with the hidden syringe.

"I am François Bellarmine," the president said, and greeted Robert Walker at the centre of the dome.

Dr Marigold found his manners: "This is Robert Walker, Mr President."

François Bellarmine reached forward, but only slightly, to accept Robert Walker's hand. The president's hand was cold, and had been oiled; the hand, Robert Walker, thought, of a reptile, but it was from the dark-blue, prismatic eyes that he recoiled - the eyes of Gertrude Smythe-Smith herself. It was all true, then, for the son shared his mother's - and his father's - stature, and not that of the lanky Sir Godfrey.

"Yes," Robert Walker said, "I know who you are. I've been following your career for some time now."

François Bellarmine stiffened; he sucked at his cigar. Robert Walker regarded the master of the island. The premier was no taller than a fourth-former; a school-boy on top of an extinct volcano.

Dr Marigold sneered: "He knows nothing. My tests indicate - an *idiot savant*."

"-."

François Bellarmine absorbed this information, and continued:

"Mr Walker, you know about me; I do not know about you. I have only *heard* you. On the radio, yes? A man of mystery, who hides behind the radio; in the same way, perhaps, as the good doctor hides behind the door."

The dignity of Dr Marigold's profession was at stake. Bellarmine puffed-out a long plume of smoke. The doctor spluttered, and turned away to supervise the nurse at the dispensary.

"Max does not approve my smoking - do you, Max? Sometimes I enjoy his disapproval more than the cigar." Bellarmine's thin-lipped grimace passed for a smile.

"So, I found your theory of interest, but entirely unconvincing. Proof. We live in a world of much speculation and so little proof, Mr Walker."

Robert Walker tried not to look at the crate in the middle of the room; it was, he supposed, of about the right dimensions. "As for the radio interview, President Bellarmine - I was only answering questions put to me; I wasn't advancing any theory."

François Bellarmine checked his - expensive - wristwatch: "You must excuse me, Mr Walker. I have been packing up some belongings. The place is in a state of general disorder."

Robert Walker happened to move, so that he stood nearer that particular crate. A label read: ANTIQUITIES - HANDLE WITH EXTREME CARE.

Bellarmine was saying, "Yet another trip overseas. Time is, as they say, short. Before I go, then, Mr Walker: any more of your theories?"

"About time? Time is all any of us have, really. It's a question of how much remains."

"Or how much has already passed?"

"That's another way of looking it - if you like."

Bellarmine's eyes had turned snake-ish. Robert Walker assumed from this short talk that he, Robert Walker, was in some danger, which smelt of a Havana cigar. . ."You're trembling, Mr Walker."

"The taxi journey," Robert Walker stated without embellishment.

"Yes, it's a rough ride. Sometimes, if there's a landslide, it's impassable."

"You are delayed, President Bellarmine?"

"I haven't decided if I should leave. My country needs me."

Dr Marigold intervened with an insolent snort.

"*You*, Dr Marigold," Bellarmine ordered, "will offer our guest some - ah - refreshment."

Dr Marigold, reduced to the status of a mere bartender, flushed with deep shame. But the doctor obeyed, and approached a substantial cocktail cabinet. In his laboratory coat, he set to work. François Bellarmine looked over the balcony into outer space. "The doctor mixes an excellent cocktail, Mr Walker," he said.

"I can well believe it," Robert Walker remarked. "I'll just have a beer, if it's all the same."

Dr Marigold made some obscure comment.

"If you please, Mr Walker," Bellarmine advised, "make yourself comfortable."

All of this seemed strangely familiar.

"There's nowhere to-."

"On that crate there." *Not that one. that one.*

"I'd rather stand."

"I insist."

Robert Walker seated himself on one of the shorter crates. Dr Marigold had poured out a BourBrew, and then made an unusual adjustment to the glass.

"I'll have that beer straight," Robert Walker observed, "if you don't mind, Dr Marigold."

"Yes, yes, yes, of course," the doctor rambled.

François Bellarmine had moved onto the balcony, where he puffed on his cigar, and looked over the great distances towards the littoral of the ocean: Indonesia, Malaysia, Burma . . . beyond.

Again, Dr Marigold fumbled, and dropped an object onto the dacha floor with a crunch. A heap of splintered glass and twisted metal oozed fluid. The doctor tried to kick the syringe under the cocktail cabinet. Then Dr Marigold turned, and - with chubby pink hands, which shook - offered the frothy beerglass. Robert Walker accepted, but he wondered about the operations those hands had performed over the years.

"You seem to have dropped something, doctor."

Dr Marigold's strange, grey-pink face turned a waxen red. François Bellarmine, irritated by the doctor's bungling, pursed his thin lips so that they almost disappeared inside his mouth. Dr Marigold's yellow-silver locks were damp with perspiration; he explained: "It's nothing, Mr Walker. For my own use. I'll prepare another. Nurse?"

The nurse, who was small of stature, and therefore - Robert Walker supposed - a favourite of the president's, stood up from the dispensary. She turned: it was Sylvia Dupin. She looked at Robert Walker with her warm, brown, silent eyes - the eyes, too, of her brother. Find her, Roger Dupin had said, but do not look for her.

"So-."

Bellarmine frowned: "Yes, Mr Walker? There is something you have to tell us?"

"-*Ssso*, how can I be of assistance to you, ah, gentlemen?"

Sylvia Dupin moved quietly aside; she busied herself with a tray, on which there were various preparations. Robert Walker was sure that Sylvia Dupin, if she really were the underground editor of the samzidat *The Black Turtle!* would, if she could, switch the tongue-wagging drug for a simple solution of glucose.

Bellarmine and Dr Marigold watched the patient.

"I don't have anything to say," Robert Walker said. "My visa is about to expire, you see. Thank you for the beer and the hospitality, President Bellarmine, but I've got to be going."

"If you would - Mr Walker - please remain seated," Bellarmine insisted. "You haven't had your beer yet."

When Robert Walker tried to stand, he was aware of the downward pressure of Dr Marigold's plump, pink hands on his shoulders. In this way, Robert Walker was re-seated on the crate. The doctor removed his hands, and then - carefully - felt inside his laboratory coat pocket.

Robert Walker said: "I can't drink this beer. It's warm. Thank you, all the same."

François Bellarmine glanced at Dr Marigold.

"There are other ways," Dr Marigold warmed to his subject, "of making bad boys take their medicine."

Robert Walker looked into the doctor's shiny eyes: Marigold, he decided, who had caused suffering, must be made to suffer - or unmasked - but not yet, and in a special way.

"Please, Mr Walker," Bellarmine smirked.

"You're not going to join me?"

Bellarmine shook his head: "Neither the doctor nor myself are. . .thirsty, Mr Walker. You must, therefore, raise a glass and toast your own health."

Robert Walker raised the warm beerglass: TO THE RETURN OF DEMOCRACY? No, that was premature, *unless-*.

Bellarmine suggested: "To your discovery?"

"My discovery? I haven't made any discovery."

Bellarmine said. "Now, concentrate: you have something to tell me?"

"About . . .?" Robert Walker took a swallow of the beer, which seemed all right, though it caught at the sides of his throat on the way down.

"Well?" Bellarmine puff-puffed on his cigar.

"No, I don't believe I have."

Bored, Bellarmine gestured at Marigold; and the doctor, in relay, signalled at a crate marked THIS SIDE UP. A black African in a pin-stripe, Saville Row business suit appeared, so that Robert Walker - who thought he recognised the man - was unaware of the nurse, who - in a flash - passed a fresh syringe to Dr Marigold.

Robert Walker was aware of a sharp prick - which went straight through his jacket, shirt - and into his arm. He dropped the beerglass, and it shattered. When he reached out, Dr Marigold had already taken a sharp step away.

"What-? What are you doing, doctor? I don't need any injections!"

"I'll be the judge of that, Mr Walker," Dr Marigold smiled.

Robert Walker tried to get up, but his legs would not move; he was stuck to the crate. By this stage, the black man in the business suit stood beside Doctor Marigold - as in consultation - and folded and refolded arms, over and over again, until the stripes of the Saville Row suit were twisted like rock candy. Robert Walker could not see how this was possible. His head throbbed as he demanded:

"Who is this man? He's out of his usual uniform of feathers, but I think he's . . .from Zanzibar."

"Very observant, Mr Walker," Bellarmine whispered.

"In my experience," Dr Marigold said, "when death comes, it is so often - unannounced."

"In your experience, Doctor Marigold?" Robert Walker taunted.

The remark flustered the doctor.

Sylvia Dupin watched the patient over Bellarmine's shoulder. Robert Walker looked at her. Her dark, warm, loving eyes seemed to say that he was all right, she had diluted the dose, but not by much, but that he must not seem all right, not in front of these criminals: a hocus-pocus madman, a sado-narcissist, and a bastard-megalomaniac with misanthropic tendencies in the extreme. He should, her eyes implied, nod his head if he understood.

Robert Walker tried to figure out who of the three was which of the three, and allowed his head - in a whoozy way - to nod forwards.

"There," Dr Marigold announced, "it is taking effect already! Thank you nurse, you can go now."

"Yes, Doctor Marigold," Sylvia Dupin automated, and - dutifully - withdrew into an ante-room. She reappeared only to say: "Farewell, President Bellarmine! The Republic and the Party are eternally grateful!"

"Oh God, no!" Robert Walker realised: she's with the BIPP! The editor of *The Black Turtle!* - itself fake samzidat, then - is a fraud, set up, by way of an underground poultice, to draw-out and then eliminate dissent!

In the ante-room, Nurse Dupin flushed the vails into a sink unit, changed into her blue-silk party costume, and - for the last time - made her own covert way back to Port Bourbon. A midnight issue had been planned: a special edition of *The Black Turtle!*

Inside the great dome of the dacha, Robert Walker confessed:

"You don't understand, Dr Marigold . . .I've had . . .all my inoculations done . . .in London. . .years' ago."

"Yes, yes, Mr Walker," said Dr Marigold, and the interrogation got under way:

"Now, relax, Mr Walker. This treatment will help you tell the truth. This service is not available on your own British National Health Service. I know, I was trained in England."

"The truth? On the National Health Service?"

"Please, doctor," Bellarmine urged, "this is no time for your jokes."

Robert Walker's head reeled: ". . .You're quite right, Dr Marigold. I don't know what I'm talking about . . .Thank you for your help. You see, I ran into some trouble up at the plantation today."

Dr Marigold leaned over Robert Walker, and frowned. "Today? How could this be so, Mr Walker? You were in custody today."

Bellarmine observed: "You must have given him too much of the serum, Max."

"Then - he must be regressing!" Dr Marigold realised.

"Bring him back, doctor! Now!"

"Well, I couldn't control the dose, sir, as you yourself were witness!"

"Enough of your excuses, Dr Marigold!" Bellarmine almost bit off the end of his cigar. "We are running out of time. I'll handle this myself, then. Stand aside!"

In a delirium, Robert Walker volunteered:

"Yes, you're a disgrace to your profession, Dr Marigold!"

The black man in the striped business suit - it was Dr Mobuto, then - grinned with agreement.

"Now," Bellarmine ordered, "let us get back to the subject at hand. You have made a discovery, Mr Walker?"

"Yes, I've made . . .a discovery."

Bellarmine produced - a photocopy? - of an original onionskin.

"Oh no!" Robert Walker groaned. "It can't be!"

"This," the president explained, "was found by the Chief of Police."

Robert Walker's eyes tried to focus on his own scribble: . . .it was the part about Lady Gertrude's soirée on the plantation. . .and Sir Godfrey's demise. . .

Feebly, Robert Walker recanted: "It's only a draft, President Bellarmine. . . More research is needed!"

"You were intending to publish this?"

"The Chief-? He must have kept the sheets, after all!"

Dr Mobuto stepped forward, and whispered into the ear of his medical colleague.

"What is it?" Bellarmine wanted to know.

Dr Marigold reported: "Dr Mobuto says this is magic paper. From - from Africa!"

Bellarmine blew cigar smoke at his two advisors. "There, that's magic for you! Now, don't be ridiculous, Dr Marigold."

"I was only informing you, sir, of Dr Mobuto's opinion."

Bellarmine stared up at the dome to collect his thoughts, and then, reasonably, asked: "You have made a discovery . . .during the course of your researches, concerning-."

"-Your mother, President Bellarmine, is alive and well. In Paris."

The cigar almost fell from Bellarmine's jaw.

"I had not realised that you were a-." Dr Marigold started, but chose not to finish.

"There's lot of things you don't realise, Max! Now, Mr Walker, Bellarmine continued. "If this is true, then *how* is my mother?"

"Mrs Bellarmine?"

Bellarmine stood away from the patient. "Mrs Bellarmine, as you call her, Mr Walker, passed away many years ago. When I was a child."

"Then why . . .are you asking me? As I have already informed Dr Goldilocks - I don't know what I'm talking about."

François Bellarmine waved his cigar at Dr Mobuto. "I'm placing you in the hands of Dr Mobuto, Mr Walker. If you won't tell me, then you will, I can assure you, tell him."

Robert Walker's head started to clear, but his legs would not yet move, and when he closed, and opened, his eyes, it was to see the same face he had encountered that night on the veranda.

"I don't recommend this," Dr Marigold said.

"It is a little too late to develop a conscience, doctor," François Bellarmine countered.

"Even so, sir."

"Enough, Dr Marigold! Alternative medicine is called for in this case!"

Dr Mobuto's eyes transfixed Robert Walker: he knew he had been asked a question, but there was nothing much to say, not anymore. When the white cloud emanated from the black man's nostrils, it was a warm, low gust of wind - the trade wind from the southwest - which was more powerful than Dr Marigold's truth serum, and held all the answers to all of the world's unasked questions. The truth, Robert Walker saw now, had many facets, not like a crystal, but in the way of the analogue ARRIVALS AND DEPARTURES flapper-board at the island's international airport. Dr Mobuto held his patient by the shoulders, and drew closer. The black man's face dissolved into a montage of kaleidoscopic images. The orbs of the Tanzanian's eyes became hollow, glass fishing floats, drifting across the great ocean. Then Robert Walker saw himself, walking along Fleet Street on a rainy day. Next, he saw himself with Harry Stone in the Wig & Pen Club. Harry Stone, the new Bureau Chief, who had deposed Vincent Mosley, gave instructions.

"I don't do that kind of work," Robert Walker complained. "I only do features."

"What's he saying, Dr Mobuto?" someone asked, but there was no answer, for Mobuto, too, was inside the same cloud.

Then, he saw Conny Trapp, packing or unpacking, it was hard to say. But then - she changed - and her face was that of one of Harry Singh's kohl-eyed maidens.

"Don't do it, Mr Singh! Don't do it! I'll tell you anything you want to know!"

"I might have guessed," Bellarmine puffed.

Then, he saw the empty apartment: Conny had gone. "Don't go, Conny! It doesn't matter if we don't know each other. Don't . . . go . . . to that place."

"Yes?" Marigold asked. "And where is that place?"

"Blackfriars," Robert Walker replied.

Dr Marigold explained: "Dr Mobuto has gained access to the patient's inner mind. His subconscious-."

"Whose subconscious? Dr Mubuto's?"

"The patient's subconscious is transforming his plight into the allegory of a street name." Dr Marigold urged: "Yes, Mr Walker, please continue!"

"Kite! He is behind everything! He would do anything to get his hands on that map. It's worth a fortune!"

Dr Marigold made a note of that name.

"He is behind . . .everything!"

"Who is this Kite?" Dr Marigold enquired.

"He is with the consortium!" Robert Walker answered, and felt immediate elation. "I am prepared to cooperate, doctor! There's no need for torture."

"Who is Kite?" Dr Marigold demanded.

"A European," Robert Walker babbled, "His name is Herr- Heeer?"

"He's regressing again," Bellarmine's voice said.

"Ah," Dr Marigold said.

"Yes, doctor? You have a proposal?"

"If he's regressing, then we should allow him to regress further, say, to the Nineteen Thirties - when you, sir, were a-."

"- Don't be a fool, Max!"

"It's all Mosley's fault!" Robert Walker shouted. "Wears those black shirts to save on the laundry bills, that's all!"

"Who's Mosley?" Marigold quizzed.

"Don't be a fool, doctor. Don't you see? You've sent him back to England! He's with the English Blackshirts!"

"All right, Mr Walker. That's far enough!"

"Tell Sir Walter I shall join him shortly," Robert Walker babbled.

"Please, Mr Walker! You are here on the island - in the Indian Ocean."

"Where is she?"

"Where is who?" Bellarmine's voice asked.

"The nurse. I'm in-. She's in love with me, so I've been told. Can't you see that, you damned fools? I'VE GOT TO OUT OF HERE!"

"She gone back to the infirmary, Mr Walker. Her duties here are concluded."

Robert Walker stared into the three faces, which shifted in- and out-of-focus. "Sylvia? Where are you? What was that you gave me?"

"Something for your nerves," Dr Marigold advised.

"THERE'S NOTHING WRONG WITH MY NERVES!"

"You're losing him doctor," Bellarmine snapped.

"He needs fresh air!" Dr Marigold advised. "He's overheating."

"Bring him out onto the balcony," someone ordered. "I'll give him fresh air."

Dr Marigold and Dr Mobuto lifted their patient from the crate. Robert Walker felt a fraction of his normal weight. On the balcony, he seemed to float wherever he was directed. Far down below, he could see the lights of Port Bourbon. In the distance, he could just about hear them: islanders cheered and shouted as they took to the streets after curfew. Out across the ocean, he saw nothing but the moonlit expanse. Below the balcony, the tops of giant conifers reached for the sky. The odour of resin from the trees was overwhelming.

"I've got to be going. I've got a flight to catch. Tonight or tomorrow, I cannot recall. My visa has expired!"

"Flight, you say? Go on then, Mr Walker, FLY!"

Out there, on the edge of the volcano, a light breeze passed over the balcony.

Robert Walker said: "Before I go, I have something for you, Dr Mobuto."

"You have? Where is it? What is it?"

"If I fly, then you fly. Your ticket is in my top pocket there. British Airways. Help yourself, old boy."

Dr Mobuto hesitated, then searched the patient's pockets. The man from Zanzibar found a card: it was the joker, the Harlequin, which Papier-Drache had left behind. Robert Walker had forgotten it, until now, when it was needed.

Bellarmine and Marigold chuckled, but Dr Mobuto howled:

"AGH! AWWWK! OG!"

"What's wrong with you, man? Get on with it!"

Lights exploded in Dr Mobuto's eyes. The joker burned a hole in the witchdoctor's hand. In agony, he reached for Robert Walker's throat. In that instant, Robert Walker and Dr Mobuto tumbled over the balcony, and into the canopy of trees.

Robert Walker felt his drugged body falling through the canopy, and into the forest. He looked up: the pin-striped Dr Mobutu was also falling. While Robert Walker's limp body floated down through the soft conifers, the witch doctor's muscular, wild movements brought deep cuts and broken bones. Mobuto screamed against the force of gravity, and then he was silenced. Robert Walker, a spectator of his own descent, laughed: what a waste of . . .a Saville Row suit.

Then, gravity kicked-in: he accelerated through the branches, and - with a rush - he crashed through a cat's cradle of dead twigs. On the forest floor, he was motionless. In the dark, half-unconscious, he looked up into the treetops: caught in a nest of broken branches, Dr Mobuto's Saville Row suit flapped in the breeze. Emptied of the witch doctor, white powder billowed from the suit's arms and legs. One last trick from the African. Another dose of powder settled on Robert Walker's face. He sneezed, waited, and listened . . .to the men up on the balcony. In the struggle, Dr Marigold had also inhaled - and been affected by - the Zanzibar-powders. Robert Walker heard the doctor spurt-out the truth:

"I've been conspiring against you for years, François!"

"Don't be a fool, Max."

"It is I, not you, who should have been president! Without me, the French elite would not have supported you! It was I who persuaded them of their historic duty to this island - and to the region. Our African friends, too. "

"But the people despise you, Max. The women, especially. As for myself, I believe they have grown to admire me. In the past, my methods may have been excessive - it is true - but then they were excessive times."

"You could never have pulled off the coup without me. I hate you, François! Do you hear me? I've always hated you. It's the truth, you see. When Anthony Montaigne returns, I shall stand against him in the free elections."

François Bellarmine had evidently had enough, for all he said was:

"GUARDS! TAKE THE DOCTOR AWAY!"

The balcony had been cleared.

Robert Walker rested on the forest floor. On the balcony, he realised, the truth had been spoken. Geo-politics? An historic grudge on the part of the French against the British? Crazy, but therefore probably true. . . He tried to move, and a twig poked him in the face. Again, he tried to move, moved, and found that he had not broken anything. A spotlight arced through the sky, and started to probe the dark forest. Voices shouted and dogs barked. Robert Walker started to move, slowly to begin with, downhill, across the forest floor. Soon, his hair and face were covered with sap and resin. Shouts, in a foreign tongue, grew fainter. The North Korean guards, their eyesight weakened by malnutrition, had already lost themselves in the forest. The moon disappeared. Robert Walker ran into a tree, bounced off its trunk, and landed on the edge of a precipice. The tree had saved him from the rocky void. After a while, the moon reappeared, and he moved on until - in a rush of fronds - he had reached the jungle belt. Already, the last dusting of Zanzibar-powder acted on his mind. His legs ran, tripped, and leapt, but he seemed to go nowhere, except down into the earth. He penetrated the dense foliage. Quickly, under the tropical heavens, he vaulted over a felled tree, where - on the other side - he landed on a black mud-slide, which conveyed him onto the next terrace below, and then another, and another, until - at last - he bounced, and landed on the pristine beach of a hidden cove.

The moonlight danced over the coral sands. The dome of stars rotated at an impossible rate. Water lapped at the island's edge. Already, he had reached the ocean, which sparkled along the shoreline. A crab scuttled into a hole. Something larger found its way onto the cove, and - sensing a human - promptly retreated into the ocean. He waited until the waters started to rise. He looked along the coast: up ahead, several ships were moored at a jetty. Inshore, there was a complex of - abandoned? fake? - outbuildings, warehouses, and a barracks.

Robert Walker was sure he had located the Soviet Naval Base at Sans Souci Bay.

A Russian soldier appeared outside the barracks: he lit a cigarette, inhaled, and saw what he thought was the Siberian Mud Man approaching from the cove. The soldier threw away the cigarette, and ran into the trees. Robert Walker made his way along the jetty. The ships were inflatable scale-models - made from a rubber fabric of some kind. A fraction of the cost of the real thing, these unseaworthy blimps were still large enough to show up on any USAF aerial reconnaissance photographs. The complex of buildings - up-close - formed a shanty of plywood. A fake radar dish rotated its wooden beacon over an indifferent sky.

Robert Walker wiped the caked black mud from his face.

At a distance, the barracks seemed real, though the scale and perspective was all wrong. A general alarm sounded. Inside the barracks, real Russian soldiers shouted, and escaped into the night. A series of flares illuminated the whole complex and beyond. A giant red flare reached for the sky, and exploded: the Hammer & Sickle formed, and then drifted. . . The image of the CCCP crackled, shimmered, and then dissolved.

Robert Walker, covered with layers of resin and mud, headed back into the jungle belt where he belonged. Along a narrow jungle path, he headed inland. A thousand fronds lapped - as with desire - at his face and body, and cleansed him of sap and sand. Dr Mobuto's damnable pick-me-up powder worked on him yet. He stopped, and wiped a fresh layer of gunge from his face. His hands seemed to pass through his face - a mere screen, then - and onto the back of his neck, where he swiped at a - a clinging bat! A bat? Out of the sky, a cloud of moisture condensed, and engulfed him. A bucketful of water was thrown - with some force - at his head.

"Who's - *spplaggah!* - there?"

No one, though, was anywhere. Again, he started along the path, and again jungle turned into forest, which meant - what? - that he was travelling in the wrong direction? The shadows of the forest appeared to trigger-off the effects of the powder, which ate into his mind, a chorus - grinding and gnashing - of inane chatter, lost souls - in hell. Water vapours rose from his damp clothes. He had done it; he had finally done it. Hell. This was it-. The cone of the volcano sucked at the soul, until a voice . . .a British voice seemed to say:

You should have left the island when you had the chance, old boy. Told you there was no treasure. Now, it's too late-!

"What-? Who's there-?"

Then, salvation: Are you all right, old boy?

"Is that you?"

Who else? Methinks you're in need of a guide. A groatsworth of wit bought with a million of repentance. Story of my life, don't you know?

"Wilson? John Wilson? Is that you?"

No, it's me. You're favourite stamp dealer.

"Oh no, oh no! This can't be right!" The drug coruscated through the vault of his brain. Robert Walker clasped his skull between his hands.

Well, there's no need to be like that, old boy. I've come all this way, and what do I get?

"I'm lost! I'm lost!"

Spiritually or geographically?

Robert Walker ran amok through the forest, and allowed the path to lead him wherever it would - as long it was away from John Wilson's vexatious spirit.

"That's enough, Mr Wilson," he demanded. "Enough!"

Still, his skull rattled. Up ahead, moonlight penetrated a clearing, where a group of boulders had gathered as for a geological convention. It all looked very tranquil, but from that observation he knew he was not yet free from the influence of the powders. Robert Walker, overcome by rapture, staggered through the boulders, and headed on through the forest, which at last gave way to the periphery of a great plantation. He felt fear, a deep fear: there would be plantation ghosts about at this time of the night. In fear, then, he skirted the edge of the plantation, and kept to the forest. If there were ghosts in there, they would not leave their own domain - would they?

Again, he made his way into the foothills. On the coast, he now realised, he might even have encountered the disillusioned American. A journey around the island. How far? Something was following him into the foothills. The something asked:

Around the island?

"Yes, Mr Wilson."

How far? I'll tell you: $2\pi r$. The circumference of the island. Very roughly, of course.

"What?"

Yes, he heard John Wilson say. It's me again: $2\pi r$ - where r strikes out a radius from the centre of the volcano.

"But," Robert Walker spoke into the forest, "not even Dr Mobuto, with all his magic, could work out *pi.*"

Don't be ridiculous, old boy, when we can safely assume - *assume*, mind you - a surd-value of 22/7, for practical purposes, then we may proceed.

Robert Walker stopped where he was, until Wilson's vexatious spirit shouted:

Proceed, I said!

"All right, all right!" Robert Walker, with his mind frazzled by the doctor's cheap potions, shouted at a giant conifer: "What about the radius?"

There was no answer.

"Who am I?"

You are Robert Walker.

"What am I?"

You are God's little soldier. No, I meant you are the creation of the Agency. You have been brainwashed. The individual is unimportant. Only the collective survives. East or West, the ideological differences are clear, but the outcome is the same.

"Brainwashed? Who, me? I have no memory of being brainwashed."

NO, OF COURSE NOT! You're a Walker! A Robot! A Robot Walker! You have been programmed by the State.

"What about free will?"

Free will? Don't make me laugh! Think I will anyway. Hahahahahah! There!

"Then, that's why-."

Dr Mobuto's powders, old boy: they have exposed the inner core of the psyche - all that kind of thing. That's your third dose. Stay away from the bloody stuff, if I were you. Drop of claret instead, eh?

"Yes, yes. . .Mr Wilson, are you still there?"

Of course I'm still here. Where else would I go?

"Well, where shall *I* go? I have nowhere else-?"

Got that bloody map on you?

"I lost it on the plantation."

What about the other one?

"I gave it to the German." Then: "How would you know about that? You'd left the island by then."

The stamp dealer did not speak while Robert Walker passed through the forest and into the exposed foothills. The moon dropped over the horizon, and the great band of the Milky Way became visible. Ahead, a giant puffball mushroom stuck up out of the ground. Robert Walker thought he ought, really, to turn his back on the puffball, which might explode, and blow him - along with a billion spores - away over the island. As his rational mind began to reassert itself, he realised this was not a puffball, or any other kind of giant mushroom, but a radome.

John Wilson's spirit would not go away:

How about an estimate of five miles for the radius?

"It must be more than that."

How about seven miles? As the albatross flies, of course.

The same distance had clocked-up in Robert Walker's knee-joints; he said:

"That's more like it, Mr Wilson."

So, the circumference of the island is πD or 22/7 x 2 x 7 = 44 miles. That is the distance Mr Beaumont will have covered. If, that is, we accept that the island is roughly circular, which more or less-.

"What about the tortuousity of his route?"

You mean hills and coves and inlets and such?

"That's the idea."

How about ten per cent?

"How about fifteen per cent?"

All right, then: that gives us 44 x 1.15 = My God! 47 miles.

"Let's call it fifty!"

As you wish, Mr Walker, and goodnight to you!

Fifty miles it was, then. Robert Walker guessed that Morgan Beaumont should have reached Port Bourbon by now, where the American would discover that Barbara West had-.

"Mr Wilson? Mr Wilson?"

There was no answer. John Wilson's spirit, or whatever incubus the magic powder had conjured up, had gone - a shooting star - over the horizon.

"Hey! Who's there? Don't move, fellah, or you'll get this!"

A backlit doorway had opened up in the side of the radome. A pot-bellied man in uniform appeared; he pointed a revolver on a lanyard in Robert Walker's direction.

"Who are you?"

"I'm Walker."

"I asked what your name is - not what you're doing, fellah."

Robert Walker waited until the last vestige of the drug cleared. "That's my name. Walker, Robert. I'm a visitor from Britain."

The serviceman with the revolver hesitated: "England? You're kidding, right?"

Robert Walker took a single step forward: "No."

"Don't move or I'll shoot!"

"I'm not moving now."

"Now," the pot-bellied soldier said, "stand forward into the light where I can see you."

"I thought you said not to move?"

"Don't be a wise-guy. You can move when I say so, which is now."

Robert Walker moved into the light from the radome's interior.

"By Christ!" the soldier said. "What's happened to you?

"I-."

"Don't move!"

"I'm unarmed."

"Yeah, I know."

The serviceman reholstered the revolver.

"Does that mean I can move now?"

"Yeah, move around all you like. I recognise your voice. We monitor all the broadcasts up here. I heard you on the radio a while back."

Robert Walker approached the radome, which, at this proximity, blocked out most of the sky. The soldier smirked, impressed by this civilian's accumulated natural camouflage of mud, sap and resin.

11

SGT. STROUD M^C CLOUD

"YOU'D BETTER COME on inside, Mr Walker. I'm Sergeant Stroud McCloud - United States Air Force. And remember: you haven't met me and you haven't been here."

"You mean, I shouldn't remember?"

"Yeah, that's what I meant."

"Then I'm pleased to meet you, sergeant."

"I'll bet you are. You look like hell."

The sergeant led the way into the facility, where he stood behind a console to watch a radar screen. The equipment inside the installation was in a state of gradual decommission. Stray wires, coils, consoles, and upended VDU's had been prepared for despatch - or incineration. Cables wandered all over the place. A huge interactive map hung askew above the sergeant's console; it showed the orbital paths of various strategic objects - unwrapped for 2-D.

"Something big coming in," the sergeant said to himself.

"From Diego Garcia?"

"Shucks, Mr Walker, you know I cannot deny or confirm that."

"Yes, I know, sergeant. Sorry about that."

"I'm the last one," Sergeant Stroud McCloud explained. "This place was built back in Sixty Three. On the equator - perfect. Now, the entire facility is being dismantled."

"Well, ah - why that's sergeant? We're still on the equator."

The serviceman frowned; blond, stratus-nimbus eyebrows spread over a pair of sky-blue eyes, but he said nothing.

"Sorry about that, sergeant."

"You're the guy who's looking for the treasure, right?"

"Well, what can I say, sergeant? If I say know, everyone on this island takes that as a yes."

"-I get the picture, Mr Walker. You've been searching all over the place? Is that why you're in such a mess?"

"Yes, you could say that, sergeant."

Sergeant McCloud said: "I'm turning fifty next week. Time I took early retirement. There's nothing else for it. Beer, Mr Walker?"

"That, I would appreciate."

"Long day?"

"Very, very long day, sergeant."

Sergeant McCloud stooped behind the console, kicked-open a military coldchest - and produced a couple of Budweiser beers.

"Bud okay?"

"Oh sure."

The sergeant, with a double fast-draw, decapped the bottles

Impressed, Robert Walker accepted a beer; he felt its deep chill against his hand.

"It's over, isn't it?"

"What's over, Mr Walker?" An atmospheric disturbance passed under the rim of Sergeant McCloud's USAF side-cap.

"The Cold War."

"I'm not able to comment on that, Mr Walker," Sergeant McCloud asserted, "but I am able to say, without prejudice, that it's great to be going home. Here's to democracy, Mr Walker," and McCloud raised his bottle.

"I'll drink to that," Robert Walker added.

Tears of sweat and sap ran down Robert Walker's face.

"You look half-starved, Mr Walker. How about a cheeseburger? I think I've got one around here *somewhere.*"

Robert Walker's stomach churned at the sound of the word: CHEESEBURGER. The promise alone was enough to dispel any lingering effects from Dr Marigold's serum and Dr Mobuto's powders.

"Hard time on the mountain, Mr W?"

Robert Walker had not been called that before. He smiled, with water in his eyes. "Yes, sergeant. It's the altitude, you know."

"Oh yeah, we in the USAF know all about that, even when we're grounded. Up here, anyway."

Somehow good-naturedly, Sergeant Stroud McCloud of the USAF opened a refrigerator unit: inside, he located a double-cheeseburger pre-wrapped in non-branded tissue. The sergeant placed the sealed bun into another piece of hardware, and pressed a couple of pressure pads in sequence. After a pre-set interval, an alarm sounded with a *preeeep!* - and the sergeant removed an overheated, melted cheeseburger, which he handed to his guest

"I'll pass on one myself," McCloud explained, and patted his potbelly: "I·have a little, ah, weight problem."

Robert Walker looked into McCloud's radar-scope eyes. Then, he clamped his teeth onto the juicy cheeseburger, which squirted hot tomato ketchup and melted cheese. The burger did not taste of anything, but he was so hungry - the lobster lunch in prison was a distant memory - that it did not matter. Away from the dacha, even the tasteless bun was a savoury from a master baker. Uncle Sam's nourishment flooded his veins. Then, he raised the bottle of beer to his mouth, and swallowed, and flooded his mouth with cold froth. The beer did not taste of anything, either, but that did not matter. Stroud McCloud had already said it: to democracy, and the sunny uplands of burgers and beer. What else did a man need?

"You would be surprised," Stroud McCloud seemed to answer.

"-?"

"I mean, how much weight I've lost just recently."

"Well, keep up the good work, sergeant."

The sergeant, though, watched the unrelenting progress of the transport carrier on the radar screen as it made its way from Diego Garcia atoll, over the Chagos archipelago, and on towards the Carlsberg Ridge. The return of democracy was, after all, only a tiny green dot moving across a radar screen in the way of a UFO.

Anthony Montaigne was on his way.

Robert Walker gobbled up what was left of the cheeseburger and drained the suds of beer. There was froth and ketchup around his mouth. He felt much, much better already.

"Thank you, Sergeant McCloud."

Sergeant Stroud McCloud, with a far away look in his eyes, studied Robert Walker at close-range. The serviceman seemed - no matter how hard he concentrated - to took through his guest, the skin of the radome, and far out across the curve of the Indian Ocean. Robert Walker did not know what to say, except, "If there's anything I can-?"

"-Do for me? Oh no, Mr Walker, all I need is my USAF pension when I get off of this island."

"How much do I owe Uncle Sam for the burger and the beer?"

"That's seven dollars and eighty five cents."

"-?"

"Just kidding, Mr Walker. The burger and the beer," the sergeant said, and looked at the interior skin of the radome, "are on the house." Sergeant McCloud laughed - a boy's laugh. Then he became serious, and said: "There is one little thing you could clear up for me, Mr Walker."

"Yes, sergeant."

"Outside: who was that you were talking with?"

"I wasn't talking with anyone."

"I was sure I heard you talking to a . . .a Mr Wilson?"

"Mr Wilson? Well, I *am* acquainted with a Mr Wilson, but he left the island about a fortnight ago."

"Then I guess," McCloud concluded, "you couldn't possibly have been talking with this Mr Wilson, then, could you?"

"No, I suppose not."

The serviceman looked at Robert Walker, knowingly.

"All right, sergeant," Robert Walker admitted, "I may have been talking to myself."

Sergeant McCloud, his instincts satisfied, looked up at the almost featureless skin of the radome. "Sometimes," he said, "I've caught myself doing the same thing. Especially, you know, recently."

"Now that you're the only one left, you mean?"

Eyeballing Robert Walker, Sergeant McCloud again observed: "You sure are in one hell of a state, Mr Walker."

"I'll clean up when I get back to Port Bourbon. Big party going on."

"So I understand. I'd better stay here, though." Then: "I'll take those, Mr Walker." Robert Walker handed over the used burger tissue and the empty beer-bottle. The sergeant placed the refuse inside a steel container. "Everything has to be shipped back home. Everything."

"Well, you've got my fingerprints on the empty Bud," Robert Walker said. "And maybe some DNA on the tissue."

"You think you're kidding, Mr Walker?" the sergeant laughed.

"Well, Sergeant McCloud, I'd like to thank you for the hospitality, but I really must be getting back to Port Bourbon now."

"Sure, I understand. Back on the trail?"

"That's the plan."

"Do you think you'll ever find it?"

"Find what, sergeant?"

McCloud frowned, so that the peak of his side-cap reached for the bridge of his nose. "Why, the Fiery Cross, of course."

"Well, sergeant, it's the search - the journey - that counts, wouldn't you agree?"

The sergeant's eyebrows knitted to form a single white layer over his blue eyes and across his brow.

"I dunno, Mr Walker, I really dunno. I'd have to think about that a while. A good, long while."

"Take my word for it, sergeant, it's the search that counts."

Stroud McCloud shook his head at Robert Walker's appearance. "I can see how you'd mean that, Mr Walker. Good luck with it, anyway. The search, I mean."

Robert Walker was already moving away from the console.

"Oh, by the way?" McCloud remembered.

Robert Walker had reached the exit.

"Yes, sergeant?"

The green radar screen illuminated the serviceman's face. "Well, I said earlier - that sometimes I talk to myself?"

"Yes, sergeant?"

"Well, whenever I catch myself doing it, I - you know? - stop myself immediately. I wouldn't want you to think that-?"

"No, sergeant, of course not."

"Okay, so long, and good luck with your search, Mr Walker. I wish I were going with you. Duty, first, though, eh?"

Once Robert Walker was outside the radome, Sergeant Stroud McCloud, who claimed he had a little weight problem, placed two double-cheeseburgers into the microwave, then, while he waited, reached for another bottle of the deep-chilled Budweiser.

PART FIVE

Regime Change

"There was no way of avoiding it: public opinion was too much for us."
The Odyssey, Homer (*c.* 750 BC)

1

BARBARA WEST FLIES NORTH

1964? 1965? WHICHEVER, the time was almost nine o'clock in the evening of 5th September 1991, and an old episode of *Sea Hunt* with Lloyd Bridges played itself out on the Marlin Room television set. Beer, spirits, and a limited quantity of burgundy in dusty bottles were being consumed, not 'on the house', but at 'special party prices' set by Mr Swann. With the Bourbrew bottling plant at a standstill, the prices were high; such had been Mario Colon's scheme to profit from the change of regime. Behind the bamboo bar, Danielle and the French waitress, Bebe, worked in tandem, but the whereabouts of Francis Long was a mystery. "Where is Francis?" the French waitress pined. "I don't know and I don't care, Bebe," Danielle scowled. "Probably the same place when his country needs him: GONE FISHING." At that, Bebe's lip curled, but she knew Francis Long would show himself soon. His affections had been wasted on Danielle, she knew, but with her it would be. . .different. The lounge, veranda, lobby and staircase were populated by half-established guests and wary visitors: diplomats, Cold War hawks and doves, footloose passers-by, those journalists who had not been deported, friends of the in-coming regime, die-hards and spies attached to the out-going regime, opportunists of all persuasions, and sensation-seekers or lingerers of no stripe, party colour or creed. One faction, though, wavered: some hardened supporters of Bellarmine had undergone an overnight transformation. These BIPP fanatics had dis-covered that they were really life-long democrats, who had always supported the exile Montaigne. Yesterday, Montaigne had been a despised counter-revolutionary stooge of imperialist forces abroad. Today, he was a hero of the freedom loving, confused, but still dynamic multi-party system. In this way, these one-party leftists had become advocates of freedom and change - so long as Anthony Montaigne survived the next 24 hours. The eyes of this *mélange* watched or pretended to watch the old programme from the USA, while everyone waited for the promised return of Anthony Montaigne. The landing of Montaigne, though, might result in an Alfonse Trouvères-style shoot-out at the International Airport. The BIPDF or militia would not, most people understood, surrender their hard-grabbed privileges without a fight, not unless Bellarmine and the BIPP elite first 'jumped ship'. Swiss banks accounts and flight schedules had to be arranged. Either way, Mr Swann's guests were able to watch events unfold from the relative safety of the Marlin Room. Why go to the airport and risk being shot, when you could stay here and drink Mr Swann's beer and watch TV? For now, Lloyd

Bridges commanded the screen in a black & white version of the great Pacific Ocean on the other side of the world. Even the parrot, No. 15, which had still not spoken (and never would), watched the television, with one eye cast sideways at the glowing tube. On the sought-after sofa, Elizabeth Greene tried to relax, and held hands - or not - with her husband. On the screen, Mike Nelson (Lloyd Bridges) plunged into the unknown depths of the Pacific. Elizabeth Greene's eyes sparkled with pleasure. The life of a senior diplomat's wife might not be so bad, after all, and her mission had been accomplished. (There had been nothing quite like this at Cheltenham Ladies College, she smiled). She might, she thought, tell her naive young husband all about it - later - and so she wriggled inside her short-cut dress, which, for the occasion, she had changed from lime-green to yellow. Yellow, the code of the mission. As for Albert Greene, he savoured a gin & tonic - and his recent promotion. You can't keep a good man down, he had remarked. Of course you can, his wife had laughed. What about Badger Browne - who had been smuggled-off the island in a khaki straight-jacket? Mode: the belly of a Hercules transport carrier. Destination: Brize Norton in Oxfordshire, then Budleigh Salterton - from where there was no return. "Don't make jokes, Liz." "I'm not making jokes, Alby!" Then she whispered into her husband's ear: "The old boy never betrayed anyone - certainly not Trouvères." And then she added: "As *you* very well know, Alby!" Albert Greene almost choked on his gin & tonic. He stared at the TV, but only to avoid his wife's eyes. *Sea Hunt? Sea Chase?* What did it matter? Liz Greene clucked and chuckled, and said no more. Instead, she thought about children (with nanny), a new wardrobe, a cottage in Surrey - anything she wanted (within reason). Once, he had asked her: What is it you want, Liz? Everything, Alby. Can't you narrow it down a bit, Liz? Can't you be more specific, Liz? Now, she would get down to specifics. Behind the Greenes, the bloated guest known as Herr Papier-Drache was uninterested in *Sea Hunt*, and played instead at a steady game of solitaire over a green-felt table (Mr Swann had found it in the cellar). The Rhinelander played the game, but he did not see cards. Wheels, axles and cogs. The universe sends gravity waves, though weak, to tease and warp a person's mind, that is for sure. *Ja!* The German snorted, and blew a card - the second joker - off the table, and onto the deck. A nearby bevy of locals saw, but turned away. Bad luck. Plenty bad luck. Again, the German snorted - *hurrrumopfhed* - and blew his straw hat off the table. Dust, from the cellar. Papier-Drache reached for his own bottle of Remy Martin, refreshed his glass, and washed the dust away from his throat. Dat is got. Mr Swann had also found the bottle in the dusty cellar - a leftover from the pre-Revolutionary days. The German had made Mr Swann a spot-offer in Deutschmarks that the proprietor had been unable to refuse. To celebrate, Mr Swann, ja? Ja, ja, Mr Swann had learned to agree. And so the

335

Rhinelander celebrated, and played cards. The Cold War was over; it had ended here, too, of all places, a small island - *Insel* - in the middle of this geo-political wilderness. Reunification would surely follow. So, now: the only sense in which Germany could, therefore, compete effectively with the crazy transAtlantic alliance (curse Herr Walter Raleigh) would be as part of a Greater European project, the global implications of which were as yet unknown. The German looked inward on the hall of mirrors that was his own mind. He, Herr Papier-Drache - or H. Kite in the Anglo-Saxon world - would thrive in this new reality. A purely economic landscape free from the distortions of ideology, he had waited all his life for this time of times. Oh, ja. Papier-Drache would soon write-up his report for the consortium, but not until he had read the Britisher's article. For this, he would pay plenty of Deutschmarks. Good, solid cash uneroded by inflation. Herr Walker had been co-opted by the same transAtlantic alliance, as much as he, Papier-Drache, had been corrupted by the consortium. Even so, the signs are promising. The report need not contain everything. He, a mere player of cards, would be ridiculed by the shareholders. The map acquired from the Italian *mafiosi* was real, though, or at least it was a *facsimile* of an antique chart from the late 1720s. In Berlin, a cartographic dealer of his acquaintance would authenticate the chart one way or the other. In the interim, the consortium was not interested in adventure stories, unless the tale involved a return on the capital deployed. A simple investment prospectus appraisal would eclipse the imaginings of romantic fools in the foothills. The opportunity for salvage remains outstanding. There might, however, be difficulties over the true ownership of the Fiery Cross: Montaigne, the Vatican, the authorities in Lisbon, Dunne's estranged widow in Southend - all would have something to say. You would only find the Cross if you did not look for it, someone had said, but whom? Swann? Robert Walker? Colon? Wilson? Beaumont? Maybe no one had said it. Poised at the end of a Camel cigarette, Papier-Drache inhaled and exhaled, and shuffled the cards. So, if there is no salvage, then there are fishing rights, which could be extracted from the new Montaigne government in return for seed capital and soft loans, and perhaps even a bond issue to underwrite tourism development. There's your treasure, old boy. The potential returns for shareholders are - well, we must all be patient for now. (Extraordinary.) Who cares about treasure? It is only an excuse, while you look for other things. Ask Herr Walker! He knows! The real treasure is in the minds of men and women, and . . .certain concessions. If things went wrong, then Papier-Drache already had his patsy. (Robert Walker would do, and, if not, the Englishman had other uses - according to Herr Harry Stein!) The long years of preliminary work had, of course, already been carried out by Mr Graham Dunne of Southend-on-Sea, now deceased, whose grave looks out over the Indian Ocean, and the carpenter-plumber Roger Dupin of Port Bourbon, who has no grave of his own but for that same ocean. So, these men have suffered, but why should not our investors benefit from the endeavours of the dead - whom anyway seek no returns? Their interests have been liquidated - amortised! After all, capital is the senior partner, is it not? In the interval, as they say, Papier-Drache's conscience whispered: to hell with the shareholders! Herr Papier-Drache drained off the rest of the Remy Martin. here! - and the German radiated sun-pink, straw-thatched satisfaction. It was then that Harry Singh entered the Marlin Room, not with his portable barbershop kit, but with a much larger box of fresh merchandise. The German was the first to buy an I♥MONTAIGNE badge, which he pinned to his straw hat. Price: 10 rupees only. Singh grinned, and showed gold and ivory teeth.

Frost!

*

ON THE FOURTH floor of the hotel, Mr Swann re-opened the Presidential Suite with his master-key. The American had gone missing, somewhere along the coast there, so the room had these last days been used solely for storage purposes. Storage? Over three hundred cases (200 had already been consumed today) of the Blue Marlin beer had now been relocated, shift-by-shift, by Mr Swann and his team. The bartender, the housegirl, the chef, and the (sullen) gardener - all had done their duty. Now, with the advent of Anthony Montaigne's return, the cargo had to be shifted again. But, where. . ?

diminishing - but certainly - not missing

*

AND WHERE WAS Francis Long? It was a hot, a very hot night. Danielle and Bebe worked without immediate prospect of relief. On the wall, the glass eye of the stuffed marlin stared down on the proceedings - unimpressed. The ceiling-fan rotated until it looked as though it might fly off its gimbals - and cut-off the head of the Listening Bird. On its perch, the parrot's feathers fluttered under the artificial breeze. By the bay window, a cell of observers had broken away from the television audience. The whereabouts of the missing bartender had been discovered. In turn, each member of the group followed Francis Long's progress through the telescope under the light of the low, ocean-dipping moon. At that moment, man and boat had slipped away from the field of view. Sharks? someone suggested. At this time of night? one man enquired. At exactly this time of night, another man replied. And then a gust of wind blew down from the plantations, over the veranda, through the lounge - the ceiling-fan precessed with a skew - then pushed its way over the television audience to reach the bay window, where it escaped onto the Indian Ocean. The bevvy of locals looked to Harry Singh for an explanation. "FruurpPmff?" Papier-Drache quizzed. "You have brought down one of those damned plantation ghosts with you, Mr Singh?" and the German played a - suspended - card. The merchant shook his head: "Dr Mobuto has gone back to Zanzibar!" he announced. There was laughter, but not from the locals. Dat is got. Papier-Drache invited Harry Singh to share a Remy Martin, and so a special friendship was born. The merchant detected the crooked game of solitaire, and suggested a new game: trade, cooperation, export-import. Ja, ja! Glasses chinked. *Prost!* A new emporium - not out on the plantation - but here in the centre of Port Bourbon. *Prost!* Harry Singh was in paradise: his eyes turned inside his head to survey some far-away vista, where kohl-eyed maidens frolicked over lush pastures. Harry Singh - tied in the middle by his elasticated belt with its S-shaped buckle - frolicked, too.

*

OUTSIDE, ROBERT WALKER slipped through the shadows until he reached the hotel. He clambered up the short flight of steps, tripped over the loose plank, and happened to block Barbara West's exit. The intrusion caused the guests on the veranda to push into the lounge for a closer view of the television. Barbara West was dressed, in a blazer-suit, for travel, and carried a military-looking overnight valise. Robert Walker looked at her, but did not know what to say.

"Why are you looking at me like that, Robert?" Her lips waxed crimson, she smiled dangerously.

Robert Walker had barely found his breath. "Going out for the evening, Barbara?"

"What," she observed, "has happened to you, Robert?"

"I'm not sure what's happened to me."

"They did this to you in jail?"

Barbara West managed to snap-close the double-locks of her efficiently packed valise. A suicide mission over the Indian Ocean? Was Bellarmine, with the heavenly Barbara West at his side, about to be blown-up in mid-flight?

Robert Walker asked: "What's going on in there?"

"They're watching television. Lloyd Bridges. I met him, once. A real gentleman. You should join them. Keep you out of trouble. The Greenes - well, Liz, anyway - have been asking after you."

Barbara adjusted her already perfect make-up.

"And where are you going, Barbara?"

"You'll have to stand out of my way, Robert."

338

She reached into her purse.

"You're going to shoot me?"

"You know I would. So, why don't you go in there and watch Sea Hunt?"

Robert Walker moved out of her way, but not my much. Barbara slung her valise over her shoulder, and moved onto the veranda.

"You *are* a mess, Robert. You should clean yourself up. This is a great day. You'll see. Soon enough."

Barbara's eyes shone under the lights of the veranda. Her face was shell-white under the night sky.

"Where's Morgan?"

"Walking around the island. Someone - I don't know who - put the idea into his head, and off he went. You knew that."

"Yes, I knew. We found him years ago. He was a doorman at a nightclub in Dallas. He'll be all right."

Out on the veranda, they faced each other.

"Maybe you should have gone with him."

Robert Walker made a snatch for her wrist, which she easily avoided. She looked each way along Revolution Boulevard.

"Expecting a taxi?"

She did not answer.

"You really did it, didn't you? How could you?"

"-?"

"With Bellarmine. Why? Why did you do it, Barbara?"

"If it's any of your business, it's my job."

"You're a patriot then, is that it? Uncle Sam's wh-?"

"-You find that embarrassing? He's only a man, you know. Just like any other. . . But, you-?"

Barbara's eyes widened over the veranda, then she stared up - at the roof of the island. "You? What is your part in all this, Robert? Tell me, now. What is it that you know? You're not a journalist, are you? Don't answer that; I don't have time."

Barbara West rearranged her luggage; Robert Walker could have grabbed her, then, but she was probably armed, not only with an automatic, but with a long bodkin needle. There, in the side of the valise-. She arched an angry eyebrow at him, and then moved - down the steps - to street-level. A taxi lurched - from a position beyond the crossroads - and pulled-up outside the hotel. The white Mercedes had been given a fast wash and polish. The meter, with that last, massive fare unpaid, had been wrenched from the dashboard. A government chauffeur had replaced the hair-primping taxi driver. In the rear passenger seat, a pair of Bellarmine's wire-headed goons waited. These BIPP thugs looked as though they wanted to kill someone. Barbara West turned, and said: "Well . . .?"

339

The chauffeur had opened the passenger door. Barbara West did not let the man touch her valise. The chauffeur climbed behind the steering wheel, and waited. Inside the taxi, the two goons watched Robert Walker with bone-crunching eyes.

"You really are a sight," she said.

"You can thank your boyfriend, and bloody Dr Marigold, and that damned Dr Mobuto for that."

"Please don't call him my boyfriend. As for those other two-. They did this to you? I don't believe it."

"Why not? They're lunatics - all of them. Marigold has been arrested for high treason. Mobuto is, I think, dead, though it's hard to say. That leaves Bellarmine. He's lost touch with reality - whatever that is."

"You're the one who's-."

"-Now, listen, Barbara, to what it is I have to tell you."

"Say, say-."

"He's still dithering. While he's dithering, it's my guess he's refuelling the Cessna at the airport. He's waiting for you, but he's not made up his mind. Montaigne is on his way in from Diego Garcia - any time now. You've got to get your man out of here - off the island. You'll need an edge: tell him this: his mother is alive and well in Paris. Top floor of the Ritz. Tell him he can take his antiques with him. Goodbye, Barbara, and-."

The memory of Dr Mobuto's powder tugged at Robert Walker's brain. For the last time, he looked at Barbara West. Viktor Chomsky, the Russian Ambassador, had been right about the honey trap. François Bellarmine, he realised, was a defeated man.

Inside the lounge, the television audience cheered as Mike Nelson wrestled into a SCUBA outfit, and took the plunge into the depths of the Pacific.

Robert Walker did not catch what Barbara West said; then she slipped into the front passenger seat, slammed the door, and the White Mercedes took off beyond the crossroads, and away up Victoria Street and into the foothills.

*

"ENJOYING THE VIEW, Mr Walker? It is you - isn't it? You are wearing a disguise?"

Questions, questions. Robert Walker turned: it was the second soup eater with the receding toupee he had first noticed in the dining room. The man's moustache appeared to be wet with beer or something. He was dressed in the same utilitarian grey tunic-suit, and carried a black briefcase.

"My name is Mr Dan. A most beautiful looking woman, if I may say so."

Robert Walker thought that Mr Dan's accent - from the American South - had been grafted, as with the toupee, onto the man.

"If you like to take risks, Mr Dan."

"You're the one who likes to take risks, Mr Walker."

"-?"

"You have been over to the Russian Naval Base, have you not? About Mr Beaumont - the American - he must be dealt with. Where is he? You know. I know you know. Any assistance you give will be well rewarded. Very well."

Robert Walker looked into Mr Dan's dark eyes. A layer of sweat had formed on Mr Dan's brow, so that it looked as though the toupee might slide off his head. Robert Walker asked: "What's in the case?"

"Nothing."

"Let me see."

Mr Dan opened the case. Robert Walker saw only an empty interior.

"There - I cooperate. Now you must cooperate with us."

"Us? Whatever you're selling, I'm not interested."

Robert Walker looked at Mr Dan's black briefcase again: it seemed too heavy for its empty shell.

"I'm not selling, Mr Walker. I'm buying. You need money. I know you need money."

"No, I don't. Not any more. You should stay away from the hotel, Mr Dan."

"I am a guest here, same as you."

"I don't believe so."

"You can't tell me what to you. You are only a journalist. You are *nothing*."

"Then stand out of the way - of nothing."

Mr Dan took a single side-step across the veranda. Then he turned on his heels - saw a group of men out on the road - and pushed a retreat into the lounge. Robert Walker waited: by the crossroads, a hundred men had gathered - stevedores, warehouseman - armed with planks, pipes and chains. The teeth and eyes of the men signalled their collective intention. This night-group started to move over the crossroads, past the Marina Hotel, and along Revolution Boulevard. Robert Walker did not budge, and the dockers paid him no attention. The group, he guessed, was on its way to BIPP headquarters. The party bureaucrats and theoreticians would, unless they had already fled, be battered beyond recognition. A reward for their graft. After a while, the men had filed past the hotel.

Robert Walker made his way into the lobby.

*

"DE CARD, IT verked, ja?" Herr Papier-Drache asked. Robert Walker merely nodded at the German; he did not want to think about Dr Mobuto any more. By the same card table, Harry Singh saw that his work on this customer had already been undone. Robert Walker, who owed the merchant money for the shave, smiled - and said nothing. Inside the Marlin Room, there was standing room only. Shot-through with fatigue, Robert Walker found the far-end of the bamboo bar from which to watch TV. *Sea Hunt* had almost finished. He ordered a bottle of beer at three-times its usual cost, and was told to wait. Behind Robert Walker, Mr Swann appeared: "A thousand apologies, Mr Walker. Anything you want, anything," and Mr Swann snapped his fingers at the barmaids. "Beer!" Danielle and Bebe obliged; Robert Walker was thus presented with *two* cold bottles of beer - and at no cost. Mr Swann chose his moment: "Do not go to your room, Mr Walker. Not yet. Later, maybe."

"Why not, Mr Swann?"

The proprietor explained: "Your occupancy has expired."

"I have one more night. And I lost two or three nights with Chief Bugis."

As usual, Mr Swann's face was torn between discretion and revelation.

"You have escaped, then?"

"I was released."

"Then that is good. I have nowhere left to hide you. Enjoy your beer, Mr Walker."

"Where's Fra-?"

Mr Swann had already returned to the lobby, where he took up his customary position behind the reception desk.

The TV set announced:

"*We interrupt Sea Hunt to bring you a special live BIRTV broadcast from the airport. . .*"

The screen flickered and buzzed. An image of a jubilant airport scene gradually emerged from the screen. After the flight from Diego Garcia, Anthony Montaigne's entourage was shown moving down the disembarkation steps. At the top of the steps, a man in a fine blue suit appeared - bearded, white-smiled - the fomer president, Anthony Montaigne, waved at the crowd. (In the Marlin Room, no one wanted to be the first to cheer.) A welcoming committee of some 12,000 people surged forwards, and the islanders engulfed the former president. The entourage was obscured from the BIRTV camera. An excited Johnny Savvy babbled meaningless platitudes, while the camera lens zoomed-in on a wave of bobbing heads, jabbing elbows, and back-slapping hands. The crowd surged again, and the entourage showed signs of panic. Mr Swann had reappeared.

"Where's Francis Long?"

"He's gone to the rock. Very dangerous. He knows nothing about boats - or women. Strong currents and sharks. I'll say no more."

"Where is Sylvia Dupin?"

Mr Swann smiled: "You have been in jail for too long, Mr Walker. Now, enough. I say again, do not go to the room under the stairs. We must show proper respect for the dead."

"-? Isn't is a little late for that, Mr Swann?"

"For the dead, it is never too late."

"Yes, I suppose you're right, Mr Swann."

In the lobby, Mr Swann's brand-new facsimile machine spewed out paper over the reception desk.

A cheer went up from the bay window area. The main galllery of guests echoed the cheer, which they had thought was for Montaigne. Elizabeth Greene shed a tear; her husband passed her a handkerchief; his face reddened when he saw Robert Walker. In the lobby, sturdy, sandy footfall passed into the lounge. The American, sun-bleached and wind-blasted, seemed to enter unnoticed. Morgan Beaumont slapped Mr Swann on the shoulder; the proprietor took it fairly well. "So, Mr Beaumont, you are still with us?"

"I'm still with us," the American agreed.

"I have had to commandeer your room, Mr Beaumont. An important visitor-."

"That's okay," the American said. "I won't be needing it any more."

"Then, we speak later, gentleman," and Mr Swann returned to the lobby. Fax messages continued to spew: Paris, London, New York - Bombay.

"I'll have that, Robert."

Robert Walker passed the American the spare bottle of beer; Beaumont drained off the beer, and then coughed. His face was bronzed, salted and mottled by the sun, and he had lost a lot of weight. The eyes were. . *,frazzled*. "What happened to you?"

"I might ask you the same question, Morgan."

"Look-."

"Let's watch TV, Morgan."

"Sure."

As the BIRTV crew found an ideal camera angle, the operator was knocked to the ground. The TV screen showed only a close-up of the concrete runway and the broken stems of some flowers. The sound had been lost entirely. The Marlin Room audience gasped, and whispered among themselves.

"Where's Barbara?" the American asked.

"Don't ask, Morgan."

"Where's Barbara, Robert?"
"I've been in jail. I don't know anything."

*

OUTSIDE, CHIEF BUGIS's heavy boots clomped over the veranda, and into the lobby. The policeman faced Mr Swann across the reception desk.
"The hotel's full, Chief."
"No, jokes, Mr Swann." The Chief had an almost empty bottle of contraband whisky in one hand and his service revolver in the other.
"How can I help you, Chief?"
Wild-eyed, Chief Bugis said: "Cargo, Mr Swann! Missing cargo!"
"No cargo, Chief Bugis!"
The policeman raised the revolver, but he could not hold the weapon steady. Chief Bugis reached over the desk, and tried to grab Mr Swann by the lapels, but the policeman's hands were already full.
"This, Chief Bugis, is a brand new suit from Hong Kong."
The Chief was capless; his normally trim, George Formby haircut stood up in spikes; and the once well-starched uniform hung, limp and dark with sweat, from the shambles of a body.
"Don't . . .say . . .anything, old Swanny," Bugis drawled. "Don't even think! That is your trouble, you think too much!"
Mr Swann flushed with anger and disgust. The Chief's whisky-breath said:
"You've got to help me. This is my last case. It must not go unsolved. It is a mystery for sure!"
"You insult my hospitality, and then ask for my help, Chief Bugis? If there is any mystery, it is there!"
A crowd had pushed into the lobby. Mr Swann tried to wave the guests away. The Chief had a policeman's notion: he released Mr Swann, and announced: "I know where! The same place nobody dares to go!"
Mr Swann advised: "Don't do it, Chief Bugis! It is dangerous!"
"As you can see," the policeman grinned, "I am armed."
"That? That is no good against them! You must take smoke!"
The Chief - without the means to make smoke - lurched towards the staircase. Out of nowhere, the boy Charlie dived into the lobby, and tackled Bugis' ankles: "Don't do it, Papa! Don't do it!"
The Chief easily tossed the boy to one side. "Stay there! Stay there, Charlie! Stay with Mr Swann!"
The boy hid behind the reception desk. Bugis mounted the great staircase. Soon, the Chief had climbed to the fourth floor. An empty whisky bottle was tossed over the balcony, and splintered onto the road

below. After a pause, the policeman was heard to kick-in the door of the linen cupboard.

In the lobby, Mr Swann decided: "Go to the kitchen, boy! Help Chef Sami there! You will be trained. You are not a spy any more, boy. You are a dishwasher."

Charlie wandered along the corridor. The boy did not make any noise and nor did he pull any faces.

Two men in grey tunic-suits had appeared on the veranda. The agents stepped into the lobby, folded their arms, and waited. Mr Swann ignored the agents, whom he knew to be part of Bellarmine's State apparatus. The implication for Mr Swann was clear enough: should Montainge's convoy fail to reach Port Bourbon, then Mr Swann would be brought to Party HQ for interrogation and disposal. As Mr Swann contemplated this possibility, the facsimile machine clicked into action - the secret policemen became uneasy - and another fax started its feed over the reception desk.

*

IN THE MARLIN room, Danielle had found an opportunity to take care of Bellarmine's portrait. Instead of its regular dusting, she replaced the image with an older portrait of Anthony Montaigne. In this way, Bellarmine seemed to look in on himself, while Montaigne smiled out at the world. Across the lounge, a voice rose in protest, but yielded to an innocuous cough. No one tried to stop her. Then she returned to the bamboo bar, where she helped Bebe to fix gin & tonics for the Greenes.

"You are brave."

"This is a great day," she told the waitress from France, "for democracy."

"You say this now," Bebe said, "but you did not say it then."

"I was young. I was a party puppet. The BIPP did all my thinking for me. Some like it that way, but not me!"

"I'll stay here, then," Bebe said. "You should go to Paris. You can stay at my lodgings!"

"I am not a waitress. I shall study politics at the Sorbonne!"

"My lodgings are at Cluny," Bebe said, "close by the Sorbonne."

Robert Walker exchanged glances with the French waitress, but said nothing. Bernard's hot breath was far, far away.

Danielle pouted: "I am not a barmaid."

"Two more beers here, please!" Morgan Beaumont ordered.

The picture on the television screen still showed only concrete runway.

"There was always something funny about that girl," the American decided.

"Which girl?"

"You know who - Barbara. I've always wondered where girls like that end up; now I know."

*

IN THE CLOUDS way above the hotel, the engines of the Cessna Citation blasted their way through the sky. The aircraft climbed to gain altitude over the wind-shedding cone of Mont Pomme d'Or, then swept over the roof of the island - and away across the ocean. Destination: Charles de Gaulle International Airport, Paris. Passengers: François Ballarmine and Barbara West. Manifest: assorted crates (contents unknown).

On the roof of the hotel, the Chief of Police staggered onto the observation deck, where - distracted by the invisible aircraft - he stared up at the night-sky over the cupola. Then - much closer - there came the sound of smaller engines. Buzzing, dark, and angry. A cloud of hairy insects swarmed out of the nest, and attacked the policeman's exposed face, neck and ears. Chief Bugis, for the first time in his career, screamed against unendurable pain.

*

"YOU HEAR SOMETHING just then, Morgan?" Robert Walker asked.

"Maybe I did. Sounded like-. Hard to say with all the chatter."

"Next," Danielle asked.

"Qui, monsieur?" Bebe invited.

Now, the barmaids had attracted a fresh group of thirsty customers. Among this onslaught, a man with a toupee asked for F & N ice-cream soda.

"What are you doing here?"

Mr Dan had not noticed he was so close to his target; he replied: "You, Mr Beaumont-. I thought you were-?"

Mr Dan tried to escape. Beaumont grabbed Mr Dan by the collar. "I've told you people before-."

As Mr Dan pushed his way through the crowd, his hairpiece came away in Morgan Beaumont's hand.

"Here - take this," and Beaumont passed the hairpiece to Robert Walker. A tag read MADE IN NEW ORLEANS. Robert Walker recalled Barbara West's words: Morgan would be all right; in other words, Morgan would be taken care of-.

Mr Dan was calm and methodical; he aimed one end of the briefcase at Beaumont's heart.

"What's in the case?" Beaumont asked.

"I'll show you," Mr Dan smiled.

Mr Dan felt for the trigger inside the handle. In the crush, a diplomat raised his glass, and elbowed Mr Dan in the ribcage. A dart under very high-pressure flew out of the case with a *phhfft!*, and lodged - with a thud - into the base of the bar. It was a bamboo dart the size of a chopstick.

Morgan Beaumont flattened his right fist against the left side of Mr Dan's face. Dan lurched, and fell - through a group of diplomats - against the base of the bar. Unconscious, he lolled to one side, and lost his grip on the case - and reality.

"Stand aside everyone," Mr Swann ordered. "Please, Mr Beaumont, you also. Now, what is going on here?"

"An assassin?" a guest speculated.

"He's out cold!" someone else observed.

"Who's out old?"

"There - there-."

Mr Swann stepped over the body to reach for the briefcase.

"Don't touch the handle, Mr Swann!" Robert Walker advised.

Mr Swann opened the case. Inside: socks, a shirt, and pair of shorts, sun lotion, and-.

"Hey! What's that?"

Mr Swann inspected the spare toupee. On the floor, Dan groaned - and was silent. . .The guests gathered around the proprietor.

"Here, let me see that," Morgan Beaumont said.

Mr Swann raised the briefcase. The American lifted the upper layer, which covered the void beneath. A compressed air unit had been rigged-up to propel a single dart, which - of course - had already been fired. To the eyes of Customs, the special scientific apparatus of an oceanographer.

Mr Swann asked: "Who was he after? Montaigne?"

"Not Montaigne," the American realised.

"You know something about this, Mr Beaumont?"

"He's gone!" someone shouted.

"Gone? Gone where?"

Behind the bar, Bebe screamed. An object crawled past her legs, opened trapdoor, and hauled itself down into the cellar. Danielle jumped onto the trapdoor, and the assassin was entombed.

"Leave him there!" Mr Swann said. "There's no way out. Not even for a rat."

"We're trying to watch television, man," one of the locals remarked.

"Then watch!" Mr Swann shouted. "Now, out of my way!"

347

The guests parted to form a human corridor. Mr Swann returned to the lobby. He stowed the evidence in the nightsafe. The two agents watched and waited. In the Marlin Room, the audience waited and watched. The television screen had begun to flicker.

"What's was all that fuss about, Alby?"

"I have no idea, dear. A renegade, maybe. They pass through here all the time. Another g & t?"

"Perfect."

*

THE STREETS HAD become unsafe. A stray bullet found its way along Revolution Boulevard, took a left-turn at the crossroads, and made its way up along Victoria Street - and into the 'Voice of the Island' studio, where the missile woke up the sleeping caretaker. Nobody, Mr Swann maintained, was to venture outside the confines of the hotel.

One curious guest enquired:

"What is that noise underneath the floorboards?"

Mr Swann had to admit: "Someone trying to find a way out."

The two agents laughed with snorts.

"You two got nothing else to do?"

The agents re-folded their arms, and said nothing. Mr Swann played with the abacus and double-checked the register: everything had to be exactly right.

*

"A QUESTION, Danielle?" Robert Walker asked.

"Yes, Mr Walker?"

"Sylvia Dupin. You have seen her?"

Danielle blushed; she blushed often these days. She replied:

"Not tonight. Maybe tomorrow. Be here: mid-day."

"Who?" Morgan Beaumont wanted to know.

"She was at the dacha. She helped me escape - I think. She diluted the dose. Then again, maybe not."

Bebe and Danielle whispered between themselves. Love potions?

The television screen flickered and crackled, and the BIRTV crew panned as Montaigne's entourage walked steadily across the runway. If there had been a disturbance, it was over for now.

Robert Walker took a great swallow of the beer, which washed away, finally, the powders of Doctor Mobuto.

After a while, Morgan Beaumont said: "They'll send someone else. They won't stop until I've been eliminated."

"You can carry on being Morgan Beaumont. What difference does it make?"

"Let's put it this way: I've got a lot of sand in my boots for someone who's not a beachcomber." The American recounted: "You know, when I was walking around the island, I came across some fisherfolk. They'd never heard of Bellarmine - or Montaigne. Three or four days, it took me. I'll tell you all about it one day. Maybe," the American had already decided, "if They let me."[*]

"Who are They?" Robert Walker asked.

A group of Chinese diplomats crushed into the Marlin Room. The Briton and the American were forced onto the far rim of the bamboo bar.

"They. Them. The Company. Who else? You know, I've heard about that kind of thing, but I never thought I was one myself. It makes you wonder - doesn't it? - if a person really has any free will at all. It's all very disappointing, really."

Robert Walker felt something unpleasant tug at the back of his mind. Across the room, he noticed Herr Papier-Drache's green-felt table. Harry Singh watched, but the merchant's eyes were elsewhere. The German's incessant shuffling of the cards unfolded only discrete facets of a grand stratagem that he would never, could never, understand.

"Ever hear of Sirhan-Sirhan?" the American asked. "Programmed, they reckon, by somebody to shoot Bobby Kennedy."

Robert Walker did not respond. It was true, though; he knew that already. John Wilson's spirit had told him on the mountainside. Even his name told him so ROBOT WALKER - an automaton for the Shoe Lane Agency. He and Morgan Beaumont were two of a kind - a pair of patsies - jokers in the pack. The American saw what he was not supposed to see:

"You, too?"

---

[*] The three chapters covering the American's three-day journey around the island have been removed from this text at the insistence of the Agency.

349

2

REGIME CHANGE

ELIZABETH GREENE, from her position on the sofa, winked in Robert Walker's direction. Beside her, Albert Greene asked if there was something in her eye, and she replied, yes - a lash.

By the bamboo bar, Morgan Beaumont confided: "I'll be deported, you know that, Robert? Credit cards cancelled, that kind of thing. No bank accounts by that name. I'm a blow-back as far as the Agency is concerned. They'll send clones of Mr Dan. Or I'll wind up in San Quinten with my mind erased."

"File your report as usual, Morgan: this time, under Travel features."

"What about you?

"About my mind?"

"No, your next assignment."

"I must return to London. A man called Harry Stone will want to debrief me. That's what they do at my agency. They have the shirt off your back, and then they debrief you. After that, I have no idea. First, I have a wager to collect. I'll take Conny on a vacation. Paris, maybe."

"Conny? That's the girl you don't know?"

"That's her."

Mr Swann appeared from the lobby.

"Ladies and gentlemen, I have an announcement to make." Mr Swann read from a fresh fax: "The USSR has this day been dissolved."

There was no response. Then: "It cannot be true," a former BIPP-man maintained. "Yankee propaganda!"

Mr Swann re-read the message from his new fax machine: "I say again, the USSR has today been dissolved!"

The Marlin Room erupted. What did it all mean? Why? How? When? Gorbachev, an hour ago the General-Secretary, was now unemployed. Yeltsin and all his men were ready to step in and take over. In sequence, Herr Papier-Drache grunted with pleasure - reunification was inevitable; Checkpoint Charlie would be placed in a museum - and played his next card, which was - being palmed - the Ace of Spades. Harry Singh laughed, and surrendered to the German. He was not really, the merchant said, a card player. The news spread through the hotel, and into the streets. Out in the gardens, someone looked up at the roof - and screamed. In the kitchen, pots and pans clattered. A pannier of knives and forks shook violently. The diplomats among the guests looked this way and then that way.

"I'll drink to that," Morgan Beaumont confirmed. A surge of guests saw fit to join the American. Behind the bar, Danielle and Bebe were -

once again - overwhelmed. Beneath the trapdoor, the assassin had failed to find a way out, and thumped for his freedom.

"You hear anything, Morgan?"

"Bats in the belfry," Beaumont raised his glass: "and rats in the basement. I wouldn't be without them."

*

THE ISLANDERS had gained control of the streets. Across the road a way, there were shouts from the abandoned brewery. After a while, the conveyor belt restarted, and distribution escalated to meet demand. In the next 24 hours, more BourBrew was consumed than on any other day in the island's history. In the distance, a great cheer went up from the establishment known as Silent Pete's. The Australian landlord had broken his oath of silence. Red firecrackers exploded beyond the crossroads and along Revolution Boulevard. Around Port Bourbon, each series of blasts brought smoke and paper shrapnel. Harry Singh smiled: a small fortune's worth had been imported and sold well in advance.

*

UNDER THE FIXED gaze of the stuffed marlin, couples exchanged kisses and danced. Mr and Mrs Greene allowed themselves an affectionate peck. On the upper floors of the hotel, the news was shouted across the marina:

"T h e U S S R has been D I S S O L V ED!"

A remote yachtsman missed his step on the pontoon, and took a dive into the water - Spur-lasshh! - but quickly resurfaced.

On the second and third floors of the hotel, there were more howls; and, on the first floor, from the summit of the staircase, a startled screech was followed by a much louder scream:

"MISTER SWAAAAAAAARGGGGGGGHH!!!"

Mr Swann took one urgent step into the lobby, and looked up the great staircase:

"In the name of God, Chief Bugis, is that YOU . . .?"

"You mean," someone asked, "you cannot recognise him, Mr Swann?"

A group of hangars-on pushed-in behind Mr Swann. In the lobby, all eyes looked to the top of the staircase. The Chief of Police, whose head had bloated beyond its usual size, swayed against a banister. As his eyes stared out from the pustule-mask that used to be his face, he pleaded:

"PLEEEASE, SOMEBODY, HELF . . .me!"

On the same landing, a woman guest encountered Chief Bugis - looked, saw - then fainted, and collapsed into the corridor. At the bottom of the staircase, an adolescent girl screamed, shook her fists, and ran outside.

351

In the lobby, no one else moved. Mr Swann advised:

"Chief, you stay there now . . . don't move too quickly!"

"Somebody get hold of Dr Marigold!"

"Haven't you heard?" another replied: "Marigold's under arrest! Treason!"

"All right, get George - the gardener - he'll know what to do!"

"Yeah, run like hell in the opposite direction!"

"Shut up everybody!" Mr Swann ordered. "Now, -!"

A middle-ranking diplomat, who was known to have a weak stomach, staggered outside - and vomited over the veranda.

Mr Swann ordered: "Everybody! Back inside the lounge! Now!"

"OH NO! Here he comes!"

The Chief's boxlike frame lurched: he crashed down the staircase, went into a tumble, and landed in a crumpled heap of bones and swollen flesh. Bugis rolled over. Inside his head, something clicked, and a sac of fluid exploded from the back of his neck.

"IT'S THOSE HORNETS!" Albert Greene realised. "They must be destroyed at once, Mr Swann!"

A dark-faced Mr Swann pressed: "Are you volunteering, Mr Greene?"

"Well, no, I - that's not my responsibility, is it?"

"Then please act like a good High Commissioner and return to your seat, Mr Greene."

"The hornets might be headed this way," a man whined, and was told to: "SHUT UP! SHUT UP YOU BLOODY COWARD!" by his woman friend.

"Now, where is George? GEORGE!"

"He's not here, Mr Swann - he's hiding in his shed."

"Shed? Shed? At a time like this? Get hold of the man and tell him to bring a blowtorch!"

Then, Mr Swann pushed his guests away to examine the policeman's quivering carcass.

"Oh Chief, Chief," the hotelier moaned, "you are dead - as dead as the dodo of Mauritius."

"He's trying to speak!" someone observed. "He wants a priest."

Mr Swann's face twitched.

"A priest?"someone said. "For Chief Bugis? You must be joking!"

Mr Swann demanded: "If he wants to speak, then let him be heard!"

Chief Bugis' black-and-purple lips were too swollen to make any sense.

"That's guilt eating his heart out," a man who had once been a gun-runner observed. Mr Swann looked at the gun-runner, who shrugged - then departed from the hotel all together.

"Now, Chief, you have something to say?" Mr Swann asked.

The policeman's blubber lips moved:

"Thu bear isth moth there. . ."

"No, Chief, I told you there was nothing up there, except . . .But you knew that anyway, and now you know for sure!"

"Whereb it be, den?"

"It is . . . Arg!" Mr Swann stood away from the expanding pustules. The policeman's head swelled again with a glug-*clack* - and Bugis, with a shudder as his heart failed, found death.

An excitable youth ran out onto the street in the direction of the Police Station. "The Chief's head has exploded!" he shouted. "The Chief's head has. . .exploded! ARRRHGGHH!" and keeled-over on the crossroads.

Inside the lobby, hardened diplomats, eager for experience of something unknown, took in every detail of the Chief wounds.

"I swear to Got," the South African said, "I never saw a ting like that before, ever, so help me Got."

"Ja, ja," Herr Papier-Drache mumbled in the background.

Mr Swann shouted at his guests: "A man is dead. Back inside, all of you!"

No one had seen Mr Swann weep before, and no one except Mr Swann wept over Chief Bugis. The crowd withdrew, gradually, from the lobby.

In the lounge, Mr Swann reached for a long net drape, and pulled it from its rail. He threw the white net over the dead policeman. To the pair of agents, he said:

"You two - return the Chief's body to his police station. Don't argue with me. Place the body inside one of the cells. There, go now."

The men in grey tunic-suits obeyed. They unfolded their arms, and - with grunts - shifted the enormous carcass, prior to the crossing, onto the veranda. Mr Swann wiped the tears from his face. "I'll send the Coroner," he advised.

"The Coroner's dead," someone said.

"How?"

"A boating accident."

*

A BREATH OF wind blew over the veranda. An old photograph of Sir Godfrey and Lady Smythe-Smith crashed to the floor. Herr Papier-Drache studied the exposed frame - a love letter hidden inside? *Nien!* - and returned to his loaded deck.

In the lobby, Mr Swann spoke to his staff: "He was a bad man, it is true, but it was not always so. I remember him as a boy. He would steal the sweets from the other children: that's where it all started. He was corruptible, that is all, like the best of us. He had his good points. . . though they elude me at this moment. Now, enough: we have a most important guest on the way! Now, to your stations!"

Mr Swann put a call through to a 24-hr undertaker, but the line was busy. In this heat, it would not do to leave the Chief for too long in his cell. He tried again, and still the line was dead. He made a follow-up call to Port Bourbon Infirmary. The porter answered, and said that no one was there: the staff and patients had made the journey to the airport.

*

A BAY WINDOW observer pointed: "Look down there!"

"Ssssssh!" a television-watcher rebuked.

"Where?"

"Francis Long - he's tying that skiff up at the pontoon. He's carrying something!"

"Something? What something?"

"I can's see; it's wrapped inside a canvas."

"I don't believe it! You mean, he found something out there?"

"In the dark, how can you tell?"

"I'm a night watchman at the harbour."

"Then what are you doing here? You should be at the harbour."

"I wanted to see what was going on over here."

"Well, that explains it, then."

"Explains what?"

"Why you can see in the dark."

On the sofa, Albert Greene looked worried.

"A limp of wrock, dat's all, min!" the South African blethered.

"It must be treasure!" a woman gasped.

"No, it looks more like a lump of rock!"

The bay window group watched Francis Long's progress along the pontoon. The bartender climbed a ladder, and disappeared from view.

Morgan Beaumont asked: "What's going on, Robert?"

"I think Francis may have done it, Morgan - Clue Number Eleven."

The television set flickered, and Montaigne's passage towards the airport terminal was lost. A legend appeared:

NORMAN PROGRAMME RESUMED
BIRTV

The screen faded, and rebloomed to show *Sea Hunt*. A drunken visitor over from Silent Pete's complained that they had missed the climax of the episode. Lloyd Bridges was piloting a boat into a dock. He smiled and then waved at a woman in white blouse who stood on a pier. She wore a headscarf against a steady Pacific breeze. Robert Walker thought the woman resembled a black & white version of Barbara West.

*

THE FAN CHURNED away at the hot, moist, smoky air of the lounge. From the mountainside, a tunnel of wind sprung up along the south-eastern escarpment, and made its way along Victoria Street, over the crossroads, across the veranda, and recharged the room with a fresh blast of oxygen.

After the off-shore trip, Francis Long appeared from the direction of the kitchen. Sea spray had soaked him through to the skin. Salt crystals formed on his face. He checked-in at reception. Then Mr Swann escorted his nephew into the lounge. The bartender was greeted with a round of applause, and - from the bay window - wolf whistles, shouts and cheers. In his arms, he bore an object wrapped in sailcloth.

"The boat is secure, Francis?" Robert Walker asked.

"The boat is secure, Mr Walker."

"Any sharks out there?" the American wanted to know.

"Not as many as in here, Mr Beaumont."

"Then let us see, Francis," Mr Swann said, "what it is you have recovered."

Bebe stepped out from behind the bar, and wrapped her arms around Francis Long. Danielle paid them no attention. Mr Swann said: "Okay, plenty of time for that later on, girl. Now, if you please, Francis - unwrap the item."

The audience crept closer. The credits of *Sea Hunt* rolled over the TV screen in silence. Francis Long dripped sea water onto the floor. He set the canvas package on the bar. Then, he uncovered the artefact, and stepped away. The audience made a spectrum of noises - surprise, disgust, awe, disappointment. Danielle spoke up:

"You risk your life for that thing, Francis? You must be crazy."

Francis Long looked at Bebe: "I *am* crazy," he said.

Albert Greene stood up from the sofa, and pushed his way through to the front of the crowd. Elizabeth Greene followed, and stood -undetected - behind her husband.

"It's the Fiery Cross!" an ambitious guest claimed.

"Don't be ridiculous," another replied. "Does it look like any kind of a cross?"

Albert Greene was ready to cross-examine Francis Long: "Are you saying you found this thing on that rock out there?"

"Le Roche de la Chien? Yes, sir, Mr Greene."

"I don't believe you."

"Please, Albert," Elizabeth Greene said from the sofa. "If Francis says he found it on the rock, then I'm sure found he it on the rock!"

"Someone else might have put it there, Liz."

"I believe that's the general idea, Albert!"

"I don't mean a couple of hundred years ago; I mean, someone may have put it there - only yesterday." Greene looked at Robert Walker. "You still here, Walker?"

"I've only just been released, Mr Greene," Robert Walker reported. "You know where *I* was yesterday."

"Looks like you've won your wager, Mr Walker," remarked an American voice. Cody? But there was no sign of William Cody.

"Wager? What wager is that?" Elizabeth Greene now stood by her husband's side. "You know anything about a wager, Albert?"

Albert Greene had turned a strange colour. "I'd rather not say, Liz, if you don't mind."

Robert Walker patted the dog's head. Its faces looked in three different directions. "This, Mrs Greene," he explained, "is Cerberus, the dog that guards the Underworld."

"You don't mean that literally?"

"As such, it represents Clue Number Eleven in Graham Dunne's quest."

"Get to the point," Greene insisted.

"The Englishman was a deluded madman!" a Belgian geologist said.

Robert Walker replied: "Well, monsieur, if Mr Dunne was indeed a madman, then why are you following his trail?"

"He must be crazy, too!" someone shouted.

The indignant Belgian puffed: "I follow no one, Mr Walker. I am here to collect samples - of the unusual, to say the least, stratum in this area-."

"-We're not here for a geology lecture!" someone heckled.

"Why are we, ah, here?" a mole-faced man enquired.

The Belgian geologist persisted: "Nonetheless, Monsieur Walker. I will offer you fifteen-hundred Belgian Francs for the hound!"

Harry Singh and Herr Papier-Drache looked ready to place their respective counter-bids.

"Ladies and gentleman," Mr Swann insisted, "this is not an auction house. The dog is not for sale!"

"All bids should, really," a junior diplomat proposed, "be made in the same currency. For the sake of clarity, I mean."

"French francs!"

"Deutschemarks, ja!"

"Swiss francs!"

"Sterling, of course."

"I say US dollars!"

"How about rupees?" a local suggested.

The Marlin Room reverberated with an uproar of counter bids, bland assurances, bogus speculations as to the true worth - or not - of the artefact, crackpot ideas, dangerous proposals as to how the dog might be acquired for nothing, and notions as to the whereabouts of the real treasure - which, of course, lay at Clue Number 12, or not.

An academic visitor observed: "How do we know this is Clue Number Eleven? Even if it is, it has been removed from its context."

"You, monsieur professor, are a fool!"

The Belgian's voice rose above all others:

"Gentleman - and Ladies - if you please. If the Dog Cerberus is Clue Number Eleven, then it is my learned opinion-."

"Get to the point, you Belgian windbag!"

"- having studied these matters for many years - that Clue Number Twelve. . . is, according to legend, the Garden of the Golden Apples. It is my further opinion that this can only be" - the geologist paused for dramatic effect - "the extinct volcanic peak we all know as Mont Pomme d'Or - the Mountain of the Golden Apples. I now propose an expedition to that windy edifice the first thing tomorrow morning! Who is with me? I ask again: WHO WITH ME?"

The geologist cowered against a barrage of peanuts, beer mats, dead (and live) cigarette butts, and ice-cubes.

*

"MY BID STILL STANDS," the defiant geologist said.

"Unlike yourself, monsieur!" a French diplomat cackled.

The lounge seethed with frustration and anger.

A local from the bevy of locals said: "This Britisher is for keeping the dog himself - and mocks us islanders! The treasure belongs to us, not these foreigners! There is a plot at work here - a European plot to rob us of our heritage!"

"It must be worth a fortune!" someone guessed.

Harry Singh pronounced: "Francis, it's yours. Out there, you risked your life for the dog. You need money, I know for sure. I offer cash in our own currency. The British, Americans, French and Germans are only here to-."

Herr Papier-Drache, who had not yet made a bid, stood up from the green card table, and threw down his deck of cards. On his way over to the bamboo bar, the German pushed through the assembly, and took a good, long view of the dog.

Francis Long decided: "It's not for sale, Herr Papier-Drache!"

"Here, let me see that thing," Morgan Beaumont demanded.

"Mr Beaumont," the German said in perfect English. "I know a fellow in Berlin, who-."

"NOT SO QUICK, GENTLEMEN!" Mr Swann warned. Then, with deft hotelier's hands, he moved between the American and German, and gently, but very firmly, took the *objet d'art* into his own arms. "Now, you listen, all of you," Mr Swann insisted. "This must be placed behind the bar here. Look, the plinth is already in positon."

"How could that be?" someone enquired.

"You see, Francis - up there on the empty shelf. Bebe, help him. Danielle, back to work, if you so please."

Francis Long looked at Robert Walker. Mr Swann said: "Mr Walker, you object?

"No, Mr Swann, it will do there above your bar as anywhere. Go ahead, please."

Francis Long accepted the artefact - a dead-weight between his hands - and stood on tip-toes to place Cerberus on a vacant plinth above the bamboo bar. Robert Walker studied the plinth, which, though plain, was familiar to him as the work of Roger Dupin.

"There," Mr Swann said, admiring the display, "see how it belongs?"

"Yes," Francis Long observed. "Here, it is in the same position as I found it on the rock."

"Is that so, monsieur?" The Belgian came forward. "You see - there - how the middle head looks up at Mont Pomme, as I had anticipated. This can only mean-."

"-Okay, okay, enough talk," Mr Swann decided. "Now, back to work, Francis and Bebe. This is not a museum! No one must touch! Plenty bad luck!"

Mr Swann returned to his post at reception. The bulk of the guests found their places around the television.

The Belgian lingered, and said to Robert Walker: "You are courier, monsieur?"

"I am no one's courier."

"Then you are aware - this artefact - you think it is soapstone? - when I know it to be of the finest jade?"

"You heard Mr Swann," Robert Walker said.

There were, of course, security considerations beyond the proprietor's warnings of bad luck, but everyone agreed that the natural place for Cerberus was on its plinth above the bamboo bar, with its three heads pointed North, West and East, but not South.

*

THE SUN-BURNT American and resin-plastered Briton looked at the Belgian geologist. A small group had gathered around the bamboo bar.

"It's jade," the Belgian whispered. "And the eyes - rubies! The same rubies that encrust the Fiery Cross, to which this dog looks."

"Soapstone," someone else sniffed. "The eyes are red glass, worth nothing. There is no Cross on this island. It was lost long ago."

"That fellow Dunne was right, after all. It must have been on that rock for over two hundred years," the Belgian geologist submitted, "placed there by none other than La Buse himself."

"A moment ago, you said he was deluded madman," a voice said from nowhere.

"Our friend Francis here," the South African mineralogist mocked, "must have put it on de wrock last week. You cannot trust these fellas - believe me, I know!"

"Whatever," Robert Walker decided. "There it stays - and let no man or woman go near it. No bids, no offers. You all heard Mr Swann. As for you, Francis, the boat is yours. You've earned it: I'll explain later."

Francis Long's journey had been completed. There was nowhere else to go and nothing more to say. In silence, he shook Robert Walker's hand, and had eyes only for Bebe

"All you have to do now," Beaumont said, "is save up for an outboard."

"It'll take him years!" someone asserted.

Harry Singh overheard: "Not necessarily," the merchant suggested.

*

"IF THERE IS no treasure in this life," Mr Swann was heard to say with Confucian simplicity, "then let us satisfy ourselves with the clues."

Herr Papier-Drache *Hummrumphfffed!* with an enormous blast of assent or dissent - it was hard to tell which - from the relative isolation of his card table.

"Please, everyone!" Danielle announced. "Now, it is time for Montaigne to speak." She reached to adjust the television set, which was brought to life by her touch. The audience stood where they were, looked, and listened.

ALIVE FROM THE AIRPORT
BIRTV

"Hello viewers, this is your old friend Johnny Savvy here again!"

In the Marlin Room, the audience applauded and cheered (along with a few groans).

The harsh lights of the mobile television unit showed the tense, sweating Johnny Savvy: the radio host, unaccustomed either to the medium of TV or the outside broadcast, partly obscured Anthony Montaigne, who, bearded, barrel-chested, and blue-suited, prepared for a makeshift press conference.

"*I give you Anthony Montaigne . . .* "

"*Johnny, stand out of the way!*" a female assistant pleaded.

Savvy fumbled, and jumped to one side: "*Ah, now, I give you Anthony Montaigne, who returns to us after fourteen years in exile!*"

The tumultuous crowd roared its approval, drowning-out anything Montaigne might have said. He looked, not at the crowd or the television camera, but up at the dark, almost invisible slopes of Mont Pomme d'Or. In the warm, night air, he motioned for silence, and the airport crowd obeyed.

"*Welcome back, boss!*" an old man shouted. "*What took you so long?*"

There was manic laughter, tears, and abrupt sobbing.

The BIRTV camera quick-panned, and showed that this was a real crowd, a spontaneous gathering of men, women, and children. Three little girls stepped out of the crowd and - shyly - handed over garlands. Anthony Montaigne patted the girls' heads, and sent them back to their mothers. He looped the garlands over an impromptu brace of micro-phones. Out of the night, from across the runway, a flowing cassock appeared: an unshaven Bishop David Chin had been released from his captivity. The priest approached, embraced the former president, and then stood by his side. After a statesman's considered pause, Montaigne spoke:

"*My fellow islanders, I return to you an older and, who knows, perhaps a wiser man.*"

A woman in the crowd wept, and gave vent to a mass outpouring of unspeakable emotion after the long years of Bellarmine's dictatorship. The BIRTV cameraman, after a wobble - achieved a good, clear, steady close-up. Anthony Montaigne moved quickly to establish his authority:

"*Please, my friends, the time for tears is over! Now, we proceed on our way to Port Bourbon!* "

That was enough: that did it: the crowd went crazy with rapture.

"*Vive Montaigne! Vive Montaigne! Vive Montaigne! Vi-!* "

"*Enough!. . .enough, my friends, enough. . .*" Montaigne delivered his broad, white, trademark smile, and the crowd managed to find reason.

Then, from across the airfield, there came rifle shots: CRACK-Crack-Cracck-crack-crack! Baaaarrrrrrp!"

The cries of adulation turned into screams of panic. The television screen showed thousands of islanders crumple onto the airfield. The

BIRTV cameraman staggered, but managed to show an isolated Montaigne - standing upright - against a hail of bullets. It was this image, above all else that night, that returned Montaigne to the hearts of the islanders, and to State House. . . as the next President of the Republic.

"STAY DOWN EVERYBODY!" Johnny Savvy shouted, and so exposed Montaigne to cross-wires from across the airfield.

"THEY'RE GOING TO KILL US ALL!" a young woman screamed.

"NO, NO! No one is going to kill anybody!" Montaigne assured his flattened audience.

From beyond, the assassin's crosswires found Montaigne's skull ... On the other side of the airfield, a triple-report - *crack, crack, crack* - counted out life or death, and the assassin died among the undergrowth.

Johnny Savvy realised he was still alive, and improvised a running commentary: *". . .Rebel forces have burst out of their barracks. . .There is no chance now. . .reinforcements. . .The renegades have been crushed."* Then, Savvy ceased his babble, and held the microphone toward Montaigne.

"Now where was I?" the former president asked.

"You were saying, sir, that it was time to proceed - to Port Bourbon."

The ocean breeze played over the airfield.

"Then, let us go!"

The crowd regained its foothold. *"Vive Montaigne!"* they cheered. *"Vive Montaigne!"*

Johnny Savvy and his BIRTV-crew followed the unsteady procession of the entourage into the terminal building. The CUSTOMS desk had been abandoned. In the ARRIVALS LOUNGE, the exile was greeted by loud, formal applause. The entourage passed through the main hallway to cheers and whistles. The flapper board announced: ALL FLIGHTS CANCELLED. François Bellarmine's massive icon was torn from the hoarding, and a placard of a younger Anthony Montaigne was hastily erected in its place. A security agent pushed Johnny Savvy out of the way, and the broadcaster smiled back. The door of a black limousine snapped open, and then closed: Montaigne was sealed-off from the island and the islanders.

*

THE BIRTV BROADCAST unit cut to a shot from much higher ground. A vast crowd - bearing torchlights, candles and lighters - surrounded the airport. Outside the terminal, a convoy had formed to escort Anthony Montaigne's sleek limousine into Port Bourbon. The crowd surged against the security cordon. The islanders hammered the roof of the vehicle, and smeared its wind-screens with their hands and faces.

"*Vive Montaigne! Vive Montaigne!*"

Inside the limousine, Anthony Montaigne paused only to look up at the dark cone of Mont Pomme d'Or.

After a short delay (Bishop Chin had been left behind), the convoy started - braked - and then crawled away from the airport. As the convoy turned onto the coastal road, the headlights of over 300 hundred vehicles stabbed the night sky, and swept-out arcs over the island. Way ahead of the convoy, the drivers of a white Mercedes and an old British Leyland bus *honk-honked* like a madmen for victory and the return of democracy to the island republic.

*

MR SWANN HAD sent for the gardener, who was discovered hiding in his shed. When George reported at reception, Mr Swann said:

"George, find a blowtorch."

The gardener refused. In the lobby, a nearby guest remarked: "I've seen this fellow somewhere before."

Mr Swann said: "You have? In the garden, maybe?"

The gardener started away from the reception desk.

"Stop there!" Mr Swann demanded. "Where are you going, George? To get a blowtorch?"

The gardener shook his head: no, he was not. Further, he would not.

"You are frightened of the hornets?"

"N-."

"They must be destroyed!"

The guest remembered: "At State House. I've seen him tending the hedges at State House."

The gardener's eyes widened. He took off his pith helmet, and looked sheepish. But: "-," he almost said.

"Yes, you're right," another guest corroborated. "Then: Mr Swann, your gardener is a coward!"

"So," Mr Swann decided: "After what happened to Chief Bugis, who can blame the man. Even so: George, I ask one last time. Save your face. Get the blowtorch."

Again, the gardener declined.

The first guest said: "He's not a coward, he's a spy. Your gardens Mr Swann: the grass has been poisoned. He only plays the coward. See how his shoulders slope, when really he is much taller."

The gardener unhunched his shoulders: he really was much taller.

"He's a BIPP spy - sent to watch this hotel over many months."

Exposed, George threw his pith helmet at the reception desk; it bounced off the register, and caught Mr Swann off-guard.

"A spy! Where?"

The two sides of Mr Swann's face became one: "I will not tolerate denunciations in this hotel. Once it is started, it will not stop!" he snapped.

Inside the Marlin Room, a television watcher shouted: "Montaigne is on his way in!"

The TV audience cheered, clapped, and drank more beer.

In this way, the gardener denounced himself: his face started to change; the pupils of the eyes became pin-points; the lips tightened; and the skin became taut and shiny. George regarded Mr Swann with hate in his eyes. Paralysed, Mr Swann wailed: "I have a traitor in the hotel!"

"Do it yourself, Swann! Do everything yourself! Down with you bourgeois scum! Up with Bellarmine! Up with the BIPP!"

"STOP, TRAITOR!"

The gardener ran out of the lobby, and onto the veranda: he tripped over the loose plank, and tumbled onto Revolution Boulevard. He stood up, and ran straight into the arms of a group of drunken stevedores. They tossed George into the air, over and over again, until all his limbs were surely broken; then they dragged the fellow's limp body in the direction of the harbour, bound and gagged him, and put the gardener-spy in the cargo-hold of a ship bound for Yemen.

In the lobby, something occurred to Mr Swann: "And this man was a friend of the carpenter?" he said to himself. "So, Dupin was betrayed."

Robert Walker appeared by the reception desk: "You asked for me, Mr Swann?"

Mr Swann regained his composure. "I did, Mr Walker. You have heard: Montaigne is on his way, and we run short of beer. Also, there is the question of your accommodation, which will once more become available. In about an hour, say? You must wash-up before Montaigne arrives. "

"My visa?"

"Never mind your visa, Mr Walker. It was issued by the old regime, which itself has expired. Now, please step this way."

Proprietor and guest approached the room under the stairs. Robert Walker reached forward, and opened the portal. Packed inside, the remaining cases of missing cargo repeated the logo: BLUE MARLIN BLUE MARLIN BLUE MARLIN BLUE MARLIN BLUE MARLIN BLUE MARLIN BLUE MARLIN BLUE MARLIN BLUE MARLIN BLUE MARLIN BLUE MARLIN BLUE MARLIN BLUE MARLIN BLUE MARLIN BLUE MARLIN BLUE MARLIN BLUE MARLIN MARLIN BLUE MARLIN MARLIN BLUE MARLIN

BLUE MARLIN BLUE MARLIN BLUE MARLIN BLUE MARLIN
BLUE MARLIN BLUE MARLIN BLUE MARLIN BLUE MARLIN
BLUE MARLIN BLUE MARLIN BLUE MARLIN BLUE MARLIN
BLUE MARLIN BLUE MARLIN BLUE MARLIN BLUE MARLIN
BLUE MARLIN BLUE MARLIN BLUE MARLIN BLUE MARLIN
BLUE MARLIN BLUE MARLIN BLUE MARLIN BLUE MARLIN
BLUE MARLIN BLUE MARLIN and so on.

*

IN A DAY or so, a sign appeared outside the Marina Hotel.

GARDENER WANTED

The advertisement was repeated in the newly re-hatched *Bourbon Island Star* - since Bougainville had elected to stay in exile - under the editorship of Sylvia Dupin. There was no response to either notice. On the Bamboo Mill, the islanders said that a gardener who is a spy and poisons your grass is perhaps better than no gardener at all. Mr Swann's response was characteristic, and led - eventually - to the orphan Charlie the Fish, who was once a boy bus-spy, being promoted from dishwasher to gardener. In time, he became known as Charles, the gardener, whose father had died in an unspeakable accident*, which anyway was talked about in Port Bourbon for decades. This was long enough to transform Chief Bugis, the policeman, into a kindly public servant and a patriot, who had once detained a foreign journalist in jail. The reporter had been able to concentrate and finish a special assignment about the Fiery Cross of Goa, the artefact of legend, which has not to this day been found.

As for Mr Dan, the assassin, his dried-up carcass was eventully located in a niche of the cellar by a group of Americans pretending to be tourists. The toupee had come away - still brand new - in their hands. No one had any idea what Mr Dan might have been seeking in the cellar. The toupee, though, was boxed, and returned to Washington, D.C. for forensic analysis, while its owner was reinterred, after some delicate negotiations, on the promontory. So Mr Dan, the would-be assassin, rests with mixed company - alongside Sir Godfrey, the lighthouse keeper, Graham Dunne, and Chief Bugis.

---

* It has been suggested that the hornets - v*espa mandarinia* - may have been provoked by a new fragrance Chief Bugis had been trying out.

The Dog Cerebus disappeared on Election Day, though its plinth remains intact above the bar in the Marlin Room. The usually verbose Bamboo Mill remains silent on the subject of a possible culprit.

Francis Long and Bebe married, had several children, and acquired a small fleet of boats - not for fishing, but for providing tourists with guided excursions offshore to Dog Rock, where Clue No. 11 had been found. The trials of Graham Dunne, too, were transformed into a visitor attraction, with Bebe Long, since Francis Long preferred the watery routes, leading the way. No one knows - or is telling - what happened either to Robert Walker or Morgan Beaumont.

At the Marina Hotel, the grass is as green as it is in England, and no longer appears parched and bleached by the sun. In the offshore breeze, though, the hornets' nest still sways from the cupola over the observation deck of the hotel.

EPILOGUE

THE CLOUDS SAILED across the white disc of the sun. Over Covent Garden, the skies opened up, and it rained - the end of a British summer - for the first time in days. Robert Walker made his way down Long Acre from the Underground terminus, and entered the building. He climbed the staircase, and passed silent doors on the way to the fifth floor. The door of the apartment opened onto the landing.

"Is that you, Robert?"

"Is that you, Conny?"

Robert Walker entered the apartment, but only as far as the potted palm. It needed water.

"I've been away for fifteen days, and you're still packing?" he asked.

"I'm not packing, Robert. I'm *un*packing. Can't you tell the difference?"

Robert Walker looked around the place. "No, I can't."

"I've been away, too. To Blackfriars. You were right - there's nothing there."

Robert Walker looked at Conny Trapp. She smiled at him. Her hair was tied back, and it had been restored to its natural chestnut brown. She wore a new mixed-tweed jacket, which suited her, with real leather buttons. Outside, the sun was going down, and - one by one - the lights illuminated the wet streets.

"You'll have to get yourself a raincoat one of these days, Robert. Now that you've joined the human race, I mean."

"Who, me? What about Harry Stone? Any messages?"

Outside, it was dark already.

"To hell with Harry Stone," Conny laughed. "Or to Brighton, I should say, to grow vegetables! You're to call in at Shoe Lane in the morning. Something about a bonus. A new assignment, too."

"The things I do for a bonus," he reflected. Then: "What about Mr Grey?"

"He's waiting for us at the Lamb and Flag. He's got something for us to sign. Time to go, then."

She ceased her unpacking. She crossed the apartment. He had almost forgotten the blue-grey of her eyes. An ocean, far away.

"Did you behave yourself?"

"I was told to stay out of politics, and leave the women alone."

"Did you?"

"In my own way. . .Yes, I left the women alone."

They stepped out onto the landing. "Then I'm your new assignment." She took him by the arm. "Isn't it time we got to know each other, Mr Walker?"

James A. Oliver
Devon, 2004

James A Oliver

Final Proof copy.
29th Nov 2004